THE
TESTAMENT

Books by ELIE WIESEL

Night
Dawn
The Accident
The Town Beyond the Wall
The Gates of the Forest
The Jews of Silence
Legends of Our Time
A Beggar in Jerusalem
One Generation After
Souls on Fire
The Oath
Ani Maamin (*cantata*)
Zalmen, or the Madness of God (*play*)
Messengers of God
A Jew Today
Four Hasidic Masters
The Trial of God (*play*)
The Testament
Five Biblical Portraits
Somewhere a Master
The Golem (*illustrated by Mark Podwal*)
The Fifth Son
Against Silence (*edited by Irving Abrahamson*)
Twilight
The Six Days of Destruction (*with Albert Friedlander*)
A Journey into Faith (*conversations with John Cardinal O'Connor*)
From the Kingdom of Memory
Sages and Dreamers
The Forgotten
A Passover Haggadah (illustrated by Mark Podwal)
All Rivers Run to the Sea

THE
TESTAMENT

ELIE WIESEL

Translated from the French by
MARION WIESEL

Schocken Books
New York

Copyright © 1981 by Elirion Associates, Inc.

All rights reserved under International and Pan-American
Copyright Conventions. Published in the United States by
Schocken Books Inc., New York, and simultaneously in
Canada by Random House of Canada Limited, Toronto.
Distributed by Pantheon Books, a division of Random
House, Inc., New York. Originally published in hardcover
in the United States by Summit Books, New York, in 1981.

Schocken Books and colophon are registered trademarks
of Random House, Inc.

The author and the translator wish to thank Mrs. Natasha
Gruzen for many hours spent researching, and Mr. Joel
Carmichael for his generous help with the translation.

Library of Congress Cataloging-in-Publication Data

Wiesel, Elie, 1928-
[Testament d'un poète juif assassiné. English]
The testament / Elie Wiesel ; translated from the French
by Marion Wiesel
p. cm.
ISBN 0-8052-1115-2
1. Jews—Persecutions—Soviet Union—Fiction. 2. Soviet
Union—History—1925-1953—Fiction. I. Wiesel, Marion.
II. Title.
PQ2683.I32T413 1999 843'.914—dc21 98-46945 CIP

Random House Web Address: www.randomhouse.com

Printed in the United States of America

First Schocken Edition

2 4 6 8 9 7 5 3 1

FOR PAUL FLAMAND

One of the Just Men came to Sodom, determined to save its inhabitants from sin and punishment. Night and day he walked the streets and markets protesting against greed and theft, falsehood and indifference. In the beginning, people listened and smiled ironically. Then they stopped listening; he no longer even amused them. The killers went on killing, the wise kept silent, as if there were no Just Man in their midst.

One day a child, moved by compassion for the unfortunate teacher, approached him with these words: "Poor stranger, you shout, you scream, don't you see that it is hopeless?"

"Yes, I see," answered the Just Man.

"Then why do you go on?"

"I'll tell you why. In the beginning, I thought I could change man. Today, I know I cannot. If I still shout today, if I still scream, it is to prevent man from ultimately changing me."

From *One Generation After*

THE
TESTAMENT

I FIRST MET Grisha Paltielovich Kossover at Lod airport, one afternoon in July 1972. A plane, just landed, was rolling down the runway. Outside, groups of welcoming relatives, friends, reporters stopped chatting and stood waiting. Reunions here do not erase the past, woven as it is of uprootings, of absences, of yearnings.

I often go to Lod to witness the most astonishing ingathering of exiles in modern times. Many of these men and women I had met before, in Soviet Russia, in the realm of silence and fear. Had I told them then that a few years later I would be welcoming them on the soil of our ancestors they would have looked at me reproachfully: "Don't make fun of us, friend; false hopes are painful. . . ."

In the crowd I would sometimes recognize a young student or a Pioneer girl with whom I had sung and danced, one Simhat Torah eve, in front of the Great Synagogue of Moscow. Once a shoemaker from Kiev burst into tears on seeing me. Another time, a university professor from Leningrad embraced me as though I were his brother, lost and found again; and, in a way, I was that brother.

I like Lod at the hour when the Russian Jews are arriving. They have a way all their own of setting foot on the ground. As if awaiting a signal, an order, they do not dare move forward. For what seems an interminably long moment they stand rooted in front of the plane, gazing up at the blue sky laced with clouds; listening to the muffled sounds coming from the government buildings. They are looking, looking, seeking proof that this reality exists and that they are part of it. No scenes, no effusiveness—not yet; in an hour, perhaps, when the first couple locks in a first

11

embrace, when father and son, uncle and nephew, camp-
mates and battle comrades recognize each other. For the
moment the two groups remain separate. Tense, nervous,
the new arrivals restrain themselves: they do not cry out,
they do not call—not yet. They hold back their silence before shedding the first tear, before pronouncing the first
blessing. They are afraid, afraid to precipitate events;
afraid to believe what they see. They seem to be clinging to
their fear; it links them to the past just one last time before
they can dismiss it.

Then one lone figure detaches itself from the arriving
crowd. A drawn-out cry reverberates, amplified by collective emotion: "Yaakov! Yaaakoov!" And suddenly nothing exists but this running shadow, this shout that rends
memory. That memory, that day itself, will be called
Yakov, will call to Yakov forevermore.

Yakov, a young officer, trembles: he wants to leap toward his father, but his legs refuse to obey. Glued to the
ground, he stands, waiting for time to flow, for the years to
dissipate and turn him into the stubborn schoolboy he
once was, able to hold back the tears that now flood his
cheeks.

As if in response to some mysterious call, the two groups
break up and then re-form, ten times, a hundred times.
People speak to one another, kiss one another, laugh, weep;
they repeat the same words, the same messages, they shake
the same hands, they caress familiar and unfamiliar faces.
They say anything to anyone. It's a celebration, what a
celebration: "When did you leave Riga?" "The day before
yesterday, no, a thousand years ago!" "I'm from Tashkent."
"And I'm from Tiflis." "What about Leibish Goldmann—
any news?" "Leibish is waiting his turn." "And Mendel
Porush?" "Waiting his turn." "And Srulik Mermelstein?"
"Waiting his turn." "Will they ever come?" "Oh yes,
they'll come, they'll all come."

A few steps away two young brothers stare at one another in silence. They are alone, without family; neither dares make the opening gesture. There they are, face to face, gazing at one another with steady, painful intensity.

"Don't ask me anything!" a stocky woman cries. "Don't tell me anything, please; first let me have a good cry— these tears have been waiting a long time."

Farther off, a giant of a man lifts up a thin young girl with brown hair and twirls her over his head: "Is that you, Pnina? The little beauty smiling at me from the picture, is that you? And my son is your father?" Drunk with joy and pride, this grandfather dances with his memories. He has only one desire left—to be allowed to dance like this all day and all night, and tomorrow too, until the end of his days.

A young man is standing to one side, forgotten on the runway. No one has come to welcome him, no one speaks to him. I address him in Russian and ask whether I can be of help. He does not reply. Too much emotion, no doubt. I extend my hand; he clutches it. I repeat my offer of help; he remains silent. No matter, he will answer later.

The man in charge of greeting the newcomers ushers the group into a large room with tables covered with white cloths and flowers, masses of flowers. Waitresses bring orange juice, fruits, cookies. "We've got something better!" a man shouts, waving a bottle of vodka. Glasses are filled and clinked. One of the men proposes a toast: "I just want to tell you that . . ." His words tangle and clog his throat. He starts again: "What I want to say is . . ." Once more his voice breaks. He is choking, gasping for air: "I *really* want to tell you that . . ." His face contorted, he casts a hopeless look over the crowd, begging for help. And he collapses, shaken violently by a sob drawn from the depths of centuries: "I don't know, I no longer know what I want to tell you . . . so many things, so many things. . . ."

Lest they betray their emotion, people lower their eyes. "The devil with speeches!" someone yells. "Let's drink, that's worth more than all the speeches and commentaries put together, isn't that so, friends?" And the cups are raised. And friends and strangers drink together: *L'chayim* —to life, to the future, to peace. Incredible what a glass of vodka can do.

I notice the taciturn young man at the other end of the room. He has not joined in either the drinking or the eating. He is tall, slender, with fine features and dark hair; his eyes are somber, his mouth is set. Everything about him suggests suffering. I try to find out: Who is he? An official scans his list and tells me, "Grisha Kossover, his name is Grisha Kossover. A special case. He's mute. Sick. You know what I mean. . . . Where he's from? Some place in the Ukraine or White Russia. Krasnograd, yes, that's it, Krasnograd. . . ."

I hurry over to the boy. I know his city, I tell him. No, I've never been there, but I know a poet who used to live there—a melancholy, generous, obscure poet, unfortunately not well known—to be quite frank, not known at all. I get confused, I mention my passion for the sacred poetry and profane prayers of that Jewish poet-minstrel whom Stalin, in an explosion of hatred, in a fit of madness, ordered shot, together with other Russian-Jewish novelists, poets and artists of the time. I talk and talk and do not see the amused wrinkle around his lips, the gleam of recognition in his eyes; I talk, I talk, until I finally understand: How stupid can I be? I did not make the connection! Grisha Kossover, this lonely, mute immigrant from Krasnograd, is . . . yes . . . my poet's son, the son of Paltiel Kossover. How could I have guessed? I didn't even know the poet was ever married. The blood rushes to my head. I want to grab the boy and carry him on my shoulders in triumph. I feel like shouting, I am shouting: "Listen to me, listen all of you! Miracles exist, I swear it!" People around us don't understand, don't seem to care. I get upset: "You don't know? You don't know who just arrived? Paltiel Kossover's son! Yes, yes, the son of the poet. You don't know him?" No, they do not know him, they know nothing; they have read nothing. A bunch of ignorant barbarians.

"Come," I say to Grisha. "Follow me."

He will not go to the hotel with the others, that is settled. He will stay with me. I have a large apartment; he can have his own room.

I push him past immigration, police and customs. I speak for him, I explain, I get his luggage—and there we are, outside. It is evening. My car is right there, the road opens up before us. We drive at high speed, in silence, pulled upward by the hills and the sky of Jerusalem.

I think of Paltiel Kossover, whose poems I discovered by accident.

Arrested a few weeks after the more illustrious Moscow writers, he was executed at the same time in the NKVD dungeons in Krasnograd. The rumor of his death made its way slowly, cautiously, through the Soviet Union until it reached the free world. It aroused neither anger nor consternation, for his work was unknown. Less famous than Dovid Bergelson, less gifted than Peretz Markish, he had so few readers that they all knew one another.

Was he a "great" poet? Frankly, no. He lacked scope and vision, also ambition and luck. Who knows? If he had lived longer . . . His only published work—*I Saw My Father in a Dream*—is quite modest: memories of childhood and war, parables, poems and nightmares. His voice is but a murmur, yet his prose seems gently lit from within. There are but few of us who savor his taste for austerity; we like his nostalgia, his melancholy. Forever uprooted, he remained a refugee to the end. His life and his death: discarded drafts.

Our memorial evenings in his honor draw only a limited

audience. But while our circle is small, its enthusiasm is great. We had eight of his poems translated into French, five into Dutch, two into Spanish. We are diehards. I comment on his work in my courses and refer to it on every possible occasion. Nothing gives me greater satisfaction than to see one of my students turning into a Kossover devotee.

And here I am, facing a task a thousand times more arduous: getting his mute son to talk. But I manage without difficulty. Actually it has nothing to do with me. The credit belongs entirely to his father.

Barely settled in my place, Grisha pulls a book from his pocket. Without a word I go to my room and return with my own copy of *I Saw My Father in a Dream*. Yes, it is the same book. Astounded, Grisha takes it, examines the binding, reads a notation or two, and gives it back to me. I think he is just as shaken as I.

"For a long time I thought I had the only copy," I say to him. "As you did, no doubt."

Grisha then takes out his pen and scribbles a few words on my memo pad: "There is a third copy. It belongs to a certain Viktor Zupanev, a night watchman in Krasnograd."

From my window I show him Jerusalem. I evoke its past, and explain the passion that binds me to this city, whose every stone and cloud is familiar. I offer some practical advice for tomorrow and the weeks to come: where to go, where to buy what, and when. I describe our neighbors—government clerks, new immigrants, soldiers. And opposite us, on the ground floor, a war widow.

"Grisha, you're tired. Go to bed."

He shakes his head. Tonight, he wants to stay up.

"Alone?"

Yes, alone. He corrects himself: no, not completely alone.

"I don't understand."

Then he makes another gesture to indicate that he would like to write.

"Are you a writer? Like your father?"

No, not like his father. In place of his father.

E.W.

GRISHA, MY SON,

I am interrupting my *Testament* to write you this letter. When you read it, you will be old enough to understand it and me. But will you read it? Will you receive it? I fear not. Like all the writings of prisoners it will rot in the secret archives. And yet . . . something in me tells me that a testament is never lost. Even if nobody reads it, its content is transmitted. The call of the dying will be heard; if not today, then tomorrow. All our actions are inscribed in the great Book of Creation: that is the very essence of the noble tradition of Judaism, and I entrust it to you.

I am writing you because I'm about to die. When? I don't know. One month from now, perhaps six. As soon as I shall have finished this *Testament*? I cannot answer that question.

It's night, but I don't know whether the darkness is in myself or outside. The naked bulb blinds me. The jailer will soon open the peephole. I recognize his step. I'm not afraid of him. I enjoy certain privileges: I can write as much as I like, and whenever I like. And what I like. I'm a free man.

I try to imagine you in five or ten years. What kind of man will you be when you reach my age? What will you know of the interrogations and tortures that have haunted your father?

I see you, my son, as I see my father. I see you both as in a dream, and the dream is real. My voice calls yours and his, even if only to tell the world of its ugliness, even if only to cry out together for help, to mourn together the death of hope and sing together the death of Death.

I am your father, Grisha. It is my duty to give you in-
struction and counsel. Where can I draw them from? I
haven't made such a success of my life that I can arrogate
to myself the right to guide yours. In spite of my experience
with people I don't know how to save them or awaken
them; I even wonder whether they wish to be saved or
awakened. In spite of everything I was able to learn—and
I've learned a lot—I don't know the answers that will have
to be given to the grave, fundamental questions that concern human beings. The individual facing the future, facing
his fellow man, has no chance whatsoever of survival. All
that remains is faith. God. As a source of questioning I
would gladly accept Him; but what He requires is affirmation, and there I draw the line. And yet. My father and
his father believed in God; I envy them. I tell you so you
will know: I envy them their pure faith, I who have never
envied anyone anything.

Perhaps you will find a way to read my poems; they are
a kind of spiritual biography. No, that's too pretentious.
A poetic biography? It's not that either. Songs—they're
simply songs offered to my father, whom I had seen in a
dream. Among the most recent is one I intend to revise in
my mind. Its title is both naive and ironic: "Life Is a
Poem." Life is not a poem. I do not know what life is, and
I shall die without knowing.

My father, whose name you bear, knew. But he is dead.
That is why I can only say to you—remember that he
knew what his son does not.

I have tried. If I have time, I'll tell you how. Let me at
least tell you this: Don't follow the path I took, it doesn't
lead to truth. Truth, for a Jew, is to dwell among his
brothers. Link your destiny to that of your people; otherwise you will surely reach an impasse.

Not that I am ashamed of having believed in the Revolution. It did give hope to the hungry, persecuted masses.

But seeing what it has become, I no longer believe in it. The great upheavals of history, its dramatic accelerations . . . all things considered, I prefer mystics to politicians.

I am going to die within a month, a year, and I should like to go on living. With you and for you. To have you meet the characters who are sharing my wait in this cell of mine.

I must tell you that in my *Testament* I did plead guilty. Yes, guilty. But not to what I take to be the meaning of the charge. On the contrary: guilty of not having lived as my father did. That, my son, is the irony: I lived a Communist and I die a Jew.

The tempest has swept over us and people are no longer what they were. I have grown up, matured. I walked through the forest and lost my way. It's too late to go back. Life is like that—going back is impossible.

YOUR FATHER

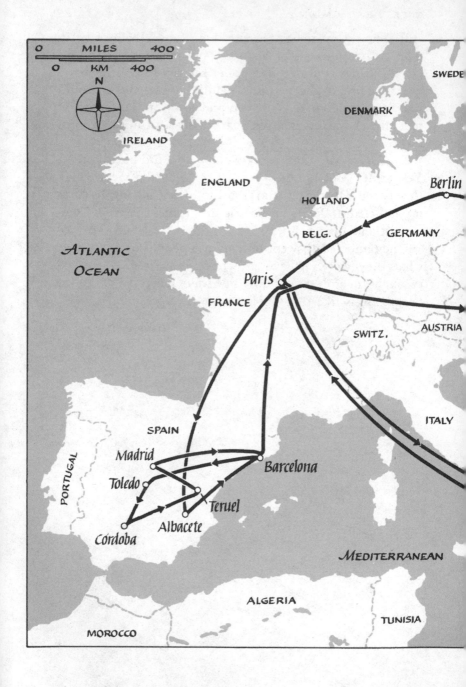

LATVIA
LITHUANIA
Moscow
RUSSIA
U.S.S.R.
Smolensk
Voronezh
Brest-Litovsk
Berdichev
Kharkov
Lublin
Uman
Barassy ←
ZECHOSLOVAKIA
Liyanov
Odessa
HUNGARY
ROMANIA
BLACK SEA
YUGOSLAVIA
BULGARIA
TURKEY
ALB.
GREECE
SYRIA
SEA
Haifa
PALESTINE
TRAVELS OF PALTIEL KOSSOVER
Jaffa-Tel Aviv
Jerusalem
PRE-WORLD WAR II FRONTIERS

OUTSIDE, THE DUSK FALLS abruptly over the hills around Jerusalem. Nothing remains of the coppery sun but a handful of sparks firing the window panes. This is the hour when Grisha likes to stand near the window, to gaze at the city reaching out for night. Not now: he's too absorbed in reading and rereading his father's *Testament*. As he turns the pages he hears the hoarse, staccato voice, unlike anyone else's, of Viktor Zupanev—the man who could not laugh—who passes on to him the story of the story of the Jewish poet slain far away.

Suddenly he tenses as he tries in vain to visualize Zupanev. Faces parade in his head—delicate or vulgar, calm or nervous, surly or happy faces—but not one of them bears the features of the old watchman of Krasnograd. He does hear his voice: "Aren't you ashamed of yourself, Grisha? Wasn't I your guide, your protector? Would you have gone to Jerusalem if I hadn't sent you? Why have you forgotten me?" Tomorrow, Grisha says to himself. Tomorrow I'll know. She is arriving tomorrow My first question will be: "Have you seen Zupanev? Describe him to me." And only then will he question her about his father: "Did you love him, Mother? Did you really love him?" Tomorrow . . .

For the moment Grisha plunges back into his reading.

". . . I AWOKE WITH A START, panting. The running, the strangled cries—all that was in my dream. The little girl

25

about to fall from the tower, and the same little girl about
to drown: a nightmare! As a child I used to recite the morning prayer: *I thank you, O living God, for giving me back
my life.* Why did I suddenly hear this as an echo? I listened
to the beating of my heart as though it were ticking away
outside myself. Instinctively, I stopped breathing, became
all ears. Silence . . . a black, evil silence rising . . . I never
knew silence could move. Was I still dreaming? A glance
at the window—it was still night, I was home in my bed.
To the right, the cradle. Grisha was sleeping a peaceful
sleep; I heard his steady, confident breathing. Raissa was
moving restlessly. What demons were besetting her? Perhaps I should wake her, tell her: They're coming, Raissa.
They're at Kozlowski's, do you hear me? Good old one-
armed Kozlowski, such a nuisance, with his foolish, useless
smiles. Did he smile as he welcomed them? No, that's not
where they were. At Dr. Mozliak's, perhaps? That mysterious character I sometimes see on the staircase—he
gives me the creeps. Was it his turn?

"All this lasted no more than a second—a second since
my awakening—and a fist of steel was already pounding
my temples. They're very close! Take care of the little
one, Raissa. He mustn't forget me, promise he won't
forget me. I start shaking her gently, but I'm petrified.
There's a knock on the door. No use clinging to foamy
waves. Listen, Paltiel. The knocks are discreet, polite,
persistent. One, two, three, four. Pause. One, two, three,
four. Raissa nudges me with her elbow. The knocking begins again. I panic: Should I wake the little one? Talk to
him, embrace him one last time? I take a deep breath—no
sentimentality, Paltiel! A pain in my left arm, near the
chest. Funny if I had a heart attack now! One, two, three,
four. They're getting impatient. A mad notion flashes
through my mind. What if I don't get up? If I don't open
the door? If I feign sickness, or death? What if it's only an

extension of my dream? A little blond girl is going to throw herself from the top of the tower, and that same little blond girl is going to drown; she cries out, I cry out, but the people are sleeping, nobody hears, nobody sees; people don't want to wake up. . . .

"No, it's all over. It's my turn. Raissa squeezes my arm. I tell her softly, This is it, Raissa. I'd like to see her expression, but it's still dark. Never mind: I look at her without seeing her, I touch her. She shakes her head; her hair falls over my shoulder; I feel warm. It's all over, I whisper. Will you watch over our son? She says nothing, but—oddly —I hear, I receive her answer. And I realize that my fear has left me. Not a trace of panic any more. I don't have to save the little girl with the golden hair, she's already dead. The anguish oppressing me for months lifts. I feel strangely relieved.

"And liberated."

THE PLANE FROM VIENNA is due tomorrow, in the late morning. In his room in Jerusalem, Grisha has one night to get ready. His mind is made up. He will go to meet his mother at Lod and bring her home with him. She'll sleep in the room, he'll sleep on a cot in the foyer for a week or two. Just time enough for her to read her husband's *Testament*. Then she'll go to stay at the Ministry's Reception Center. Perhaps then, she too will feel relieved.

A year has passed since Grisha left Krasnograd. He remembers his mother's pale, distraught face: "Are you leaving because of me?" When Grisha did not respond at once, she lowered her voice and asked again, "Because of me? Tell me." In shame, she covered her mouth with her hand:

she knew well enough that her son could not speak his answer. But Grisha had learned to make himself understood by moving his lips, his hands, his shoulders, or simply with his eyes. "No, not only because of you," he answered. Reassured, she said, "Because of the doctor?" "I'm going because of my father."

That was only partly true. His mother surely had something to do with it. By tomorrow you'll have read the final sentence in the story of the arrest, Grisha muses, and I'll look at you as I never have before. And you will live the death of my father.

And Raissa, what will she say? "Grisha, my son, don't judge me; I beg of you, don't judge your mother. Try to understand." That's what she'll say, as she had each time she tried to justify herself, and failed. "Make an effort, Grisha. Try to imagine the past years, the terror, the loneliness. Especially the loneliness . . ."

Enveloped by night, Jerusalem holds its breath.

I have never laughed in my life, said old Viktor Zupanev, as if explaining something. Can you understand that? Even when I was kidding around, even when I was playing, my heart wasn't in it: I wasn't laughing. You don't seem impressed. And yet . . . Have you met many people incapable of laughter? Tell me. So what? you'll say. One can do without laughter. One can do all sorts of crazy things: one can love, eat, dream, chase skirts, jump on a high wire, set the clouds afire and tear down trees, thumb one's nose at the world, one can even be happy—and still not laugh. True. But as for myself, Grisha, I wanted to laugh, to have one really good laugh, to roar with laughter, laugh until I

*croak. But I never could. I'd look at myself in the mirror
and sink into one of those depressions. . . . That's why you
won't find a single mirror in my place. And then a poet
different from the others, a crazy Jew, burst into my life
and changed it by telling me about his own. And then . . .*

I N WRITING HIS *Testament*, Paltiel Kossover had sought
precision first of all. Every word contains a hidden meaning; every sentence sums up a wide range of experiences.
Could he have imagined that his writings would survive
him? That his words would be read and reread, studied
and restudied by his son? Like all prisoners, all condemned
people, this singer of Jewish suffering, this poet of dead
hopes knew what could be expected: in the dark solitary
cells of the Secret Police people wrote only for the inter-
rogators, the torturers, the judges. Awaiting death, they
wrote only for death. Did Paltiel Kossover, in spite of
everything, believe in the impossible? He hinted at this
somewhere. Page . . , which page? Grisha leafs through
the manuscript. There on page 43, at the bottom:

". . . Y OU ASK ME why I'm writing. And for whom. At
one time these questions were easy to answer. In fact, at
the time I was touring the collective farms and communes,
I was asked these two questions after each of my lectures.
The Soviet people wanted to understand, and the Jewish
poet tried to supply them with explanations. I am writing

in order to vanquish evil and to glorify that victory; I am writing to justify the thirty or forty centuries of history I bear within me. Grandiloquent? Pretentious? So what? My words reflected what I felt. As for the second question—for whom was I writing?—I answered: I'm writing for you, for you who are alive today, my contemporaries, my allies, my companions, my brothers. I should like to take your arm, watch you smile as you listen to my story, which is also yours. . . .

"Today I no longer know. I am writing, but I do not know for whom: for the dead, those who abandoned me en route and who are waiting for me? I am writing because I have no choice. As in that story of olden days: King David used to love to sing, and as long as he sang, the Angel of Death could not approach him; composing his Psalms, he was immortal. Like me. As long as I write, as long as I put ink on paper, death will be powerless against me: you will keep me here, between these hideous walls. And when I shall have told my last story, completed my last reminiscence, your emissaries will come to fetch me, to lead me to the dungeons. I know that, I live without illusion. So it is because of you, if not for you, that I shall go on writing. And since I have the right to tell everything—that is the only right I have—let me add this: these words, which you think you will be the only ones to read, are intended for others beside yourselves. You can destroy my notebooks; no doubt you'll burn them, but a voice within me tells me that the words of a condemned man have their own life, their own mystery. Does the word 'mystery' make you sneer? Well, I'm beginning to believe in it. The words you strangle, the words you murder, produce a kind of primary, impenetrable silence. And you will never succeed in killing a silence such as this. . . ."

Grisha TURNS THE PAGES. Would his mother be able to read the handwriting? What a pity I'm mute, he tells himself. I should have liked to give my voice to my father, to be the narrator of his broken life and his hidden death. Poor Father! Your son, your heir, can articulate only unintelligible sounds; your only son is mute.

While reading, he moves his lips, as though talking to himself in a low voice. From time to time he raises his eyes, passes his hand through his tousled hair; his thoughts wander off into the distance, beyond the years and the frontiers: a sad child, harassing his mother, an unhappy child humiliated by a stranger, a bewildered orphan, a rebellious, frenzied adolescent who attached himself to a mad old man, to that night watchman who was so anonymous as to be faceless. A mother he loves and no longer loves: "Try to understand," she tells him. Grisha rubs his eyes as if to chase away a painful memory; he rubs his eyes each time he thinks of his mother. Yet there was a time he refused to leave her for a single hour, even to sleep; he loved her and only her. There was a time they were alone in the world. Alone, Grisha thinks, and his heart twinges.

He gets up and walks over to the open window. The fresh air does him good. Night is a living presence in Jerusalem; it roams the streets, accompanies passersby, hides in the doorways. In Jerusalem night is a messenger.

Tomorrow, Grisha thinks, the plane arrives tomorrow morning. Friday, the eve of Yom Kippur.

Who will go with him to the airport? Someone must, to do the speaking. His friend, the writer in whose house he lives, who knows everyone. For years, he has been fighting for the Russian Jews. Many owe him their freedom. It was he who informed Grisha, "Your mother has just arrived in

Vienna, she'll be coming here in three days." Grisha felt
dizzy. His friend put his arm around him protectively. "You
love her, don't you? You never thought you'd see her
again, did you? You're excited, I understand, so am I. The
family—what's left of Paltiel Kossover's family—reunited
in Israel, well, that does something to me. . . ." Poor fellow,
Grisha tells himself, he thinks he knows and understands
everything.

What about Katya? Of course she would go with him.
She'd know when to step aside. But she might say something better left unsaid. No, I'll go alone, Grisha decides.
Police and customs, my mother can handle all that, she's
not the timid sort. A former Red Army officer knows how
to take care of herself.

Tomorrow. Moment of truth, day of judgment, eve of
Yom Kippur. A strange coincidence. Grisha breathes
deeply, strains to catch the thousand and one noises rising
from the street and neighboring buildings. The radio brays
out the news of the day: commentaries, commentaries on
commentaries. Israelis love to comment. Everybody has an
opinion on every subject: the Russians, the Chinese, the
Left, the Right, abortion, psychoanalysis, men, women, and
those in between. And the coming elections. And the Day
of Atonement: should one fast or go to the beach? Politicians' speeches, religious exhortations. God wills, God
exhorts: how many spokesmen He has, all so sure of themselves! Thanksgiving for the year gone by, prayers for the
year to come. No war—above all, no war.

It's ten at night, perhaps later, but the street still brims
with activity. A rabbi and his disciples, in winter kaftans
despite the hot weather, are on their way to the Wall to beseech God to give them the strength and wisdom to better
beseech Him tomorrow evening. A worker makes his way
homeward breathlessly. A tourist asks someone to decipher
an inscription on a yeshiva: "This building will not be

sold or rented until the coming of the Messiah." How
Paltiel would have appreciated that quiet affirmation!

Children call to one another. Their parents, new immigrants from Odessa, exchange complaints and advice:
"You want a tax-free car? All you have to do . . ."

Katya lives across the street, in the gray, three-story
house, on the ground floor. Should I pay her a visit? Quite
a girl, Katya. If there were room in his life for such things,
he would try to marry her.

Excitable, amusing, warm, Katya is a mute in her own
way when it comes to her husband, fallen in Sinai or in
the Golan Heights. She never speaks of him. A war widow,
she refuses to be a dead man's prisoner. Not like me, Grisha
reflects. I live with the memory of my father, I incorporate
him into my own memory; I live in his shadow. It is to
him that I dedicate all my free hours, all my passions, all
my energy and willpower. I am the shadow of a shadow;
we disappear at dawn.

No, he will not go to Katya's. Not tonight. He knows
how it will end and he does not want to be distracted, not
tonight.

Since his arrival in Jerusalem in 1972, since settling
down in the apartment loaned to him by his father's ad-
mirer, Grisha has led a solitary life except for his relationship with Katya. He spends his days copying, recopying
and studying his father's poems and *Testament*. In the
evenings he visits Katya.

When he first went to her, he hesitated whether to ring
the doorbell or knock on the window. He chose the
window. She came to let him in, showing no surprise. "Who
are you? What do you want?"

Grisha found her attractive. A little on the plump side,
but attractive. How explain to her that he was mute?

"All right, come in," said the young woman, after looking him over attentively.

"I'm letting you in because you knocked at the window," she added. "I don't like the door, people ring to bring bad news."

Grisha inspected the room as though interested in its cleanliness. Beneath the mirror were some framed photographs of an officer in various poses: saluting the Minister of Defense, surrounded by comrades, on the beach, holding hands with a young woman, a little on the plump side but attractive.

"My name's Katya, what's yours?"

Grisha did not answer. He looked at her. More than once, seeing her silhouette through the window, he had been attracted and troubled by her. He feared her rejection as much as her pity.

"You're not saying anything? Why not? Have you lost your tongue, maybe?"

Grisha nodded—yes, in fact he had. She backed away.

"Forgive me."

Grisha shook his head again—no need to ask forgiveness.

"How did it happen? When? The war?

No, not the war.

"Then what? Have you been mute since birth?"

No, not since birth.

"Then I don't understand."

He made a gesture as though to say "You can't understand." In any case he was not going to tell her his life story. Or tell her about his father's work. Or talk to her about his mother. And surely he was not going to confide in her the secret adventure of an old watchman of ghosts called Viktor Zupanev. Even if he were not mute he would have remained silent.

At first he stayed to one side, without touching her. He had the feeling they were not alone; you don't make love, Grisha, in the presence of the dead.

Then he had yielded. He had succumbed to the urgency

of his desire. Forgetting his mother and father, forgetting the fallen officer, he let himself be carried away by his body. He wanted to love this young woman, open himself up to her one day. . . .

No, not tonight.

I'll go see her tomorrow morning. I'll ask her to take me to the airport. Better her than anyone else. On the way back, there'll be two widows in the car. Is there some link between them? I know why Katya will be there; but my mother? Why was she coming? What forced her to leave Krasnograd? How did she manage to free herself from Dr. Mozliak? Grisha muses about his mother, her lover and their hostile city. Still, the city did have hospitable hideaways known to him alone. . . . Then his thoughts brought him back to Jerusalem, a city of distinct contours, wrapped in its legends and its kings, a city of changing colors, of voices near and far. And above it all, gray and white clouds contending for the sky. And my father? Grisha shivers. My dead father who wants to talk to me. And what about me? Me? Me—nothing.

W<small>HO'S THIS, MOMMY?"</small>

A man with a melancholy, anxious smile, a man both very old and very young, very sad and very happy. How could one tell? The picture was frayed, dusty. Grisha must have been three at the time.

He had held out to her the book with the picture.

"Where did you find that? Give it to me!"

She had snatched the book from his hands and quickly put it back in its place on the highest, most inaccessible shelf, behind a pile of dishes, glasses and pots. Grisha did not understand why his mother was so upset—he had not done anything! Finding the book on the floor, he had opened it casually, not knowing why, hoping perhaps to find some funny drawings of animals having marvelous adventures. But there was only a single photograph on the cover.

"Mommy, that man—who is he?"

"Can't you see I'm busy?"

Grisha could not forget the man in the picture. The way his hands were clasped, palms out . . . He seemed to be looking for something or someone, or perhaps telling a story about wild animals, hungry children, a story about . . .

"But who is he, Mommy?"

"Don't bother me!"

Grisha had never seen his mother in such a bad mood. She usually talked to him calmly, explaining what he was supposed to do or not do, say or not say. And here she was turning her face away from him, dodging his gaze. She washed the dishes, hung up clothes that were lying about, all the time avoiding the little boy's eyes.

"What did I do, Mommy?" he asked, feeling guilty.

"Nothing."

"But you're angry!"

"I'm not angry!"

Grisha felt like crying, he who always prided himself on not crying. His eyes wide open to keep them dry, his jaw set, he held his breath. Raissa took him in her arms.

"I don't want to cry," said Grisha, crying.

"I know. I know. You're a big boy, and big boys don't cry."

He wanted to start questioning her all over again, but changed his mind; why make her angry? He loved his mother and told himself how lucky he was—she could have been some other little boy's mother.

"Promise me something," Raissa whispered. "Promise

me never to touch that book again. And if someone asks you, say you've never seen it."

"Who is that man in the picture?"

"Forget him. You've never seen the book or the picture."

At that point, a confused Grisha, feeling misunderstood, started to sob. He saw himself floating in the air, sitting on the highest shelf, the book on his knees, and the man was saying to him: "Grisha, my boy, aren't you ashamed of yourself, crying like that?"

"He's your father," Raissa said.

And Grisha calmed down. My father is not a man like other men, my father is a picture. Then, a moment later, he corrected himself: My father is a book. And for years he was to carry this discovery within himself like the most precious of secrets.

Often when he was alone in the apartment, he would climb up on the table, then on the sideboard, from where on tiptoe he could reach the forbidden book. And feel his father's presence, his warmth. Or sitting at the foot of the bed, ready to hide the book at the first warning, with pounding heart, he would leaf through its pages though he could not yet read. Then his father would speak to him in a language he did not understand. He didn't care: he moved his fingers over the lines, over the words, and that made him happy.

One day Raissa came back unexpectedly. He thought she was going to scold him, but she took off her coat and sat down on the floor, facing her son. She looked more worried than usual.

"Forgive me, I didn't mean to hurt you," Grisha said. "But Yuri has a father, little Natasha has a father, Vanya has a father, and I too have a father. I want to love him, to see him, caress him. . . ."

Raissa's eyes filled with tears. "One day you'll understand."

"You promise?"

"Of course I promise—one day you'll understand."

She took the book and, opening it at random, in a melodious voice recited a few verses in Yiddish, then translated them:

> I offer you
> My memory
> And its wellspring,
> My light
> And its shadow;
> And I ask
> Your own
> In return.

"Again," asked Grisha, without understanding, but overcome by an excitement he had never felt before. "More, I want more."

> You tasted the forbidden fruit
> Before I did;
> You felt the breath of life
> Before I did;
> You measured eternity
> Before I did.
> But the hungry child,
> The thirsty stranger,
> The frightened old man,
> All ask for me.
> And I take pride in that.
> You—are too far away.

"It's Yiddish," Raissa explained. "Your father wrote in Yiddish."

"What's that?"

"A language."

"Like Russian?"

"No—it's a Jewish language. A language unlike any

other, it tells of sorrows and joys unlike any others, it's a very rich language given to a very poor people."

"More," Grisha begged, his cheeks on fire.

She started reading again. Then, closing the book, she said to him:

"Remember—your father is a poet."

"What does that mean?"

"It means poets live in the present."

"What does that mean?"

"It means that . . . that your father was different from other men; he lived, dreamed, suffered, loved—differently. For him, life was a song. He thought everything could be accomplished through words."

Grisha clapped his hands. "I love it when you read. It makes me feel like opening the window and shouting— Come here, come and hear my father's songs!"

"Don't," murmured Raissa. "Don't ever talk about it."

"Why?"

"Because it's dangerous."

"For my father?"

"Of course not. Your father's dead."

"Dead? My father? How is that possible, if he is a poet? You told me poets live forever."

"They do."

"Well then . . ."

"They are dead, but they live on."

"No, Mommy. My father is not dead. My father is a book, and books do not die."

There was so much pity in Raissa's eyes that he was overwhelmed.

"Don't be sad, Mommy. I love you just the way I love him. The way you love him yourself. You do love him, don't you?"

Raissa's gaze became remote and Grisha was seized by fear.

"What's the matter, Mommy?"

"Nothing."

"I want to know."

"You're too little. Too little to understand."

The tremor in her voice made Grisha fall silent. He felt threatened. His room was no longer his room, his toys were no longer his toys. He was being separated from his mother as he had been separated from his father; the world was filled with thieves, stealers of souls, who kill poets and destroy their books. And in that kind of world, orphans are doomed to solitude.

THE TESTAMENT OF PALTIEL KOSSOVER I

WITH YOUR PERMISSION, Citizen Magistrate, I should like, before I begin—and I shall begin with the end, which I know to be near—to express my gratitude to you.

You were kind enough to allow me to continue to exercise my profession here. You even suggested a subject: "Your life."

Thus, thanks to your kindness, I enjoy a privilege that, in our tradition, is accorded only to the *Just*. They are forewarned of their end so as to enable them to live their death, and, above all, put their affairs in order. And their thoughts. And their memories.

A *Just*, me? Of course I'm joking. But I find that religious notion strangely appropriate here: have not our relations, Citizen Magistrate, developed, from the beginning, under the sign of religion? You have been urging me to *repent*, to *confess*, to *purge myself*, to *expiate*, to *atone*, to seek *pardon*, to be worthy of *salvation*: these acts are all essentially religious. Priest or inquisitor, you serve the Party whose attributes are divine: great and magnanimous, omnipotent and merciful, infallible, omniscient. . . .

If time allows, Citizen Magistrate, I shall return to this another day. But first my confession.

You have interrogated me a thousand times on the crimes of which I stand accused; and a thousand times I have answered you that none of it made any sense.

To show you my appreciation, I have today the honor of informing you that I have changed my mind: I plead guilty. Not on all points—not on those that implicate other persons. Only on those that for me—and hence for you too—have symbolic value.

I plead guilty to having felt something akin to hatred for the glorious Russian nation into which I was born and for which I have fought.

I plead guilty to having nurtured—a little late, too late —an exaggerated, boundless love for an obstinate people, my own, whom you and your people have endlessly denigrated and oppressed.

Yes, today, I break my links with your world, a world protected and represented by this prison; I espouse the Jewish cause, I espouse it entirely and totally; yes, I declare my solidarity with the Jewish people everywhere, always. Yes, I am a Jewish nationalist in the historical, cultural and ethical sense; I am first and foremost a Jew, and regret not having been able to declare this earlier and elsewhere.

And now the facts.

You will laugh: I should like to express myself in verse. But that would take a lifetime. . . .

Name, given name, patronymic: must I write them down? You know very well who I am. It is true that, under the pressure of your interrogations, one reaches the point of forgetting one's own identity. And you, do you learn any more from that? Forgive the impudence of a maker of words, Citizen Magistrate. His history binds you to him forever, for one day you will be old and alone with your reflections, as I am now. And you will ask yourself who you are. And you will answer: I am the one who was seen by a Jewish poet before he died, I am the one whose image Paltiel Gershonovich Kossover carried with him to his death.

Yes: Paltiel Gershonovich Kossover, that is my name. Poet by avocation, Jew by birth, and—forgive me—Communist, or former Communist, by conviction. I know: you are wincing. You deny me the right to refer to my various titles of service. I am an enemy of the people—you have drummed that into my head often enough. You do not *become* an enemy of the people; it is something you have always been. Even if you never knew it, never wanted it, even if you spent your life fighting the people's enemies, you are still an enemy. It is like grace for Christians—you have it or you don't; you are born with it.

The transition is perfect: I was born in this very place in 1910, in this lovely city of Barassy, better known since the Revolution as Krasnograd.

I am sorry I cannot be more precise. It was at the end of May, or the beginning of June. All I know is that I came into the world the second day of Shavuot. My father, you see, like all middle-class Jews, was profoundly religious and lived according to the Jewish calendar, from one holiday to the next, from one Sabbath to the next. The week began on Sunday, the year began on Rosh Hashanah, in the fall.

Strange coincidence: my grandfather, whose name I bear, died on the same day of the same holiday, but three years earlier. All I know of him is that he owned a sawmill in a neighboring village and was respected throughout the province. The wandering beggars used to pronounce his name like a blessing; he housed them and fed them like honored guests, making them feel that they were honoring him by accepting his alms. He was respected equally for his erudition and his piety. In order to attract Jews to his village, he had a House of Study built where he taught Scripture and the commentaries to both adults and children. The most famous rabbis, it seems, attended his funeral.

As an adolescent I stumbled upon a photograph in one

of my father's books. It showed a stately Hasid, tall and vigorous, with kind and noble features. I asked my mother who he was.

"Your grandfather," she answered, "Paltiel Kossover. Be proud to bear his name."

And I, foolishly, contradicted and hurt her, "Why should I?"

The insolence of the Communist in me went even further: "Proud of a Hasid, me? I'm ashamed!"

My mother began to weep silently, and, instead of stopping and begging her forgiveness, I continued with the same idiotic insolence:

"You forget the age we're living in, Mother; we believe in Communism, we reject God, and even more those who use faith in God, who use God to prevent the Jews from freeing themselves, from emancipating themselves, from claiming their rights as citizens and human beings."

In a frenzy of arrogance and stupidity, I tore up the yellowed photograph, in a way annihilating my grandfather, right under the horrified eyes of my mother. That memory still haunts me. . . . Today, Citizen Magistrate, I regret that act. In fact, I regretted it immediately, though for other reasons. Rather than scold or threaten me, my mother said quietly, "I won't tell, Paltiel, I won't tell your father."

I wanted to beg her pardon, to nestle against her and . . . But I did nothing of the sort. I was too ashamed—or not ashamed enough. I regret it today. I regret having hurt my mother; I regret having betrayed my father; I regret having torn up the face of my grandfather, whose name I bear. I so wish that my son could have seen his picture one day; my son will not even see mine. My son . . . Don't make me speak of my son, Citizen Magistrate, have pity, you who are without pity. Question me about anything you like, but leave my son out of your games: he is only two years old.

He bears my father's name: Gershon, nicknamed Grisha.
My father was strict and gentle at the same time. The
youngest of eight boys, he seemed incurably shy. Yet his
presence was imposing. He rarely raised his voice, but we
paid attention even when he coughed before speaking. He
said what he had to say in a few sentences, sometimes in
a single word, always clear, concise and to the point. You
are sneering, Citizen Magistrate; my love for my father no
doubt amuses you. So what! I loved my father; I admired
him. I never told him, so you will be the only one to know
it. He himself, you see, must have thought the opposite.
Admit it—I *was* a good Communist; one who repudiated
his forebears.

I made my father suffer, but in so doing, I suffered too.
I tormented and tortured him. Yet, whenever he chose to
answer me, to refute an argument, or simply to speak man
to man, I listened without interrupting.

Of his three children—I had two sisters—I was the only
one who caused him worry. He dreamt of seeing me grow
up to be a good Jew, and I spent my time distorting that
dream. I am trying now, while writing this *Testament*, to
return to the origins of that revolt of mine. How old was
I? All I know is that it was sometime after my Bar Mitzvah
and that by then Barassy was far behind me.

I remember Barassy, I remember my childhood in
Barassy. A Jewish home, on a small Jewish street in the Jewish quarter. If I may paraphrase our great poet Y. L. Peretz
—in Barassy even the river spoke Yiddish; and the trees,
month after month, preened themselves or lamented in Yiddish; the sun rose so as to send Jewish children to *heder* and
kabbalists to the ritual baths. Time flowed in harmony
with the rhythms and seasons of the Torah. We observed
the repose of the Sabbath, we ate matzo during Passover,
we fasted on the Day of Atonement, we drank to celebrate
the Giving of the Law; we lit candles to illuminate victories and miracles thousands of years old; we prayed for

the reconstruction of the Temple, whose ruins still saddened us. King David and his Psalms; Solomon and his
parables; Elijah and his companions; the Baal Shem Tov
and his disciples: all of them lived in our midst. Rabbi
Akiba, Rabbi Shimeon Bar Yohai, little Rabbi Zeira
of Babylon were all intimate parts of our landscape: I
listened to them, spoke with them, played with their
children; we linked ourselves to the present while living
in the past.

When I was three, my father wrapped me in his immense heavy ritual shawl and carried me to Reb Gamliel-
the-Tutor. He was a stern-looking man with bushy eyebrows and an unkempt beard, and he spread terror around
him. There were a dozen or so of us children whom he
taught how to chant the holy eternal letters, with whose
help God was supposed to have created the universe—and
with whose help you, his adversaries, fierce rationalists,
think you can explain it. The dunces would tremble
every morning, the others too; Reb Gamliel never hesitated to crack his whip over the backs of those whose
thoughts wandered—he accused them of idleness, laziness,
even banditry, why not? . . . How I could hate, at the age
of three! But now, when I take stock of those distant years,
I recall my old teacher with nostalgia and affection.

Please don't tell me that is natural; don't tell me Jews
like to suffer. We are not so stupid. If I feel tenderness for
an old man who once used to hurt me, it is surely not
because I love pain but because I love knowledge. I
would even say that, at the time, I hated Reb Gamliel, the
man and all he stood for—education by fear, forced study,
stifling prisons where words were suffused with hostility,
a hostility that scarred our minds.

Every evening I came home in tears. But I let myself go
only in front of my mother. Since my father often stayed
late in the store—he sold piece goods—I had an hour or

two to wipe away the traces of my torment. To calm me
down my mother would sing sad lullabies: A Jewish child
goes to sleep with a goat under his cradle and receives the
tears of a sweet, lovely widow called Zion. . . . And my
mother would tell me, "Learn these words that make you
dream today; tomorrow you'll make them sing."

Little by little I grew accustomed to the rhythm of that
life: I would cry during the day, and smile in the evening.
That lasted two years, two years of pain and repressed
anger. The twenty-two letters of the alphabet mocked me;
they fought me and I had to tame them.

When I left Reb Gamliel for a more learned teacher, I
realized I was not to be free of fear; it clung to my body,
to my life. And I understood I was not the only one to
endure it; my parents too were marked by it, and their
friends, and all the other Jews in our town; all were victims of fear. All were afraid, not of Reb Gamliel, of course,
but of the world surrounding us, the world whose dark
threat made Reb Gamliel himself tremble.

A recollection: Christmas Eve. Sent home in the early
afternoon, before prayers, I ask my mother why. This
night, and until the following morning, she explains, it is
forbidden to study our holy texts. Why? She does not
know. Taking my courage in both hands, I ask my father,
who knows everything:

"This is the night," he answers, "when a curse passes
over us; it's better not to expose our secret treasures."

Later I learned that on Christmas Eve, throughout
Christendom, the enemies of the Jews would chase them
in the streets to punish them in the name of their Lord, in
the name of His love; it was more prudent not to go to
school or to the Houses of Study and prayer; prudence
obliged Jews to stay at home.

I was growing up, maturing, understanding better:
being a Jew in a Christian world meant to know and be-

come accustomed to fear. Fear of heaven as well as fear of man. Fear of death and fear of life—fear of everything that breathed outside, of everything being plotted on the other side. An obscure threat hung over each and every one of us. Now it was becoming more precise, taking shape. I was going to witness my first pogrom, I was going to live through it, survive it. My age? I don't recall, I remember only that it was before the First World War.

I especially remember the day, shortly before Passover, when my father, looking distraught, appeared unexpectedly in my class and took the teacher aside. It was clear he was giving him bad news, because the teacher decided once more to close the *heder* for the day. He sighed: "Oh God, Oh God of Abraham, Isaac, and Jacob, have pity on their children and on yours, have pity."

Bewildered, we gazed at him. All those hours of freedom, what a gift! We had already begun rejoicing when my father brought us back to reality.

"Go home," he said, "run fast; God willing, you'll come back tomorrow."

I took his hand and followed him quickly. I had never seen him walk so fast. My mother was in the courtyard, holding a broom; she was beginning to make preparations for Passover. She saw us, and with her free hand covered her mouth to suppress a cry: she had understood everything.

"Where are the girls?" my father asked.

"Inside."

"Let them stay there. We shut down the school," he added.

"And the shop?"

"Also shut. Everything must be shut."

My mother did not look surprised; for her it was not the first time.

It was around noon. A splendid April day. Trees in bloom; a feast of fragrance and color. Blue sky flecked

with white; a golden sun, full of promise. Far off, the
parks in all their freshness. And the river, serene and
luminous. And in the midst of it all, a small, brutal and
barbarous word—pogrom—ringing out like the scream of
a mangled woman heralding visions of disemboweled
bodies and smashed skulls. Yes, Citizen Magistrate, it must
have been noon on one of those spring days when man
feels in harmony with Creation. And Barassy was beautiful. Never shall I forget the beauty of Barassy, the serenity
of Krasnograd on that day.

Nothing about that day shall I ever forget.

My father called my older sister, Masha: "Would you
run an errand for me?"

"Of course, Father."

"You're not afraid?"

"No, Father. Anyway, it's less dangerous for a woman.
Where would you like me to go?"

"Hurry over to the House of Study; tell the out-of-town
students, those who have no place to go, to come here."

Masha left and brought back three young men, one of
whom—a whim of fate—was to become her husband.

Standing in the bedroom—where, I remember, an old
painting of the Western Wall hung above the two beds
separated by a night table—my father revealed his plan:

"We have five or six hours—let's put them to good use.
The main thing is to remain cool. God willing, we shall
get through the ordeal safe and sound."

"What will you do, Reb Gershon?" asked Masha's future
husband. "Put up barricades? Do you really think, Reb
Gershon, that bolted doors will stop the murderers?"

"Let's prepare to die like good Jews," cried his friend
Senderl, a thin, intense-looking adolescent. "Let's be
worthy of our ancestors!"

"Have you a plan?" asked the third student. "A plan to
stop the murderers?"

My father listened patiently, stroking his beard, which

he wore trimmed short, and thought for a long moment
before answering:

"My friends, God alone can and will stop the murderers.
Or disarm them. Or strike them with blindness and deafness. As in Egypt long ago. Who are we to give Him
advice? He knows what to do. As for us, listen. With God's
help, here's what we're going to do. . . ."

We opened all the drawers, all the closets; we scattered
dishes, silver and clothing all over the floor in order to
give the impression that we had taken to our heels in the
grip of panic. Having thus set the stage, we went out into
the courtyard surreptitiously and one by one filed into
the barn. My father lifted a floorboard and made us
descend a narrow ladder. After joining us, he carefully
put the board back in place. In the semi-darkness I saw
spiderwebbed beams and old furniture. Perspiring, my
father pushed everything together to block the opening;
we helped as best we could. He wiped his face.

"God willing, the enemy won't find us; we must have
faith."

The enemy, the enemy. I tried to visualize him. Egyp-
tians in the time of Pharaoh. Looters in the time of
Haman. Crusaders in the shadow of icons, their faces
twisted by hate. The enemy never changes. Nor does the
Jew. Nor does God Himself, thank God.

A few sunbeams made their way into our shelter. Instinctively we drew away: if the sun could get to us, so
too might the enemy. If only we could make ourselves
invisible . . .

God willing, everything is possible—God willing. Those
were the only words my father had on his lips. He had
faith; he was convinced that the Divine Will would prevail. But how determine what God wants or doesn't want?
If the enemy were to discover us, would that mean God
wanted him to? Endless questions swarmed in my childish

head, but I had no right to ask them. I had to keep quiet, breathe without a sound, enveloped by silence, my senses on the alert. At that time I still didn't know, Citizen Magistrate, that silence too could turn into torture. I thought of that in this very place a few weeks, or a few months, or a few eternities ago, when you deemed it useful and profitable to lock me up in the "isolator." Silence as a source and harborer of hostility and danger: the density of silence, its pressure, its violence—all seemed familiar to me. Except that in that dusty hideaway in Barassy, now Krasnograd, I was not alone, and that the enemy back there was an enemy of long standing.

I remember the silence towering like a wall, separating the two sides. I remember the silence going beyond its own limits and becoming omnipresent, becoming God.

Desolate streets. Closed shutters. Drawn curtains. Night in full daylight. Here and there a cat walked lazily about, followed by a thousand invisible eyes. A horse whinnied, and a thousand ears listened. A board creaked, and a thousand throats went dry. As did mine.

The hours went by, slowly, heavily, unnerving. Waiting for danger, anticipating disaster—do you know what that is like, Citizen Magistrate? Do you know what it is to wait for the massacre, you who never wait?

My mother distributed some small rolls she had managed to prepare, I don't know when. The three students ate heartily. My father didn't. Nor did I or my sisters.

Later, when the sun disappeared, my father whispered, "Time for *minha*."

The men recited the prayer in voices so low I could hear nothing. The darkness became total and I touched my mother's arm to make sure she had not abandoned me.

"Paltiel! Say the *Shema Yisrael!*" my father commanded under his breath. "You're not to leave God just because the enemy is close."

I obeyed. I knew that prayer by heart—I still do—
having recited it every morning and evening. Reb Gamliel
claimed it chased demons away—we would see, soon
enough.

Strange sounds, begotten and expelled by silence, were
approaching the Jewish quarter. Suddenly we all froze.
My heart—or was it my father's?—was beating so loud it
threatened to wake the whole city. The unknown was
going to be revealed to us, the unknown was going to take
hold of my imagination and never let it go. I was going to
learn what men are capable of. Their madness was going to
burst into our universe: black and hateful, a savage madness thirsting for blood and murder. It was approaching
slowly, cunningly, with measured steps, like a pack of wild
beasts encircling a victim already overcome by terror.

And then, madness broke loose. A primeval shriek
slashed the silence and the shadows: *Death to the Jews!*
and it was taken up by countless throats, until it echoed
through the city and beyond the forests to the farthest
reaches of the earth. It penetrated trees and stones, rivers
and rocks, hell and paradise; groaning or sneering angels
and beasts transmitted it, offering it up to the celestial
throne in remembrance of an adventure that had come to
an end, of a failure on the scale of Creation . . . *Death to
the Jews!* Suddenly these four words, among all the words
used by men, meant something, something real, immediate, true. As I listened to them, endured them, felt them
ravage my brain, my ears rang, my eyes burned, I ached all
over. I could not control my trembling. I clung to my
mother, who held me close. She too began shivering. I
would have liked to feel my father's hand on my head, but
he was too far away. Just as well: I would have been
ashamed to admit my weakness to him. Anyway, what good
would it have done? Much better to hide. To be paralyzed,
or dead. My teeth chattered and I was sure they made more
noise than the pogrom outside.

It had already reached our street: the harrowing shrieks, the cries of terror and the death rattles. And the roaring of the pillagers, the murderers, the strippers of corpses. Their hatred, their joy were unfurling over our homes. Who was still living, who had ceased to live? I kept thinking of the prayers for the Day of Atonement: someone—was it God? —was reviewing his records, checking off one name here, erasing another there.

The turmoil was coming nearer and nearer; here it was in our courtyard, inside our house. Chaos—smashed windows, broken dishes, wardrobes hacked to bits with hatchets: *Death to the Jews, Death to the Jews!* The voice of an enraged drunkard: "Hey, Yids, where are you hiding? Come out, let's look at your ugly faces. They've run away! Ah, the cowards! The rats!" Another voice: "They're worse than—worse than wild animals. There must be more silver!" First voice: "That's what they're like, those Yids. That's all they're interested in—money and silver!" Another voice: "To do that to us!" Another voice: "Or maybe—" Another voice: "Maybe what?" "Maybe Ivan's boys were here ahead of us?"

They ransacked the house and then went out bellowing like savages. They were about to leave the courtyard and take care of the next house when one of them caught sight of the barn and yelled to his followers, "Hey, boys, let's take a look in there." They entered, torches in hand, they peered into the dark corners, turned the wheelless cart upside down, tore apart a sack of potatoes, then a sack of dried nuts. Stubbornly, the leader climbed as far as the loft and came down again, disappointed. He flung himself down on the floor, listened, and then yelled: "Hey, you Yids, come out! Show yourselves! Don't be cowards, show your dirty faces. . . ."

We could almost smell his breath. My teeth would not stop chattering, my eyes bulged, the blood throbbed in my head, and an iron fist kept pounding, pounding in my chest, preventing me from breathing, from living. I wanted to scream in terror, in pain, in anguish. . . . But my father stretched his arm out toward me and put a finger on my lips with a pressure as gentle and soothing as my mother's lullabies: You must not, you must not give in, you must not moan, you must not even blink; you must merge into the night, melt away into the silence, into oblivion. And for one interminable moment, the enemy, nose to the ground, alert to the slightest sound, seeking out the smallest crack in the floor, the enemy was the sole inhabitant of heaven and earth.

Then the pack retreated. We waited before opening our mouths. My mother, in a murmur: "Is everyone all right?"

Everyone was all right. Masha's future husband exclaimed, "It's a miracle! A real miracle, Reb Gershon. They were there, right there, and God made them deaf and blind. . . ."

. . . "And us He made mute," said another student.

". . . Like Egypt, long ago," my future brother-in-law went on. "Thank you, Reb Gershon, for having brought about this miracle!"

"It's too early to rejoice," said my father. "They may still come back."

I fell asleep and awoke only after the pogrom was over. The sun, in all its glory, was shining on a spectacle of horror. The street was piled high with mutilated bodies. In their ripped-open homes men, women and children lay massacred, disemboweled, shriveled. Reb Gamliel: a cross of blood cut into his forehead. Asher the gravedigger: crucified. Manya, his wife: her throat slashed. Their eight sons and daughters: beaten to death.

Where to begin? What to do first? Whom to help?

The three Houses of Study that had graced our street had been desecrated and sacked. The holy scrolls, soiled and torn, littered the ground. Shimon, the beadle, lay in a pool of blood.

With my father, my sisters and the three students, I went from house to house, from family to family. I looked, I listened, I wept with rage and bitterness. I wept at being a child, at not being able to help the victims, at not being able to strike back at the killers. An immense love welled up inside me for the Jews of my town. I wanted to bring them back to life, to console them and make them happy; I longed to have them share the miracle God had granted us.

The funerals of the victims made a deep impression on me: a long procession of coffins covered with black cloth, carried by rabbis and scholars in mourning. The ceremony took place in the courtyard of the main synagogue in the presence of dignitaries who had come from as far away as Kharkov, Odessa and St. Petersburg. Under a gray sky, a dense throng listened to the funeral orations, then moved toward the cemetery. Three beadles, like living scarecrows, led the procession, shaking money boxes and crying out, *"Tzedaka tatzil mimavet,* charity will save you from death, charity is stronger than death. . . ."* Everyone approached timidly to deposit a coin. My father had given me five or ten kopecks, but I couldn't bring myself to come close. I know it's stupid but those three tall thin men, walking ahead of the dead, of death itself, paralyzed me. I feel the terror to this day.

As for the murderers, the looters, I hated them, I wanted to see them on their knees, whipped, chained—yes, Citizen Magistrate, I felt a profound hatred, monstrous and without pity, for the population of Barassy, and thus for Krasnograd and its people, and for the Russian people and the whole of Russia.

Yes, Citizen Magistrate, I loved my people and I hated yours. Therefore, I, Paltiel Gershonovich Kossover, resident of Krasnograd at 28 October Street, I, a Jewish poet charged with subversion, deviation and treason, plead guilty: from the age of five—or was it four?—my love has been centered on one people, my own, who obey only God, and that God is not yours. In other words: even at four or five I was already guilty of nationalist Jewish plots and agitations against your law, for your law is the enemy of mine.

KRASNOGRAD AFTER THE SECOND WORLD WAR—how can it be described? Those born there swear their city is a real metropolis. But in fact, Krasnograd is a provincial town, neither better nor worse, neither uglier nor more stimulating than any other.

Perhaps more picturesque. At night you can hear the distant roar of a waterfall. In the summer, young couples venture into the woods. The bolder ones climb the mountain, a mountain whose summit seems a challenge, especially to children. If you don't care for either the mountain or the river, you can stroll through one of the five parks that are the pride of our municipality. Gorky Square is the finest spot. But it is often deserted. For good reason: the Security offices are nearby. People prefer the small romantically unkempt park that lies in the shadow of the Hill of the Seven Repentant Bandits, named in memory of seven eighteenth-century bandits who saw the light and changed professions.

Krasnograd numbers one hundred to one hundred and fifty thousand inhabitants of very diverse origins. This is hardly surprising in this region, since Krasnograd is the third point of a triangle between Zhironev and Tosahin. Five languages are used here, plus two just for bickering.

Like all Soviet urban centers, Krasnograd boasts tramways, factories, daily newspapers and houses of culture, theaters, movie houses and all kinds of schools. The city has its share of heroes and villains, drunkards and whores. There are two churches and a synagogue: the aged must be kept busy, after all. The young people prefer the "special" clubs, most of them under the aegis of the Pioneers and

57

the Komsomol, notwithstanding the spate of lectures they must endure. They go there to play chess, to meet friends, or simply to hear the local news. It's pleasant enough; the rooms are spacious, the canteen offerings passable.

As happens elsewhere, people live among their kind: old with old, young with young, and the same is true for engineers, war veterans, the sick, the retired, the bureaucrats and the Party members. Teachers socialize only with other teachers, members of the Secret Police associate only with other members of the Police, Jews see only Jews.

Not many Jews are left in Krasnograd. Large numbers were massacred at the beginning of the German invasion; others joined the partisans in the forest. The young people fought, the old took care of supplies. They had to defend themselves against both the invaders and the local inhabitants. The Jews had no friends at all at that time. Their isolation continued after the occupation. That Jewish aloneness tinges Grisha's earliest memories; it comes back to haunt him whenever he thinks about the past.

He was very young when, on his own, he discovered the walls and limits of his world. His solitude was magnified by his mother's. She seldom spoke to him, and encouraged his conversation even less. Mother and son lived as outcasts, pariahs of the community; people pointed at them and whispered as they passed. The father's absence was enough to create a void around them: after all, you don't rub shoulders with the family of a saboteur, a spy, an enemy of the people; you don't smile at a schoolboy whose father has been involved in a political plot; you don't shake hands with a woman whose husband has vanished.

Every morning Raissa left Grisha at the school gate and rushed to the factory where she worked as a bookkeeper. As he watched her being swallowed day after day by the morning crowd or carried off in a jammed streetcar, Grisha feared he would lose her forever. To hide his anxiety he had to conceal his happiness at finding her again in

the afternoon at the same spot. He did not let her out of
his sight for the rest of the day, and followed her into the
communal kitchen, the grocery store, even the bathroom.
He left her only to get into his bed in the room they shared.

It was not much fun for a boy to grow up in an atmosphere of anxiety and rootlessness. He devoted his energy
to comforting his mother—who spent her time comforting
him. How did they bear it? They themselves did not know.
There was no other way.

Then one day everything seemed to change for the better. Khrushchev, launching a policy of liberalization,
opened the camps, the prisons, the universe of slow death.
Files were reviewed, sentences reversed. And so Raissa
Kossover received a visit from three solemn-looking
officials.

"We have a communication of the gravest importance
for you."

"Please sit down." She seemed agitated and anxious:
"There aren't enough chairs, I'll run and borrow one from
my neighbors. . . ."

"Don't bother, the bed will be fine."

Grisha was trying to follow the adults' conversation, trying to understand: "What is it, Mommy? What do they
want?"

They informed Raissa of the purpose of their visit—an
official communication of rehabilitation—and she explained to her son, "It's good news, Grisha."

"But who are they?"

"They're sent by . . . by the Central Committee," said
Raissa.

"Why?" said Grisha impatiently. At eight, he already
mistrusted strangers.

One of the men, the spokesman, heavy-lidded, with a
face that exuded kindness, drew Grisha close and gently
explained their presence:

"We've come to talk about your father."

Grisha became frightened. He cast a glance toward the bookshelf to see whether his father was still there, in his place, and breathed easier: the visitors had not discovered him. Suddenly, to his great surprise, his mother climbed up on a chair, took hold of the forbidden work and presented it triumphantly to the spokesman.

Grisha protested: "You mustn't, Mommy! You mustn't show them my father, you mustn't take him out of his hiding place!"

The man smiled at him: "Why not, Grishinka?"

"It's dangerous, you know that, don't you?"

"Oh, no, my little Grisha Paltielovich, it's not dangerous any more—times have changed. . . ."

He examined the book, passed it to his aide, who studied it seriously, conscientiously, before giving it to his colleague. All three shook their heads sadly, compassionately, and let out whistles of admiration and long sighs:

"Yes, yes, no doubt at all, a great work . . ."

"He was a real poet, that's what we heard from high places, you know."

"A martyr. What a tragedy, what a tragedy . . ."

"And what an outrage!"

Grisha was lost. Why these outbursts? His mother was drinking them in. Grisha had never seen her so joyful, so exuberant. The visitors took their leave, promising to return to discuss practical arrangements: pension, compensation. . . . Raissa showed them to the door. She came back, excited, almost in a trance:

"You see, Grisha, you see, they came! They spoke about your father, that means that from now on you too will be able to talk about him; it also means we can keep his book right here, in the open."

For Grisha things also changed at school. His teachers and classmates no longer treated him as a nuisance. Still, whenever he mentioned his father, he was left alone again.

During that period of his childhood he made two important acquaintances: first Dr. Mozliak, and then the night watchman for the group of buildings they lived in, a strange fellow called Viktor Zupanev, who was to become his protector, his guide, his ally, his best friend.

Dr. Mozliak was a physician of sorts. Grisha was convinced he spent hours at a time in front of the mirror admiring himself, perhaps even talking to himself. Surely he thought himself irresistible, with his mustache, his hard, cold, piercing eyes, the eyes of a man who thought he knew everything and was entitled to everything.

Grisha couldn't understand his mother: how could she become attached to someone like that? Of course, she was alone, she needed a man in her life, while he, Grisha, made her feel even more alone.

Grisha detested Mozliak and made no secret of it. Because of him Raissa would slip out in the evening and go up to the floor above. To make her feel better Grisha would pretend to be asleep. Besides, she would have left anyway. Often, eyes aching, sick with anxiety, he would wait for her return: when would he finally hear the door creaking? His anguish endured until the door opened. Then he would close his eyes and pretend to be fast asleep. On one occasion, he didn't succeed. It was impossible to close his eyes: he tried and tried—in vain. Raissa turned on the bed light and saw her son's twisted face.

"What's the matter, Grisha?"

"Nothing, nothing at all."

"Weren't you sleeping?"

"Yes, I was. I just woke up, I had a bad dream."

"I'm here now. Go to sleep."

She put out the light. "You should spend more time with your classmates, make some friends," she said in the dark. "Now it's all right, it's possible."

"I know that," he said spitefully.

She was startled. "What are you talking about?"

"Nothing."

She was silent a moment before going on: "Are you angry with me?"

"No."

"Dr. Mozliak is a fine person, you know, you'd like him too, if . . ."

"If what?"

"If you'd meet him. In fact, he'd like nothing better."

Grisha thought it over: "What do you do in his place when you're together?"

"Nothing," she answered quickly. "We talk, that's all. We drink tea and chat. He's a good talker, Volodya, I mean Dr. Mozliak."

"And my father?"

"What do you mean?"

"Was my father a good talker?"

The hostile silence created an abyss between them.

"Your father didn't talk much, Grisha. He was a poet. And poets, in order to sing, need silence. Your father was often silent."

Grisha promised himself that one day he would be silent too. And that he would learn to understand words before they were born and after they had disappeared.

I have never laughed, said Viktor Zupanev, the night watchman. I have never laughed in my life.

My parents tried to make me laugh; my neighbors tried to make me laugh; my adversaries tried to make me laugh. Life and death, intertwined like drunkards, did everything to make me laugh.

My parents took me to doctors, who made me vomit; then to gypsies, who made me drink; then to fortune-tellers, showmen, monks, scoundrels, witches, acrobats, clowns, fakirs—I always left with a frown on my face.

At boarding school, my teachers swore on their honor to make me laugh; they beat me and deprived me of food, water and sleep; they laughed, not I.

My schoolmates persecuted me. Girls tickled me, their mothers caressed me and bubbled with laughter. Nothing worked—I didn't laugh.

I had no real friends, no real enemies, no mistresses, no illegitimate children—I had no one, I was no one. And all because I didn't know how to laugh.

At the office, I watched everything that went on, I observed, listened and took notes—but there, too, I had no desire to laugh.

THE TESTAMENT OF PALTIEL KOSSOVER II

SOON AFTERWARD World War I broke out, but I had nothing to do with it, I swear. No doubt this will shock you, Citizen Magistrate, since you are convinced that everything evil that happens in the world is arranged, directed and willed by the Jews. Not this time. Sarajevo—not my fault.

To tell the truth, I was a little bewildered by it all. Those names, those titles, those thrones: too much for the head of a Jewish child. The adults were worried and so was I. It was dismal, distressing. Those church bells, ringing for hours across fields and mountains, were announcing to men and women that it was their turn to meet death, some as messengers, others as victims. The bells rang out, they chimed; would they never stop?

"What does that mean—war?" I asked my father.

He tried to explain: politics, strategy, territorial ambitions, national pride, economic factors. All I understood was that the Austrians loved their king, the English theirs, the Russians theirs, but that all this royalty envied and hated one another.

"But then," I asked in astonishment, "why don't *they* do the fighting? Why do kings send their people to kill and be killed in their place? It would be so much simpler. . . ."

My father agreed. "Unfortunately, kings don't think the way we do."

Another time he gave me a better explanation: "War is a sort of pogrom, but on a larger scale."

"Against the Jews?"

"Not necessarily. You see, in war, all people become Jews without realizing it."

Barassy was being emptied of its arms-bearing citizens and filling up with strangers. Sons and husbands, called to the colors, were leaving for the train station singing, while recruits mobilized elsewhere were arriving in our midst. At first the war was one long journey, an endless displacement, a national uprooting.

My father having been discharged for medical reasons, there were no changes in our family life. On the other hand, my maternal and paternal uncles had all donned uniforms and were already fighting for the glory and honor of the Tsar of All the Russias.

I can still remember. Most evenings, neighbors and friends would gather in our home, in the dining room during the winter and under the poplar in the summer, to discuss the situation at the front. The three students, our companions in misfortune during the pogrom, paid us frequent visits. Two of them came for the meals, the third for my sister.

The conversations also touched on the future: What was better for the Jews—a victory for the Tsar or a triumph for the Kaiser? As it happened, both of them, one after the other, lost that war, and neither's loss benefited the other—or the Jews.

At the time there was much talk in our families about a highly placed monk, his evil power and great influence at the Imperial Court; about the misery of the country, its weakness, the soldiers who were fighting badly or not at all, about the rich and the dignitaries who spent their nights drinking and making merry; about the discontent taking hold of the people. . . .

I learned some new words—Bolshevism, Menshevism, Socialism, Anarchism. I questioned my father: " 'Ism'— what's that exactly?"

"It's like a fickle woman ready to marry . . . the first word that comes along."

There was talk of leaders—courageous or rash depending on one's point of view—who clandestinely or from abroad claimed to be able and willing to depose the Tsar.

"That's a joke," someone said. "Depose the Tsar—no more, no less. They can't be serious."

Then the talk turned to revolution, counterrevolution, the Brest-Litovsk armistice, peace, the White and Red armies.

Why did my father one fine day decide to leave Barassy and move us all to Romania? He was probably as afraid of civil war as of Communism.

The move was painful and filled with incidents; we had to abandon a good part of our belongings on the way. My mother was a poor traveler but never complained. Masha was upset at having to leave her future husband; but Goldie, a year younger, was helpful and good-natured. As for myself, I found the adventure strangely exciting— towns and villages devastated, men and women in flight seeking shelter, and above all, the stories they told between handshakes—never before had I heard such stories. I experienced this time of upheaval with every fiber of my being. In my child's mind I sometimes fancied this war had been declared just for my education.

Welcomed in Liyanov, a small town on the Romanian border, by Sholem, a cousin of my mother's, a devout Hasid, we adjusted quickly. What do you expect, Citizen Magistrate? Jews remain Jews wherever they are: united, charitable, hospitable. Every Jew knows the roles can easily be reversed; the person who welcomes a homeless stranger to his home can so easily be in his place next time.

You condemn Jewish nationalism for its internationalist character, and in a way you're right: between a Jewish businessman from Morocco and a Jewish chemist from Chicago, a Jewish rag picker from Lodz and a Jewish industrialist from Lyons, a Jewish mystic from Safed and a Jewish intellectual from Minsk, there is a deeper and more substantive kinship, because it is far older, than between two gentile citizens of the same country, the same city and the same profession. A Jew may be alone but never solitary, for he remains integrated within a timeless community, however invisible or without geographic or political reality. The Jew does not define himself within geographical categories, Citizen Magistrate; he expresses and identifies himself in historic terms. Jews help one another in order to prolong their common history, to explore and enrich their common destiny, to enlarge the domain of their collective memory.

I know: what I say now constitutes additional evidence of my guilt; I've just acknowledged that I'm a bad Communist, a traitor to the working class and an implacable enemy of your system. So be it. But my father's opinion means more to me than yours. In fact, it is his alone that counts.

At the hour of my death, it is his image that will rise before me. It is to him that I must justify my life. And in his presence I have a feeling close to shame. I wasted too many years seeking something that could never be part of me.

To please him, all I would have had to do was to follow the divine path, obey the Law of Moses, accept God's grace. I must have been a disappointment to him in this area. As in many others.

At Liyanov I was old enough to study seriously. Accordingly, my father enrolled me in the best schools. He introduced me to famous religious masters, and let me taste the joy and magic of a good Talmudic argument. I wonder today whether his efforts were not in vain.

I loved Liyanov, and Barassy seemed far away. I loved Liyanov because Barassy seemed far away. I was an expatriate, a refugee, a Romanian subject. Memories of the pogrom vanished into the past. War, flight—I no longer thought of them. My studies were supposed to absorb me, and that is precisely what they did. In short, life returned to normal.

My father resumed his trade as a piece-goods merchant. Goldie helped him in the shop. A radiant Masha was counting the days until she would once again see her student from the Barassy yeshiva—and marry him.

I remember that wedding. I remember because it brought me face to face with misery and despair. It was 1922, the year of my Bar Mitzvah.

The marriage was celebrated with joy and pomp. Uncles, aunts, cousins—I never knew I had so many— all attended together with friends, companions, acquaintances. Fortunately, my father could afford it; the festivities might well have ruined another man.

In accordance with custom, a special meal had been prepared for the poor. Masha danced for them and with them. Did she really see them? Yes, she did—and she wept, though she may have been moved by love, not pity. I looked on, holding back my tears. The seeds of my future Communist sympathies were planted at that wedding.

The table for the poor was set up in a long spacious room. It was stifling in there. Pitiful, grotesque men and women scurried about trying to snatch a piece of fish, a little white bread. Here and there quarrels broke out. People spat, yelled, exchanged insults, came to blows. It was to be expected—they were hungry, these children of poverty. Dressed in rags, a mad glint in their eyes, their features distorted by greed and hate, they appeared to be living in a bewitched, accursed world. But in the next room, where the distinguished guests were, there was such feasting and merrymaking, such enthusiasm, that nothing else seemed to matter. It was as though evil and distress had already vanished from earth.

It was painful to go from one room to the next. I no longer paid attention to the songs, happy or sad, of the entertainers. The rabbis said the blessings and made the usual speeches but I didn't even listen. Everyone seemed happy except me. I felt torn; my place was among the beggars.

At my Bar Mitzvah, which took place a few months later, I devoted my discourse to the scandal of social injustice in the context of Jewish tradition. I quoted the Babylonian Talmud and the Jerusalem Talmud, Maimonides and Nahmanides, Menahem Harecanati and the Maharal of Prague, the poets of the Golden Age and the Vilna Gaon. I was indignant, I protested: "Long ago, it was thought that if a Jew was poor it was because of society; if he suffered it was because of Exile; people forgot that it is also our fault, mine and yours." And I concluded: "If it is given to man to commit injustices, it is also up to him to repair them; if the creation of the world bears the seal of God, its order bears the seal of man."

My speech created something of a stir. One purist reproached me with having twisted a quotation; another claimed he had heard some blasphemous "insinuations." As for my father, he came directly to the point.

"Remember this, Paltiel: with God everything is possible; without Him nothing has value."

That same week Reb Mendel-the-Tactiturn accosted me in the House of Study and announced he had chosen me as a disciple. That was a consecration; Reb Mendel did not accept just anyone into his intimate circle. Often he would reject candidates without the slightest explanation. Incredibly, he deigned to tell me why I had found favor in his eyes:

"I'm taking you with me to keep you from choosing the wrong path," he said in his hoarse voice. "You are looking for the bark, not for the tree; you seek understanding, not knowledge; you aspire to justice, not to truth. But poor soul—what would you do if you learned that truth itself is unjust? You may tell me that's impossible, but who's to say? No—we must do everything in our power to *make* it impossible. And that is what I shall teach you."

I entered the most fervent, the richest, most exalting phase of my life; I discovered the boundless humility and yearning of mystical experience. I pursued silence in words and words in silence. I was determined to take my self apart if that was required to attain self-realization. I stooped so as to see the summit. I mortified myself so as to feel a purer joy. To believe in salvation, I danced on the brink of the abyss.

Guided, challenged and shielded by Reb Mendel-the-Taciturn, I explored the pathways of messianism. I strained to unveil them, to comprehend them.

I passed my days and nights in the House of Study. When I wasn't praying, I was studying; when I wasn't studying, I was praying. If I allowed myself to succumb to fatigue and sleep, it was only to dream of Elijah the Prophet, who, according to tradition, holds the answers to all questions.

My questions revolved endlessly around the Messiah. I was aching to hasten his arrival, knowing that he would surely abolish the distance between rich and poor, sad and happy, beggar and landlord; put an end to pogroms and wars; unite justice and compassion, making certain that both were true.

You smile, Citizen Magistrate. I pity you. I pity you for not having experienced this kind of dream. But no, Paltiel Gershonovich Kossover, you are not being fair to the good Citizen Magistrate who is reading you: he too has experienced this dream but his masters called it by another name —his Messiah was Marx. . . . Yes, Citizen Magistrate, but ours has no name. That is the majesty of our tradition: it teaches us that among the ten things that preceded Creation was the name of the Messiah—the name no one knows and no one will know before he appears.

And indeed, Citizen Magistrate, I was actually a Communist without knowing it. I too wanted to help the poor, the hungry, the damned of the earth. Except that I believed I could do so by appealing to the Messiah: he and he alone would heal the scandal of human injustice, alleviate the pain of human existence.

But this Messiah, how could we hasten his arrival? Reb Mendel-the-Taciturn knew how: We needed to study our holy texts closely, immerse ourselves in our esoteric tradition, learn the names of certain angels and free certain forces. Such is the disquieting beauty of the messianic adventure: only man, for whose sake the Messiah is expected, is capable and worthy of making his advent possible. What man? Any man. Whosoever desires may seize the keys that open the gates of the celestial palace and thus bring power to the prisoner. The Messiah, you see, is a mystery between man and himself.

One evening the door of the study opened, and a figure appeared. I held my breath as a man dressed in a huge kaftan cast furtive glances around the room. Not seeing me, he grew bolder and stepped forward. Elijah the Prophet, without a doubt, I thought as I got up to welcome him and solicit his help. I could hardly control my happiness. At last, I thought, my wishes are coming true; the prophet is here and he will lead me to where all is

light. Rejoice, O Israel! The hour of thy deliverance is
at hand! But prophet though he was, the night visitor was
not expecting to see me at that hour in that place, he
made a gesture of alarm, almost panic. It was then I became aware of my error.

"Ephraim," I exclaimed, a trifle disappointed. "What
are you doing here so late?"

"The same as you," he said, irritably.

"Are you studying Kabbala?"

"Yes, I am."

"With whom?"

"I don't have the right to reveal that to you."

"Are you also looking for the ultimate secret?"

"Of course."

"And you're trying to get an *Aliyat-neshama*, to let your
soul ascend into heaven?"

"What else?"

His answers excited me. So I was not the only one who
wanted to upset the plans of Creation. And Reb Mendel-
the-Taciturn was not the only master in this domain.
I scrutinized Ephraim more closely. He was known to be
erudite and pious, and a glorious career was predicted for
him; he would probably succeed his father as rabbinic
judge. I was gratified by his visit. We could be friends,
study the same works and together overcome the same
dangers. But why was he behaving so strangely? His kaftan
was hiding something bulky.

"What's that?" I asked out of simple curiosity.

"Oh, it's nothing."

Faker, I thought, he must have come across some rare
treatise.

"Come on now, Ephraim—show it to me!"

"No—I'm not allowed to. Besides, I really must go. I'm
in a hurry, someone is waiting for me."

I didn't insist. He turned on his heels, and clumsily

bumped into a desk. As he put out his hand to keep from falling, he dropped his package. And you'll never guess, Citizen Magistrate, what it contained—pamphlets and booklets of a very nonmystical nature.

Yes, indeed, my first lesson in Communism was given me by Ephraim that very night, at the House of Study. Funny, isn't it? Ephraim, a Communist agitator. Ephraim, the future rabbinic judge, distributing clandestine tracts.

"Let me see!"

Ephraim shrugged his shoulders and agreed. I sat down on the steps leading to the podium and started reading. Eerily bloody stories glorifying the terrorist activities of the revolutionaries at the beginning of the century. Attempts on the lives of the Tsar and his family, bombs flung at the governor's motorcar, the assassination of the Minister of Police. . . . How stupid, I thought, how childish. All these adventurers, these criminals whose inevitable destination was Siberia—what did I have in common with them? The Tsar had not harmed me personally; his Secret Police, the Okhrana, had never touched me; no one had taken it into his head to shut me up in a fortress. I read those pamphlets with their tales of long ago without really understanding them. Though their authors wrote in Yiddish, their language was not mine.

I looked at Ephraim in confusion, not knowing whether to be angry or laugh. "Have you gone mad, Ephraim? You're abandoning the holy texts for *this*?"

Embarrassed, he put his head between his hands and didn't answer.

"Seriously, Ephraim, is this how you intend to hasten redemption?"

"Yes," he said defiantly.

"My poor friend! Our sages were right to forbid the study of mysticism until a certain age: it endangers the mind."

"I haven't lost my mind, Paltiel. Now listen to me carefully. I still want to save the human race and rid society of its ills; I still wish to bring the Messiah. Only—I've found a new way of doing it, that's all. I've tried meditation, fasting, asceticism, but with no success. There is only one path leading toward salvation—"

"Which one?"

"The path of action."

"Action? But I believe in that too. What is prayer if not an action? What's the practice of mysticism if not an act of faith in God?"

"I'm talking to you about an action related not to God but to history, to the events that produce history, in short, to man himself."

Seated on a bench between two desks, I with my Book of Prayers according to Rabbi Itzhak Luria, he with his idiotic pamphlets, we made a fine pair, Citizen Magistrate.

"Would you like to have a real discussion?" said Ephraim.

"Why not?"

"Then first of all promise to say nothing to anyone."

"I promise."

"It's not enough to promise—swear."

"I swear."

"It's not enough to swear—swear before the open Ark, while touching the sacred scrolls."

I refused, of course. One doesn't play around with the Torah.

"If you don't trust me, too bad," I said. "Let's drop the whole thing."

"I do trust you. If I demand an oath from you it's for your own safety as well as mine: you'll watch what you say; otherwise you might let something slip at the wrong time and place."

"So, what could happen to me?"

"It's better not to know, Paltiel. You've heard of the Secret Police, haven't you? Well, they exist, and for them torture has become a science. If they catch you in their net, it's all over for you. They'll never believe you weren't mixed up with . . . with all that."

"Mixed up with what?" I cried.

"The Revolution," he said gravely.

Ephraim tried to give me a quick course in political science in the manner of a Talmudic lesson, but I didn't take him too seriously, at least not that night. And yet his fear was real: though he seemed to be more afraid of his parents than of the Secret Police. In spite of his arguments and exhortations I stood my ground and refused to take an oath before the holy Ark. My word had to be enough—take it or leave it. He stood up; I thought he was leaving. Not at all. Deliberately, methodically, he started his work: one pamphlet in each desk, tracts in the *talith* bags. Incredulous, I watched him without moving. But he, entirely at his ease, had the audacity—and the ingenuity—to ask for my help, without which he could not finish in time. And like an idiot I could think of nothing better to do than to agree.

And that is how, without my realizing it, without even thinking about it, I became his accomplice. He was kind enough to promise to return the following week to continue our discussion—and our work. And, of course, he kept his word.

His explanations and arguments could be recited by the youngest of our Pioneers. Simple and simplistic, yes— but sincere. And persuasive for a romantic adolescent of sixteen like myself, for they played on my sensibilities. The emphasis was on human misery and not on religious defiance. If Ephraim had used real Marxist propositions I would have turned my back. But instead of quoting Engels, Plekhanov and Lenin, he invoked the messianic

hope we shared. And I could only approve: he was pleading for justice for the victims, and the dignity of slaves,
amen.

"My father is one of the Just," he said. "He has never
done anything to harm a living being; and he's poor.
We often go hungry, did you know that? Two hot meals a
week, that's all we can afford. Why are we condemned to
hunger, to poverty?"

"Because it's God's will," I answered. "Who are we to
wish to pierce the secret of His ways? Let the Messiah
come and . . ."

"I have four older sisters; there's no money to marry
them off. Why do you want my sisters to remain old
maids?"

"God's will is unfathomable; it is not up to us to question it, you know that perfectly well. Let the Messiah
come and . . ."

"The Messiah, the Messiah! For two thousand years
men worthier than we have been imploring him to make
himself known and to establish his kingdom, and century
after century injustice goes on. Do you know Hanan-the-
Coachman? He has nothing; he doesn't even own his horse
or his coach; nor his hovel either, nor even his body. He
toils from dawn to dusk and often late into the night.
Occasionally you can see him, eyes red from lack of sleep,
lips parched, driving Jonah Davidovich. Think of Jonah,
sitting comfortably in the coach behind Hanan, and dare
deny that so much injustice makes it imperative for us to
wait no longer. Dare tell Hanan to be patient! And what
about Brokha-the-Laundress, do you know her? Pious and
humble, she has lost her husband and kills herself working to feed her seven children, to send her three sons to
school, to buy ingredients for a Sabbath meal. She does
the housework, the laundry and the cooking for Ksil
Messiver, the greengrocer. Ksil has the time and the means

to wait for the Messiah—but Brokha-the-Laundress! Think of her before you answer."

Ephraim expressed himself passionately; he disturbed me. We were alone, as usual, in the House of Study. Outside it was snowing. And as he talked, one by one, the candles burned down and went out. Ephraim swayed back and forth while talking as though we were studying a tangled commentary submitted by Rabbi Eliezer, son of Hyrkanos, on the purity and impurity of certain objects.

"You'll tell me it's all up to God," he went on. "You're right, but only partly. Human suffering concerns God, of course, but it also affects us. Why do men make their fellow men suffer? Paltiel, that question concerns you and me!"

"Who makes his fellow man suffer? The wicked and the miscreants. Their victims' fate affects me, their own leaves me indifferent. The presence of the wicked in the world is a problem for the philosophers, and that I'm not. How can we explain the imperfection of Creation? And evil, and its appeal and power? Since the mystic response doesn't satisfy you, read Maimonides. As for myself, I prefer to wait for the Messiah."

"Well, I feel sorry for you, you've got a long wait ahead of you."

"Why? Don't you believe in the coming of the Messiah?"

"Yes, Paltiel, I do. Every morning I pray for his coming, his early coming. Like you I recite the prayers. But he's taking his time; meanwhile exile is a heavy burden to bear, especially for the poor: the laborers, the beggars. Do you understand, Paltiel? I'm willing to wait a year, a century—but the less fortunate can't wait!"

Little by little, slowly and systematically, he instilled in me his concept of the world. Only Communism allows man to overcome oppression and inequality swiftly. According to Ephraim, Communism was a sort of messianism

without God, a secular, social messianism while waiting for
the other, the true one.

"Look around, Paltiel, look around here in Liyanov.
On one side, the rich; on the other, the destitute. On one
side, the powerful, on the other, the exploited. The rich
are rich because the poor are poor—and the other way
round. If the rich had no one to exploit, nothing would be
left of their fortune. Conclusion: the wealth of the rich
is just as scandalous as the poverty of the poor."

Our nocturnal meetings became more and more frequent. I helped him distribute his tracts; sometimes, quite
as a matter of course, I accompanied him to other synagogues. We were a team, but he had still not confessed to
me his adherence to the clandestine Party. We talked of
mysticism and liturgy, history and poetry, everything but
ideology. I helped him because he had become my friend;
he was my friend because he allowed me to take action.
We were friends because—because we were friends.

Together we believed that ultimate redemption depended only on us, as our ancient texts kept affirming. God
had created the universe and made man responsible for
it—it was up to us to shape it and make it resplendent.
In helping our neighbor, we were helping God. In rous-
ing the slaves and invoking their pride and dignity, we
were accomplishing God's work on His behalf. That was
how we reconciled divine omnipotence with human freedom. In His omnipotence, God has made us free; it is
up to us to restore the primordial equilibrium by returning to the poor what they had had to yield to their ex-
ploiters; it was incumbent on us to change the order of
things—that is, to start the Revolution.

"Don't you understand?" Ephraim cried, eyes ablaze.
"We must start the Revolution because that is God's command! God wants us to be Communists!"

In spite of all Ephraim's explanations, I still didn't

know what that word meant, just as I didn't know that it linked us to the Soviet Union. I didn't even know that in Liyanov, among our God-fearing Jews, there was a clandestine Communist Party.

I was very naive, Citizen Magistrate. I was a Communist and didn't know it.

WHILE WASHING THE DISHES in the communal kitchen, Raissa eyed her son, who stood in the doorway, ready to return to the attack:

"Please, Mother—tell me about my father. Now we're allowed to talk about him, you said so yourself."

"Don't you see I'm busy?"

She was irritated, as usual. Her irritation was contagious.

"You're always busy. And when you're not, you're upstairs with Dr. Mozliak."

"Are you starting again?"

Grisha seemed about to run off, then turned back. What good was it to get angry? That was no way to make her talk.

"Please, Mother. I hardly know my father, I don't know him at all. It's not normal. A son should know his father, even if his father is no longer alive."

"What do you want to know?"

"Everything."

A pot in her hand, a kerchief on her head, Raissa seemed to resign herself. Grisha found her pretty, vulnerable. A melancholy smile, like a memory of her youth, brushed her lips.

"Everything?" she asked with a smile. "And what does that mean—everything?"

Grisha hesitated. His assurance left him. In his mother's presence he had for some time felt himself both accuser and accused. Why was she making him suffer? Why was she so evasive? And—why was he so insistent? Because he loved her or because he didn't?

"Yes, Grisha, what is—everything?"

Grisha blushed. His mother was right. Everything—
what a stupid word—meaning one thing for the living,
another for the dead; another for Mozliak, and yet another for Kossover. For the living, it was perhaps the sun-
beam dancing across the kitchen, playing with the dust; or
the noise of chairs being moved on the first floor; or certain
silences tormenting an abandoned child.

"Tell me—was he happy?"

"I think so. Sometimes. Why do you ask?"

"I told you. I want to know everything about him."

All of a sudden it was vital for Grisha to know whether
his father had been happy. And only Raissa could tell him.

"He was happy, Grisha. Like most people."

"I don't like that answer. My father wasn't like most
people."

"That's true, Grisha. He wasn't, except in matters of
happiness; he was happy and unhappy like the rest of us."

"What made him happy?"

"Everything or nothing. A smile. A babbling brook. A
word, the right word."

"What made him unhappy?"

"A smile. A babbling brook. A word, the wrong word."
Raissa paused; there was a silence. Then:

"He *was* unlike anyone else."

"Did he love you?"

It was important, urgent, for Grisha to know whether
his father had loved Raissa.

"Yes, he loved me."

"How do you know? Did he tell you?"

"He told me."

"When?"

"I don't remember."

"How did he tell you?"

"I don't remember."

"Try. Think!"

"I don't remember."

Raissa had raised her voice as she said those last words. A neighbor came in, scowled at them, took a teapot and left.

"And you?" said Grisha. "Did you love him?"

"Why these questions? Why now?"

"Did you love him? Answer me. I have the right to know whether you loved my father."

"What right? Who gave it to you? I will not allow you to . . ." Raissa spoke harshly.

She controlled herself: "You're still young, Grisha. You can't understand. Between man and woman there are many ways of loving."

She took a deep breath. "You, it was you he really loved."

She had finished putting away the dishes and dishcloths.

"You didn't know," she went on, "you couldn't know, but he loved you so much . . . so much it made me jealous."

And since Grisha didn't respond, she hastened to end the conversation. "It's all so complicated. Others besides me will be able to explain it to you. For instance . . ."

"You mean Dr. Mozliak?"

Grisha went out without waiting for his mother's answer. An idea haunted him: his father had not been happy, not been happy, not been happy. And his son? Not happy, not happy either. Because of what? His mother, maybe?

KATYA LEFT THE WINDOW and went to open the door.

"Oh, it's you? Come in."

It was a ritual: he rapped on the window, she opened the door. As usual, she looked him over carefully.

"You seem depressed," she said. "Oh well, I forgot you

may do everything, feel everything without explanation.
You're depressed and that's that. All right, I'll do without
your explanation; I have no choice."

Grisha sank into the sofa, his usual place.

"Are you thirsty?"

No, he wasn't thirsty.

"Some fruit?"

No, he wasn't hungry.

"*Something else?*"

She smiled at him. No, he didn't feel like *something
else*. Not this evening.

"You're sure?"

Yes, he was sure.

"All right, let's watch television."

Politics, literature, gossip: everything was there. Orators
of both the right and the left promised the citizens happiness and good fortune; skeptical journalists answered
with "Oh, no! Oh, yes!" The daily news: eight hundred
tourists arrived yesterday; twice as many were expected
tomorrow for the Day of Atonement. Austria: the government is shutting down the transit camp for Russian immigrants. And those already there? Grisha jumped up.
What about his mother? She'll get here, don't worry. Besides, Golda Meir is doing her best to get the decision
rescinded. She went to visit Kreisky, who didn't even offer
her a glass of water. A spokesman for the government:
Everything's fine, things will improve; a spokesman for the
opposition: Everything's bad, things will get worse, money
will lose its value and youth its faith, unless . . . The election campaign is at its peak. The people ridicule it. The
speeches are just a joke. Start again, start all over again.
Trust us; help us help you. The politicians, another joke.
Only the army is serious: Remember the victory of '67?
The Israeli Army is always on alert. It is powerful, more
powerful than ever. It sees everything, knows everything.

The Arabs are lying low; they wouldn't dare do anything foolish. Tomorrow is Yom Kippur.

"Happy holiday, Grisha. Are you fasting?"

Yes, he's going to fast.

"What? Are you observant?"

No, he's not observant, but he's a Jew. If his people fast, he'll fast. How explain this to her? Luckily she doesn't ask for an explanation; she asks questions and answers them herself.

When Grisha makes her understand *not this evening*, she starts moving around the room, restless, sullen, dragging her feet. She's always slow, Katya. Was she like that *before?* Probably not. Life stopped for her with Yoram's death. No more plans, no more interests. Katya is listless; even when making love she's slow.

"Sometimes I think I envy you," she said. "You're mute. People ask you questions and all you have to do is frown to let them know: Sorry, go to the next window, this one's closed. . . ."

She comes and sits down beside him on the sofa. "I'm sorry, Grisha, are you sure you . . . ?"

Yes, he's sure. He writes something on a scrap of paper: "My mother's arriving tomorrow." As if that explained his behavior. Katya doesn't see the connection, but she does not insist. Grisha continues: "I'd like you to go to the airport with me tomorrow."

"Gladly, if that'll make you happy."

There she goes again, touching on her favorite subject—happiness. She clings to it and won't let go.

"Yoram was happy," Katya says thoughtfully. "Before him there was Eytan. He was serene, Eytan. And before him was my friend Miriam. Miriam—so delicate, so graceful, made for joy and happiness. All those I loved, all those who loved me . . . I speak of them, I think of them in the past. Death is jealous—the slut! She took from me all who

were dear. You're right to hold back, Grisha. You mustn't
. . . you mustn't get too close. The Angel of Death is never
far away, the bitch. I sense her, lying in wait, spying on us.
I sense her, Grisha. Who will be her next prey? You or
me? Maybe your mother? I feel she is armed and ready as
in wartime. . . ."

She gets up and goes to look at herself in the mirror as
if seeking someone else, an image of a lost image. She
shakes her head with resentment.

"Tonight you don't want to," she says. "I understand,
Grisha. You can't make love in the presence of death."

Is she offended? Does she feel rejected? Grisha doesn't
know her well enough; she knows him even less. All she
knows is that he's a Jew, a Russian Jew, and that he's mute.

"Don't try to be happy with me," says Katya. "It's dangerous for you. The slut is jealous, jealous of the happiness I give you."

Happy? Grisha is hardly that. He thinks of his mother,
who killed his taste for happiness. Has he ever been happy?
Yes, in a way perhaps, in Krasnograd, after the accident.
That was when he met the extraordinary old man, the one
he looked upon as his father's messenger, and who was to
become his best and only friend. Oh, those evenings spent
with Viktor Zupanev, the watchman with his tales of a
thousand and one nights of solitude. The stories, the reminiscences he made Grisha learn by heart. The secret
places they met. The mission suggested, defined and accepted. Yes, Grisha had been happy. His father's unpublished poems, the chapters of his *Testament,* the agony of
silence, the secret laughter and its liberating explosion.
Grisha smiles as he recalls the various stages of the project.
His victory over Dr. Mozliak and his mother. Can Katya
understand why a mute young man feels the need to smile
as she tells him about sad events?

Katya, too, reviews her own past, her own struggles and

defeats. She brings to life for Grisha those bright years in the kibbutz with her parents—now dead—and the sunlit years with Yoram—now dead—and her idyllic liaison with Eytan—now dead—and her entertaining, scintillating, solid friendship with Miriam—now dead. And Grisha thinks of his own life, his parents, his mother. Is it normal to hate one's mother? Normal to want to hurt her in the name of a dead man?

Outside it is night. And suddenly the city stretches toward heaven as though to wedge itself among the stars that see and retain everything.

"You understand, Grisha?" asks Katya as in a dream, and with maddening slowness. "You understand, my darling mute lover? Sometimes I wonder whether I'm not death's accomplice, whether I'm not being used to attract her chosen victims. First I make them happy, then I hand them over. . . . You're in danger, Grisha. Tomorrow you'll leave me. You'll see your mother again. Make her stay with you. Your writer friend won't object, I assure you. You need your mother, she needs you. And as for me, forget me. It's safer that way. Far from me, you'll be able to go on living. . . ."

Through the window the city appears unreal, suspended between the clouds and the hills, between nostalgia and premonition.

THE TESTAMENT OF PALTIEL KOSSOVER III

I CONTINUED MY STUDIES. There was no conflict between my mystic quest, the old debates about the cult in the Temple, and my "political" work with Ephraim.

My father seemed satisfied with his son and proud of him. If I persevered, I would soon receive my ordination; I would marry an intelligent and beautiful girl, well brought up and virtuous, and from a respectable family; we would have children who would grow up to be good Jews; and, God willing, we would all have the privilege of going to welcome the Messiah at the gates of Liyanov, and afterward—there would be no afterward.

In his naiveté my father congratulated himself on my friendship with Ephraim, which had become well known. Why not? Together we were exploring the dazzling texts of the Talmud. Nothing objectionable in that. Our sages urge students not only to select a master but also to find themselves a companion.

Appearances were kept up: Ephraim, a master at the seduction and corruption of the mind, carefully set about initiating me into profane reading. First he made me read the religious authors, then the free-thinkers. Poems, short stories, essays. Mapu, Mendele Mocher Seforim, Frishman, Peretz, Bialik, Shneur . . . Ephraim's task was not easy. The Talmudist in me, deeply rooted in tradition, resisted

him. I could not bring myself to get interested in the
dramas and psychological conflicts of imaginary beings at
a time when I found myself personally involved in every
lesson formulated by Rabbi Yohanan ben Zakkai or Hillel
the Elder. Memory fascinated me more than imagination.
But Ephraim, a patient mentor, did not lose heart. We
would attack a social novel as though it were a page of the
Aggada, analyzing it from within. And finally I would
succumb to its spell. And admit that there were indeed
books worth discovering outside the "Tractate on Idolatry
or Divorce." I promptly set out to devour the Russian
and French classics, in Yiddish translations of course.
Victor Hugo and Tolstoy, Zola and Gogol: my horizon
was expanding. I was abandoning Safed to stroll through
Paris. I was following the path of emancipation.

The next phase was slower, more difficult. To liberate
me completely, Ephraim brought me works of philosophy:
Spinoza, Kant, Hegel—still in Yiddish translation. I
balked: What, how dare they cast doubt on the existence of
God, deny Biblical truth, the divine origin of Creation?
Calmly, Ephraim set out to show me that blind faith is
unworthy of man; that it is permissible to formulate questions: even Maimonides had done so. And Yehuda Halevy.
And Don Itzhak Abravanel. In order to refute the un-
believers, one had to know their arguments. That is written
in the *Ethics of the Fathers*. Does criticism of the Bible
frighten you, Paltiel? But why? It's just the scientific study
of Scripture. Is it science you're afraid of? But our greatest
thinkers, our most illustrious commentators were scientists
. . . Ephraim knew how to go about it. He drew me along,
and I let him. He gave me copies of Schlegel, Feuerbach
and Marx. We discussed the exile of the *Shekinah* less and
less, and *The Critique of Pure Reason* more and more. You
will not believe me, Citizen Magistrate, but that year I
learned by heart entire passages of *Das Kapital*. And its
commentaries.

Ephraim, in his methodical way, succeeded in awakening in me the love of the homeless for a homeland—I mean this one. And I, who had little sense of geography or economics, was obliged to learn everything about the cities and republics, the steppes and mountains of Soviet Russia, the Revolution, the government and its structure, its social system, its benefits to mankind. Newspapers, journals, schools, military heroes, revolutionary writers—I became better acquainted with the life of the Soviet Union than that of Romania, my adopted country. It became as familiar to me as celestial Jerusalem. If one were to believe Ephraim, the Messiah had left Jerusalem for Moscow.

"Do you understand?" he would ask me in a frenzied voice. "They've fulfilled Isaiah's prophecies, they've justified Jeremiah's consolation. No more rich or poor, no more employers or employees, no more persecutors or persecuted. No more ignorance. No more terror. No more poverty. Do you hear me, Paltiel? Over there all men are brothers in the eyes of the law: they don't have the right not to be. Just think what that means. The Jews are no longer threatened with death; they no longer live in fear and uncertainty; they no longer have to buy their right to happiness or education. They are free and equal. Neither feared nor envied nor isolated. They live as they like, they sing in their own language, they build their homes according to their taste and shape their dreams according to their vision. That's what counts, Paltiel: if there is a single country where Jews feel at home and live in security, it's the Soviet Union. Why? Because the Revolution has triumphed. It has produced a new man—Communist man —who has overcome the power of capitalism, the dictatorship of the rich, the fanaticism of the superstitious. . . ."

Since at home in Liyanov and its environs anti-Semitism was rampant, and since the suffering and misery of its victims tore at my heart, and since Reb Mendel-the-Taciturn had died before teaching me how to hasten the

coming of messianic times in accordance with mystical
procedures, and since my soul yearned for romance as
much as idealism and since my friend was as persuasive as
he was seductive, I let myself be dazzled, tempted. I
responded to what he described as the call of the Revolution.

One evening, at the home of a comrade from a bourgeois
family, I met other comrades: two students from the
Yeshiva, a seamstress, a barber, and Feivish, an employee
of my father's. On seeing the latter, I experienced a mixture of indignation and sadness. Like the others, Feivish
condemned the greedy capitalists who drank the workers'
blood. And I felt myself blush: My father, a drinker of
blood? My father? I raised my hand and asked to speak:

"You're lying, Feivish! My father is gentle and kind. He
works harder and longer than you or anyone. And he
shares what he earns. He gives, he loves to give. And you
know that perfectly well. You know we never celebrate the
Sabbath meal without inviting poor persons to our table.
And after the prayers, my father goes from one synagogue
to the next to make sure no stranger, no beggar is left
without lodging or food. And every Wednesday there is set
up in our courtyard a kitchen for all the beggars of
Liyanov, or for travelers who are hungry. You know all
that better than anyone else, Feivish. So why do you
slander him? Is that what your Communism is? Malice
and lies?"

As we left that evening, Ephraim tried to set things
straight. "It's my fault. I was wrong to bring Feivish and
you together."

"That's not what upsets me," I said, getting upset all
over again. "The point is that Feivish is telling lies, and
you encourage him. Whether he lies in my presence, or
when I'm not there, has nothing to do with the fact that
he's telling lies. And if Feivish tells lies, that means the

other comrades are also lying. Is that what your Communist *truth* amounts to?"

"You're furious, I understand," said Ephraim. "But you're exaggerating. Don't take the general statements of one comrade as a personal offense. Communism is valuable only as an objective system; to individualize it is to distort it."

He was right, but so was I. I was distressed for my father. As for Feivish, I nursed a grudge against him and never spoke to him again. I wished I could send him away: I found it difficult to live with him under the same roof. My mother was aware of my uneasiness; she would often look at me furtively, as if inviting me to confide in her. Did she guess the nature and gravity of my commitments? There was never a shadow of reproach in her eyes. Even the day I came to tell her I intended to go abroad, she gazed at me sadly but uttered no word of blame.

I had reached the age for military service, and had not the slightest desire to find myself a soldier of His Majesty the King of Greater Romania. I therefore made a pact with Ephraim to slip away and go abroad: Berlin, Paris, and—God willing—Moscow.

"When are you leaving?" my mother asked, turning pale.

"In a few days."

"Does your father know?"

"No, I'll speak to him this evening."

She shook her head. "Try not to cause him too much grief."

What was she alluding to? I cleared my throat and asked her.

She answered with a question that seemed to have no connection with mine: "Where are your *tephilin*?"

"My phylacteries are in the House of Study."

"You won't forget to take them with you?"

The very fact that she asked such a question proved to

me she had guessed my secret life: I was still observing the
fundamental precepts of Torah, still practicing our religion, still studying sacred texts, but I was already moving
away. My departure would mark an irrevocable break—
and my mother knew it.

"Do you seriously think I'm going to stop being a Jew
when I go away?"

"Nothing's impossible, my son. Far from your parents,
anything can happen. That's why I tell you now: to
chase away the Evil Spirit, remember your parents."

She knew—my mother knew. She knew we would be
living far apart from one another for a long time, but she
managed to hide her grief. I remember that conversation
as if it were yesterday. We were in the kitchen. My mother
was straightening a drawer and arranging the dishes. There
was a smile on her face, a smile I had never seen before, a
smile that shattered me. I wanted to ask her forgiveness; I
didn't. I don't know why.

That evening my father came home a little late, accompanied by Feivish.

"I'd like to speak to you, Father."

"Right away," he said. "I haven't said *maariv* yet."

Feivish looked panicky; he was afraid I would denounce
him. He went out and left me alone in the kitchen with
my mother.

"Don't keep anything from your father, but don't hurt
him. Tell him why you have to leave. Tell him you've
received your mobilization papers, that you must present
yourself at the recruiting center next week; tell him that
you and I both think it would be a mistake to spend years
serving an army where you can't observe Jewish law—but
don't talk about the rest."

Oh yes, she knew. She knew I had changed and would
change even more.

My father joined us.

"Come into the living room," he said.

I followed him. He took his favorite Bible commentary and put it down on the table in front of him; he was never without it. Even in the shop he kept it before him, on the counter.

"Well, I'm listening," he said, sitting down.

I brought him up to date in a few words. He seemed saddened but not surprised. Absentmindedly he leafed through his book while listening to me. We had discussed military service more than once. The regime was corrupt, and with a bribe one could get a discharge or even hire a proxy. But that solution was unacceptable to him. Corrupting someone else is worse than being corrupted, he told me firmly. Only one possibility remained—to flee abroad. And wait for the first amnesty.

"When are you thinking of leaving?"

"In a few days. At the beginning of next week."

"Will you go to Bucharest first?"

"Yes, for a day or two. Just long enough to get the necessary documents, and then I'll go on to Vienna or Berlin."

"Is someone helping you? Who is it?"

"Ephraim and a friend of his," I said.

My father, his right hand on the open page, seemed lost in thought. Where was he? What ancestor was he questioning in his mind? His words seemed to come from far away:

"I have three children—you're my only son. Will you say Kaddish for me? You'll remain a Jew, won't you?"

The anguish in his voice startled me. So he too knew what was going on!

"Of course," I stuttered, "of course. Why—why do you ask me that?"

His eyes straying over the open page, his hand caressing it uninterruptedly, he made clear to me that I had been

wrong to hide my activities of the last few months. He
hadn't been fooled at all. He had understood a long time
ago that Ephraim and I had been occupying ourselves
with illegal matters. He hadn't intervened out of respect
for me. Especially since, as far as my religious duties and
studies were concerned, he had nothing to complain about.

"You hope to change man," he said. "Very good. You
want to change society. Magnificent. You expect to eliminate evil and hatred. Extraordinary. I'm in full agreement."

He expressed himself slowly, with great effort; I listened
with every fiber of my body, with all my being. Suddenly
he changed the subject. "Do you remember Barassy?"

"Yes, Papa, I remember."

"And the pogrom?"

"I can still smell the mustiness, see the darkness. I can
still feel the silence."

"The funerals—do you remember them?"

"They will live within me until the end of my days."

"The coffins . . ."

The images remained vivid. The black coffins, the
throng, the three men in black with their money boxes.

"Those three beadles who marched before the caskets
shouting *Tzedaka tatzil mimavet*. Charity will save you
from death—what did they mean? What a strange idea!
Suppose a man takes it into his head to distribute his
fortune to the needy, suppose he gives charity day after
day, and even at night—does that mean he'll never die?
Would the rich thus have, in addition to their money, an
assurance of immortality? Of course not. That admonition
means something else: in helping the poor, in looking after
and listening to those who need us, we are but exercising
our privilege of living our life, of living it to the fullest.
And what a privilege it is! Without it we would not feel
alive. That is the meaning of the formula: charity saves
man from death . . . *before* death! That is my farewell

present, my son. Do you understand now why I didn't stop you from doing what you were doing? I don't know your Communist friends, except for Ephraim. I only know that their aim is to diminish unhappiness in the world. That is what counts, that is all that counts. They're said to rebel against the Almighty; that's between them and God. Let Him take care of it. What matters is that they are fighting for those who have neither the strength nor the means to fight. The essential thing for you is to be sensitive to the suffering of others. So long as you persist in fighting injustice, defending victims, even victims of God, you'll feel alive, that is, you'll feel God within you, the God of your ancestors, the God of your childhood. You will feel within you man's passion and God's. The real danger, my son, is indifference."

My father had never taught me so many things in so few words. My eyes followed his hand moving over the yellowed page. I had to force myself not to lean over and kiss it as I used to kiss it on the Day of Atonement.

"Having said that," my father resumed, "I must ask you to remember one thing and remember it always: You're a Jew, a Jew first and foremost; it is as a Jew that you will be helping mankind. If you care for others to the detriment of your brothers, you will eventually deny everyone. You may, if you wish, consider this my last will and testament."

He broke off. His hand lay motionless on the open book: "Promise me you will remain a Jew."

"I promise."

"Promise to put on your phylacteries every morning."

"I promise."

"Try not to eat pork. Don't forget your studies. Keep our festivals. And you will fast on the Day of Atonement, that I know."

His certainty moved me. How could he be so sure? The

following week I would be in the capital, then in another city, then in yet a third; I would meet new people, hear new words. I might have to deny myself, deny him. How could he know what I would do?

He closed his book and took out his handkerchief. He didn't say another word, nor did I. Then we joined my mother in the kitchen. She smiled at us, happy at seeing us silent but reconciled.

The week passed both too quickly and too slowly. I had to prepare for my trip, yet I tried to stay near my parents as much as possible. Finally the day of departure arrived. My suitcase was ready, I only had to pick it up. An envelope stuffed with banknotes was waiting for me on the table. In the kitchen my mother was preparing tea. We drank standing, exchanging trivial remarks heavy with suppressed tenderness. Will you be careful? I'll be careful. Don't forget to eat. I won't forget. You'll write? I'll write. Tell Masha . . . The children . . . Goldie . . . her fiancé . . . Explain that . . . Never before had I felt this close to my parents, so disarmed and humble before their son, before life itself. Never before had I loved them so intensely. If that's a crime, Citizen Magistrate, I plead guilty. Guilty of having loved my father and mother, two gentle, upright people, sincere and honest, who nevertheless belonged to the cursed middle class; they believed in God and practiced the religion of their ancestors; theirs was a pure ideal, and yet they weren't Communists. I plead guilty to having loved them more than our beloved leaders, more than anyone else in the world—I plead guilty to loving them still today, and a thousand times more, six million times more than during their lifetime.

My father reminded me that it was time to go; we had to say farewell. I swallowed hard. A child was screaming somewhere, scolded by its mother.

"It would be wiser," said my father, "if you went to the station without us. Better not to attract attention."

He was right. There was no shortage of informers among us. Ephraim would carry my suitcase and I would accompany him as if he were the one going to spend a week or two with the Rebbe of Wardein.

I took my mother's hand and kissed it. Then I took my father's and kissed it. My heart was pounding. I was glad that Ephraim arrived just then. No tears, Paltiel, he commanded quietly. I left quickly. It's embarrassing to cry when you're old enough to wear a uniform, when you feel strong enough to go off to war against the forces of evil in the name of what is beautiful, just and human—in other words, in the name of the Revolution.

A thousand glints of gold and copper were playing in the trees bordering the street. Passersby greeted one another, shadows followed one another, birds twittered, children jostled me, premonitions churned within me. I walked slowly, forcing myself not to turn back, sensing my father's burning look and my mother's veiled eyes; and it was as if the two of them, motionless, preceded me. Until the end, they would watch over me.

Did I know then that I would never see them again?

*I hear you had an accident, Zupanev, the night watch-
man, said. They had to take you to the hospital. You
didn't cry. Bravo, little Grisha. I like that. You're an intelligent boy, and brave too. Come with me, let's talk. Oh
I know—you can't talk. Never mind. We'll have a chat
anyhow. Let's go to my place where we'll be more comfortable. You don't know me? But I know you. That's
my job: I know everyone around here and everything
that goes on in every apartment, in every family. I know
your mother, your neighbors; I know the one you hate
and, believe me, I hate that Dr. Mozliak too. A strange
doctor. . . . All right now, come along. We'll be able to
converse better at my place. Since you are mute, how will
I manage to understand you? Don't worry, I'll get along.
I've learned to hear the words people leave unsaid, to read
the words one promises oneself never to utter as they take
shape in the mind. Just make believe you are speaking,
and I'll hear you. Make believe you are speaking and you
will be speaking. Do you trust me?*

GRISHA DID TRUST HIM and they became friends—confi-
dants, allies. Grisha needed a father, Zupanev a son.

They had first met one unbearably hot summer evening.
Krasnograd could scarcely breathe—the slightest movement required an effort. Even the flies and mosquitoes
were buzzing in slow time.

Raissa had gone swimming with Mozliak. Grisha, alone in the apartment, was filled with self-pity. He had had a quarrel with Olga, a schoolmate. And then his accident had added to his isolation. At fourteen, he felt trapped, defeated, and ready to provoke yet another accident. So as to punish his mother? Mozliak would have consoled her quickly enough. That could wait. Tomorrow, next year.

He picked up a newspaper lying on the floor: nothing in it. A book on the night table: boring. He turned the pages without stopping at a single line; he didn't even know what this novel, written by the most famous of the fashionable writers, was about. He was going to pour himself a glass of water when someone knocked at the door. A short, baldheaded man stood on the threshold.

"May I come in?"

Grisha nodded.

"I saw you, so I said to myself . . . Excuse me, I haven't introduced myself: I'm Zupanev, Zupanev the watchman. May I sit down?"

Grisha pointed to a chair and motioned to him, asking whether he wanted something to drink.

"No, thanks. I just came over to talk. At this hour there's no one else in the whole building. They have all gone swimming or to the park. Does it bother you, my coming?"

Grisha shook his head. Nothing bothered him; nothing annoyed him; nothing excited him.

"Wouldn't you like to come to my place? We would be more comfortable," said the watchman.

Grisha studied him. The man said he was a watchman. How is it I've never really noticed him?

Zupanev guessed what he was thinking. "You've undoubtedly crossed my path a thousand times but you never stopped to look at me. That surprises you? That's how I am—I don't attract attention. I'm a human chameleon, or something close to it. I blend into the landscape; there's nothing about me that catches the eye. Everything about me is so ordinary that people look at me without seeing me. But I see them. After all, a watchman's duty is to watch."

How old was he? Sixty? More? Less? He was ageless. As a child he must already have had that round expressionless face, those pale expressionless eyes. He was right: with his rounded shoulders, balding head and heavy walk, he was unlikely to arouse any interest. His features were so monotonous that one skipped immediately from forehead to eyes, from eyes to nose, from nose to lips without a single wrinkle or line to catch one's eye. Anonymity.

"Come, my boy," said Zupanev. "I'll speak for the two of us. I'll tell you stories you don't know and should know."

They went down to the ground floor. Zupanev opened a door, asked him to enter, offered him a glass of soda water, which Grisha drank in small sips while looking over the room. A cot, a table, two chairs, a trunk, a bookcase with some volumes whose titles the young boy's eyes scanned. A shock: one was *I Saw My Father in a Dream*, his father's work.

"What is it, my boy, what's the matter?"

He saw Grisha's eyes fixed on the bookcase.

"Ah, I see! The book of poems. You're surprised. But why? Don't I have the right to like poetry? It's in Yiddish, so what? I understand Yiddish."

He took the book and opened it at random to a poem called "Sparks." He began to read in a hesitant voice; soon Grisha was on the verge of tears. So many questions flashed through his head: Who are you, Zupanev? This book, how did you get it? How long have you been a watchman here? Did you know my father?

Zupanev seemed to understand. "Some day I'll tell you

more. You'll come back. I'll tell you everything; you should know it all." He lowered his bald head abruptly as if to press it forcibly into his chest. To hide his pain? Grisha felt overcome by an inexplicable uneasiness.

Zupanev kept his word. There was no end to his stories. A spellbound Grisha listened to him without missing a single word or intonation; had his father himself been speaking to him, he could not have listened with greater intensity.

Who was Zupanev? Why had he not seen him before? What did he do with his free time? Whom did he see? Who kept him informed and whom did he inform?

In time Grisha understood that his friend never bared himself. He spoke of others to avoid speaking of himself.

"David Gabrielovich Bilamer—does the name mean anything to you?" murmured Zupanev. "A writer, a great writer. A Jew, a Communist, and a friend of the big shots. Listen: one evening he is summoned to the Kremlin; he gets there early. He's received politely, taken to an anteroom, told to wait. He's so terrified that he develops an urgent need to go to the toilet, but unfortunately the door is locked, and no one is there to open it. What has to happen, happens: he wets his pants. Just then the door opens, an officer asks him to follow him. Bilamer tries to explain his problem, but the officer tells him: *He* is waiting for you. There they are in *his* presence: Stalin, in person. What a nightmare. Bilamer thinks: They'll shoot me. He feels a huge icy hand on his back. And suddenly, he hears the familiar voice: 'Comrade, I wanted to tell you personally how much I liked your article on myths in literature.' Soon Bilamer finds himself back in the corridor, then outside where the wind takes his breath away."

A sickly smile, or rather, an unwholesome grimace on his face, Zupanev pauses a moment before reaching his punchline: during the anti-cosmopolitan purges, Bilamer was arrested and charged with crime against decency and offense against the Head of the Party. And he was of course shot.

How does Zupanev know all that? Grisha wondered. The watchman knew a lot more. A whole procession of men, well known and obscure, ordinary and odd, peopled his stories. Grisha could guess what was coming just by keeping an eye on his companion's right hand: if it stroked a glass of tea, some contemptible people were about to be described; if it fiddled with a cigarette, the character would be admirable.

"Do you know the story of Makarov?" Zupanev asked one evening, taking out his tobacco from an inside pocket. "I guess you're too young. Ah, Makarov! Massive as a bull, gentle as a lamb, he really believed in the acceleration of history. That's what the Revolution is, isn't it? For centuries and centuries nothing moves; then, all of a sudden, mountains collapse and everything happens at once. Instead of wasting his time learning a trade or looking for a woman, Makarov joins the Party and suddenly—there he is, raised to the position of an official—excuse me, a high official; he'd skipped several ranks without knowing it. Congratulations, Makarov. Especially since he's doing a good job. And the glory doesn't go to his head. He retains his modest life style, goes on seeing his old friends, drinking with them, and even goes so far as to protect them with his authority. Then, one fine morning comes his downfall, as abrupt and unforeseen as his rise. One night he's yanked out of bed; he struggles, he protests; he's told: 'Later—you'll tell all that later.' Before the investigator he voices his anger and threatens to complain high up. The investigator laughs in his face. 'But you *are* as high as you can get now, you idiot!' And he comes straight to the point: 'We know your loyalty to the Party. There's a mission awaiting you, a mission only you can carry out.'

He gives him some details; tells him it's all about—
Antonov. 'Antonov absolutely must be broken. He's your
childhood friend. I know, and that's why there's no one
better qualified to unmask him.' 'But what's the charge?'
'He belongs to the Zinoviev gang.' 'Impossible! I know
Antonov as well as I know myself. I'll vouch for him. You'll
never make me believe that my friend Alexeyevich Antonov
has betrayed the working class. Why, he's given his life
to it. You'll never make me say he's an enemy of the Party,
after he's shed his blood for the triumph of the cause.'
Makarov screams—he's taken back to his cell. The interrogation is repeated ten times, a hundred times. The usual
methods are used—in vain. Specialists are called in—in
vain. Then the investigator appeals to ideology, patriotism,
dialectic, individual conscience confronting the collective
conscience, means and ends, self-sacrifice and the Communist ideal. Throughout his discourse, the investigator
keeps playing with a sharp black pencil on his desk.
Makarov can't tear his eyes away from it—and that's what
saves him. He answers, 'My life and my soul belong to
the Party, but I would disgust myself if I destroyed my
best friend; I would be unworthy of the Party.' 'In short,
you refuse to carry out a Party order?' 'Not at all. The
Party demands we tell the truth; I'm telling the truth.'
'But what if the Party says one thing and you another,
who's right?' 'The Party.' 'Listen: the Party has tried
Antonov, the Party declares him guilty. And you, you
proclaim he's innocent!' 'Impossible! The Party can't
condemn my friend Antonov because the Party can't lie.'
The investigator gets angry. Makarov, no intellectual,
couldn't care less about logic. And—this case is unique in
the annals—the affair does not end in tragedy. Ten years in
the clink instead of the bullet in the back of the neck,
which the 'gentleman of the fourth cellar' had been ordered
to administer. Why the reversal? Well, neither Makarov

nor Antonov ever signed anything at all. Their dossiers were lying around for so long that the gods finally changed both tools and victims."

Grisha's astonishment grew. Where did Zupanev get all these stories? Had he known the heroes he was talking about?

"One fine day," Zupanev went on, "Makarov and Antonov meet in the prison courtyard. They fall into each other's arms. 'How did you manage to hold out?' Makarov asks. 'It's simple. They were trying to persuade me that I ought to confess for the good of mankind. To which I answered, "How can I hope to work for the good of mankind if to do so I must become a traitor?" It wasn't easy. The interrogations went on and on, but you see? I'm here. And how did *you* manage to hold out?' 'Oh that was even simpler: I kept staring and staring at the investigator's pencil, telling myself, I'm not a pencil, a human being is not a pencil. . . .'"

Oh yes, that watchman knew a lot of things. About prisons and torture sessions, judges and clowns—as if he had forced open mysterious doors to bring back secrets no one dared name. But why was he revealing all this to his young friend? How did he get access to the forbidden memories of an entire people reduced to silence? What was it that those expressionless eyes of his saw when he sneered in the middle of a phrase or gesture? Zupanev sneered frequently, he kept on sneering, uttering sounds that seemed to want to turn into laughter. He would shake his head, moisten his lips, move his hands to sketch strange shapes, and then expel a forced guffaw: "*Ha ha ha*, you see what I mean?" Grisha did not always see, but he listened.

Sometimes he felt his mind reeling. "The prison world is a sort of hereafter," Zupanev would say. "In it, nothing can be understood, nothing seems true. Often the condemned are joined by their judges. Prosecutors and prisoners, torturers and tortured, false and true witnesses, they are all there, pell-mell, reduced to subhumans. . . ."

Grisha and Zupanev met often. For Grisha, the watchman's lodging had become a refuge which neither his mother nor Dr. Mozliak could invade.

Who are you, watchman? What prison do you hail from? How many languages do you speak? And why do you talk to me? Why are you teaching me Yiddish? And why are you so anxious for me to hear your stories?

"Did I tell you the story of Hersh Talner, you know, the historian? He kept working on his history in his cell; and as he was not allowed to write, he used to repeat, sometimes aloud, sometimes in a whisper, what he would have put on paper. One night a miracle takes place: someone slips him a pencil stub and a sheet of white paper. Try to imagine that, my boy, just try to imagine it: he's finally going to compose his *J'Accuse* and set it down for eternity. He has so many things to say, too many for a single sheet. How can he sum up on its two sides the nightmares and agonies of a whole generation? Holding his head in his hands, he reflects; this is worse than torture. His memory is overloaded; too many facts, too many images. How can he convey them without mutilating them? Conscious of his mission, he weighs the haunted faces and broken bodies, the confessions and denials, the testimony of the dead and the appeals of the dying; he questions them, consults them, judges them: which should he rescue from oblivion? Dawn breaks; he has not yet written a single sentence. Then, gripped by panic, he bursts into sobs; will the historian fail in his task? He weeps so hard the warden enters his cell and confiscates pencil and paper. Unfulfilled the mission, the unique opportunity lost. Later the historian is led once again before the examining magistrate. In the raw light of the court, someone sees him and suppresses a cry: Hersh Talner's red hair had turned completely white. Can you understand that, my boy? A single sheet of blank paper had turned him into an old man."

The watchman's eyes were moist; so were Grisha's. And my father? the boy wondered. Did he too get old? Did the watchman know? Zupanev seemed to know everything.

"Listen, my boy," Zupanev said to him in his monotone, bringing him back into his own era, his own world, where men pray and lose hope for the same reasons. "Try to understand what I'm telling you. Each generation shapes its own truth. Who will tell our truth whose witnesses have been murdered?" He paused and began grimacing again: "I know who. The crazy historians, the paralyzed acrobats. And do you know who else? I'll tell you: the mute orators. Yes, my boy, the mute poets will cry forth our truth. Are you ready?"

And the adolescent could only nod: Of course I'm ready. I want to get old fast.

THE TESTAMENT OF PALTIEL KOSSOVER IV

BERLIN 1928. I WAS ALMOST NINETEEN and life was beautiful. The world was crumbling around me, but I didn't mind. On the contrary: I felt alive—living, as the expression goes, intensely.

I had begun writing poems and more poems. They were not worth much, and I no longer like them; I prefer those I wrote later, here in prison. But what was important was to keep myself busy, to express myself, to say what I thought about people, what I felt for them—not for everyone, of course, not for the industrial tycoons with their pompous, sinister manners, but for their pitiful slaves, the wretches like myself—and there were a lot of us.

Life was funny. Though housewives no longer went marketing with suitcases stuffed with banknotes, and shopkeepers no longer went home pushing wheelbarrows filled with money, the poor were still poor and hungry.

I gave, I kept giving as much as I had, sometimes less, mostly more. The money I had brought from Liyanov still represented a veritable fortune. Compared with my new friends I was a Rothschild. Compared with Rothschild, to be sure, I was . . . But why should I have compared myself with Rothschild? That was the fashion at the time. People used to say, "Oh, if only I were *like* this one, or *like* that one." It made me laugh. One day I quoted Rebbe

Zusia, the famous Hasidic master, who told his friends and disciples, "When I appear before the celestial tribunal, the Prosecuting Angel will not ask me, 'Zusia, why weren't you Moses?' Or, 'Why weren't you Abraham?' Or, 'Why weren't you Jeremiah the Prophet?' No, he will ask, 'Now, Zusia, why weren't you Zusia?' "

To which my new friends responded by laughing at me. "So now you're quoting rabbis? Here? What's the matter with you, poor Zusia?"

They all belonged to that phantasmagoric milieu in Berlin where intellectual and artistic clowns, political and antipolitical militants flitted from one pastime to another, from one profession, lover, mistress or confessor to another.

We would meet at Chez Blum, at the New Parnassus or at one of the other clubs and carry on noisily, going into artificial flights of ecstasy, getting into fights but being reconciled the same day. We discussed the Versailles Treaty, Rosa Luxemburg, Nietzsche's madness and Plato's homosexual tendencies. Politics, modern literature and philosophy, theories of art or Communism, Fascism, pacifism—we never stopped talking. We were drunk on words, invariably the same ones: progress, change, realism, the proletariat, the sacred cause, the cause that recalled into question all other causes.

I was happy, I'm not ashamed to confess. I was as happy, that is, as the next person. Berlin 1928: even the unhappy were happy.

Happy? I am exaggerating, of course. Let's say, I was in a good mood. We were having a good time and we were amusing. We were living in the very midst of a farce. The cabarets, the humorists and caricaturists set the tone: those who did not join the laughter were laughable.

Germany in defeat gave the impression that on its soil everything was permissible except taking oneself seriously. Idols were smashed, clergymen defrocked, the sacred was ridiculed and, to get a laugh, laughter was sanctified.

My friends considered themselves Communists, some more so, some less—or at least fellow travelers. They admitted me into their circle, thanks to Bernard Hauptmann, the internationally famous essayist and specialist in medieval poetry, to whom my mentor Ephraim had written of my impending arrival. Where had they met? Had they friends or memories in common? Unlikely, unthinkable. Ephraim in his kaftan and Hauptmann with his foulard were so different. Still, the scholar received me as a friend.

"Oh, so you're the one dear Ephraim has sent us from Liyanov? Welcome! Berlin needs you."

Was he making fun of me? He took my suitcase and carried it into what was to be my room. "Come," he said, "A cup of bad coffee will do you good. A little sandwich too, I imagine."

We had coffee in the living room. Hauptmann, elegantly dressed as if for the opera, inspected me from head to foot. "Your sidecurls," he said a moment later, "I see them, or rather I see their traces. You were right to cut them off."

I blushed. In Bucharest, before boarding the train, I had gone to a barber near the station: "What kind of cut would you like?" "Well, uh, modern, very modern." A few snips of his scissors and I no longer looked like a Jew, that is, a religious Jew. I knew my father wasn't going to see me, and still I felt guilty—I was betraying him. But I had no choice, Father; after all, I couldn't get off the train in Berlin sporting beard and sidecurls, kaftan and black fur hat. I was not exiling myself to advocate Jewish orthodoxy or deepen my studies of Rabbi Shimeon Bar Yohai.

"Is it that obvious?" I asked, embarrassed.

"Oh, no! Your sidecurls aren't visible, it's just that I see them anyhow. Forget it, my dear traveler from Liyanov. We'll soon see which gets the upper hand with you—Berlin or Liyanov."

Astute and eloquent, Bernard Hauptmann, from adolescence on, had singlemindedly indulged his passion—to turn young religious Jews away from their faith—and he used his fortune, time and intelligence to further that end. With me, the task proved both easy and complex. In theory, I willingly accepted his Marxist atheist influence, but in practice I resisted; I had not forgotten the promise made to my father. The result was rather odd: at night Hauptmann would take me to hear Hayim Warshower thunder against God, but the next morning I would put on my phylacteries, pray to God to protect me from His enemies and bless me with a thirst for knowledge and divine truth, and, above all, to rebuild the holy and eternal city of Jerusalem *in* Jerusalem.

Why this split personality? Out of loyalty to Moses? Oh, no—I did not think of Moses; I had left him in the desert. But I did miss my parents. And a childlike voice in my head whispered that if I stopped putting on the phylacteries, *they* would be punished—a risk I refused to take. Hauptmann, of course, made fun of me, and logically he was not wrong. In his eyes I represented the kind of human weakness that stands as an obstacle between the individual and his salvation; my old attachments alienated me, I was unworthy of his friendship. I felt guilty toward him *and* toward my father. My conflict became deeper. Unable to cope with it any longer, I summoned up enough courage to flee. I moved to an attic in Asylum Street, where I could pray and chant as I liked without having to explain or defend myself.

However, Hauptmann, with the tenacity of a policeman, albeit a friendly policeman, did not let go. At Chez Blum or during gatherings with our cronies he often provoked me. I recall one incident at the café:

"So, Mr. Rabbi? Did you speak to your God today? What does He think of the situation? Don't forget to keep us up to date."

Intimidated, I shrugged my shoulders. I was familiar with his arguments about the nefarious power of religion, the sterility of superannuated rituals, the paralyzing effect of our customs and ceremonies, as well as with his ideas on the dangerous influence of the prophets, the sages and the righteous.

"I prefer not to discuss it," I said.

"Do you hear? He prefers not to discuss it. And he calls himself a Marxist! And what about dialectics—did you ever hear of them?"

"I prefer not to discuss it," I repeated stubbornly.

"You're just running away. You refuse to see, you refuse to hear, you can't bear being contradicted. And you consider yourself an intellectual? And pretend to sympathize with the Communist Party? Really, Paltiel, you are still in Liyanov with your blind, fanatical, ignorant Jews! Admit it, Paltiel. Admit that you've never left Liyanov, admit that you go to the synagogue morning and evening, that you admire the backward fools who put their faith in miracle workers! Admit it and stop putting on an act!"

He stopped to catch his breath.

"You lack understanding, Hauptmann," I said in a choked voice. "And refinement. You're free to offend God and insult the masters. But you're wrong to poke fun at their poor followers who need a little warmth, a little hope. What do you reproach them with, Hauptmann? They're unhappy and in exile, they haven't read the books you feed on, they've never gone to the schools you teach in— they don't even know of their existence. Is that their fault? Why poke fun at them, Hauptmann?"

"Hey, how about that, he really loves them!" Hauptmann cried. "He loves them with a passion. Didn't I tell you? The train has left Liyanov, but our friend is still standing on the platform."

A roar of laughter greeted this attack. As a speaker, as a polemicist, Hauptmann had no equal. I had to face him alone, I stood alone against all of them.

No, not entirely alone.

"Idiots! What are you all sneering at? You're a bunch of decadent drunks. What's happened to your sense of comradeship? Shame on you!"

Stunned, I took a moment to regain my composure. Someone was coming to my defense? I lifted my eyes—it was Inge, Hauptmann's girlfriend. There was a silence.

"It's one of two things. Either the God of these poor Jews exists, in which case they do well to address themselves to Him. Or He doesn't exist, and it's our first duty to pity them, then to enlighten them—they themselves exist, after all. By what right do you despise them? Since when do Marxists despise human beings?"

Everyone round the table looked at her incredulously but submissively. Challenging Inge entailed risks: no one but Bernard Hauptmann had enough stature to counterattack.

"You'd make a first-class Talmudist," muttered Hauptmann, trying to hide his annoyance. "If only you spoke Yiddish you could go on a mission to Liyanov."

This time the barb fell flat. Was this their first quarrel? It certainly was their last. It marked the split between them, and the beginning of a new couple. Inge, my first infatuation, my discovery of love, my first love. I think of her now and I smile. She must have been thirty, perhaps a little less. Beautiful enough—no, the most beautiful of women. Well, I had fallen in love—what else?

Why had she chosen me? Was it her maternal instinct that prompted her to protect a youth assailed by spiteful adults? No matter: I was grateful to her. I would never have dared take the initiative and court her. A rejection, however gentle, would have destroyed me. Inge must have guessed as much. Inge, my first guide, my first refuge, the angel and the demon of my adolescence. Cultured, headstrong yet feminine, she terrorized people; they were afraid of her explosions, her stinging repartee. As for me,

I loved her long dark hair, her black eyes, her sensual lips; looking at her was to follow her into the primitive jungle where anything goes.

I liked the casual, almost untidy way she combed her hair and dressed. It would not have occurred to anyone to ever criticize or compliment her. She allowed no one to judge her. She considered herself free, and was. So was I. I did things with her that would have repelled me with anyone else. All she had to do was look at me, touch my hands or forehead, and every taboo was lifted. If anyone succeeded in making me forget Liyanov, it was she.

Hauptmann was to confide in me later that his former mistress had merely been carrying out the Party's instructions. She supposedly had been given the mission of completing my political education, which, frankly, left much to be desired. Maybe so. Would I have been less enamored with her had I been aware of that? The fact is I loved her even when she was trying to instruct me in the theories of Engels and company. And I think, in her own way, she loved me. She loved my innocence, my ignorance, my total lack of experience. She loved making me do things for the first time.

The first time . . .

We had just left a political meeting where Bernfeld, the one with the silly little goatee, had been vehemently defending the revolutionary theories of Trotsky, whom, in fact, he emulated. Hauptmann had contradicted him. In that smoke-filled parlor floor at Chez Blum tension had mounted as in a circus when the acrobat is about to slip and break his neck. Violence was in the air. Interruptions, catcalls, insults: both sides had become inflamed. And, Citizen Magistrate, take note: I was applauding Hauptmann. But when we had to shout to drown out Bernfeld's answers, I was not up to it. I confess: my accursed timidity once again stopped me from doing my duty. Instead of

bellowing along with the comrades, I murmured my indignation with a weak "No, no, enough." Luckily the
comrades were too busy to see or hear me. Suddenly I felt
someone jabbing my ribs. It was Inge, her face alight with
passion, obviously enjoying the brawl she seemed to be
directing. She was shattering our opponents, making them
give in, annihilating them. . . .

"Paltiel!" she commanded. "Louder! Go to it—louder!"

"I—I can't."

"Are you dumb? Shout—that's an order. Shout, yell!
Make some noise!"

"I can't, Inge, I'm sorry, but . . ."

"You must! To keep quiet is an act of sabotage."

Angrily she took my arm and squeezed it hard, very
hard, as if to hurt me. But what I felt was pain mixed with
pleasure. So confused was I that I could no longer utter
even the slightest sound. Bernfeld was singing the praises
of Leon Davidovich, Hauptmann those of Vladimir Ilyich,
Inge those of Hauptmann. As for myself, I regretted having
left my home, my parents, my small provincial town where
men and women did not hate and fight one another over
a word or a name. Inge kept squeezing my arm and I
felt dizzy. Instead of encouraging me, Inge was weakening
me. And then her hand slid over mine; our fingers intertwined, and what I felt then, Citizen Magistrate, is not
your concern. I was, we were, at the core of the universe.
Desire, violent yet soothing, pierced me, scorched me,
roused me. And Inge went on shouting, and I went on
being silent. My comrades and their adversaries were
quarreling over history and human destiny; they were
predicting torrents of blood, victory or death for the Revolution, and all I could feel was my own body and Inge's. I
did not dare look at her for fear of losing her. And because
I was so afraid of losing her, I repressed my fear and my
shame, I smothered my desire and began to shout louder

and louder, like a wild man. Bernfeld could not finish his speech; he lost the battle and so did Trotsky. As for me, I discovered that evening the bond that can exist between the Revolution and a woman's body.

With Hauptmann and the whole group, we went off to celebrate our victory at the Hunchback's Tavern, where our credit was still good. I gulped down some wine and promptly passed out.

"It's the excitement," said a voice. "His first fight."

"The boy hasn't seen anything yet."

"Are you sick?"

"Too much emotion," suggested Hauptmann.

"I don't feel well," I said weakly. "I'd better go home."

"I'll go with you," said Inge firmly.

Hauptmann tried to dissuade her. "Are you playing nurse? That's really not your style, my sweet."

Inge shot him a look filled with such contempt that he was silenced. With considerable effort, I got up. Inge guided me toward the exit. A fresh breeze whipped my face. I breathed voluptuously.

"Shall we go?" said Inge.

She was strong, my guardian angel, stronger than I. I could not have hoped for a stronger support.

"Let's go."

What would my landlady say? I decided bravely to worry about that some other time. For the moment I had better things to do. Leaning on Inge, my heart in my mouth, I was aware of my body as never before. My eyes searched the small, empty streets, my ears listened to the sound of our footsteps, my nostrils caught the multitude of stale odors from closed restaurants. Beneath the heavy gray sky, as we skipped over the garbage cans, I discovered in myself a blossoming and beckoning new fear, the fear of learning to know this body that was pulling and pushing, hurting and healing my own. What will my landlady say? The hell

with my landlady. But Inge—what will Inge say if I
ask her to stay with me? And I—what shall I say if she
accepts?

My landlady said nothing. She was asleep, the whole
house was asleep, so was the street, the whole neighborhood. We stopped in front of the door. I took out my key,
I hesitated: Open the door very casually and show her
in? Or say goodnight, au revoir, see you soon? Inge made
the decision for me. She took the key from me, put it in
the lock and turned it.

"What floor?" she whispered.

"Fourth."

She was about to press the switch for the staircase light.
I stopped her. The landlady, what would the landlady say
if we woke her? Never mind. Inge always carried matches.
Let's go up. Softly, softly, I first, let's go up the stairs. I
stopped in front of my door. There again, Inge took the
key from my hands. She found the switch and turned on
the light. The disorder did not seem to shock her. She
removed my jacket, my belt, unbuttoned my shirt, and
without the slightest embarrassment, said, "Into bed!"

I looked at her aghast: What did she mean? Into bed,
just like that, in front of her? I, the son of Gershon Kossover, whose head was still buzzing with the divine commandments heard at Sinai, get into bed in her presence,
and maybe, maybe . . . ?

"A night's rest will do you good," she stated matter-of-
factly.

She flung off her coat and set to work undressing me.
Bewildered and embarrassed, I wondered what my role was
supposed to be: Protest or cooperate? Close my eyes or
stare at her? Talk or keep quiet? Pull her toward me or
turn away? A thousand contradictory thoughts raced
through my mind. Suppose she stayed—would I be able
to measure up? And then, a stupid question, so stupid I

could have screamed: How was I going to put on my
phylacteries with Inge in the room, or—heaven forgive
me—in my bed? By then I was already in bed. Alone, still
alone. Inge was busy in the other corner.

"What are you looking for?"

"A hot plate."

"I haven't got one."

"I'll bring you one tomorrow. A cup of tea is what you
need. Or a glass of milk."

"But I'm not thirsty."

"You're sure?"

"Quite sure."

She inspected the room, the bed, one last time. "Good, in
that case I'll let you sleep."

She moved toward the door and put out the light. I
held my breath. Sleep? I did not want to sleep. I was suffering because I was disappointed. Here I had had all those
ideas. And invented all those situations. Liyanov, I thought
—Hauptmann was right; I had never left Liyanov. I had
misinterpreted everything. I was an imbecile, a village
idiot. I had had the nerve to read intentions into her
mind. . . . My fault. I should have suggested she stay, spend
the night here, on the pretext I was not feeling well, and
needed her. After all, I could hardly have expected her to
humiliate herself by offering herself to me, could I? Too
late. Inge was gone, probably for good. Gone, the woman
who had bewildered me to the point of actual pain. Gone
—gone back to Hauptmann.

But, strange, I had not heard the door open and close
. . . not so strange . . . Inge, Inge's hand in the dark, Inge's
hand on my forehead . . . a stinging sensation. . . . Absurdly,
I suddenly remember the old Rebbe of Drohobitch.
What's he doing here, in my room in Berlin? The last
time I saw him, at his brother's, in Barassy, I was still a
child. He had questioned me about my studies and given

me his blessing by placing his hands on my head. I had had the same stinging burning sensation. . . . Inge must have gotten down on her knees, her face brushes mine, her breath mingles with mine. I am ill, I shiver; the fever will carry me off. The old Rebbe of Drohobitch speaks to me of God, but God is silent; I am silent. Inge is silent and her silence penetrates mine. I do not dare move or breathe —besides, I am unable to breathe; my lungs are not my own; nor my lips, now sealed by Inge's. So this is love, I tell myself. A man and a woman love each other and the presence of the old Rebbe of Drohobitch does not disturb them. Two persons embrace and the chasm in their lives is lit up. A man and a woman intertwine and human misery is conquered. It is simple, so simple. No need for words, no world-shaking projects: mankind can be helped with much less. Other reflections, equally naive, float around in my head while Inge teaches me to kiss her gently. Inge is skilled, agile. Without moving away or stopping for a second, she takes off her blouse, her skirt, and the rest, and there she is in my poor, creaking, narrow, uncomfortable bed—with me, on top of me, under me; she hurts me, she shatters me, she hardens me, the better to embrace me; her fingers, her lips, her tongue kindle a thousand flames in my body—and I do not know what to do. I twist and turn, I imitate her, I invent things, I venture in the dark, I see in the dark, I see two bodies mingled, knotted, and freed. And what about the Rebbe of Drohobitch? And my land-lady? To hell with my landlady. To hell with everyone. I am alone and free; alone with Inge, free as she is free; we are united in freedom, nothing else matters: we are united in the same cry of pain, pleasure, liberating agony; I have left one world for another, a deeper, more enveloping one. A thought: So it's true, paradise exists.

What made me think of paradise? Because in Haupt-mann's speech the day before—only the day before?—he

had said Trotsky was deluding himself by trying to transform paradise into hell; what had to be done was transform
hell into paradise. No—Trotsky, Hauptmann and their
arguments have nothing to do with it. If I thought of paradise, it was because of Adam and Eve: I was not a Talmud
student for nothing; everything comes back to Scripture.
I had just experienced the joy of the first man who came
to know himself by knowing his woman.

"Why are you smiling?" asked Eve—Inge.

"I'm thinking of our grandfather Adam."

"Was your grandfather named Adam?"

"Yours too, Inge."

I had to explain. She raised herself halfway and began
caressing my face as though I were a child, perhaps hers.

"My poor little Paltiel, you really believe in that? The
Bible, the holy Bible, you read it too much; it's time you
read something else."

And there in bed, between two kisses, she gave me a
cram course: Darwin and evolution, historical materialism,
the origins of the universe, the myth of divinity. I listened
without reacting, I heard without listening. God, a capitalist invention? Abraham, a big landowner? Moses, David,
Isaiah—enemies of the working class, that is, of the people? A strange place, a strange time to teach me the
philosophy of the sciences, I thought, laughing to myself.
But Inge was teaching me something else too, something
better, lucky for me.

I fell asleep at dawn, in her arms. Later I woke with a
start: How could I put on the *tephilin* in front of her? I
looked at her and an unspeakable shame engulfed me: I
had committed a sin, I had just broken one of the Ten
Commandments, and, now, like a hypocrite, I was preparing to put on my phylacteries.

Inge was smiling in her sleep: at whom? and why? Perhaps she was laughing at me. I had left Liyanov, but

Liyanov was following me. I wanted to wash, cleanse myself, mortify myself, hide, but Inge opened her eyes and drew me to her without a word. My body tensed with desire, I thought of other things, then I stopped thinking.

She left toward noon. She had barely closed the door behind her when I rushed over to the drawer where I kept my phylacteries. I unrolled the leather straps and put them on my left arm and on my forehead and recited the morning prayers. I sighed with relief: a narrow escape—what would I have done had she decided to stay in bed the whole day? Thank you, God, thank you for having permitted me to serve You while loving your adversary.

Later on, Inge must have become aware of my religious infidelities. She often tried to keep me with her, or at her place, to prevent me from being alone, that is, alone with God. She was too astute and too intelligent to restrain me completely; she set me free for an hour or two, but would come back unexpectedly, as if to catch me red-handed. Afraid of this embarrassing possibility, I began praying more and more rapidly. I behaved like a small boy caught stealing candy, like a man hiding a liaison from his wife. Well, I *was* lying to Inge, and on many levels. She thought she had converted me to the ideal of the atheist Communist Revolution. She was wrong; I was deceiving her. Laugh if you will, Citizen Magistrate, laugh: I loved Inge, I loved her passionately, and I was betraying her with God, whom I no longer loved.

But that's another story, beyond your authority.

Still, Inge succeeded in influencing my life. One night I accompanied her and a group of comrades to fight Nazis in a tavern near the zoological gardens. There were twenty of us and three times as many of them. Until then I had never been in a free-for-all: I was not meant for that. Puny, skinny, poor at sports and even worse at fisticuffs, I was too cowardly and inept for this type of expedition. But what won't you do for a woman in love with you and whom you love? So there I was in the midst of a fight. Not for long—a second later I was out. I found myself in the street, on the pavement, my face swollen, spitting blood, half blind, half deaf and possibly dead. Comrades helped Inge take me home. She nursed me. She pampered me. She loved me. And the next day, exhausted, the next day, I am ashamed to admit it, I forgot my prayers. Was it because Inge had not left me for a single moment? Had she deliberately stayed there to force me to break with her rival? Fact is, I did not think of the phylacteries until two days later. Too late, I thought, to resume my habits.

Thus my break with religious practice resulted not from a decision taken after mature consideration but from an accidental lapse of memory, a lapse for which I could never forgive myself. To break with God, all right—but to forget God?

I did not forget Him. I remained attached to Him, hoping He did not hold it against me too much when I left Him at night to meet Inge. I needed her lessons, her presence. As for God, He could manage without my prayers.

My phylacteries? I tucked them away in a corner.

YORAM SANG OF LIFE," says Katya in her slow monotone. "No—it was life that sang through him. Here's a question you should be able to answer: Do mutes sing, even without words? Yoram sang, and I sang with him. And if there is a God, He sang with us."

Katya rises, sits down again; she talks a great deal, that's normal: widows talk a great deal when they have someone to talk to. Sometimes she stops in front of the window and contemplates the night, ostensibly addressing herself to it rather than to Grisha. Other times her eyes move to the door and she falls silent. She is afraid to continue just as she is afraid not to continue. Then her face takes on a haggard, slightly mad look.

"In our youth, in the kibbutz, we belonged to a choir," says Katya, "but I sang flat. I annoyed everyone except Yoram. He loved me, and he didn't care. People complained: Why couldn't we love each other without getting on their nerves? But Yoram would say: Better to love each other well and sing flat than the other way round."

Grisha thinks of his mother, who never sang, and of Olga, who did nothing else. His mother and Olga. Yesterday. And tomorrow?

Olga, in high school: a pretty blonde, excitable and exciting; a ball of fire whenever she did not get what she wanted. In the beginning, Grisha would try to avoid her. To no avail. Whether going to or from school, running an errand for his mother or picking up a newspaper, there was Olga, right in his path. This amused the little minx; she rocked with laughter.

One day she blocked his way on the street: "I bet you've never kissed a girl on the mouth."

"A girl? You mean only one? How old-fashioned can you be?"

"How many have you kissed?"

"Who counts?"

Hands on her hips, she eyed him provocatively: "If you kiss as badly as you lie, I feel sorry for them."

"You want me to show you?"

"You couldn't if you wanted to."

"Yes or no?"

"Yes."

Grisha hesitated; how could he get out of this? "Not here."

"Coward!"

"In front of everyone? Your father, your mother— suppose they see us?"

"You make me sick," she hissed.

"Let me pass," said Grisha.

He did not dare push her aside; he did not know how to do it without touching her; he wished he could touch her without touching her. His brain was a mass of confusion. Did he want to escape or prolong this contact, this encounter? Precocious and bold, Olga made a gesture of scorn.

"Men are so stupid," she said, with a sigh.

She stepped aside. He took a step forward and she followed. They walked on together, in silence. When they got to Olga's house they stopped.

"You're not very gallant," said Olga. "Open the door for me." He obeyed. She went in and called to him, "What about this one?"

Grisha opened the door to the courtyard.

"I bet you've never looked into a woman's eyes," said Olga.

The schoolboy did not have the courage to challenge her remark; his head was spinning, heavy with images and suppressed visions of his mother and Dr. Mozliak speaking to one another, being silent with one another, embracing one another.

"Please, Olga. I have to go back. They're expecting me."

"On one condition: look me in the eyes."

Unable to resist her any longer, Grisha yielded. His head whirling, he felt himself transported to the top of a mountain. There was so much gaiety in the young girl's smile, and such intensity in the appeal she radiated that he very nearly fell. To keep his balance he held on to her.

"You see?" she said mocking him. "You're falling into my arms."

He went home, feverish and breathless. His mother asked him what was wrong. He answered evasively, out of habit, but also because he was surely not going to admit that a little girl had turned his head. The cheeky little thing—he resented her having conquered, that is, humiliated him. He kept holding it against her while thinking of her. He spent a sleepless night followed by a second and a third.

Since they were neighbors, they walked to school together. By accident, of course. Great loves are born without reason and die for very definite reasons. For Grisha and Olga, there were problems of nationality, religion and fear of anti-Semitism: Olga was not Jewish. This detail meant little to Grisha, but his mother interfered:

"It seems you're going out with Olga?"

"What do you mean?"

"You know perfectly well what I mean."

"I don't. Olga is a classmate, I see her just as I see other boys and girls."

She vanished into the kitchen and returned.

"Olga's not for you, and you're not for her," she said. "Think of your father and hers. Your father's pride came from his poetic vocation, his Jewish past; her father is the great-great-grandson of a lieutenant of Bogdan Khmelnitski, whose glory it was to have taken part in thirteen pogroms in nine Jewish communities in less than three days. Did you know that? Did you think of that?"

"Congratulations—you know everything. Do you know as much about *your* boyfriend?"

Their relations were deteriorating daily. Difficult to talk to each other, difficult to understand one another.

"If you take that tone with me I prefer that you keep quiet," said Raissa.

"As you like."

Grisha felt uncomfortable in her presence. Because of Mozliak, of course, who had taken his father's place. If Raissa and the doctor were not living together, it was because of Grisha. This heightened his feeling of being unloved, an intruder. He represented a dead poet.

"Feeling down?" Olga asked him one day as they left school.

"A little."

"Why?"

"It'll pass," Grisha answered gloomily.

He had never told Olga about his mother. He changed the subject. "If your father knew we were—let's say, close, he'd give you a thrashing."

"He'd never dare. It's against the law. The Soviet law is strict with degenerate parents who hit a member of the Komsomol."

"Anti-Semitism too is forbidden by law," said Grisha, "and yet . . ."

"Not the same. Weak, helpless minors have to be protected, that's natural, but the Jews? The Jews are powerful, in fact, they're supposed to be almighty."

She burst out laughing. "Seriously, Grisha, all this is unimportant. Whether my father approves or not is his problem, not mine or yours. Your religion? You know what? I'm glad you're a Jew—and it's just too bad if it enrages my father. We all liberate ourselves as best we can. As for me, I liberate myself by loving you."

For her, Grisha's origins created no problem. As a Communist, she thought of inequality only in terms of social classes. Communists fight against discrimination, fine! Communists struggle against ignorance, superstition, obscurantism, fanaticism and religion in individuals as well as in society—wonderful! They struggle against the individual for the benefit of society—still better! Olga and her friends in the Komsomol firmly believed these slogans.

"You're really a bore, you and your Judaism," she would say, annoyed. "What is this Judaism of yours? A religion? You're not religious as far as I can see. Are the Jews a race? You're not a racist, thank God. Is it a sickness? Your health is fine. So—is it an excuse? That's it: you want to break up, and you're looking for an excuse—"

"Oh, no, Olga, no! You're wrong about me and about Judaism. It's . . . it's more than an excuse—it's something else."

"Something else, you say, something else, but what? A culture? You know nothing about it. A civilization? You don't live in it. A philosophy? You don't practice it. A fatherland? You don't live in Israel."

Olga had a good head. How could one explain the Jews to her?

"Let's say that for a Jew being Jewish is an act of conscience."

"All that's just poetry."

"Let's say that for a Jew being Jewish is creating poetry."

"What do you know about it? You don't happen to be a poet, do you?"

"No," said Grisha. "But my father was."

"May I read his poems?"

"No, they're written in Yiddish."

"But you could translate them for me, couldn't you?"

He yielded once again. One May afternoon, sitting under a tree, he showed her Paltiel Kossover's collected poems. He recited:

> I dream of a cursed day
> and I am afraid.
> I dream of a fiery dawn
> and I am thirsty.
> I dream of a burnt-out sun
> and I am aching.
> I dream the dream of the poor
> and I am hungry.
> And cold.
> And then I bless the day;
> And turn dawn
> into an offering.
> For I shall light the sun's fire again
> with the spark
> of my soul.

"Your father wrote that?" Olga asked.

"Yes, he did."

"Well—was he crazy?"

"Perhaps."

> I listen to the wind
> sweeping across
> submerged continents.
> I listen to the night
> carrying away
> children never to be born.
> I listen to the prayer
> of a condemned man
> who can no longer pray.
> I listen to life

deserting
the solitary man
about to die.

"That too is by your father?" Olga asked after a long silence.

"Yes, the whole collection is his."

"Was he really so unhappy? And so alone?"

"He was a madman. And a Jew."

Olga stopped asking questions. She took his hand in hers and lifted it to her lips. Grisha never forgot that gesture. During the next few days she asked him to read other poems to her. She knew how to appreciate them. She would listen with closed eyes, her head in her hands. For each poem she had a brief comment, half ironic, half affectionate, that brought her closer to Grisha.

Their reading sessions were interrupted by the accident that took place in Dr. Mozliak's office. Olga did not see Grisha until a couple of weeks later, when he was already mute. Not knowing this, she asked him to read more Paltiel Kossover. Grisha shook his head. She wanted to know the reason for his silence. He went on shaking his head. Then, for the first time, tears filled her eyes.

"I don't deserve that," she said.

How could he explain, how could he tell her what had happened? All he could do was shake his head.

"All right, then," said Olga. "Till tomorrow, in school."

But he never went back to school. From that day on he spent his free time with Zupanev, the night watchman, who showed an uncanny taste for Jewish poetry.

Yoram used to sing, you know why?" asks Katya in a constricted voice, as if every word is a struggle. "I'll tell you—he sang because his parents never had any reason to sing. His parents, you see, had gone through the concentration camps. Yoram was their only son. They were lucky; they didn't have to mourn his death. They died before him; they died knowing him to be happy; they took his happiness with them."

She breaks off; she must stop. She must drive Yoram from her thoughts.

"Come, Grisha," she says, "Come over here, to me."

But Grisha, grappling with his own past, makes her understand that he cannot—not tonight.

Abruptly, a mad, delirious notion crosses his mind: Katya may be right. This night is unique: why not mark that uniqueness in a special way? What if I said yes? Yes, Katya, let's make love. I'll father your child, a son who will look like me, who will look like my father. . . .

Poor Yoram—he died without leaving an heir. With his death a whole line vanished. And what if I too die without leaving an heir? That would be the end of me, the end of my father and of his father.

Katya senses the change in him. She does not let the occasion slip by.

"Come," she says.

As always, she pulls him into her untidy room, stretches out on the unmade bad and waits. And through his desire, through his madness, Grisha sees Olga. He knows he should not do what he is about to do, but he will do it anyway. Katya's eyes are moist, so are her lips.

"Come," says Olga.

And Grisha, facing the young virgin of his dreams, the anti-Semitic judge's daughter he had coveted, can only obey. He lies down on Katya's body without seeing it, without feeling it, thinking only of the young girl back in Krasnograd, whom he had followed with his eyes every morning, his heart beating impatiently, his blood in turmoil. He does not hear Katya's little sounds of satisfaction

or amusement. He hears nothing, nor does he answer when
Katya asks him gently, softly, whether he is happy, whether
he likes this or that, whether he sometimes opens his mouth
when he makes love, whether the fact of being mute, of
being unable to cry out in joy prevents him from feeling
that joy. He loses himself in her, scorched by a sun of
ashes.

THE TESTAMENT OF PALTIEL KOSSOVER V

MAD, CAREFREE, ANXIETY-RIDDEN and, above all, irresponsible, such were the years of the golden age of the wonderful, stormy Republic of Weimar. We were poor, we lacked material goods, but what did it matter? The future was calling to us, belonged to us. I wrote my parents: "More than ever I am convinced we are destined to save the world." We who? My father must have thought, We Jews. My thought was, We idealists, we the young revolutionaries.

Berlin was sliding into a sea of grimaces and tears, dancing on the brink of the abyss, alternating between excesses of pleasure and poverty, goaded by absurd delights and approaching terrors. Which was more dangerous? The blindness of fanatics or the shortsightedness of free men? We refused to look ahead; we refused to look at all. Was that why Bernard Hauptmann killed himself?

Inge and I were now living together, but we went on seeing him. He was older than we, he was our guiding star; the comrades clung to him and so did we. We admired his prodigious gifts of analysis and intelligence. On the surface our relations had not changed. He showed us neither hostility nor resentment; he seemed to hold no grudge against me for stealing Inge from him. Nor did he seem angry with her for leaving him. He would often observe us with a benevolent, slightly mocking air.

He was known to have new liaisons, but none brought him happiness—that was obvious. He talked more but enjoyed himself less. Courses, students, comrades, public debates, brawls with the Nazis—he was everywhere. He took part in every operation, even the most insignificant, just to fill his days; he seemed afraid of being alone.

I confess that in his presence I felt ill at ease. He did not resent me, but I had betrayed him. It was no use for Inge to repeat that she had taken the first step and thus was responsible. I still felt guilty. And the more magnanimous Hauptmann was the more disturbed I became—and also the more I sought his company. Masochism, need to atone, to redeem myself? I had not yet freed myself from my Liyanov inhibitions.

Yet Berlin was the ideal place for self-liberation. The capital, in continuous effervescence, was reminiscent of the sinful cities of the Bible. The Talmudist in me would blush and look away. Prostitution, pornography, debauchery of mind and body, perversions of every kind; the city disrobed, painted its face, humiliated itself, flaunting its degeneration like an ideology.

A few steps away from Chez Blum, in a private club, there was nude dancing: men with women, or women with women. Elsewhere, people took drugs, flogged one another, wallowed in mud, pushing back all accepted limits; it reminded me of the mores of the followers of Sabbatai Tzvi, the most notorious of the false messiahs. Values were reversed, prohibitions abolished. Did people sense the approaching storm? Before entering into the night they wanted to try everything, to give life and substance to all their hallucinations.

Our group did not follow the stream. We were more disciplined, we had other goals. Our social conscience saved us from corruption. Our experience was on another level: we played with ideas, we tried to strip them of their masks, yet we respected those who defended them. Among us, everything began and ended with words. We would discuss Tucholsky's latest essay, Brecht's latest play, the stage productions of Stanislavski and Wachtangov, Moscow's new economic policy, the march of the Revolution. As for the Nazis, we spoke of them as of a disagreeable disease, not serious and surely not fatal. We told ourselves: Every society has its misfits, and so does ours; one day they would be discarded, thrown into the trash can of history. The threats, the ramblings, the obscene delirium of a Goebbels or a Goering or their ridiculous Führer did not even annoy us. We thought: They are barking, let them bark, surely they will wear themselves out. Hauptmann called Nazism a marginal sect. Lacking education and mass support, it could not possibly influence events. History cannot be changed by a few anti-Semitic speeches. Fighting them would give them too much importance, do them too much honor. Better not turn them into adversaries. Our real adversaries were much closer: the trade union movement, the Socialists, the Social Democrats. The Nazis were no more than a diversion.

The opposite thesis was formulated by an essayist called Traub, a specialist on both Master Eckhardt and Hegel. Tall, skinny, and as long as a day of fasting in prison, this friend of the famed revolutionary Paul Hamburger used to harangue us in his cracked, panting voice, trying to convince us that Nazism meant the decline of civilization, liberty and morality, and that it must be crushed before it could be organized, before it was too late.

In all honesty I must acknowledge that my own position was closer to Hauptmann's. Traub's warning sounded hollow. For me the Nazis were rabble, wretches who needed to hate in order to live. Where I came from, they were called pogromists, here they were Nazis. It was all the same. Sadists, yes. Disgusting, yes. Bloody, capable of any

crime. But the idea of *those people* in power was unthinkable. What about the intelligence of the German people,
its culture, its rationalism, its common sense, its contribution to the spiritual evolution of mankind. Never in the
land of Goethe and Schiller could such uncouth bastards
come to power.

The facts seemed to vindicate us. In the elections of
1928, the Nazi Party received only eight hundred thousand votes. Pathetic—and reassuring. Congratulations, Weimar. Congratulations, Germany. The Nazis had fallen on
their faces.

Epecially in Berlin. Unlike Liyanov or Bucharest, Berlin seemed to be dominated by Jews like myself, or, rather,
like Hauptmann. Newspapers and publishing houses,
theaters and banks, department stores and literary salons.
As far as Germany was concerned, French anti-Semites
who saw Jews everywhere seemed right. The sciences,
medicine, the arts: Jews set the tone, imposed it on others.

How different from Liyanov. At home Jews, in order to
survive, had to lie low, hiding their talents, their accom-
plishments. In order not to die, we had to play dead. A
Jewish cabinet minister, a university professor, or an
editor in chief of an influential review: impossible even to
imagine in Liyanov. To get a position in politics or the
arts, Jews had to detach themselves from their Jewish
origins and deny their Jewishness. To enter the Conserva-
tory or the Academy, a Jew had to show a certificate of
baptism. Not in Berlin, where Jews not only were part of
the landscape but gave that landscape its color, its cultural
texture. One could imagine Berlin without Nazis but certainly not without Jews.

Hauptmann said this, and I supported him. I remember
his measured words and their effect on Traub. This friend
of Paul Hamburger's shouted like someone possessed.
Stormy discussions, passionate debates were held on all

the current subjects: pacifism or war? patriotism or internationalism? Where would salvation come from? The official Communists defended Moscow's changing theses; their fellow travelers, cautious and clear-minded, looked to Paris, the traditional haven of political exiles. Hauptmann took the Moscow line; so did Inge. I did not. I belonged to no party. I leaned toward Communism because of Ephraim, and even more because of Inge. Had Inge known how to speak of the Messiah, I would have followed her straight to the Kremlin.

Hauptmann was the typical faithful, unyielding Communist. He had known Kurt Eisner and Ernst Toller at the time of the Red Republic of Bavaria, in which he had been involved. How had he managed to escape? At the moment of the debacle he had taken refuge with some workers, who had hidden him during the critical months. "I trusted the masses," he would often repeat to us, "and I was right." He still believed in the masses; they were his religion. This elegant intellectual felt a deep harmony between himself and the anonymous, shapeless masses; he was totally taken with them and believed that they had invested him with a lofty mission. Thus, his resolution reflected theirs. Whenever he pronounced the words "the masses" his voice became grave and solemn.

Inge was a Communist like Hauptmann and just as fervent and ready to sacrifice herself for the party of the Revolution. Where did they differ? Hauptmann could, on occasion, speak about the Party in a relaxed way; not so Inge.

I used to accompany them, with some of our cronies, to public meetings where speakers would preach, lecture, teach, thunder, vociferate, condemn and make demands depending on the slogans of the day. I liked to look at the throngs and merge with them. I liked the composed and confident atmosphere of "the masses," I liked their way of accepting the Communist gospel with raised fist; I liked the brotherhood, the sense of common destiny they radiated; I envied them.

I had asked Inge whether she could help me become a Party member. She advised against it. "Later," she said. "You're not mature enough." "Later—but when?" I wanted to know. "Later," she decreed. And once she made up her mind, there was no way to change it.

She may have been right. I was still too attached to my parents, to Liyanov. I no longer practiced the religion of my ancestors, but I missed it. Sometimes on a Sabbath I found myself humming a Hasidic air, or quoting an old parable or conjuring up some mystical figure in whom to confide my distress or bewilderment. Inge knew this.

I seemed to be leading the life of a Communist, but appearances deceive. Inge often reminded me of that. "You're not a Communist; I mean, not really."

"That's true. I think too much about the Messiah. Some people wait for him; the Communist runs toward him. You're helping me run."

Talk like that enraged her: the Messiah, for her, was a sort of rabbi and she hated rabbis. She hated them as much as she hated priests.

"You see?" she would say, upset. "You're not ready yet."

"Because I mention the Messiah? Do you know, Inge, that there's a tradition of messianic *surprise?* It speaks of the redeemer emerging unexpectedly, just when mankind least expects him."

"I don't like that kind of surprise, nor that kind of redemption. Communism is something else. It means working in the here and now, it means provoking upheavals not by dint of magic formulas but by work and political action. You still have a lot to learn."

To please her I worked hard. I shared with the Party— that is, with some Party members—the money my father sent to meet my needs and pay for my "studies." To be more precise, I subsidized needy pals and comrades. If on rare occasions I had any money left, I gave it to Inge, who handed it over to Hauptmann, who added it to his special fund.

The 1932 elections were approaching. I turned that campaign into a personal matter, as though my future depended on it. I hardly ever slept. I wrote articles and edited tracts in Yiddish, which Inge helped translate into German; I ran from meetings to demonstrations; I shouted with the masses so dear to Hauptmann, demonstrated with them, fought for them with slogans, and soon, even with my fists. Leading their march, I carried the red flag just as my father, in Liyanov, used to carry the sacred scrolls—with love and resolution.

I was expecting a decisive victory. And so, I thought, were Inge and Hauptmann. Hauptmann had changed; he was getting thinner, as if consumed by a secret flame. Did he doubt the results after all? Was he more lucid than we had thought? He fought hard like all of us, but as the elections drew nearer, he looked increasingly worried.

One evening, as we were going to a demonstration in the suburbs, I told him how worried I was about him.

"What's wrong with you, Bernard? You're not your usual self."

"I'm tired, that's all. Overworked."

"Another few days and you'll be able to rest."

"Another few days and the real work will begin."

"Explain that, Bernard."

"We're going to win, the people will conquer; then we'll have to assume our responsibilities," he said with a smile.

Whatever doubts he had concerned *his* ability to assume the responsibilities of power, for he was convinced that the masses would carry him in with them. We shared his confidence. We were conducting an earnest struggle for the people, for the militant working class, and our triumph was inevitable. History wanted it that way, and we alone, not the Social Democrats, not any other party, were marching with history.

In the higher levels of the Party, to be sure, coalitions and alliances with other parties, except the Nazis, were under discussion. For us, matters were simpler: all we could see were the contours of the platform the voters were going to shape with their ballots. The poor, the unemployed, the homeless numbered in the millions—they could not help but elect us Communists, who spoke for them, and who proclaimed their right to dignity.

I remember the speech Hauptmann made shortly before the election.

"Workers! Workers' wives! Pause and reflect. Ask yourselves whether you prefer the shame of alms to a good salary, whether you prefer hatred to solidarity! Pause and reflect, comrades, before committing your future. . . ."

Inge too spoke that night.

"My parents are rich, so are their friends, they have never put in a day's work in their lives. Others work for them. I have turned my back on them, and do you know why? To break the chain of evil. To help forge the brotherhood of the workers. I choose you, comrades, I choose you over my parents. . . ."

And I applauded, I applauded until I was exhausted. As for myself, I never took the floor. Only once did I make a speech—in Yiddish—before a Zionist group. I no longer remember whether the people hissed because of my political ideas or my language: they had expected an address in German. I fled, only to be jeered by Inge:

"Oh, yes, it was a triumph—for the Zionists!"

Election day came. Ensconced at Chez Blum since morning, after a sleepless night, we gulped black coffee while waiting for the first results. Hauptmann made regular trips to Party headquarters and came back shaking his head: too early to know what was happening. The hours wore on. Inge, unable to sit still, left for the offices of the *Weltbühne*, where she knew one of the political commentators nothing. She ran back over to the Rumänisches Café on the Budapest Strasse, and came back, out of breath and upset: the first results showed astonishing gains for the Nazis. Hauptmann, with a motion of his hand, kept us from panicking: that particular precinct had been carefully worked over by Goebbels; it did not prove a thing. . . .

After a second sleepless night we had every reason to panic: it was definitely a Hitler tidal wave. The figures were going up and up; they were entirely out of control. After only two years of political presence, Hitler had won six million votes.

Inge collapsed; she sobbed without restraint. Hauptmann, ashen, put his arm around her shoulder, and, strangely, I was more touched by his gesture than by the tears of my beloved. Was he still in love with her? Had I been wrong to separate them? United, they might, perhaps, have carried off a victory. . . . Once again I was gripped by old Liyanov complexes, my old guilt feelings. Fortunately, no one was paying attention to me.

For some reason that eluded me, Inge decided not to go home with me; she went to rest at her parents' villa shaded by linden trees. After parting that night, the three of us went our separate ways.

It was the end of our group. We went back the next day to Chez Blum; we followed our usual routines, but our hearts were no longer there. We saw the inexorable onslaught of the curse: it was soon to strike each one of us in turn.

Inge moved; she rented a room in the apartment of an

actress doing one of Reinhardt's plays. She was no longer in love with me. At least, so I thought and told her.

"With what's happening these days, we have no right to think of love," was all she could find to say.

To which I should have answered, "With what's happening these days, love is precisely what we must think of."

Bernard spoke less and less. I questioned him. "And the masses, what do you make of them? Their wisdom, their gratitude—have they suddenly disappeared? Explain to me how six million miserable wretches managed to vote for even blacker misery, more unbearable wretchedness! Explain to me, Bernard, the rabble's triumph over decency and reason."

Hauptmann gazed at me without wincing, a penetrating gaze. He said nothing; there was nothing to say. Moscow's instructions had been unequivocal; there was to be no united front with the others opposing the Nazis. Why not? None of us understood; Bernard was no exception.

Then came the fateful New Year's Eve. One of Hauptmann's chic girlfriends had offered us her home to celebrate—celebrate what?—a hope gone up in smoke? It was to be our last party together. We drank, we clinked glasses, we forced ourselves to be merry. Loud laughter, noisy kisses, falsely gay songs, promises of love and fidelity: we were actors determined to play all the roles before leaving the stage.

Someone insisted Hauptmann give a toast. He raised his glass and said hoarsely:

"To defeat!"

We were too shocked to respond. Inge, on the verge of tears, implored him with her eyes to add a sentence, a single word of hope. Hauptmann smiled at her and at every one of us in turn. Then, without drinking a drop, he set down his glass.

That night he put a bullet through his head.

THE TESTAMENT OF PALTIEL KOSSOVER VI

I NEVER WOULD HAVE THOUGHT that one day I would be happy and proud to be numbered among the subjects of His Majesty the King of Greater Romania, but here I was. Perhaps I exaggerate. But it surely was useful. Thanks to my Romanian passport, valid in spite of my irregular military status, I was able to leave the Third Reich without difficulty.

My German friends could have come along or followed. It was 1934, and the frontiers were still so loosely guarded that all the Jews could have crossed to the other side; the police actually encouraged them to do so.

I tried over and over again to convince Inge and Traub to leave everything and set themselves up in Prague, Vienna or Paris, to go somewhere, anywhere. . . . Animated discussions that led nowhere. We each clung to our position.

Inge maintained that it was her duty to remain in Berlin. The Party needed the vital strength of its militant members. The Nazi regime would not, could not last; it was necessary to stay in order to hasten its fall.

Traub answered that this was wishful thinking. The Nazi victory was due not to political or economic considerations but to a mystical situation. Hitler embodied a desire for power and domination he had drawn from the depths

of the German people. Germany might not be Hitler, but
Hitler was Germany. One had to be blind not to realize
that. He concluded: The Nazi regime would last; it would
weigh upon an entire generation.

Though lucid enough to have given up hope, Traub
refused to leave. Paris, Vienna or Prague? His friends, all
the people close to him, were still in Berlin. And then,
despite all the taunting, cruelty and public humiliation
that sporadically marked the onset of the Hitler era, the
Jews went on living among themselves as well as before, if not better. Ostracized by the Christians, they had
fallen back on themselves. The result was an unfolding
of cultural activity unprecedented in the history of German Jewry. Forced to renounce all assimilationist ambitions, a substantial number were attending seminaries and
evening schools to discover their own identity; that was
reason enough to remain in Germany.

Is this the right moment to mention this? Later, much
later, I learned that my father, Gershon Kossover, of
blessed memory, had confronted the same dilemma in
Liyanov. Some friends had offered him refuge in Bucharest; from there, with some money, he could have made
his way to Palestine. But he could not make up his mind.
He discussed it with my mother and sisters, with neighbors and friends. Should he leave the community to its
fate? Or wait and see? What was his duty as a Jew, his
responsibility as a man? To settle down into uncertainty,
or confront the unknown elsewhere? My mother was of
the opinion that he should liquidate the business, sell the
house and flee; my father chided her for thinking only of
their own situation. They stayed on. You know the rest,
I imagine.

On the eve of my departure, Inge and I had one final
discussion. She was packing my suitcase and I implored
her to pack her own. She had no valid reason to remain.

Her parents were seeking buyers for their department store and luxurious apartment; they had business connections in England and planned to go there. Her friends and comrades were on the run or in prison. The Party, in disarray, was barely functioning any more. Did she belong to an underground network? Undoubtedly. In fact, she hinted at it.

"I've got work to do here."

"You will always have work. In France, just as here. The same kind of work."

"No, not the same," she said, and changed the subject.

She did not go so far as to tell me the exact nature of her work; she didn't have to. I understood what she meant but did not accept her argument.

A feeling of failure oppressed us. We had failed on every level, as militants, as friends and as individuals. Since Hauptmann's suicide, Inge and I had drifted apart, though we still met daily. The shadow of our friend, his mocking, indulgent smile haunted us. We avoided talking about him but he remained present. Like remorse, his memory kept gnawing at us.

That evening, again, he was in our thoughts. Why did he commit suicide? Had it been fear of what was to come, or disgust with the events of the year just ended? Traub claimed Bernard had been toying with the idea of suicide for a long time, often citing Seneca's praise of suicide: *The wise man lives as long as he should and not as long as he can.* According to Traub, Bernard was afraid of old age, impotence, decrepitude. Inge, however, maintained that Hauptmann's act was related to mankind and not to his own person. He had killed himself because, in his view, we had just witnessed the decline, the death of the human race.

An idea crossed my mind: Inge insisted on remaining in Germany not because of the Party but out of loyalty to

Hauptmann. I asked her, "Is it Bernard who keeps you here?"

"Not really."

"Inge, when you say 'not really,' that means yes."

"This time it may mean no."

For the first and last time we spoke openly and honestly about our dead friend, that is, in relation to ourselves. Had we behaved badly toward him? Were we responsible for his despair, therefore his death? In spite of what Traub thought, Hauptmann's suicide was not in character; it surely was not a solution for a revolutionary intellectual of rigorously logical bent. A man such as he, capable of resisting impulses and irrationality, of fearlessly confronting deepest despair and even integrating it into his own system of values, would not opt for suicide. And yet. How to explain an act that denied his very life? Could it have been Inge's relationship to me, our love? I rather thought so, Inge did not. She leaned toward the obvious explanation: disappointed by the elections, betrayed by his "masses," his illusions vanished, Hauptmann drew the most radical conclusion from the situation. Suicide: his way of saying to the German people and to German history, I've had enough of you, you've chosen to dance with the devil, go ahead, enjoy yourselves—without me.

The question still troubles me today in this cell, where everything seems more remote, yet closer at hand. There are men whose impact is greater dead than alive, and Hauptmann was one of them.

What causes an intelligent, dynamic and creative person to decide one evening to kill himself? Why this choice, this fascination with self-destruction? Why this refusal to live, this implacable, irrevocable refusal? So as not to suffer, not to debase oneself? To punish the survivors and make them retroactively responsible? A man like myself, imprisoned without reason and with nothing to lose, why should I not play with the same idea? Why have I never thought of it? I might, like Atticus, Cicero's great friend, refuse to eat, and so die hungry and alone, rather than in the presence of the executioner. Why have I not been tempted? Because I have a wife who . . . ? Let us not speak of Raissa, Citizen Magistrate. She is not the one who binds me to life; it is my son Grisha. Will I see him again one day? Will I ever speak to him of my father, whose name he bears? Is it he, or my father, who keeps me from becoming my own executioner? Sometimes, during these interrogations—painful, to put it mildly—I find myself wishing to die—but never to take my own life. To kill myself means to kill; and I refuse, most emphatically, to serve death.

In our conversation—our last—Inge and I did not go to the bottom of the matter. She was reticent. She had had enough of tracking down words which, she said, proved hollow as she grasped them. To make up for this, she announced her intention of spending the night at my place. I was glad. I think I still loved her. She seemed more beautiful to me than ever; her melancholy made her more seductive, more reserved. I began undressing; she turned away.

"Would you rather not?"

She would rather not. She preferred to lie down on the bed fully clothed. Very well—I did the same. Silently we contemplated the night. Others haunted the room. My father was urging me to take along my *tephilin*, my mother to take care of my health. Ephraim was laughing. Chez Blum's proprietor was asking for the seventy marks I had owed him for three months. Bernard was explaining that, speaking philosophically, history meant movement, hence change, hence . . . Hence what? someone asked. I did not hear the answer because I fell asleep. But I know that Inge did not close her eyes all night. Of what, of whom was she thinking? That I do not know; that I shall never know.

My train was not leaving until the evening. Inge, preoccupied by who knows what, no doubt some clandestine errand, decided to leave me in the morning. It was better that way. Standing at the door, we embraced.

I renewed my invitation. "Come to France, Inge. You'll be more useful there than here."

She seemed not to hear.

I insisted, "If you change your mind, if you decide to come, will you know how to get in touch with me?"

She looked at me without seeing me.

"Inge! Will you know how?"

"The comrades will know," she said, her face a blank.

She was already in another world, that of Bernard Hauptmann. She turned away and left without looking back.

And I, remembering her first visit to this very room, felt an almost physical laceration; I wanted to shout, to scream. I wanted to run after her, force her to come back, come with me, live with me, live, period: if I shook her hard enough, if I loved her hard enough, she might agree. But I could not move. The die was cast with irrevocable certainty. Inge would stay in Berlin and I would plunge into the surrealism of Parisian life. I reasoned with myself: Inge will come, you'll see her again. Sooner or later, they will all come, Traub, Blum and all the other comrades, the liberals and the anarchists, the Communists and the Jews; they'll suffocate here, they'll push through to freedom. . . . Deep down I knew that it was a childish hope. Inge would stay in Berlin. Inge would die in Berlin. And I would live somewhere else, I would take another woman somewhere else. Let's turn the page, Inge. Thank you for helping me discover love, thank you for initiating me into political action. Thank you for giving me pleasure and pain, thank you, Inge.

My last day in Berlin: farewell visits; debts to settle at
Chez Blum; a last talk with Traub, who insists on paying
for my coffee, and tells me he has written Paul Hamburger
about me; a last letter to my parents. Next time, Father,
I'll be writing you from Paris, God willing, of course,
God willing. Don't worry, Father—your son will take his
phylacteries along.

A last walk. A splendid April day. The crowded avenues
pulse with life. Brown, gray, black uniforms. Countless
swastikas. Happy faces. The city is at peace with itself.
Hitler in every window: his people gaze at him with un-
disguised pride, with love. Poor Bernard Hauptmann: the
masses do stupid things sometimes, but is that a reason to
commit suicide? Poor Inge: these people have repudiated
you; they spit on you and yours, and you persist in want-
ing to sacrifice yourself for them; do you really believe
they deserve it—deserve you?

Suddenly, near the Zirkus, a strange figure emerges from
the throng: a regal Jew. Dressed with austere elegance, he
walks tall and with a firm step. Dignified, majestic, he
moves forward in the crowd of pedestrians without fear
or mistrust. What makes me think he is a Jew? I could
not say. But I know that he is and that he is not from
Berlin. He attracts attention. A Nazi, catching sight of
him, looks outraged; people stop and stare; he seems to
have come from another place, another time. Is he a
prince of Israel? A messenger of God? Trimmed beard,
eyes sparkling with intelligence, he projects such uncanny
strength that it disturbs the passersby. Another second
and the whole district will be petrified: all eyes are on
this noble, haughty Jew sauntering through Berlin as if
the capital were not under Nazi domination.

I catch myself trembling for him; he is in danger and
seems unaware of it. What if some lout were to attack
him? What if the crowd were to surround him and beat
him up? Would I go to his rescue? I like to think so, but

who knows? In any case, my problem is purely theoretical. People are so stunned, they do not move; they let him pass. He turns the corner and by the time they recover, he has vanished. Should I rush after him? What's the use? Besides, it's getting late. I have to get home quickly. Quickly, Frau Braun, I am in a hurry. How much do I owe you? Will you be kind enough to forward my mail, I'll send you my address, all right? Thank you in advance, thanks for everything, and so long. Ah, *liebe* Frau Braun, don't look so sad, we'll meet again some day—at home, my people say that only the mountains never meet. Quickly, the suitcase. Is everything inside? Shirts, books. The phylacteries. My briefcase. The passport, where's my passport? Damn, I have lost it. No, it's in my pocket. Where's the ticket? Inside the passport. And I am holding the passport in my hand. I am getting all confused, I am losing my mind in this demented country. Quickly, a taxi. No taxi? Never mind, I'll walk. There's a taxi. "Quickly, the station." "Which station?" "I am taking the Paris train." "Paris?" asks the driver, startled. "You're late." But he adds with a laugh, "Wait a few years and we'll all meet there." Not funny, his joke. "Oh, well," says he, "Oh, well," say I. He steps on the accelerator. Hard. The streetlights are coming on. The traffic policemen wave their arms. The shop windows are blazing. In the prisons the torturers stretch, and their victims murmur, "It's only a dream, a bad dream." A dull uneasiness takes hold of me: Who will come to the station; who is there? Inge? Traub? I run to platform Number 11, the train is still there. I board; jostling the passengers, I find my seat, drop my suitcase on it and start looking for a familiar face. Of all my friends, all my companions, none has made the effort. I am somewhat disappointed. I shouldn't be. They are afraid, and I am going to a world free of fear. *Will I ever see them again?* For days and days this question has tormented me: *Will I see them again one day?* An impersonal, twangy voice answers, "Train for Paris, now departing." My heart explodes, it hurts and I know why. There is a moment when a man knows everything, and I am living through such a moment now; I think of my comrades, happy and unhappy, wise and bold. I know they will be swept away by the tempest of blood and fire, while I, a lucky deserter, shall go on living.

The train tears itself away from Berlin. Leaning on the window, not daring to turn around, I look into the night. Finally, overcome by fatigue, I sit down. A man in the corner smiles at me: it is the mysterious prince I had seen that morning near the Zirkus.

Weary and drained, I close my eyes and at once open them again to return his smile. Suddenly I want to cry—to cry for Inge and her dark future, for Hauptmann and his buried illusions, for Traub and his comrades, for Berlin and its Jews. I want to weep but my traveling companion is smiling at me. And this is how I leave the Third Reich, holding back my tears and smiling against my will, like an idiot. Was it weakness, cowardice, desertion? I plead guilty, Citizen Magistrate. I plead guilty of having fled prison and death in Berlin.

WHO ARE YOU, Zupanev, my friend? Where do you come from? What planet dropped you into my life? What have you done, whom did you see before taking charge of this district at night? What kind of man are you, watchman friend? What secrets, whose secrets are you protecting? On whose orders? These unpublished poems by Paltiel Kossover—how did you get them? Who gave them to you? You say someone entrusted them to you for me. How did that stranger know we were going to meet? You say so many things, Zupanev, and I wonder why? And will I ever know what you're keeping from me?

More and more intrigued by the watchman, Grisha asked himself the same questions again and again. Zupanev must have known his father—in prison, maybe? Unable to put his questions into words, he implored him with his eyes, hoping the watchman would understand. Did Zupanev understand? His answers concealed as much as they revealed to his young visitor.

They met weekends or evenings. Sitting on his cot or on a stool, his notebooks on his knees, the watchman became the teacher: he taught Grisha things the boy had not learned at school. He explained the events of the day: the zigzags of Russian policy with respect to Jewish citizens, what was happening in Israel, the problems of emigration. He imparted to Grisha rudimentary Yiddish and some episodes of Jewish history. In sum, he was preparing him for the great departure.

"Me they won't let out," he said. "You they will. Some of the writers' children have already left; your turn will come. Then you must be ready."

Ready for what? Grisha wondered. But Zupanev changed the subject: no use insisting with him.

One day he surprised his young protegé. "I have a present for you. Some of your father's unpublished poems. He wrote them in prison."

Burning, incandescent verses. Grisha imagined his father, crouched in his cell, setting fire to a darkened world with simple everyday words; let loose upon a maddened age, they delayed redemption; the world does not deserve redemption.

"The sum of a lifetime," said Zupanev. "Agonies, friendships, separations: words. Everything begins and ends with words."

Soon, Grisha mused, soon I'll know my dead father better than my mother ever did.

"You see?" said Zupanev. "Everything is possible."

He repeated, "Yes, my boy. Everything is possible and always will be." And he winked.

UNPUBLISHED POEMS (*Written in Prison*)

BY PALTIEL KOSSOVER

He is not in his movements,
he is not in his words,
nor is he in his anger,
or his confession,
or even in his time.
But then,
then
where is he?

Night,
before the assault.
A pale rumor swelling
and roaring.
A rumor before the cry,
it flows and kills
and dies.
God,
before the prayer.
A harsh throbbing silence
that strikes.

Memory:
Temples and barbed wire,
corpses and walls
of Jericho and Warsaw;
ghettos for the enlightened,
prisons and darkness,
rocks and whips,
gunfire and convulsions;
dead children,
children of the dead.
Keeper of eternity,
how do you succeed
in not drowning
in the madness
of those who give you life?

Gravedigger,
give back to earth
the mud and the clay
of heaven.
Cover your face,
gravedigger,
and shame God
who has veiled
his own.
Abandon the dead,
gravedigger,
as they have abandoned you;
the living are calling you
because they are afraid
of you.

Life is a poem
that is too long
or not long enough,
too simple
or not simple enough,
life is too long
or not long enough.
Life is a poem
that is too sad
or not sad enough,
too clear
or not clear enough.
Life is too long
and not long enough.
Life is a poem?
Too short
and unfinished.

                    Translated from Yiddish

THE TESTAMENT OF PALTIEL KOSSOVER VII

Paris, city of light? Why not? Getting off the train at the Gare de l'Est one rainy day, unshaven, exhausted, covered with soot, I had no idea where to go. I knew no one, no distant cousin in leather goods, no uncle in the Rue des Rosiers. I had only one address, which I knew by heart —that of Paul Hamburger.

Traub had given it to me. "Get in touch with him. You never know, you might be able to be useful to each other."

Easier said than done. I could hardly present myself at his home, just like that, fallen from the sky, suitcase in hand, empty stomach and all. I had eaten nothing since Berlin. Too tense, too nervous. And also, my traveling companion had intimidated me to the point where even if I had been hungry, I wouldn't have let him see it.

We were alone in the compartment. He sat near the door, I had the window seat. Knowing nothing about him —not even whether he was Jewish—I kept looking out at the landscape, the sky, the telegraph poles, the houses and thatched cottages so as not to have to start a conversation. I was being cautious. We were still on German soil; what if the fellow were a spy? He didn't look the part, to be sure, but informers and policemen never do. No, it was better to hide behind my thoughts and my home-

sickness. I was still pleading with Inge; I kept finding new
arguments, and never had I been so eloquent, so persuasive. . . .

Suddenly, I turned around, bewildered: my companion
had spoken to me—in Yiddish. "In this cursed land, one
has the impression of witnessing the end of the world,
don't you agree?"

I answered in the same language, but with a certain
anxiety. "You shouldn't speak of such things, not out
loud."

Disdaining my advice, he went on, "Fear is one of the
Biblical curses. Fear of speaking and listening, of awakening and sleeping: oh, yes—we are witnessing the apocalypse."

His Yiddish was from Lithuania, pure, melodious, in
contrast to his raucous voice. "At the same time I tell myself that since the world was world, there has always been
one man who looks around and declares the end is at
hand—and he is always right."

His recklessness intrigued and disturbed me. I turned
and studied him more closely. In Berlin I had taken him
for the prince of a royal tribe of Israel, so majestic was his
bearing. As I said, he was dressed austerely and elegantly,
with waistcoat and gold chain. He had a free and easy
manner, an aquiline nose, and a faraway, preoccupied
look. In Barassy and Berlin, in Liyanov and Bucharest, I
had seen all types of Jews, believers and nonbelievers, rich
and poor, affectionate and vain—but this one resembled
none of them. Radiating a mysterious power that transcended his own person and mine, he was in a category all
his own.

"Who are you?" I asked.

"Forgive me. I have not introduced myself. I am a professor, my name is David Aboulesia."

His looks and demeanor were neither those of a professor

nor those of a Spaniard. A man named David Abou___
would express himself in Castilian or in Ladino, but su___
not in Yiddish. I suspected him once again of havi___
disguised himself for some unavowed purpose.

"What do you teach?"

"The history of Jewish poetry. Or, if you prefer, the
poetry of Jewish history."

And he started talking to me of Biblical, prophetic,
midrashic poetry; medieval litanies; songs commemorating
the martyrs of the Crusader period and the pogroms; of
Yehuda Halevy and Shmuel Hanagid, Eliezer Hakalir and
Mordechai Yoseph ha-Kohen of Avignon. He had such
mastery of his subject that I became oblivious to the
constant comings and goings in the corridor of suspicious
characters in dark raincoats and uniforms. We were approaching the frontier.

"The work of the poet and of the historian are identical," said my companion. "Both illuminate the summit
and proceed by the process of elimination, retaining only
one word in ten, one event in a hundred. The difference
between poetry and history? Let's say that poetry is history's invisible dimension."

He carried on so long about all this that he was beginning to annoy me. We were crossing a barbarian land
where Jewish history and poetry were continuously threatened, yet here he was, erect and dignified as a statue,
playing with words, juggling ideas—and in Yiddish, to
boot. After all, there's a limit.

"David Aboulesia is a Spanish name—where did you
learn Yiddish?"

The explanation was simple: his maternal grandparents
were Russian Jews. And on his father's side?

"Sephardim from Tangiers."

Where did he live? Where did he teach?

"All over. I've been traveling for some years now. I

e through towns and villages, I go from country to
.ntry."

What was he looking for?

"Someone," he said. "I am looking for someone."

"The Messiah?" I asked, by way of a joke.

My tone displeased him. He stiffened.

"Why not? Why not him? He's of this world, young
man. The Talmudic sages place him at the gates of Rome,
but in fact he lives among us, everywhere. According to the
Zohar, he is waiting to be called. He is waiting to be
recognized in order to be crowned. Remember, young
man, the Messiah looks like anyone at all except a Messiah.
His name, which preceded Creation, also preceded him.
The story of the Messiah is the story of a quest, of a name
in search of a being, or of the being itself."

His digressions irritated me. Who did he think he was?
An initiate? A madman, I thought. We're still in Hitler's
Reich and all he has in his head are messianic theories.
He must be mad. But I had no chance to let him see my
irritation. The train stopped, we had reached the frontier,
and other preoccupations gripped me. What if my name
was on a blacklist? And if they arrested me? The agony was
interminable: police and customs officers were turning my
passport over, searching my suitcase. Aboulesia watched
them with a calm, almost haughty look. Because he had a
British passport? I detected no trace of alarm in him. The
Germans saluted us politely and left. But the strain did
not relent for me until the train started again and crossed
the border. I sighed with relief. I looked at my companion
in a new way: Now let's begin. But he beat me to it.

"I saw you yesterday, young man," he said. "I caught a
glimpse of you, near the Zirkus in Berlin. I was waiting
for you to follow me."

He really *is* mad, I thought.

"But—I have followed you, haven't I?"

"So you have," he answered. "That places me under an obligation. Make a wish, no matter what."

There he goes again. He was no longer playing at being the Messiah; now he was impersonating Elijah the Prophet. One more, so what! They were not hard to find, those prophets and messiahs, they were a dime a dozen. I quite liked them; and they liked me too. There had been many, ever since I was a child. Maimonides is right: a world without madmen could never exist. But those of my childhood were all poor, lost, stray devils, searching for a morsel of bread or an attentive ear—not like this Sephardic professor who had gone to look for the Messiah in Germany.

"I'm waiting—your wish?"

"Very well. Answer one question: What were you doing in Germany?"

He left his corner and sat down opposite me, near the window.

"Our sages believed the Messiah would come the day mankind was either entirely guilty or entirely innocent. I went to Germany—on a mission. To assess the country's guilt."

"So?" I said, playing the game. "What did you find?"

"The world isn't altogether guilty yet, but don't worry, young man, it soon will be," he said with surprising detachment. "But—"

"But what?"

"Now it's my turn. I'd like to ask you a question."

"Go ahead."

"I noticed some phylacteries in your suitcase. Now, you're not wearing a hat, you didn't say your prayers this morning. What kind of Jew are you?"

Ah, the phylacteries.

"I am not a practicing Jew."

"But then I don't understand. . . ."

Soon I was telling him about Liyanov, my father, my promises. Aboulesia took an interest in my past. He spoke to me of his own. He had studied in a famous yeshiva in Lithuania, had taught in Galicia, in Greece, in Syria, in the Old City of Jerusalem. He had masters and disciples everywhere. . . . As I listened to him, I recalled an incident from the time I was studying under Rebbe Mendel-the-Taciturn.

His pupils were young, devout, fervent, engaged in penetrating Scripture's secret splendor, a splendor linking mortals to their immortality. Each of our words resounded in the Celestial Palace where God and those near to Him fathom the story of our sufferings; each of our silences suggested another silence, more sublime, more holy.

I remember one evening, before midnight, Nahum, the youngest son of the *mikvah* attendant, asked a question: "We have reached the threshold of knowledge, Rebbe, but what use is it?" Nahum was trembling like a leaf about to drop from its branch. It was a dead-end situation, and he knew it. Means or end, knowledge inspires the same degree of fear.

Rebbe Mendel-the-Taciturn hid his head between his hands and raised it only after a long moment. "You want to know the use of knowledge?" he said. "Well, listen, all of you listen: it helps us understand Creation, that is, to grasp it, to work on it and even on its Author; it helps to bring us close to the beginning and the end simultaneously; it helps to bring about a liberation of the being inside beings, of the eternal in time. . . ." The Master seemed in a trance. He kept saying that knowledge is a key, the most precious of all keys, and also the most dangerous, because it opens two identical doors: one to Truth, the other to the abyss. Nahum cried out, "And what if I refuse the key?" "Too late," answered our Master. "We have crossed the threshold; from now on, doubt is no longer permitted." A silence heavy with apprehension fell over us. No one dared break it. It lasted until the morning prayer—no, it drove away prayer. We passed that day without prayer, without food, without rest. Shortly afterward, Nahum lost his faith, his brother lost his life, and I myself felt the ground shaking under my feet.

David Aboulesia was speaking and I remembered Rebbe Mendel-the-Taciturn, whose eyes flashed with rage whenever a text refused to reveal its meaning. I remembered Ephraim and his politico-religious games. Inge and Traub. Hauptmann and Bernfeld. And now David Aboulesia. . . . They all were trying to hasten events, to prepare man for the Messiah or the Messiah for man. The goal was the same—impossible to attain. Impossible? Not for Inge. In a guilty Germany she represented salvation. Aboulesia was speaking, and I was imploring Inge to drop everything and come join me in Paris.

". . . Since he refuses to appear in our midst," said my companion with complete seriousness, "I shall continue to pursue him wherever he may be in heaven or on earth."

"Good luck," I said.

The corridor had become livelier. Some of the passengers, half asleep, were going to the dining car while others, half awake, were coming back. We were approaching Paris. Glimpses of dreary, rainy suburbs. Laughter, yawns, exchange of addresses. Do we arrive soon? Soon. Stiff legs, headaches, heavy, burning eyelids. The train was slowing down.

"Don't forget, young man," David Aboulesia said. "Don't forget—the great thing is not to be the Messiah but to seek him."

"And if I find him?"

"First find him, then we'll talk about it."

"The three of us?"

We shook hands, got off the train together, and were

separated by the crowd. I never thought I'd meet him again, but there too I was mistaken. As I was looking for the information desk, I heard his voice behind me: "I know Paris, young man; why not come with me?"

I could not help smiling. What if he were Elijah the Prophet after all? Or the Messiah? Not the real one, not the great and only one, but a more modest messiah: my own? Paris, city of light, wake up—I am bringing you a messiah! And he took me to his hotel.

His "hotel" was a dingy lodging for the poor, not far from the Place de la République. Cramped, smelly, it was always dark inside. The second floor—I was to find out later—was reserved for very special clients who slipped upstairs for *un petit moment* and left looking guilty.

"The advantage of this hotel," Aboulesia explained, "is that it's cheap and the police show themselves only rarely for fear of stumbling upon an important personality—a cabinet member or industrialist perhaps."

The proprietor, a drunkard with a puffy, sleepy face, managed a smirk as he welcomed us:

"Ah—Professor," he exclaimed from behind the desk, "so you're back again? Let's see—what room shall I give you? Ah, here you are. The same as usual. As for your friend . . ."

Unfortunately, my room, on the second floor, was occupied—but only temporarily—by a customer of the hurried kind.

"Sit down here," said the proprietor. "Have a cup of coffee. By the time you're finished, the room will be ready, I promise."

That was my initiation into the ways of tourists and hotels in France. The disorder was shocking. In Berlin such things would never happen.

"Don't be upset," said the proprietor two hours later. "The customer up there, who knows? Just put yourself in his place. . . ."

I would have been delighted to put myself in his place;
I was collapsing from fatigue. What could I do? Since I
knew no French, I couldn't even allow myself the luxury
of complaining. David Aboulesia was fluent; he served as
my interpreter.

"Ah, *now* you can go up," the proprietor announced
sleepily.

To make up for having inconvenienced me, he was
ready to offer me—exceptionally and temporarily—what,
or rather, who, came with the room, but he saw me blush
and did not insist.

I stretched out on the bed and fell asleep. David Aboulesia woke me at the end of the afternoon and took me to
a kosher restaurant for dinner. He invited me again the
next day and the day after that, and throughout his stay
in Paris.

I don't know what he had come to do; he would leave
early in the morning without telling me where he was
going or for how long. Upon returning, he knocked on my
door and we would go to the restaurant. Later we would
go up to his room to chat. Funny: two floors below, men
and women were buying and selling one another, enticing
one another, indulging in pleasure—we could hear them
squeaking, laughing, groaning, we could smell a mixture
of nauseating odors—while in his room, the professor-
rabbi, the adventurer-magician was describing his jour-
neys. Two floors below, men and women were offering one
another simple, immediate pleasures, and David Aboulesia
was talking of the End of Days, of the Ultimate Experience,
of the explosion of language to the limits of the absolute.
The end, the end. It was an *idée fixe* with him, an obsession. Now I was really getting irritated. I had not come to
Paris to listen to speeches on the apocalyptic outcome of
history—I had already been subjected to them in Liyanov.
But I couldn't hurt him. I've already told you, Citizen
Magistrate: there was something about him, something

singularly noble—yes, noble, even in that flophouse—that
commanded respect. And I certainly owed him that.

"Well, your famous anonymous fellow, did you find
him?" I asked, to show my interest.

"Not yet, not yet."

But he was continuing his inquiries. He was going from
market to market, from synagogue to synagogue, from one
hotel to the next.

"He too likes to move around," he explained to me. "He
too changes settings."

"And what if he's intentionally avoiding you? Fleeing
from you? Hasn't that ever crossed your mind?"

"It's possible," he admitted morosely. "It's possible I
am frightening him. I am free not to call him; he is not.
I mean, he's not free to refuse to respond to my call. . . .
Listen to what happened to me yesterday. I visited the
mental hospital at Charenton. A friend of mine, a famous
psychiatrist, introduced his patients to me. It's partly
because of him and partly because of them that I had to
pass through Paris—all of them claim to be the Messiah."

He paused, to stress the point. "All of them—the psychiatrist too."

That's what we were chatting about in my room, or
his—I sitting on the bed, he on the only chair—while on
the second floor, good, ordinary, and not-so-good, not-so-
ordinary people were busy exorcising their depressions,
filling their loneliness, or, as they say here, *making* love—
like making coffee or making beds.

The week of my arrival I went to the office on the
Rue du Paradis where foreigners such as I received help
and advice. I had found the address in a Jewish Communist daily, *Dos Blättel*. I had also bought a copy of
Pariser Haint, a publication whose literary quality I approved, though not its politics. Too Zionist for my taste:

I preferred Communist internationalism to Jewish chau-
vinism. Yes, Inge's influence was proving more lasting
than Rebbe Mendel-the-Taciturn's: I dreamed of Moscow
more than of Jerusalem.

The Aid Committee in the Rue du Paradis mainly took
care of special Jewish refugees: Communists, fellow travelers or sympathizers. Its offices were jammed with men
and women of all ages who needed residence permits in
order to get work permits, or work permits in order to get
residence permits. Polish workers, Russian grocers, Romanian merchants. Haggard and frightened, they reminded me of Liyanov and Barassy-Krasnograd.

After waiting an hour or two, I was asked by a buxom
bespectacled woman with hair piled high on her head
whether I needed money or papers: door A for the former,
door B for the latter. Like a schoolmarm, she lifted her
index finger to explain it in Yiddish, but with a heavy
French accent. "If it's money you need, you'll need documents proving you have none, documents if it's . . ."

"I have both."

She jumped. "What?"

"I have money to prove I have money; and I have documents to prove I have documents."

"Then you don't need anything?"

"Nothing, madame. I have a valid passport and enough
money to live on."

"But then . . . what do you want?"

"I'd like to meet people who speak my language and
think as I do."

The poor lady was bowled over. She had never run into
a character like me. I explained my situation. I did some
writing, I came from Berlin, I felt close to the working
class—close, but not part of it—I wanted to make myself
useful. . . . She listened attentively, but incredulously,
then got up and went into another office. She reappeared

ten minutes later and announced solemnly: "Comrade
Pinsker himself will see you."

Following her directions, I went up to the first floor,
where an old gentleman in shirtsleeves told me to knock
on the last door on the right at the end of the corridor.
Sitting behind a mountain of journals and newspapers, a
man with a huge pile of papers stacked in front of him
was writing; he didn't bother to lift his head to nod or
even look at me. I moved forward. No response. The
scribe was very busy, every minute counted. Was he re-
writing *Das Kapital?* I stood there for what seemed an
endless time. I coughed. No response. Sucking on an unlit
cigarette, he went on writing. He gave the impression he
was going to write until the end of his days and mine. I
lost patience.

"I was told to—to come see you."

Nothing, still nothing. He was undoubtedly beginning
a new chapter that would revolutionize the philosophic
thought of our generation.

"I was told downstairs to come see you—I mean, to
speak to you," I said, annoyed.

Without moving, he deigned to open his mouth.

"Wait," he said in a cutting voice.

Very well. I observed him with growing hostility. Who
did he think he was? No one had ever kept me standing
and waiting so long. What did he want to prove? That each
office had its own little dictator? Finally he put down his
pen and addressed the intruder who had come to disturb
his work.

"Yes? What do you want?"

"To sit down."

With a movement of his right arm, which he had to raise
high in order to clear the mountain of papers, he granted
me permission to take a seat on a chair laden with diction-
aries. His left hand was groping impatiently for something

in the mass of papers. He emitted a grunt of satisfaction
as he found the matches and lit his cigarette. I sat down.

"Well, speak up," said Pinsker. "What do you want?"

"I want to do something. Preferably something useful."

"Who are you?"

Good—Pinsker was not a writer but a police inspector.
I introduced myself quickly.

"You say you are a writer?"

"I would like to write."

"What?"

As if I knew! Does one ever know what one is going to
write? One writes, then one knows.

"All right, so don't answer. Another question: *Why* do
you want to write?"

He was picking a fight, for sure. Why, why did I want
to write? Does one ever know why one does this or that
without knowing why?

"Well?"

I explained as best I could that I was sorry but . . . I
could explain nothing. To hide my literary incompetence,
I expanded on my "activity" as Ephraim's right hand, my
"work" as Inge's collaborator.

He interrupted me: "Are you a Party member?"

"No." I hastened to add: "But I am a poet."

Caught off guard, he forgot to suck at his cigarette, but
he recovered quickly. "That explains it; now everything
makes sense. I haven't read the morning paper *but* I am
hungry. Okay, okay . . . what are your poems about?"

I started to stammer. I never could—I still cannot—
speak about my "work."

"Show me," Pinsker ordered.

"I've nothing with me," I apologized.

"Recite something," he said with an air of extreme
weariness.

"I—I can't."

"But then what are you doing here, young man?"

So he was capable of getting angry, this Pinsker, he could show some human emotion: he wasn't a machine for writing but for offending. Intrigued, I observed him like a spectator: Will it fall, won't it fall? I am speaking of the cigarette butt, of course.

"Do you think I have time to waste? Why did they send you to me?

He was getting angrier. He slammed his fist on the table, raising a cloud of dust.

"I am sorry, Mr. Pinsker. I was wrong to come. Wrong to bother you. I interest you less than the most insignificant journal there on your desk. I'll go speak to the editor-in-chief of *Dos Blättel*; he'll be more encouraging."

I got up. So did he. A disappointment—I had thought he was taller.

"Really?" he said, brightening. "Are you sure of that? So you really think the editor-in-chief will be nicer?"

"I surely hope so."

Will it fall, won't it fall? The butt fell. Pinsker had just flung his tousled head back and snorted:

"Keep on hoping, young man, keep on hoping."

"Oh, that won't be a problem. Absolutely anyone would be more pleasant than you."

"Anyone? And what if I told you I am the editor-in-chief?"

He burst out laughing, and I felt like sinking into the ground if not lower. Only then did he come to my rescue. He shook my hand, asked me to hurry over to the hotel and come back quickly with my poems.

Unbelievable but true, I swear—he liked my poems, and promised to publish them. He kept his word; the first one appeared in the following Sunday's issue. It was called "How." How to return to the hungry their pride, to the humiliated their strength? How to speak to the disinherited

of love, and to orphans of happiness? And how to sing of
hope in the face of mute suffering? How can this be done?
Ask the humiliated, the suffering, it is they who will show
you how. . . . And if you do not ask them, watch out! They
are jealous—more jealous than the gods; demanding—
more demanding than the prophets; truer and stronger
than the judges. Yes, the workers will build the kingdom
of man! And you, poor maker of words, you will knock at
the doors until madness overtakes you, and no one will
tell you how to open them. . . .

The poem, too declamatory, wasn't good, and I knew
it—it's not included in my collection. Pinsker knew it
sooner and better than I, but his interest had been
aroused by the Talmudist, the mystic in me. He could announce to his readers another victory for the enlightened
Jewish proletariat: Paltiel Kossover, Jewish by birth and
poet by profession, had abandoned the God of his ancestors for the working class, the superannuated Torah for
the Communist ideal, idle contemplation for the class
struggle. . . . His editor's note was on the level of his newspaper, but that hardly bothered me. What was important
for me was to be published.

As a result, I began giving Pinsker two or three poems
a day; he kept them about a week and returned them to
me: too simple, too complicated, too personal or not
personal enough, too lyrical, too dry—and surely too
numerous. And yet, not all were bad. I included seven in
my collection.

Pinsker advised me to try prose. Once he accepted a
story of mine, a short pseudo-Hasidic meditation; another
time even a poem, and that was cause for celebration.

As for David Aboulesia, he read only the first poem. He
read with raised eyebrows, moving his lips and looking sad,
sad to the point of tears:

"We're all knocking at the gates," he remarked. "Are

they the same for everyone? And then, young man—what's
waiting on the other side, tell me?"

"I used to be excited about the other side; now it's this
side I care about."

"Really? What a pity. Yes, Paltiel, I mean it: a poet who
doesn't look beyond the wall is like a bird without song."

One day he announced his departure. He had friends to
see, missions to accomplish in Italy, Greece, Palestine.

"I'd like very much to do something for you," he said.

"What—you want me to make another wish?"

"No," he said, with a friendly smile. "Something else.
I'd like you to entrust me with your *tephilin*. You don't
put them on any more. I'll return them to you, I promise."

No, not that. My phylacteries and I were inseparable.
That was my father's wish.

"I understand," said the mysterious messenger. "And I
am happy you refused."

We shook hands. The question of questions during those
years was burning my lips: *Will we see each other again?*
My friend was sure of it, I was not. I left the hotel the
same day—to the regret of the owner and a few pretty
young girls who loved to tease me. I moved in with a passionate activist recommended by Pinsker, or rather he
had recommended me to her. "She adores poets," he
had told me, his eternal cigarette dangling from his mouth.

Sheina Rosenblum was her name. I especially remember
her lips, quivering, fleshy, always ready to swallow. Her
arms, her head, her eyes, I noticed them only afterward—
after the first night.

A strange activist, Sheina Rosenblum. At twenty, owner
of a luxurious apartment on the Rue de la Boetie, she was
a Communist by temperament. She housed illegal foreigners sent to her by the Party, but she selected them with
care. As soon as I crossed her threshold, I was submitted
to a full-fledged inquisition.

"Who sent you?"

"Pinsker."

"You haven't any papers, is that it? Are you here illegally?"

"Not at all."

"But then, why does Pinsker . . . ?"

"Because," I said, blushing, "because I am a—a poet."

And following Pinsker's exact instructions, I handed her the paper containing my first poem.

"Oh, good," she said. "Sit down, there, in the living room. Let's have a talk about your work."

Was she being ironic? Nasty? I couldn't have cared less. Throughout the conversation I saw only her lips; they opened and closed at regular intervals. From time to time her tongue licked them slowly, very slowly, as though teaching them patience.

"You often knock on doors?" she asked suddenly, after reading my poem.

Her voice troubled me: voluptuous, too voluptuous. I cleared my throat and said nothing.

"It's stupid to knock," she went on. "Doors are there to be forced open."

Hypnotized by her lips, I guessed her allusion; I would have liked to say yes or no, you're so right, mademoiselle, or you're so wrong, comrade, but—inexperience? Shyness? Memories of Inge?—not a sound escaped my mouth.

"I'll take you," she said. "I mean, as a lodger. Go and get your things."

I made a superhuman effort. "But—how much will that be?"

"Don't worry about the rent. You'll pay me according to your means; nothing pleases me more than being able to assist our admirable Jewish poets."

I wanted to protest. I, admirable? But she was already pushing me outside.

"Go, my dear poet, let's not waste time. Come back quickly. I'd like to know you better. I mean, your poems, of course."

I did not have to be persuaded. Fortune was smiling on me: I caught all the metro trains, made all the connections, without losing a second. Hardly had I left before I was back, installed in a little room facing the courtyard, and then seated on the living-room sofa with my notebook of poems. On a table was a coffeepot with an intoxicating aroma. Outside it was getting dark. Sheina was preparing to go into a trance.

As I read, my mind strayed: to my father praying in Liyanov, to Inge running through the streets of Berlin; I saw my mother's disapproving eyes and the resigned look of my former girlfriend. Read, said a strange voice. I read without knowing what; I was elsewhere. Read, don't stop, read, read, said a panting mouth . . . vast and deep, inviting me to explore and devour it. A mad idea: that mouth was an opening to a secret world where I would find my people.

Then, in the middle of a bad poem, in the heart of a dream in ruins, I lost my head. And my voice was extinguished in the dark.

Paris: city of encounters, of furtive and painful discoveries. All isms converge there, including the anti-isms, all the revolutionaries too, including the counterrevolutionaries. Nowhere else on earth is there so much talk about so many subjects with so much passion, if not sincerity. Bergson and Breton, Blum and Maurras, Drieu and Malraux, Stalin and Trotsky: I spent my evenings at Le Chénier in Montmartre with the editors of *Dos Blättel*, listening to their talk about political, poetical, philosophical events as seen from the Communist angle. A speech of Daladier's excited us no less than Davidson's latest review in the *Pariser Haint* of a work by one of *our* authors.

I didn't take part in the debates; I preferred to listen, learn and absorb. I felt too young, too much of a beginner, to take a position. There was only one subject on which I allowed myself an opinion—Hitler Germany. Unfortunately there was no lack of experts on the subject, and they all talked louder than I.

I finally met Paul Hamburger, and that meeting changed my life once more.

Hamburger received me in his hotel room. Yes, he remembered Traub. He also knew Inge and kept in touch with her.

"I am glad you've come," he said. "Stay with me. We'll do good work together."

He had the style of a business manager. People came to ask him questions and went off with his instructions. They brought him slips and messages, to which he gave brief answers. Everyone spoke German—so did I. An immediate, intimate contact was established.

"But what sort of work do you do?"

"You'll know soon enough."

"When, Paul?"

"You'll know, believe me."

Paul Hamburger was a giant. Like Aboulesia, but more heavyset. His was an intelligence that was rare, cultivated, generous and bold. He could do anything. He organized networks, selected emissaries, wrote pamphlets and propaganda manuals, supervised the liaison agencies, those already existing and those about to be set up among the various underground movements in Germany; everyone knew him and he knew everyone. Though a Communist, his influence reached beyond the Party structure. People loved working with him, for him.

He immediately assigned me the "poetry" column in the multilingual journals he published. In this way I made some friends and not a few enemies. I used the little power

I had reluctantly: to praise a work, denounce an author. I was as loath to flatter as to demolish. Still, it had to be done. Paul often said, "We're at war; your personal feelings and tastes are useful to us only insofar as they help us fight the Nazis."

I had his confidence, and yet I was not a Party member. I had actually implored Pinsker to propose my candidacy to the Yiddish cultural section, but Paul had advised me against this while scolding me affectionately.

"What do you want? A card? What for? A piece of paper with your picture on it, like an identity card from police headquarters; I have a dozen of them. The name changes but not my picture. That's how it is."

"You don't understand. . . ."

"I don't understand what? Your need for membership, your desire to belong to a fine loyal brotherhood? But that's romanticism, my poor Paltiel. With or without a card, you're one of us, isn't that true?"

It was true. Paid out of the Party's secret funds, I was working for the Party, taking risks for the Party, living for the Party. I even suffered for the Party: the editors of the reactionary *Pariser Haint* never lost a chance to shoot poison arrows at me. The war was on. My writings irritated them, my poems sent them into a fury. Nor did we handle them with kid gloves in our own newspaper. Our public fights were ferocious and transcended our political differences. Everything they preached was evil; everything we did was sublime. We were defending truth and justice; they were practicing falsehood and idolatry.

Bizarre: we were Jews, they too; we spoke Yiddish, so did they; we came from Central Europe, so did they; our parents were brought up on Torah, theirs too; and yet, and yet—an abyss separated us.

We faced the same enemy; the same danger threatened us. In the eyes of the Fascists, we were Jews—Yids. Hateful, all of us, and contemptible, fit only to be driven out of the country, expelled from society, eliminated. We answered—but not together. It was impossible to come to any agreement on organizing joint meetings, demonstrations, or acts of solidarity and protest. Impossible to unite our strengths and wills. We were fighting our battles separately; one might have thought we were fighting against one another much more than against the German or French anti-Semites.

An article of mine, appearing at the end of 1935 or the beginning of 1936, brought down on my head an avalanche of hateful replies in the *Pariser Haint*. In that piece I explained my opposition to the principle of Zionism. A choice must be made: either you are religious and are forbidden to rebuild David's kingdom before the coming of the son of David; or you are not religious, in which case Jewish nationalism would jeopardize the Jews it claims to safeguard. And I was specific: a Jewish state in Palestine would be a ghetto; and we are against ghettos. We are struggling against walls, against discrimination, against divisions everywhere. We view the phenomenon of the ghetto as a defect, a mark of shame; we favor a humanity without frontiers. Religious beliefs arouse distrust and rancor among peoples; rather than cutting Jews off from humanity, we are trying to integrate them, to weld them together. It's not enough to liberate the Jew, let us liberate man, and the problem will be resolved. . . .

For a whole week the Zionist paper would not let go. They called me a propagandist in the pay of Moscow, a renegade, a traitor. The more moderate critics chided me for my ignorance, not to say stupidity. Poets who mix into politics, declared the polemicist Baruch Grossman, are like sleepwalkers who apply for jobs as guides.

Secretly I was jubilant: Baruch Grossman had recognized the poet in me. That was worth all the insults in the

world. Nevertheless, I responded. Why should poets stay
out of politics? What about the prophets? Isaiah, Jeremiah,
Habakkuk, Amos and Hosea: they were poets, weren't
they? And they mixed into politics, didn't they? And what
about the French revolutionaries of 1789?

For a week the Yiddish world of Paris was plunged into
real tumult. The two camps quarreled with a verbal violence unprecedented even in *our* annals, and all because of
a few lines signed by a certain Paltiel Kossover. I was the
only topic in the cafés and clubs. In the leather-goods
workshops, among the tailors and pressers, the only discussion was of the battle opposing the two Jewish dailies.
We were graded, criticized, congratulated; one day I won,
the next I lost; my stock went down, up, then down again.
One might have thought nothing else, nothing as important, was taking place in the world.

Echoes of the polemic reached as far as Liyanov. My
father, in one of his short, moving letters, wrote: "It
seems there is a man in Paris with your name; he is a poet,
a writer; our local weekly has reprinted excerpts from an
article he wrote about our people. . . . What a pity he's
sullying your name and your family's. . . . Perhaps you
ought to insist on a statement in the paper saying you are
not the author. . . ." He ended by reminding me that I
had sworn to put on my *tephilin* every morning.

Of all the reactions to my article, his was the only one
that hurt.

A painful irony, admit it, Citizen Magistrate: today it
is *Dos Blättel* that disowns me and the Zionist press that
comes to my defense. The newspaper clippings you showed
me last week—or was it last month or last year? I have lost
all sense of time here—made me laugh: Pinsker saying I
had *always* been an *agent provocateur*. That was why he had
opposed my joining the Party at the time. And another colleague, Alter Yoselson, writing his political confessions in

the columns of the same paper: "I admit the snake really took me in." And in a New York Yiddish Communist newspaper, someone named Schweber covers me with mud, when only ten years earlier he praised me to the skies. Yes, it is painful: my comrades, my friends of yesterday, so quick to judge me, to condemn me.

Why did you show me those articles, Citizen Magistrate? To prove the extent of my isolation? You have succeeded. Not one of your other arguments has caused me such grief. "So, prisoner Kossover, you think I am the only one to consider you a traitor? Are you perhaps expecting some testimony in your favor from Paris? Just take a look at these newspaper clippings. You'll see what your 'friends' think of you. They're accusing you of treason—and they do so with more venom than we. Look and look well, prisoner Kossover: they justify your condemnation even before your trial opens. . . ."

That hurts—yes, that hurts.

You let me see the Zionist articles too, for tactical reasons, right?—to be able to say later, "But look, prisoner Kossover—who is coming to your defense? Reactionaries, imperialists, the worst enemies of Soviet Russia—and you persist in denying you were their accomplice? But then, tell us, why would they be trying to save your skin?"

There you have failed. For, you see, I am glad I finally have a good press among the Zionists—among committed, dedicated Jews, among *Jewish* Jews. Their attitude comforts me. This time your ruse did not work, unlike the first, which filled me with disgust. Even now, when I think about it, I feel nauseated. To cleanse my thoughts, I think of my father's face, his voice, his request. The *tephilin*, oh, yes, my phylacteries. I had forgotten about them, tucked away in a drawer, beneath my shirts, at Sheina Rosenblum's. Because of your tricks I almost forgot about her—her too.

You'll laugh: I speak to you and think of her, and it is

her mouth I see—nothing else. She drove me crazy. She had only to open her lips and my body arched toward her. Sometimes I would come home late, after exhausting days of meetings; I would see Sheina, sleeping in her bed or mine. And despite my fatigue and need for sleep and rest, I would lie down beside her—to embrace her, embrace her until morning.

At the paper I saw other girls who pleased me. There were always beautiful, mysterious women around Paul Hamburger. I remember Lisa: delicate, angelic; she was liaison to a secret group in Germany. I desired her; she never knew it. I remember Claire: tall, full of laughter, she flirted with everyone, told spicy stories and gave the impression she spent all her time making love and yet . . . it was said she was a virgin. There was Madeleine, one of Paul's secretaries, who translated his articles into French, scowling as she worked. She was not pretty, but I liked the way she concentrated. I could have initiated some short-lived affairs, but I lacked the time—and the courage. The little I had of both I devoted to my landlady. Our ritual never varied. She made me recite a poem and closed her eyes. She understood nothing—so what? She paid me royalties all the same.

Did she love me? Perhaps. Did I love her? Sometimes. I insisted on paying rent; symbolic amounts. I addressed her with the formal *vous*, at least in the beginning. She never called me by my first name but by fanciful nicknames. It was "my poet" here, my "great poet" there . . . "Is my little genius hungry by any chance?" or "Is my great Rimbaud cold?"

From Pinsker I knew she had had many lovers, but she never alluded to them. The past is the past, she would say, shaking her finger at me: don't touch it.

It was the future that fascinated her. Had she needed it, she could have made her living as a fortune-teller. The accuracy of her premonitions alarmed me. She got up one morning and said, yawning, "I feel I'll be going to a funeral soon." That same week one of her aunts died. Another time: "We're going to have something to celebrate." The next day a comrade escaped from a German prison. Hence the fear I had of deceiving her. She would have guessed.

I suppose she was faithful to me; otherwise I would have stumbled on another poet in the house. I never did. Sometimes I would glimpse an anonymous visitor sent by the Party, who stayed a night or two; I gave him my room and shared Sheina's.

I seldom "went out" with her, for lack of funds. Under no circumstances would I have let her pay the check in the restaurant or the café. Pride? Vanity? Both. And while we're at it, we might add self-respect and the remnants of a bourgeois education: in Liyanov a well-bred young man would never have let himself be supported by a woman, however rich and impassioned by Jewish poetry.

One evening, however, I invited her to dinner. I had just cashed a check for a long novella published by my paper and translated into French by a contributor to *Ce Soir*. It was the first time I was to be published in French; I was feeling somewhat exuberant. We were drinking to that, Sheina and I, when Paul appeared at the door of the restaurant. He knew Sheina; she motioned to him to join us. Paul was my closest friend, but for some inexplicable reason his presence embarrassed me. Would he judge me? Did he resent my living with a rich woman? I was still a puritan. I became surly. Sheina was in top form; superb and enticing with her resonant laugh, she attracted attention. A doubt: Paul and she . . . was it possible? Surely Paul would have told me. His style was to be forthright, open; truth above all, on the same level as friendship. He would have sat me down in front of him, in his office; he would have closed the door, and, looking me straight in the eye, would have said, "Listen, friend, I know you're living with Sheina; that doesn't bother me as long as you do your job." Also: "I want you to know that Sheina and I used to be intimate but it's been over for a long time." That's how Paul Hamburger would have handled the matter. No, there had been nothing between them.

Then why was I so troubled? What irritated me was not knowing what irritated me. As for Paul, he behaved very naturally. He commented with humor on current events, described the situation in Germany: anecdotes, predictions, rumors. He was more brilliant and fascinating than ever. The meal over, he had the tact not to come with us. "I have some things to take care of in the neighborhood," he said, kissing Sheina on both cheeks. He shook hands with me and vanished in the direction of the Opéra. I was grateful to him; I was happy.

Was I really? In this cold, barren cell where the sun never penetrates, not even on orders from on high, the answer seems obvious to me. Yes, I was happy, free, without care, blessed with love and companionship. Moreover, I knew I was doing good useful work, fighting the good fight. Everything seemed simple. In a sick society we represented the only chance for a remission. We were raising the banner of revolt against complacency and resignation. I knew where I was going, I knew what I wanted and from whom and how I was going to get it. I knew my enemies and was exposing them. And I knew my allies too. Is that true happiness? Today I say "yes" without hesitation, without qualification. At the time I would have said "I don't know." I would have said, "Happiness? I am much too busy to think about it; happiness, gentlemen, is for the bourgeoisie; we the proletariat have something better to do just now."

And yet I experienced moments of happiness—conscious and fully felt—and I remember them. There was that visit with a family in the north, then in the middle of a strike. A miner and his children receive me. Sad but proud, they invite me into their home. "We have nothing to offer you, we have nothing."

"But you do," I say to them. "A good word or two, a story will be enough. I'll put them in the paper."

They consult each other silently, then the father turns to me and says, "Ordinarily we don't speak about ourselves. But since you're our guest, this will be our way of offering you hospitality."

I ask questions, they answer. How do they live, how are they managing? The mother's illness and death, the solidarity of the fellow miners . . . I listen, I take notes and I am ashamed. I am ashamed of not being hungry, of not being unemployed. And what if I went to the grocer's now? I am afraid of embarrassing them. I'll do it later.

The grocer opens his eyes wide, astonished at the size of my order. I tell him where to deliver the food. "All that?" asks the grocer. "Yes, all that." I pay and walk toward the station. The train is not leaving for an hour. Suddenly, I hear footsteps. My miner sits down next to me on the bench and says, "What you did there is—how can I say it?—it's beautiful."

His familiar way of talking moves me. Awkward like myself, he has difficulty hiding his emotion.

"I didn't know," he says.

"What didn't you know?"

"That Santa Claus was a Communist."

"Santa Claus? I am a Jew, comrade. Our Santa Claus is called Elijah the Prophet. He variously disguises himself as a peasant, a beggar or a coachman."

"And he's a Communist?"

We burst out laughing at the same time. That is what I call happiness.

Another example: a demonstration from the Place de la

République to the Bastille. The Popular Front is the rage.
Leon Blum and Maurice Thorez are beaming; Socialist
and Communist embrace. We shout our hopes at the top
of our lungs. With fists raised, I march past the platform;
I am every workingman's brother, and like him, bubbling
with enthusiasm. Together with our comrades from the
paper and our aid societies, we march, heads held high,
joyous, confident, inspired by an unshakable faith in our
power: we shall triumph over Nazism. I am not a French-
man—so what? I am part of an immense family that
carries history on its shoulders. Behind us, in front of us, all
around us, intellectuals and stevedores, winegrowers and
bricklayers advance with firm and equal step, irresistible,
ready to conquer the earth, and the sun too, if necessary.
Forgive me, Citizen Magistrate: a sally of Trotsky's comes
to my mind: "And if they tell us that the sun shines only
for the bourgeoisie, well, comrades, then we'll extinguish
the sun." No, Trotsky—what's the good of extinguishing
the sun? We'll turn it around to our side, that's more
practical. . . . Suddenly, I see some Zionist groups in the
crowd. They, too, have Socialists in their ranks. Come to
think of it—their paper stopped attacking me weeks ago.
Once again my thoughts go to Elijah the Prophet: there's
no end to his miracles! And while marching and shouting
the usual slogans, I address a silent prayer to the most
democratic, most political and most militant of our
prophets: I thank him for involving himself in our affairs.
My thoughts also go to my father; I am grateful to him
for having taught me to pray and give thanks. If he ever
comes across my picture in a Jewish or Romanian newspaper, he'll surely write me a letter that will not hurt.

Secret mission to Hamburg: I hand over a sum of money
to a network entrusted with the escape of an underground
leader. Later I will learn it concerned Brandberg, the dep-
uty, Rosa Luxemburg's friend. Three rendezvous in three

different public places: the railway station, the harbor, a stop of the Number 3 streetcar. Secret codes, passwords. A waiter takes charge of me first, then a streetcar conductor. Finally I find myself in a restaurant beside a dowdy housewife. Following instructions I put my *Völkischer Beobachter* next to me on the seat; the money is folded inside. I let my neighbor take over. She substitutes her paper for mine. We eat without haste, without greeting one another; two strangers. She leaves before me. Furtively, I follow her with my eyes. *Will we see each other again one day?* The teams keep changing, the question remains the same. I think of Inge. No doubt she's performing similar missions; how much time will go by before she is jailed? I have an idea: What if I stopped off in Berlin? For one day, one night? My heart beats like a drum. No, the orders are explicit. It's forbidden to see old friends again, to expose them to useless risks. I never see the Hamburg housewife again. But a few months later at Paul's I meet a sick, elderly man. Paul introduces us. "That's him," he says, pointing to me. And the man shakes my hand, does not let it go. "I owe you my life; believe me, I owe you my life." And my only thought is, That is what I call happiness—when a man owes you his life.

Oh, yes, I was happy in Paris: as only a Jewish activist —and a poet to boot—could be.

There was also that trip to Palestine. An unforgettable lightning trip. I experienced it intensely—I was about to say, religiously—from beginning to end. And, from beginning to end, my father's eyes never left me.

One gray, rainy morning, Paul calls me into his office. "The Holy Land—what would you say to going there?"

Emotion—at the moment inexplicable—leaves me speechless.

"We're hearing about serious events, riots," says Paul. "A complicated, tangled situation. Englishmen, Arabs,

Jews; intrigues, plots; religion, politics, finance: it's one big mess. We can't make head or tail of it, and we'd like to."

His hand on my shoulder, Paul speaks to me softly: "Will you be up to it—I mean, will you try to remain neutral, objective? You won't forget that passion blinds judgment, and thus is dangerous?"

My face changes color. Yes, I am moved, I don't deny it.

Paul's office takes care of the arrangements: visas, steamship ticket, my "cover" as a special correspondent for a prestigious weekly, *Images de la Vie*. Unlimited expenses. Best hotels. And I'll be carrying an important amount of money to turn over to someone who will introduce himself in a certain Jaffa café as "Wolfe's lost cousin."

The crossing is awful. Hardly have we weighed anchor in Marseille when the sea breaks loose. I never imagined that so large and heavy a steamship could toss around like a matchbox. The ship seems to rise and fall simultaneously, and simultaneously lunge right and left, and I remain behind, always behind, snatched up by the monstrous jaws of the black waves. Vomiting makes me long to flee, to die, to disappear in the dark waters.

The sun returns and the calm restores my zest for life. I spend hours on the bridge, I feel the pull of the sea; I love the murmur of the waves suggesting an endless song; I love the thick white foam stressing the inadequacy of all fixed forms. Peace and depth—I do not resist. I look, afraid to look too much. I go off to read or chat with an Austrian explorer, a Frenchwoman who is an Egyptologist, an emissary from a kibbutz. Unbelievable how quickly one forgets. Yesterday, I was suffering so much I thought of death. Now, I am so at peace with myself I am thinking of death.

The last night I could not close my eyes. Excited, troubled, my heart beating furiously, the Talmud student from Liyanov remained on the bridge so as not to miss that first contact, that first image. Other passengers too must have yielded to the same curiosity, the same impatience. Here and there I caught a whisper, a sigh. The steamship was gliding toward the shore and holding its breath.

At dawn I saw Carmel rising from the sea into a blazing sky of deep blue shot through with red. The beauty of the landscape hit me with almost physical violence. Wide-eyed, I scrutinized the horizon and heard my father saying: "This is the land of our ancestors, my son. Don't you think you should say a prayer—for yourself and for all those who can't pray any more?" I went down to my cabin, and obeying the wish of Gershon Kossover, his son put on the phylacteries from which he had never been separated.

Haifa, Tel Aviv, Jerusalem. Taken in hand by the Political Affairs Department of the Jewish Agency, I traveled throughout the country, studying its problems, penetrating its multifaceted drama. I wanted to meet with members of the Socialist communes: Degania, Ein-Harod and Givat-Brenner. I could have spent the rest of my life there. I feared for the activists, so young and handsome, so open and determined, who were preparing for armed resistance against the Arabs *and* against the English.

I was astonished: "There are so few of you, and you hope to beat them all?"

"Here history counts more than statistics."

"But you're mad! To fight, you need men, arms. You don't go to war with ideas and words. The Bible may be very useful, but it will not protect you against bullets."

"You're thinking in political terms. If we thought the way you do we'd abandon the struggle immediately."

"You're mad!"

I loved their madness. The British colonial policy, on the other hand, scandalized me. As imperialists they

despised both the Jews *and* the Arabs, amusing themselves
by turning one against the other. In matters of duplicity
and intrigue they needed no lessons from anyone. If one
were to believe them, the Jews and Arabs could not survive without them; without them, there would be a
massacre.

In Jerusalem I walked through the narrow, bustling
alleys of the Old City, looking for a memory, some sign of
another age. I loved the sky hanging low over the cedars,
the incandescent clouds above the domes, the motionless
shadows hugging the hovels and shops. I loved the camel
drivers and their camels at rest, at the gates of the city. I
loved the muezzin whose calls to prayer and faith were lost
in the distance; it filled me with nostalgia. I loved, above
all, the stone pathways leading to the Wall of the Temple.
I always took the last few steps at a run. There I found
pilgrims, beggars, mystical dreamers seeking illumination.
I joined them without knowing why; as for them, they
did not ask me why, and I asked nothing of them.

One night a figure emerged from the shadows and
joined me. It crouched beside me and greeted me. In
the silvery half-light of the moon I recognized Aboulesia,
my Sephardic friend. Was he smiling at me or just studying
me? And where did he come from anyway? From the sky?
We shook hands and, foolishly, I wanted to weep.

"It's natural," said David Aboulesia. "Everyone feels
like weeping in this place. This is where God Himself
weeps over the ruins of His temple and His creation."

We strolled around the city. The air was balmy; the
wind was playing in the mountains, rustling through the
trees, descending to the valley to rest. A star flickered. Behind the walls of the houses, men and women were trying
to interpret the meaning of their encounter, and perhaps
of ours.

"Well, and what about the Messiah?" I asked my companion. "Are you still pursuing him?"

"When he's not looking for me, I'm running after him."

But that wasn't the only reason for his coming to Palestine. He made a point of being there during the riots.

"My place is among my persecuted brethren," he said. "Among those being pushed toward the abyss. I am going to prevent them from falling, I must. I know how to go about it. I am a secret agent; I am making my report. To whom? You know perfectly well. I tell Him my fears, point out the dangers. My role is to sound the alarm; I did it in Germany, I am doing it here; I do it wherever the Eternal People are in danger of death. For, unfortunately, this is only the beginning."

I shuddered.

"The beginning of what?"

"I don't know. Of redemption perhaps? Great suffering is to precede the luminous explosion of the messianic age, our mystics tell us. It fills me with fear."

"Fear? Of suffering?"

"Yes. Suffering is meant to frighten. But I am even more afraid of what it means: namely that evil plays a role in the cosmic drama of ultimate redemption. Well then, poet, is it possible that those who bring about suffering, hence injustice, hence evil, are doing the work of salvation?"

While wandering through the silently brooding old city, listening to the insane words of my strange friend, I could not keep from smiling. I thought: This professor-adventurer-mystic expresses himself like a Marxist without knowing it: he is a revolutionary in spite of himself. Paul says that to save the world you must amputate it; to save the arm, you must cut off the little finger. The old metaphor: The worse things are, the better they will become. The more blood flows, the nearer peace. But I cannot stand the sight of blood. If, in order to appear in his immaculate glory, the Messiah has to have himself announced by shrieking nations massacring one another, let him stay home. And yet, both my friends are invoking him, each using methods repugnant to the other. Poor Messiah! All the things done for you in your name—all those things you're made to do.

We parted at dawn. From the Old City, opening up, came an unexpected sound, as of a tent canvas being brutally ripped apart—then a long silence followed by other sounds: doors slamming, shutters squeaking. A mule driver and his recalcitrant mule. A water carrier. Aromas of baked goods and of vegetables. The man sidling along the wall—is he a watchman returning home, a criminal? A mother's strident cry: "Ahmad, are you coming?" And a child answering, "Coming, coming."

I left Jerusalem intending to return, but had to change my plans. Instead, I went to Jaffa, to a noisy, crowded café where "Wolfe's lost cousin" was supposed to single me out. I tried hard not to look like a tourist, but I probably did anyway.

Surprise: the "cousin" was a girl. A *sabra* of Oriental background, she was quiet, simply dressed, with a round face, flat nose, brown hair and black eyes.

"Ahuva," she said, introducing herself. "Call me Ahuva."

We swallowed strong, bitter coffee and went out to take a turn around the market, an ideal place to shake off any inspector with the absurd idea of tailing me.

"I've an envelope for you," I said.

"Not here."

As in a cheap novel, she led me to a shady hotel—even shadier than the one in Paris. I rented a room there for several hours. The obsequious porter handed me the key with a knowing leer. Once in the room, we drew the curtains. I double-locked the door.

"Now," said Ahuva, "show me what you have for me, comrade." She squinted while talking, as if to make herself look more severe. "Well, comrade?"

I handed her the envelope containing the money. She slipped it inside her blouse. "Count it," I said.

"I trust you."

"Count it, I tell you."

She pulled the envelope out of her blouse, opened it and counted. Mission accomplished. We could say good-bye, but Ahuva advised against it.

"That fellow downstairs," she said. "What'll he think of you? And of me? We'd better be careful and remain up here at least an hour, to . . . to make believe."

Was that an invitation?

"Let's talk," she said.

I started questioning her about the situation, the future, the Party, relations with the Zionists, the Arabs. Less educated than Inge, she expressed herself more primitively but better. She burned with a somber, mysterious flame which I found irresistible. Had she made one gesture, I would have forgotten Sheina and Paris; I would have stayed in Palestine. I was ready to break with Europe, ready to fling myself into a new adventure, a new love. But there was no gesture, no word of encouragement. She undoubt-edly had a boyfriend. Or else I was not her type. She answered my questions, asked her own, like a good comrade-in-arms; nothing more.

At the end of an hour, or two, or three, I knew the essentials about her. Her thirst for brotherhood, her ideal of justice had led her to a kibbutz. Then, under the in-fluence of a friend, a greater desire for a vaster brother-hood, a loftier ideal of a more universal justice, she had left. A Party member, she maintained the liaison between certain of its Jewish and Arab sections. What did she think of the tensions agitating the country? She was not entirely pessimistic.

"The English are sowing hatred, but the soil is arid: it doesn't take. At the opportune moment, Jews and Arabs, led by the Party, will unite in a common front against them."

"You don't see any Jewish bloodshed ahead, Ahuva?"

"No bloodshed—neither Jewish nor Arab: for me, Jewish and Arab blood are the same."

Nobody could have foreseen that ten weeks later, during the bloody riots in Hebron, she herself would be attacked, raped and murdered by a band of Arab marauders who knew nothing of the Communist ideal of human brotherhood.

But that I was to learn years later. In Soviet Russia, I met a Jewish comrade from Palestine and asked for news of Ahuva.

"Ahuva? Don't know. Maybe she goes under another name. Describe her to me."

I did, and he cried out, "Of course—you're talking about Tziona! Didn't you know that . . . ?"

I didn't know. There were many things I didn't know. But one thing I did know, and wrote about to my father: From my trip to the Holy Land, I brought back a spark taken from its flame, a star from its sky, a teardrop from its memory.

I did not say all the prayers I should have, and certainly not every day, but in spite of everything, my father would have been pleased with his messenger.

There was one cloud, however. I forgot it a moment ago; but I must face it. Now I can speak of it without fear. Here, in this enclosure that serves you as temple and altar, Citizen Magistrate, I am no longer afraid. Here, the victim lays claim to his own truth. What I speak of has to do with old, old, forgotten events; ancient history. It has to do, if I many remind you, with your predecessors and mine.

Where were you at the time? What were you doing?

Western newspapers everywhere were waging a campaign against the spectacular trials (Kamenev, Zinoviev, Bukharin) unfolding in the Soviet Union. They were shouting about the judicial scandal, the mockery of justice, the gross, indecent lies . . . as they are doing now in connection with my case.

At Pinsker's request—amusing, isn't it?—I put the press in its place. I published article after article proclaiming my faith in Soviet justice. I ridiculed the indignation of the *Pariser Haint*, I pilloried and denounced its moralizing sermons: "So, you take up the defense of your opponents? Their fate suddenly preoccupies you, you shed bitter tears for men whom, only yesterday, you cursed and consigned to damnation. Shame on you, gentlemen—your hypocrisy is matched only by your blindness!" It was a brawl to end all brawls. I shouted as hard as our enemies. Being a novice at such things, I was convinced of the guilt of the accused—especially since they admitted it themselves. The great heroes of the Revolution would not behave like traitors if they had not been traitors. Torture? Humbug. They had stood up to the Okhrana, resisted the Siberian prisons and defied the Tsar's torturers; they would have done as much now if they were innocent.

Paul did not share my conviction. I can tell you now, now that he's no longer alive. Having lived in the Soviet Union, he was better informed about the secret, hidden life there. In his day-to-day relations with us, his collaborators, he masked his worries and his perplexity. But sometimes they came through. I would find him slumped at his desk, staring into space, looking distraught. The helplessness of this giant, usually so full of good humor, became unbearable; I would withdraw, closing the door behind me.

He was not fooled, Paul Hamburger.

One evening I surprised him in his room. I had dropped in just like that, without telephoning, thinking that if he was busy, he'd tell me. He was alone, a bottle of cognac in front of him on the table.

"I'm down in the dumps," he says without looking at me. I don't respond; I don't know what he wants to hear me say.

"I am in a monstrous depression," he repeats. "And you?"

"Not yet."

I sit down.

"I feel like getting drunk," says Paul. "And you?"

"Not yet."

With his fingers he caresses the bottle, turning it round and round without opening it.

"It's funny," he says wearily. "I feel like getting drunk, but I don't feel like drinking."

"With me it's the opposite. I feel like drinking but not like getting drunk."

As a rule, he is too generous not to laugh at my jokes, even if they don't deserve it. This time he just shrugs his shoulders.

"I don't understand," he says after a long silence. "You— do you understand?"

"Understand what?" I say, knowing perfectly well what.

He gives me a fixed, stern look, and insists on an answer.

"Yes or no—answer: Do you understand?"

"I think I do. The Soviet Union is not paradise. There are some good people there and some rats. The good people deserve respect—the traitors, punishment."

"So you think the accused are all guilty, is that it? Rats, traitors and morons?"

He has raised his voice; I begin to feel nervous, but I recite my lesson: "Why shouldn't they be? They've confessed."

Paul studies me with a kind of horror mixed with condescension I had never seen in him before.

"There's a big difference between you and me. You're

too young to understand. There's this difference of age between us, which is expressed by another difference no less essential than the first: *I know*."

"You know what?"

He makes a gesture as if to pour himself a glass of cognac, but doesn't. "It's a game, Paltiel. A cruel and terrible game, but a game nevertheless."

"So what? One more reason for you not to get upset. Is the game cruel? Well, one day it'll be over. . . ."

"Not for the accused, Paltiel. And I know the accused. And the accusers too, I know them all, for heaven's sake."

He gets up, paces about the room, sits down again, seizes the bottle and says, "The worst of it is that either the one *or* the other have betrayed the Revolution. Either way, it's horrible and hopeless."

I am hypnotized by the bottle Paul is turning in his hands. He looks at it, but doesn't see it; he sees something else, something my eyes cannot grasp.

That evening he speaks to me more frankly, more openly than ever before. Sheina must be getting impatient —I told her I would be away for just an hour—but I can't help it; she will *feel*, she will *know* it was urgent for me to come here, to remain here. After all, I cannot abandon a friend who needs to unburden himself, offer himself. As a rule Paul is guarded about his private life. We, his colleagues, know no more about him than on the first day we met him. Where does he come from? What is his background? Is he married? What makes him sad or happy? All I know is that he is highly placed in the apparatus; that he performs some more or less public functions and others that are entirely secret. What kind of man is he in private life? Where is his Achilles' heel? For the first time, he is opening up. And I shrink back on my chair, make myself tiny, afraid he'll stop if he sees I am there in the flesh in front of him.

Wolfe, Petya, Paul: the evolution of a given name, the

flowering of a destiny. That is what I learn. It takes my
breath away. So Paul and I are linked by the same origins.
Wolfe: a Jewish child from eastern Galicia, educated in
poverty, his conscience inflamed by rebellion. Fervent,
dangerous friendships in Vienna, where a chance meeting
catapults him into the stormy world of conspiracy.
Finished, the past with its Sabbath songs; finished, the
warm household where a widower surrounded by six
hungry children glorified the heavens and God's grace.
Finished, the Hasidic kingdom where masters and disciples invented reasons to hope, to believe, to beg for faith
by singing. . . . Long live the Revolution, long live the
World Revolution!

Then came special courses, illegal trips, intelligence
training, familiarization with the closed system of the
Komintern, and then of the Military Intelligence abroad,
the Fourth Department. Now called Petya, Wolfe made
his way into the nerve center of the Party, the one con-
nected to the outside world. The Revolution was young
and pure. Like Petya. The most ambitious dreams seemed
possible and necessary. No more hatred among nations, no
more oppression, no more ruling class, no more profit, no
more hunger, no more shame: life was an offering of
friendship, a thrilling call to solidarity. Petya took up with
Tartars and Uzbeks, fell in love with a White Russian then
left her for a Spaniard. This universe in flux where Jews
and non-Jews embraced one another, where all cultures
are equal, where all religious beliefs are mocked, this universe made him proud and strong. Gratefully he accepted
his first mission to the West: Paul, messenger of the
Revolution, went to Germany invested with unlimited
powers. His was the right to destroy everything in order
to rebuild everything, to abolish everything, to make a
clean slate; he considered himself authorized, indeed commanded, to dethrone kings and gods, and in their place, to
elevate mankind, a frightened and hungry mankind.

Wolfe, Petya, Paul: the history of a legend in three phases, the history of an ideal in three movements. . . .

As he talks, the rhythm of his speech gains in intensity. He describes his village and its artisans, his father's helplessness in the face of helmeted, booted gendarmes demanding bribes; he recalls the last time he observed the Day of Atonement or attended a Seder; he flares up as he relives his encounters with the Just Men of the Revolution. Usually so lucid, so restrained, he expresses himself now like a drunkard. He becomes intoxicated in front of me; he is getting drunk without drinking.

I feel closer to him than ever before.

"The powerful, cleansing breath of the World Revolution, you felt that in those years," says Paul. "It was the dawn. The birth of a movement whose breadth equaled its depth. We made it a point of honor to throw all the capitalist games—and everything there is a game—into the garbage can. Rank, titles, distinctions—we didn't give a damn about them. You could visit anyone without having to announce yourself. Trotsky, for instance: I saw him at the War Commissariat without even going through his secretary. He was still our hero then—not yet a traitor. He transfixed me with his piercing, friendly eyes: 'Well, comrade, tell me, have you read a good novel lately?' I was flabbergasted: A novel? Me? In those times? The world was on fire, the masses in upheaval, and Trotsky expected me to talk about literature! Oh, how proud I was. There, I thought, was the real Communist humanity, a simple Communist meets one of the armed prophets, one of the chief actors of the Revolution, and what do they talk about? A novel I have not read, for the simple reason that I never could allow myself to read any novel. I told him that. He asked me how I spent my time. Courses in theory, political training, practical work, languages, propaganda. . . . He did not hide his dissatisfaction: 'I'll have to pass a word to the people in charge,' he said, shaking his head. 'We began our career with reading; on this point there's no reason for you to be different.' Whereupon he launched into an astounding analysis of the revolutionary dynamics in literature, quoting novels and plays, with some parentheses for music and the arts. It was the finest lecture I've ever been lucky enough to attend. And all that while he was at the head of the Red Army. . . .'"

That meeting had left its mark on him. I envied him. I was about to confess this to him, but he stopped me.

"And once," he went on, "I also had the honor of making the acquaintance of Comrade Stalin—who was not yet our beloved leader and father. One commissar among others, that's all he was. If my memory serves me, he was in charge of national minorities, not of the services to which I was attached. But, I no longer know why, the two of us at the head of our class, before going on our mission, were received by certain top leaders. Puffing on his pipe, Stalin watched me without a word. There I stood, trying to hide my uneasiness, sweating, afraid of fainting, when finally he spoke to me. 'Comrade Petya! What's your real name?' I guessed it was a test: he had my dossier spread out on his desk. 'Wolfe Isakovich Goldstein, Comrade Commissar,' I answered, stiff as a telegraph pole. 'Good,' he said, exhaling smoke. 'Good, so Petya is Wolfe Isakovich. Tell me something—do you know the Bible?' That question dumbfounded me even more than Trotsky's about the novel. 'No, Comrade Commissar. I have no desire to read the Bible. I am not interested in stories that the rich use to oppress and trick the poor.' 'Well, well,' said Stalin, starting to clean out his pipe. 'You're a Jew, your name is Wolfe Isakovich Goldstein, and you've never opened the Jewish Bible. I studied it at the seminary. . . .' 'But I did open it, Comrade Commissar, a long time ago.' 'You opened the Bible without reading it?' 'Yes, without reading it.' Stalin was savoring my embarrassment; entangled in my responses, I did not know how to extricate myself. 'One might think you're afraid of confessing,' said Stalin, letting a fresh puff of smoke escape. 'You must never be afraid, not under a Socialist regime. Comrade Wolfe Isakovich. The innocent have nothing to fear, right, comrade? . . .' That was true, and how! In the Soviet Union, only the criminals, the White Guard assassins, those nostalgic for the White terror had to be afraid—not their victims nor their conquerors. I believed that, Paltiel, I believed that. I still believe it, but . . . there are . . . there are, you know what there are. Trials . . . deviation, opposition, sabotage: those words are knives. Lenin's companions—traitors to the fatherland of the Revolution? Double or triple agents? Is that conceivable? If it's true, we're done for; and if it's not . . .''

Paul was speaking—and becoming a different man before my eyes. Once again he was Wolfe.

Finally, it was I who began to drink one glass after another. I emptied the bottle, and for the first time in my life I collapsed like the last of the drunkards at the Liyanov fair.

So I plead guilty, Citizen Magistrate, to having caroused in a capitalist city in the company of a former friend turned enemy of the people, and to having succumbed to intoxication in his presence.

By tacit agreement, during the weeks that followed, neither Paul nor I ever referred to that night. Paul became more and more taciturn; he was being recalled to Moscow. He was not the only one: the Komintern was recalling its agents by the hundreds throughout the world. We could not have guessed it was in order to liquidate them. Yet Paul's intuition told him something was amiss. He could have refused and sought shelter with influential friends in France, but that was not his style. Besides, to trick him, they had not summoned him to report immediately, but had allowed him six weeks to prepare himself. That reassured him. I spent those weeks almost constantly in his company. He was calm; so was I, and even more than he. I thought he would go to Moscow, meet his superiors, gather some explanations, and return; and then I too would understand. Nevertheless, from the very depths of my being, the old question kept surfacing: *Will I see him again?*

Could I have guessed that the moment he arrived in the Soviet Union he would fall into the hands of your people, Citizen Magistrate? That they would fling him into prison? Which one? This one perhaps.

I remember our final evening. A dinner for two in a Latin Quarter bistro. We spoke of one thing and another, activities suspended, contacts to renew, German comrades to rescue and hide. We were taking stock; we were satisfied with each other. I asked him about his return to France. Would he stay on in the same section? Would he keep me on his staff?

He did not answer right away. He scanned the room, glanced at the street to make sure we were not being observed, and said to me in a toneless voice, "I've got some advice for you. Follow it and don't ask too many questions."

"What's that, Paul?"

"Don't wait for my return."

"What? But . . ."

"You heard me. Leave Paris. Do something else. Go away."

I pretended not to understand. "Why do you want me to go away? And leave the comrades? And who will do the work, tell me?"

"I hate repeating myself. I have given you my advice. If you choose to disregard it, that's your problem."

"But . . . where do you want me to go?"

"Far away. As far as you can go."

"But why? Why, Paul?"

My lack of maturity angered him. I should have understood. . . . He stared at me. Could he trust me? He made a decision.

"You're too well known," he went on. "People know that we're close, that we're friends."

Like an idiot I went on arguing. "We're friends, so what? I am proud of our friendship!"

"Don't shout. Do me the favor of controlling yourself. The things I know, it's better you don't know; I hope for your sake you'll never learn them. You have the luck not to belong—officially—to the services I represent. You can travel freely, you can go anywhere. Get out!"

His words pained and confused me: Leave? Again? When? To do what? To flee whom? And that fist inside my chest: *Will I see him again?*

"You are surely mistaken, Paul. You're imagining things. You're overworked, exhausted. So am I. . . ."

He lowered his head to prevent me from seeing his defeat. "Follow my advice, Paltiel," he repeated. He paused to swallow.

"Listen," he went on, "go to Spain. If I can, I'll meet you there first chance I get. It's a fight I don't want to miss."

He gave me the name of a liaison agent who would help get me into the Brigades and across the border. *Will we see each other again?* I murmured to myself. God willing we would.

"What are you saying?"

"That we'll see each other again."

"God willing," said Paul, after a silence.

Wolfe, Petya, Paul: pseudonyms and passwords learned by heart; that's what my friend transmitted to me as a farewell present, together with those few images of his youth and his blessing.

Here, Zupanev was muttering as he blew his nose, here are some words. Not mine, but yours, what I mean is: they belong to you; they were meant for you. And I think that's funny. These words, snatched from a dead man, from death itself, in order to be repeated, transmitted and kept alive, I am entrusting to a mute! Will this farce never end?

Read these tales, Grisha, and you will learn about the life and death of a Jewish poet, your father.

He was somebody, your father. Difficult to get on with. In the beginning, during the first interrogation, he annoyed us to the point of exasperation.

I was only a clerk, you understand. Nothing more. A stenographer. I took notes. From my corner, I observed the prosecutor, the colonel, the magistrate—to hell with all these titles, anyway, they all added up to the same thing —and I observed the accused without being seen by them.

I was a piece of furniture. An instrument. Part of the scenery. The invisible man from whose attention nothing escaped. So you can believe me, son, when I tell you that he was somebody, your father.

Now don't jump to conclusions: he did not succeed in resisting all the way: the one who will has not been born yet. Oh, yes, we broke him, as we broke those before him and those after him. The fact remains that he was, forgive the expression, a rare bird, a unique case. He held out longer than anticipated, he took punishment better than the most hardened politicians. Do you know why? Because he was not afraid of death. And that, my little one, is what is referred to in our circle as "foolish and hypocritical behavior"; everybody is afraid of death, let me tell you.

*Man is meant to live and meant to want to live. Only
your father was different. You may be proud of him, my
boy.*

*I remember as though it happened yesterday. That
night, they had really let him have it. He could no longer
stand on his feet, his body was swollen and bloody—and
yet, he resisted. I don't even remember now what the
particular charge was. He simply, stubbornly, refused to
sign the official minutes of the session. The examining
magistrate offered him a cigarette—they all do that. Your
father declined; anyway he could not have put it in his
mouth, which was a gaping wound.*

*The magistrate addressed him with a semblance of pity:
"Why are you so foolish, Kossover? Why are you so obstinate? There is nothing to be gained that way. Why are
you determined to suffer? I'd like you to explain."*

*The magistrate seemed truly, sincerely interested. Sens-
ing this, your father made an effort to stand straight.*

"Very well," he said, "I shall explain."

*He spoke with difficulty: the words scorched his tongue.
He swallowed his saliva, his blood.*

*"I am a poet, Citizen Magistrate. And it behooves a
Jewish poet to safeguard his dignity."*

*And you know what, Grisha? For a moment I was flab-
bergasted—I don't mind telling you—and so was the
judge.*

*From that moment on, I began respecting poets. Be-
cause of your oddball of a father. And I began reading his
poems and even transcribing them, for you. Yes indeed.
Your father helped me discover poetry.*

*You see, before that, I had no use for scribblers. How
can one live with words alone, I wondered, with nothing
but words? Now I know that one can.*

*Another discovery. Because of your father I began ask-
ing myself questions which triggered more questions: How*

can a man spend a lifetime hurting other men, in the
midst of cries and screams of horror? How can he lie down
to sleep at night, rise in the morning, knowing that he is
living from one death rattle to the next? You may laugh,
son. I was working for a magistrate whose function it was
to ask questions; but as far as I am concerned, it was your
father who taught me how to ask them.

Why does one man inflict suffering on another—do you
know why? I have seen executioners panting with pleasure, I have seen wretches becoming excited every time
their prisoner moaned, and worse: I have seen officials to
whom all this represented nothing but a job, a duty. Told
to strike, they struck. Told to whip, they bludgeoned their
victim and drove him into madness. They were just doing
their job, approved and rewarded by the law. And yet, my
boy, for the life of me, I don't understand: How can one
man hurt another? I mean, how can one man hurt another
who is without defense, senselessly, without reason, I mean
without personal reason? I don't know what makes some
people try to overcome suffering while others give in to
it. In truth I never understood either the victims or the
torturers, I never felt close to either. But, yes, I did feel
close to your father. I'll explain that to you another time.
He made me care, and, listen to this: in the end, he even
made me laugh, me, who had never laughed in all my
life.

You listen to me, you look at me and you resent me,
admit it. You are wrong. I have never struck a prisoner, I
have done nothing but take notes. And I feel guilty, that's
normal. Guilty of having seen evil, of having lived with it,
side by side. Sure, I could have protested, resigned. For
example, I could have pretended to be ill. But I would
have been liquidated the following day: I knew too much.
And I wanted to live; I clung to life. That's how I am,
like everybody else. I still haven't found a good substitute
for life. Like everybody else, I am afraid to die.

As for your father—you won't believe this—in the very beginning, he seemed happy, yes, happy to find himself there, facing the magistrate, poised on the threshold of pain and death. Poets are a queer lot. Could it be that they wish to endure and know all there is to endure and know?

As I said, in the beginning, he amused me. He was still in good health. His eyes were red from lack of sleep, yes, he was a little pale, but that was all. He stood erect and answered routine questions in a calm voice: name, first name, father's name, profession. He amused me because . . . Listen. The magistrate asks him whether he knows why he has been arrested. Your father responds that yes, he knows. "Why?" asks the magistrate. "Because I have written a poem." The judge almost chokes with laughter. Your father, you understand, was about to be accused of sabotage, of conspiracy, of treason. They were getting ready to attempt to have him implicate the most illustrious names in Jewish literature and he comes out with his poem. "And this poem," says the judge, "where is it? May one read it?" "No," says your father, "you cannot read it." "Why not?" "Because it's in my head, only in my head. . . ."

He often referred to it, to this poem he had written in his head.

Oh yes, that father of yours was quite a character, he was somebody all right.

I remember the first question he asked the judge: "Where am I?" Did you notice, my boy? Not "Why am I here?" which is what all the prisoners ask when they arrive, but "Where am I?" Later he explained. "Some people define themselves in relation to what they do—not me. I define myself in relation to the place where I happen to be."

I had been struck by this because he could not know, none of the prisoners knew where he was. In what prison, in what section. They didn't even know the name of the city. They were blindfolded and disoriented, like beaten blind men.

In fact, your father was languishing in an old fortress of our charming city of Krasnograd; but that was kept from him. He was variously led to believe he was in Leningrad, in Kharkov or even in Tashkent. One day they stuffed him into one of those vans popularly referred to as "black marias." He was driven around and around for hours, with many stops. Taken back to his cell, your father did not recognize it. Sometimes the examining magistrate was replaced by a colleague who pretended to be him. All these games, designed to shake and unsettle the prisoner's mind, to disgust him with himself, I duly recorded, at first for them, later for your father. The hunger pangs, the agonies of thirst, the wounds of memory: I have recorded them all. Which was the worst? Silence. There, your father recorded it all. Wait, let me find it. Here it is, do you see?

I WONDER WHO INVENTED the test of silence, the torture of silence. A madman? A poet of madness, of vengeance?

As a child in Barassy, as an adolescent in Liyanov I yearned for silence. I dreamed of it. I begged God to find me a mute master who would impart his truth—and his words—to me, wordlessly. I spent hours with a disciple of the Hasidic school of Worke, whose rebbe had turned silence into a method: the faithful converged on Worke so as to link their silences to the Master's. Later, with Rebbe Mendel-the-Taciturn, we tried to transcend language. At midnight, our eyes closed, our faces turned toward Jerusalem and its fiery sanctuary, we listened to the song of its silence—a celestial and yet tangible silence in which both voices and moments attain immortality.

No master had ever warned me that silence could be nefarious, evil, that it could drive man to lies, to treason; that it could break man rather than make him whole. No master had ever told me that silence could become a prison.

You taught me more than my masters, Citizen Magistrate. In this "isolator"—the word is well chosen: in it one becomes isolated not only from mankind but from oneself as well—I have attained a level of knowledge I had despaired of reaching.

In the beginning I was comfortable there; I rather liked it. After the screaming, the blows and the constraint of having to remain standing, the silence was a welcome haven, a soothing embrace.

Upstairs, on the second floor, I would faint in order to avoid the questions, the sneers, the insults, the spitting abuse. Sentences became amplified until they weighed on my skull and inside my brain and the pressure became intolerable. The slightest noise—the blinking of an eyelid —reverberated inside me as in a metallic drum. I floundered, I sank into nothingness. I had the feeling that every object in this universe was moving, dancing, creating a roaring hubbub as of a carnival: the lamps were hissing, the pens were squeaking, the curtains were bellowing, the chairs were rocking back and forth like vessels in distress.

They carried me, like a wreck, from corridor to corridor, they dragged me down the stairs and threw me into this cell. "From now on, not another word, understood?" The last human voice, the last echo. Beyond that, nothing. Time itself came to a halt. The earth no longer turned, dogs no longer barked. The stars, far away, went out. Man's universe was transfixed forever. And up above, on His motionless throne, God silently judged His hushed creation.

When I came to, I thought for a moment that an un-speakable curse had struck all of mankind; man had lost his faculty of speech. Guards in their special slippers were gliding from door to door. Through the peephole or from the doorway, they conveyed their orders with signs only: get up, lie down, swallow. The outside world had ceased to breathe. I no longer heard my neighbors, the old and the new, the weak and the brave, as they scratched the walls, as they muffled their moans. Nothing, anywhere, had a voice. And then, anxiety took hold. I understood that silence was a more sophisticated, more brutal torture than any interrogation session.

Silence acts on both the senses and the nerves; it unsettles them. It acts on the imagination and sets it on fire. It acts on the soul and fills it with night and death. The philosophers are wrong: it is not words that kill, it is silence. It kills impulse and passion, it kills desire and the memory of desire. It invades, dominates and reduces man to slavery. And once a slave of silence, you are no longer a man

Once—was it morning? night?—when I could go on no longer, I began to talk to myself. The next instant the door opened and the guard signaled me to stop. I whispered, "I didn't know it was forbidden." In truth, I did know, but I wanted to hear myself pronounce those words; I was overwhelmed by an irresistible need to hear a human voice—mine or that of the jailer, it hardly mattered. But he was not duped. He punished me by tying me to the cot with heavy rope, and his threatening index finger made it clear: "Don't try it again, or else . . ." During one day and one night, and another day, that was how I remained, nailed down, choked by the cries that filled my chest. And yet, I did it again. Not out of heroism but because I was exhausted, crushed by the silence. I began to hum, very quietly but not quietly enough: the door opened without a sound, as in a dream, and the guard shook his head with displeasure and sealed my lips with tape. If this continues, I thought, Paltiel Kossover will turn into a mummy. Fine. I imagined myself dead.

Only, in my imagination, the dead are not mute; they speak, they cry out. The massacred Jews of Barassy and Liyanov, the fighters struck down in Spain, the men and women of so many forgotten or burned cemeteries, they pray, they sing, they lament: how is one to silence them? How is one to explain to them that because of them I was risking more punishment?

Once the guard surprised me as I was staring at the wall nodding: new reprisals. He made it clear to me that it was forbidden to speak to the wall—even in my head. I had to force myself to keep silence within as well; mind and body became one: no more dialogues, no more discourses, no more challenges, no more memories. I *saw* myself moan, I *watched* myself agonize, howl or sob; the images ceased to be transformed into words.

The Rebbe of Worke is wrong. He says that the loudest scream is the one that is stifled. No. It is the one that is not heard; the one that is *seen*.

As time passed—but did it really pass? And as it passes does it not emit a sound?—the intensity of the pain increased. I didn't know that it was possible to die of silence, as one dies of pain, of sorrow, of hunger, of fatigue, of illness or of love. And I understood why God created heaven and earth, why He fashioned man in His image by conferring on him the right and the ability to speak his joy, to express his anguish.

God too, God Himself was afraid of silence.

And yet, Grisha, your father overcame this test.

And, thanks to the brilliant idea of one magistrate—the one who had the honor of being my superior—Paltiel Kossover did find a kind of happiness. It's silly, I know: Can one be happy in prison? Yet ask those who are confined there; some will retort: Can one be happy anywhere else?

Such is the ultimate test a prisoner faces: happiness. The examining magistrate knew how to use it and, my boy, your father fell into the trap. Will that diminish your esteem for him? That would be wrong. There are no tough guys. Our system, erected by the companions and disciples of the great Vladimir Ilyitch in person, tested during more than three revolutionary decades by the philosophers and scholars of torture, always prevails over its opponents.

Our experts are masters in the art of breaking the former minister, the fallen dignitary, the commissar in disgrace; they know how to overcome the mistrust of the politicians and the faith of the believers and bring them to the point of spilling the beans. Oh, yes, I've seen them all. Yesterday they were famous and powerful; today they're on their knees, whining and repeating the speeches prepared for them, and they don't even remember that these discourses are not their own.

But not your father, I told you that. After three days and three nights without sleep, following three months of anguish, the examining magistrate would throw him a name, any name, as bait, to engage the conversation. And your father would respond: "Who is this you're speaking of, Citizen Magistrate? Someone living or someone dead? As for me, I only know the dead."

211

And the judge, my sadistic superior, had to restrain him-
self in order not to strike him down on the spot. Stubborn
as a mule, your father; impossible to make him yield! So
as not to risk sliding down the path of confession by re-
acting to the names of innocent men, he resisted from the
start. The interrogation dragged on and on. Did he think
that was the way to save his skin? He was too intelligent
and too clear-sighted not to know that, with or without
confessions, his fate was sealed: his appointment with the
"gentleman of the fourth cellar" was set. And yet, he put
up resistance. His is a unique case in our annals: though
totally alone he placed our entire apparatus in jeopardy,
and he knew it.

To appease the judge trembling with rage—he was on
the verge of a nervous breakdown, my poor chief—your
father one day asked, "Why do you get yourself into such a
state, Citizen Magistrate? Because I dare oppose my will
to yours? I cannot possibly be the only one to do so. You
have won so many victories; consider me the exception to
the rule and turn the page."

"I cannot."

"Think of all those you have subdued and my case will
no longer matter."

"I cannot. Because of you, it is the other cases that no
longer matter."

At which point your father, from under his dirty and
sticky beard, attempted a smile. "This reminds me of the
Book of Esther."

"Esther? Who's that?" exclaimed the magistrate, pleased
to have extracted a name from my father at last. "She has
written a book? Where does she live?"

"You're way off, Citizen Magistrate. The Book of Esther,
that's ancient history. . . ." And he began to tell us about
the old king and his adviser Haman and about the beauti-
ful Jewess. Why did Haman hate Mordechai so passion-
ately? Listen to your father the poet's explanation:

"*Because this solitary Jew was the only one who refused to greet him. Haman states it clearly: 'When I see him, erect and dignified, so different, the rest no longer matters; as I face his determination, the honors bequeathed on me by others lose all value.'* "

Your father interrupted his Biblical lesson to wet his lips.

"*But you, Citizen Magistrate,*" *he continued,* "*you live in the present, not in ancient history, thus draw your own conclusions from Haman's mishap. Think of how he ended . . . but, above all, think of his victories and let me have mine. . . .*"

This gives you an idea, my boy, of just how much he irritated us. We were preparing a trial and he was pestering us with Haman!

And yet, my chief did get his way. If I told you how, you'll think I'm exaggerating, inventing . . . embroidering—but I'm not making up anything. I am conditioned by my profession: I arrange facts as in a police report. Nothing but the facts. The judge trapped him by appealing to him as a writer. Your father derived his strength from his talent, from his writings; and the judge succeeded in transforming his talent into a weakness. Had he been a plain laborer or municipal employee, your father would not have given in; but then, of course, he would never have been thrown in prison in the first place. Still, the examining magistrate did catch him in the end, and how. He outsmarted your father. One night, after a particularly long and exhausting interrogation, the judge said with feigned lassitude:

"*I give up. You are strong, stronger than I expected. None of our methods has proved effective. And so, I shall make you a proposition: you are a writer, write. Anything, in any way you choose. Any time. I promise not to badger you any more. You will not speak of the living? Very well. You will write poems? Better yet. What I need is some-*

thing to fill my dossier. I must be able to tell my superiors: See, he has made his confession."

His smile was friendly and your father was too worn out to understand its meaning.

"If I were you, I would write the story of my life. After all, why not? What a project for a writer. What do you say? I offer you the time and the means. What author worth his mettle would refuse such an offer?"

Well played, Magistrate. Bravo, Chief. Paltiel Kossover had a vulnerable spot and the judge had found it. Your father, completely snared, allowed himself to be manipulated. My idol became a puppet. The writer in him succumbed to the temptations of writing, to the mysterious spell of the word. The poet relented even as the man yearned to remain whole, unshaken.

The judge ordered pencils and notebooks brought to him. Yes, that's how it was: home delivery. Your father, wary nevertheless, fearing a new ruse, did not touch them for a week. But the words were consuming him, asking to be born. He began to write. First an innocent poem, then another. A meditation on solitude. Another on friendship. Then a letter to his wife. And a letter to his son. And finally, an intimate journal he entitled The Testament— the very one we are reading at this moment, my boy. Don't worry: I filched it, and one day I shall tell you how, and why—but that's another story.

And so your father wrote and his work met with huge success: the examining magistrate no longer read anything else. Every evening the prisoner's pages were taken to him. He studied them as though they represented the confession of the century. He took notes, compared names and dates, transmitted excerpts here and there to interested parties and entrusted me with them for addition to the dossier resting in our inviolable and inviolate vaults.

Let me give you an example. The passages relating to Wolfe-Petya-Paul circulated through various services.

Since they contained references to Stalin, the dossier was immediately brought to the attention of Abakumov, who personally broached the subject to Beria. Beria in turn demanded an additional inquiry and, as a starter, the arrest of Ehrmanski—who had represented the NKVD in Paris during the thirties—for lack of vigilance. You cannot imagine, my boy, the uproar created here by this nasty business. Our "services" were hard put to lay their hands on that bastard Ehrmanski. He was on the wanted list in every Socialist republic, he was hunted by our men everywhere. But day after day, we had to concede to an enraged Abakumov that Ehrmanski continued to elude us. Weeks and weeks later we understood why; he had been liquidated in Paris before he could inform on anybody, by his lieutenant, who was our man. Oh, yes, we had informers spying on our informers. Such was the rule: our executioners ended like their victims—a bullet in the neck. Even executioners are mortal.

At times your father gave birth to a poem I read with pleasure—it distracted me. Not that I always understood your father's poems, but I loved them anyway. As for the examining magistrate, he hated them; they contained no useful information.

If you must know the truth, my boy, I once was very upset. Your father had just finished a philosophical poem of which I didn't understand one wretched word. Neither did the judge, but as was his wont, he congratulated your father, who abruptly turned his head, as though to hide.

"What's wrong with you?"

"Nothing, Citizen Magistrate."

"Don't you feel well?"

"I do. Only . . . it hurts. I realize my son . . . my son will never read me."

And I, who have no son, felt unspeakably sad. And I, who have never cried or laughed all my life, felt tears springing to my eyes. Is that when I decided to make off with a few pages here and there and stuff them into my drawer where the devil himself couldn't find a thing? You never know . . . is what I was thinking.

The judge, clever as always, tried to placate your father. A writer, said he, must never think of his reader as he writes; all that should matter is his truth. So write the truth, Paltiel Gershonovich, that is your duty.

Thus your father had at least two devoted readers. I liked the stories, whereas the judge focused on the names. Before I put away the notebooks I transcribed the names onto an alphabetical index I had to keep up to date. Inge, Paul, Traub, Pinsker . . . then the writers and poets, both the acclaimed and the unknown writers and poets of the Soviet Union—many in prison like himself.

In this index, there was one name which, literally, made us fly into a rage; we came close to howling every time your poet of a father chose to mention, with glee, this incredible, impossible character whose hobby it seemed to be to appear unexpectedly, in the weirdest, most outlandish places, be it the market in Odessa or a brothel in Paris. You know who I mean: that David Aboulesia, if perchance that was his real name.

If you knew, my boy, how many agents were set on his trail. For weeks and months they searched, never uncovering the slightest clue. Abakumov himself had signed the warrant to detain him, abduct him and bring him back at any cost. He was convinced, Abakumov, that your father's friend directed an international network on a huge scale; that he had placed his accomplices even inside the Kremlin walls, perhaps even among the insiders of . . . Our services mobilized our finest sleuths. Result: zero. David Aboulesia mocked the world, and, in particular, all of us.

Do you know that he even managed to follow your father into Spain—in the middle of the civil war?

THE TESTAMENT OF PALTIEL KOSSOVER VIII

I KNOW THIS PLACE, I know this sky, I know these walls, these courtyards, these trees. Searing, spellbinding, that was the thought that never left me, that obsessed me.

I was walking through the streets of Barcelona after training in Albacete, and the landscapes seemed eerily familiar. The hills overlooking the city. When had I experienced this blurred nostalgia—as I arrived or as I left? I ambled through the streets ready to halt before a window to converse with a woman who had smiled at me centuries earlier; I cut through cemeteries, my favorite haunts, and deciphered barely visible Hebrew inscriptions. These names, these numbers recording births and deaths, I remembered them as though they were linked to my past, to my life as a man.

I was sorry that I could not write my parents the truth; it was forbidden to me to inform them of my enlistment in the Brigades. I entrusted my letters to an emissary who carried them to France and posted them in Paris. My address: care of Sheina Rosenblum. Pity. I could not tell Spain to my father.

As a child I had studied the history of the Jews in Spain—the poets, the philosophers, the scholars, the ministers in their period of splendor, then at the time of their distress—and I had loved it. I rediscovered Abulefia of

Saragossa and his messianic divagations, Yehuda Halevy and his poetic visions, Shmuel Hanagid and his prayers, Don Itzhak Abravanel and his acts of faith. I saw myself among my brothers as they were being coerced into choosing between exile and disavowal; I took my place among those who left and those who remained. I understood them all: the ones who chose disavowal made me sad, the others made me proud, and both added to my sense of richness. I felt as much at home as back in Liyanov.

And this war—atrocious, horrible but imperative—in which I was involved was mine more than I realized.

Granted that every war is madness—civil war, fratricide, is the worst of all: it reaches deeper into ugliness, cruelty and absurdity. It is like a man lacerating his own flesh out of self-hate; he kills himself so as to kill the enemy within.

Oh, yes, I wished I could have told my father about it. Told him that the Jew within me was possessed of a memory more ancient than the Communist's. The Communist conceded to the Talmudist. During the nights of waiting at the front lines, during the long watches, from Toledo to Córdoba, from Madrid to Teruel, I dreamed of the Jewish poets of the Golden Age more than of Marxist ideology. My first poem composed under the tormented skies of Spain addressed itself to Abraham Abulefia, that unfortunate false messiah who, unable to gain recognition from his brethren, traveled to Rome to try his luck with the Pope, whom he planned to convert to the Jewish faith, no less:

> The Pope?
> Why the Pope,
> poor Abraham,
> innocent dreamer?
> Say, brother, tell me,
> supposing you succeeded,
> supposing the Pope had

> bravely
> taken Joshua's side
> against Christ,
> would you have won the battle?
> There would have been
> in the world
> one more Jew,
> that's all,
> one Jew
> another Pope
> would have sent to the stake.
>
> (Translated from Yiddish)

One morning, among the ruins of a cemetery, much gray on a background of dirty yellow, I came upon a tombstone whose inscription made me shiver: *Paltiel son of Gershon, born the 15th day of the month of Kislev 5118* and returned to his ancestors the 7th day of the month of Nissan 5178.†* . . .

To us Jews, all cemeteries seem familiar.

Contrary to my fears, Sheina did not make a big fuss when I announced my decision to enlist. She neither burst into sobs nor did she threaten to commit suicide. She did not pull me into her arms to dissuade me from leaving. Quite the opposite: she declared herself delighted and proud.

"You shall write poems," said she, all excited. "You shall read them to me and we shall make love."

"And if I don't come back?"

"There'll always be someone to read your poems—and to make love," she answered laughing and inviting me to come closer to admire her lips.

---

* Winter 1358
† Spring 1418

She bought me a knapsack, underwear and shirts, hand-kerchiefs and—one of her whims—a pipe.

"But, Sheina, I don't smoke a pipe!"

"You're a poet, yes or no? Poets who go to war smoke a pipe, don't you see?"

We elaborated a detailed plan to enable her to forward my parents' letters and money orders. *Will I see her again?* Some day, Sheina, some day. After the war, after the victory. We exchanged promises and appropriate wishes, and one rainy evening I took myself to Austerlitz station.

As I boarded the "Volunteer Train" I recalled my departure from Berlin. There, too, no one had been on the platform to wish me bon voyage. The compartment was jammed, but I slept through the night.

Arrival in Perpignan. The hotel is pitiful. Again! Clearly it is written that I shall never see the inside of a palace.

It is forbidden to leave the room to mingle with the regular clients, to be noticed, to attract attention.

Amusing: my ancestors left Spain and I am returning. . . .

I wrote a letter to my father, informing him that I was doing well—as fabulously well as "God in France" as Jews were fond of saying in Odessa, or as "God in Odessa" as they said in France.

The "guide" called at the hotel shortly before midnight. There were some twenty of us who were to follow him, including two nurses, an American—he had seen my photograph in a Communist newspaper in New York—a few Germans, Austrians, a British journalist. . . . There were among us former soldiers, engineers, experts in explosives. But only one poet.

The "guide" knew his way in the Pyrenees as I knew mine in my father's orchard in Liyanov. He was familiar with every path, every brook, every rock. He knew pre-

cisely at what moment the border guards would appear
and where; he seemed able to predict what subject they
would be discussing and in which direction they would
turn to relieve themselves. In five minutes we had crossed
the border. Another "guide" took charge of us and es-
corted us to the camp at Albacete, where a first selection,
according to skills and inclinations, took place. I had to
start from scratch. Skills I didn't have, and my value as a
fighter was surely negligible. And so I was dispatched to
the "Leningrad" camp near Barcelona, where I was taught
the use of light weaponry, how to throw a grenade without damage to myself, and the Communist method of
moving forward under fire without ever pulling back. I
carried on as best I could in order not to embarrass Sanchez—my alias of the moment—but my instructors, soon
discouraged, had to give in to reality: I was too clumsy,
too inept in battle, I simply wasn't made for the noble
profession of soldier. I was assigned to the service of
"Propaganda and Culture."

Of the camp and all those who gave me shelter during
my stay in Republican Spain, I have retained an abun-
dance of memories, good and bad, depressing and exhil-
arating. I shall always be proud to have known these men
and women who had forsaken homes and families to defend this land of freedom; one can never say enough about
their spirit, their comradery and courage. Physicians and
taxi drivers, academicians and cesspool cleaners, disillu-
sioned intellectuals and idealistic laborers, romantic young
girls and serious and devoted activists, they came from
countries near and far, peaceful and tormented, to prevent
Franco from trampling on this generous people in love
with sun and sacrifice. Communists and libertarians addressed one another with the familiar *tu*, we helped each
other, we shared everything. In the evenings we would
sing around the campfires or inside the barracks, we would

sing alone or in groups, Flamenco and Russian, French, Yiddish and English melodies; we would get drunk with words, anecdotes and hope. We felt mobilized by history in its war against the barbarians; we yearned to be strong and pure like saints anxious to sanctify the cause that ordered them to kill and die: oh, yes, Citizen Magistrate, you are too young, you cannot know. . . . In those days, there was still room for hope and friendship.

But . . . there was also sadness and horror—even more than in earlier conflicts. This war fed upon itself. The battle was suicidal—the struggle of a people challenging its own existence. Naturally, there were fundamental differences in principles, faith, ideals. Our side was fighting on behalf of human dignity, the opposite side on behalf of spiritual slavery. Yet the cruelty on both sides was identical.

Near Córdoba, in a village reconquered by our men, I saw what the Fascists had done with their prisoners: I saw the obscenely mutilated corpses, piled up in the *casa del pueblo*, and I went on seeing them in my sleep for a long time, and, for a long time, when I was with a woman, all desire dissipated at the memory of that scene. Castrated men, disemboweled women. Three Reds drowned in the same well, heads down, their feet on the ledge. Never have I felt so sick. Never have I hated so much.

I saw a group of men buried up to their eyes. Three prisoners were hanging from the branches of the same plane tree. And there were those who had been driven insane by thirst or by pain. The Fascists played with their victims before finishing them off—debasing, sadistic games they prolonged even beyond death.

Being a good propagandist, I visited the *centurias*, the Brigades, and my hatred was contagious. Our cause is just, I proclaimed, for the savagery of our enemies makes man ashamed of his humanity.

To be fair, the Loyalists did not distinguish themselves by excessive charity. Churches in ruins, crucified priests, dismembered nuns: I have seen them. And I shall not forget.

A church of the Paloma, somewhere in the region of Teruel. I remember: the statue of the Virgin on the ground; next to it, a young woman, dead, her skirts in tatters, her thighs spread apart. Next to her, another statue. And another young woman, raped. And so on, from the portal to the altar.

The International Brigades, on the other hand, behaved honorably. Because there were such a large number of Jews among them? And because Jews seem less likely to commit certain ignominies, even when vengeance is involved? A Stern, a Gross, a Frenkel, a Stein, who had come from various dispersed communities of Eastern Europe, all were humane with the other side. Not that they would ever have attributed their aversion to cruelty to their Jewish origins; rather they would have related it to their Marxist ideology. But I am certain of what I say. I *know* it to be true. Ideology had no effect upon people. With all due respect, Citizen Magistrate, some Red militiamen, Communists though they were, indulged in the same kind of butcheries as the adversary. Court martials, summary executions, torture . . . I was appalled.

Yes sir, Citizen Magistrate. Both sides took part in a horrible and debasing cult in which the sacrificial offerings were men and women. The war chants were different but the results were similar: *Arriba España, No pasarán,* words charged with hatred, blood and death.

In battle, though, my comrades were admirable. Their behavior under fire was heroic. One against ten, rifles against machine guns, machine guns against cannons, they undertook large-scale operations and displayed incredible bravery. No situation was desperate; no position was re-

linquished without a fight: a hill would change hands six
times in a single night and our men would give ground
only when they ran out of ammunition. That is what I
saw; that is what I saw above all.

I admired their gallantry, their regal contempt for
danger, but recoiled from their cruelty. I didn't understand: Could man be great and ferocious at the same time?
Be as inspired by evil as by good? As seduced by vengeance
as by solidarity? I didn't understand then; I still don't
understand. Though I saw both, I acknowledged Fascist
terror, but rejected the concept of Red cruelty. The
Russian comrades I met in Barcelona reassured me: "Back
home, it happened differently. The Whites—Kolchak and
Wrangel's mercenaries—did not succeed in imposing their
methods on us; the honor of the Red Army remained
unsullied." But then, why was it so different here in Spain?
Was our mission here less lofty?

In those days I couldn't understand. But now, in the cell
where you have me locked up, I have brooded over many
things. It seems idiotic, Citizen Magistrate, but it is only
now that I understand the cruelty in Spain. It is linked to
Jewish history. You may laugh if you wish, but I believe
that the Spanish civil war is linked to Jewish history. If
the Spaniards massacred one another, if they set their
country on fire and bled it, it is because, in 1492, they
burned or drove away their Jews. It seems idiotic, but
I believe it: the cruelty they exhibited toward us back-
fired. You begin by hating and persecuting others and you
wind up hating and annihilating your own. The stakes of
the Inquisition led to the destruction of Spain during the
time of Franco's Fascists.

Of course, there must be a more rational explanation:
every war releases demented forces. Once released, they
are impossible to restrain. The Talmud says it: If allowed
to have his way, the Angel of Death will rage indiscrim-

inately; he will cut down the wicked *and* the just. In time
of war, mankind goes insane.

I thought of that in Spain, and later in Soviet Russia,
during the attacks and counterattacks. Human beings
collapsed, moaning, gasping, cursing the enemy or heaven,
or both. Some died praying, crying for their mothers, their
wives, their lovers—and I said to myself: This is madness,
this is madness.

Am I a romantic or just a fool? Or both? Death, in
times of war, always brings me back to madness, a meta-
physical madness. Children grow up; they learn to
walk, to run, to talk, to laugh, to praise life, to denounce
evil. At the cost of tears and effort, men and women come
closer to happiness, a very small happiness. For themselves
and their children they build a home with their hands
and imagine a future filled with light—surely not without
clouds, not without obstacles and surprises—and then,
suddenly, a chosen one—*their* chosen one?—issues a command and the very rhythm of time is altered: the gesture
of one single being cancels years, centuries of work and
hopes. Immortality rushes toward death, and I feel like
shouting, But this is madness, this is madness.

I accompany Carlos, my German-French-Hungarian
friend whose name here is Carlos, as Stern is called Juan
and Feldman is gunner Gonzales, as Paltiel Kossover now
answers to the name of Sanchez. Sheer madness, all these
first names borrowed from operettas, ludicrous masks we
donned to run to the battlefield or possibly to death?
Whom do we deceive? The Angel of Death is not fooled;
he couldn't care less about our games; he too must whisper
that this is madness.

And so I accompany Carlos to Madrid. The capital is
besieged, wounded, but it vibrates with enthusiasm. The
proud city seems exhilarated. *No pasarán*, the Fascists will
not pass, howls Madrid, knowing that sooner or later the

words will give way to the guns, that sooner or later this white and red and purple city will be turned upside down, invaded, punished, despoiled and brought to her knees. Why does she cry *No pasarán?* To bolster her own courage? Why do a hundred other towns, on every continent, echo her: *No pasarán?* To earn themselves a good conscience?

I ask my friend Carlos this question and he answers: "Because. After all, they must shout something. If you want people to fight, tell them to shout."

"This is madness, Carlos, this is madness."

"I prefer the madman who shouts to the one who keeps silent."

"Not I, Carlos."

"That's because you have not yet learned to shout, nor to make war."

Notwithstanding my visits to the front, my knowledge of things military had hardly improved. Prone to palpitations, to violent migraines, I made a wretched soldier. A rifle in my hands would have endangered my life more than the enemy's. I did in fact carry a revolver in a leather holster clipped to my belt, but that was meant primarily to impress the militiamen and convince them that Comrade Sanchez was somebody.

The street battles are raging. The bastards fiercely defy death. Fiercely, the Reds show their mettle. It is Stalingrad before Stalingrad. Every house is a fortress, every citizen a hero. *Salud,* a captain of twenty or so calls out to us, as he wipes his mouth. *Salud,* cries a young woman bending over to avoid the bullets. The university complex nearby resembles a cemetery where the dead perform macabre dances.

"I am looking for Commanding Officer Longo," says Carlos. "He must be in this sector."

The young girl knows nothing, the young captain has heard nothing. We meet wounded fighters and others carrying the wounded, we ask them whether they know this Commanding Officer Longo, whose real name is no doubt less exotic: Langer? Leibish? Yes, some do know him but they have no idea where he might be, others do not know him but say that he is commanding officer and, moreover, in charge of this sector. He may, in fact, be there, in the shelter, near the entrance to the park: *Salud*, greetings and good luck. Fine, let's get across to the park, Carlos. The gunfire is intense. Hunched over, crawling along the open road, we advance, greeted by our boys: *Salud, salud*. We answer: *Salud* and *No pasarán*. Finally, in a shelter beneath a three-story building in ruins overlooking the park, a Brigade soldier escorts us to Commanding Officer Longo. He is squatting, studying maps. Sweat is running down his neck. Unkempt, exhausted, red-eyed, he looks like a wild man.

"What do you want?" he barks in a guttural voice without raising his head.

"I have orders to deliver to you," says Carlos.

"Then, what are you waiting for? Let's have them."

"Not here," says Carlos, looking him over.

"Are you insane? Where would you like us to go? To the drawing room?"

"These are secret orders," Carlos insists.

"What do you want me to do? Send everybody outside to get knocked off?"

He runs his hand over his forehead, leaving a streak of black grease.

"All right," he says irritably, "I understand. Let's go to the corner, over there."

They are alone in their corner, Carlos, who hands over the orders, and Longo, who receives them. Their eyes meet, a shell explodes and the two borrowed names are no more. *Salud*, Carlos. *No pasarán*, Longo, Leibish, Langer. This is madness, I say to myself.

Salud, too, to the orders transmitted but not received,
Salud to the orders lost with Carlos and Longo. They
might well have resulted in an important initiative for our
side, one that might have been essential for victory. I shall
never know. I returned to base, a single thought throbbing
in my head: This is madness; war is madness, war begets
madness.

Particularly in Barcelona . . .

In Barcelona another war was being fought within the
larger one. A sneaky, ugly, stupid war; I see it now, I
didn't at the time. I knew that the various armed groups and
mini-groups of the different movements and factions, leaning more or less toward Socialism or anarchy or Communism, were jealous of one another, opposed one another
and on occasion killed one another, but I didn't know
that it was systematic. Comrades, particularly leaders,
disappeared into the night: Sent on a mission? Arrested by
the NKVD? Doubt lingered for a few days, until one forgot,
turned the page and dealt with other crises, only to discover
other disappearances. Then one day, it was disclosed by
"well-informed sources," that, in fact, the first to disappear
were still—or were no longer—in the sinister dungeons of
such and such a prison and that they were suspected of subversive, divisive, therefore criminal, activity. Should one
have reacted with indignation? There were more urgent
priorities; there was the war against the Fascist enemy.
And so the NKVD people carried out their mission as
they saw fit, without shame and even without provoking
shame. Their victims fell, often without knowing why.
And even if they had known, what difference would it
have made?

It was stupid, Citizen Magistrate, stupid and absurd,
confess it, you who usually make others confess.

On one side, there were the Fascists, united to a man.
On the other, the Loyalists and their allies: divided, frag-

mented, pitted one against the other, always ready to fight one another.

The Trotskyites—who were staying at the Hotel Faucon, on the Ramblas—were first to disappear. Then followed their old friends. Then came those who were nobody's friends: the anarchists. Politics above all, you'll tell me. No, Citizen Magistrate: victory above all, justice above all.

You think I'm naive, don't you? I was. I am not ashamed to admit it, I even state it with pride. This Spanish war, I am glad to have taken part in it. I believed in it. I was on the right side, I fought for everything that stands for the honor of being a man. I was conscious of that. That is why I disregarded the nocturnal arrests and the executions at dawn of my Trotskyite and anarchist friends—for they were all my friends. Am I indicting myself now? Never mind. I am speaking to myself as I speak to you and I refuse to lie to myself.

I rather liked the Barcelona anarchists—their courage, their bravado, their absurd but poetic slogans. I envied them a little; why couldn't I sing as they did, with the same kind of carefree, childlike enthusiasm? Interesting: there were only a few Jews among them.

They were grown children. Smiling, exuberant children confronting a society that defied them with its logic, its laws, its hypocritical calculations, its efficacy.

Their ideology did not hold water, that's true. Anarchy does not exist, cannot exist as a system, for it denies the future by preventing it from being born. One does not militate against an established order by opposing to it another established order: the void is not a tool, nor is disorder. The concept of chaos contains its own contradiction. A true anarchist must eventually repudiate anarchy, become anti-anarchist, therefore . . . Nonetheless, I loved to walk along the Ramblas or drink in the picturesque bars

of Montjuich with García from Teruel, Juan from Córdoba, Luis from Malaga—were those their real names?
Does an anarchist accept the ties and responsibilities of
a name? Whenever they repeated themselves too much or
uttered a grandiose statement that was meaningless, they
would begin to laugh loudly and clap their knees. As for
me, as drunk as they, I recited for them—yes, you read
it correctly—mystical poems which they inspired in my
dizzy head. For they were all unavowed mystics, reluctant
mystics, obsessed by the mystery of the end, the explosion
of time. They tried to rush into it to reach nothingness
and drown in it in a flash of laughter. Anarchists and
mystics use the same vocabulary, did you know that? They
use the same metaphors. In the Talmud, God forbids
Rabbi Ishmael to cry lest He plunge the universe back into
its primary state. Is that not the first anarchist image, the
first anarchist impulse?

I remember Zablotowski—pardon me, José—a painter
of talent, full of fire and fury, explaining to me his in-
volvement with the movement: "I hate white; I like to see
it exploded. Covered with mud and blood."

And Simpson, the student from Liverpool, said, "I hate
this life that has been imposed upon us, this earth that has
been given to us as one is given charity, this world that
is putting us to sleep. I'd like to see them caught in hell,
twisted by the flames, terrorizing the gods who have created them. That is why I have broken with my people and
my past. Here I feel free!"

Don't let these declarations lead you to the conclusion
that the anarchists were attracted by death. The inane
battle cry "Long live death" did not originate with them
but with a senile Falangist, General Milan d'Astray. The
fool. He did not understand that to express desperate anarchy required both superior intelligence and a sense of
humor.

In fact, that beribboned ass was rebuked by Miguel de Unamuno, whose work I didn't know at the time. I began reading it after learning what had happened at the University of Salamanca, whose rector he was. In a crowded and emotion-charged amphitheater, facing Falangists howling their admiration for General d'Astray by repeating his "Long live death," the old philosopher spoke slowly, soberly: "I cannot remain silent. . . . Not to speak up now would be to lie. . . . I have just heard a morbid, senseless cry: Long live death. For me, that is a loathsome paradox. . . ."

A speech of astounding courage and nobility. Its echoes reverberated through all of wounded and bloody Spain. It was discussed in the *casas del pueblo* during the long nights under the tents and even in the trucks transporting us to the front. At the time, I was able to recite his entire speech from memory: "This university is a temple to intelligence and I am its high priest. . . . You, General d'Astray, will prevail because you have the might; but you will not convince. . . ."

That was his last public speech; he stopped teaching and died shortly thereafter. But there was renewed interest in his writings. I read his *Life of Don Quixote and Sancho Panza* at the time of the Teruel campaign. His *Tragic Sense of Life* I devoured in '37 at the time of the battle at Guadalajara. I remember that as I read, I thought that the author had to be a descendant of the Marranos. His concept of exile reminded me of Rabbi Itzhak Luria. The tragic sense reflected in his work had been expressed, centuries before, by the disciples of Shammai and Hillel who considered that it would have been better for man never to have appeared in this world. But "Since he was born, let him study Torah. . . ." Funny, everything seems to bring me back to Jewish memory. Everyone I meet is an old acquaintance.

Would you like another example? It was back in 1938, shortly before the great debacle, shortly before I was repatriated. The German army had just entered Austria, welcomed by a delirious population. The vise was tightening, the clouds were gathering. Night was about to descend on the continent, as it had over Spain. Spain's history foreshadowed Europe's. Might prevailed over right, even over divine right. The aimed rifle was indifferent to human values; it was pointed at mankind and mankind first began to notice. Republican Spain was lost and so was Europe. History was tumbling into shame and fear.

I was depressed, we all were. The end was approaching, we were moving toward unspeakable disaster. Nothing remained of that early enthusiasm when the Brigades were forming under the sign of solidarity. The governments of France, Great Britain and the United States had abandoned Spain to its fate, delivered it to its executioners. How was one to explain, without any attempt at justification, such cowardice in otherwise honorable, honest and politically lucid men? We no longer even tried to understand.

Soviet Russia remained faithful, she alone remained faithful. That made us proud and determined. But the die was cast. There was no more chance of winning. We were still fighting, but it was for the sake of honor, not victory.

My depression also had a personal side. Bercu, a Hungarian-Jewish comrade whom I loved like a brother, had disappeared.

I went to see Yasha to solicit his intervention. Yasha was working for the Security services, everybody knew that. In certain quarters he was even thought to be their all-powerful chief.

He was lodged at the Hotel Monopol, renamed Libertad. He received me cordially. Large head, engaging smile, curly hair, swarthy face: the archetype of the Jewish Communist intellectual, such as one imagined him in the thirties. To put me at ease, he discussed with me—in Yiddish—the general situation, and his views appeared to me less pessimistic than my comrades' and my own. The Spanish war is only an episode, said he; others will follow. What matters is to have an overview. What matters is that Soviet Russia honored its commitments. The workers, the outcasts, the free men who have been betrayed know that they can rely on her; the rest is not as important, the rest will change and be forgotten. Make a jump, a jump of ten years, and you will see: these painful episodes will no longer be of concern. . . .

I was sitting, playing with Sheina's unlit pipe—I enjoyed playing with it; I didn't smoke. Obliquely I observed my powerful friend. His right hand in his pants pocket, he was striding back and forth in the room as he talked. To listen to me, he stood still. At intervals he took out a cigarette, lit it slowly, savoring the smoke as he closed his left eye, only to open it again as he exhaled.

Knowing him to be very busy and not wishing to take advantage of his generosity, I came directly to the point.

He interrupted me: "I know. I know why you asked to see me."

"So?"

"So, nothing."

"What do you mean, nothing? Listen, Yasha: Bercu has disappeared and . . ."

"And nothing, I am telling you."

"What does it mean, Yasha? That you have nothing to do with it?"

"It means that you'd do well not to get involved."

"But Bercu is one of ours, an idealist, you know that. . . ."

In the hall, outside, there was a noise. He stiffened, his

voice turned harsh—but not the look in his eyes. He continued in French:

"In fact, we have nothing to say to each other, in any case, not on that subject. If Bercu has been arrested by our services, which is possible though not certain, that is their business; they know what they're doing and do only their duty. . . ."

He went to the door and opened it; there was nobody.

"Sorry," he whispered in Yiddish, squeezing my hand. "Your friend is lost. Forget him."

And, aloud, in French, "Think of afterward, of the total picture. We shall win, Sanchez, we shall win."

In that hour, I aged ten years. I thought of Bercu: Was he still alive? Was he suffering? What crimes could he have committed to deserve a traitor's fate? A chilling thought occurred to me: Where was he being held? Perhaps in the very cellars of our Hotel Libertad?

Drained of energy and life, I wandered aimlessly down the Ramblas, losing my way in the twisting alleys where a few months earlier I had walked with Bercu.

Born in a village close to the Romanian border, he had rebelled against his father, a rich merchant. To administer punishments to his son, his father had hired the butcher's apprentice. Every time the young Bercu came home from school declaring that he would not go back—and this happened frequently—his father, without a word, would send for the butcher's apprentice and his stick, "It hurt," my friend told me, "I suffered like a thousand devils in hell; but I bit my lips so as not to show it; I never did show it. This went on for weeks and months. I don't know whom I hated more: my father who impassively witnessed the canings or the butcher's helper who, equally indifferent, was breaking my bones for a few coins. One day I met somebody who belonged to the clandestine Party; I followed him and that is where the real surprise was waiting for me: the butcher's helper had preceded me there; in fact, he was already chief. . . ."

Thus it is possible, I discovered, to serve rich and pitiless merchants, to punish defenseless children at their behest —and prepare the liberation of mankind! It is possible to be chastised first by religion and then by Communism. It is possible to be both Bercu's friend and Yasha's. Yasha . . . What would I have done in his place? He knew Bercu; we had spent evenings together, singing, comparing our adventures. Now Bercu was his prisoner. His victim?

On the market square, I saw an anarchist convoy, red and black flags fluttering in the wind, preparing to move toward the front. Antonio, in the first vehicle, motioned to me:

"Sanchez, Sanchez, why so grim?"

"I've lost a friend. One? Two."

"Come with us and you won't think about it any more," said Antonio. "You'll see one of those battles. Why don't you come?"

"No, thank you. I'm not good at battles, you know that very well."

In truth, I was tempted by his invitation. I refused because, unexpectedly, Yasha's image appeared before me, scolding me: You should not have gone with the anarchists, no, you should not have joined them. . . . Yasha asked me: Why did you follow them? And Antonio, how long have you known him? Why do you consort with our enemies?

"No, Antonio," I repeated. "I cannot."

Cowardice? Caution? Let's not play with words: it was cowardice.

The result: monstrous, all pervasive gloom. The moon sought refuge behind veils. The stars went into mourning. The town became accursed. I could find no place for myself; I felt out of tune with the world, with the body that linked me to the world. For the first time, I regretted having come to Spain. I would have done better staying in France. Or Palestine. Or Liyanov . . . Once again, my father's face loomed before me, as in a dream: Be a good Jew, Paltiel, be a good Jew, my son. . . . Was I still? I no longer observed the commandments of the Torah, I transgressed its laws, I no longer put on my phylacteries, but . . . but what? They are in my knapsack, the *tephilin*, I am dragging them from camp to camp. I don't put them on because . . . because I am fighting a war. A war, for whose sake? Spain's? Also for the sake of the Jews, Father, and for you, and for all the oppressed people on earth. But you came to fight in Spain, for Spain, says my father, but it wasn't my father. Who was it? He had appeared out of nowhere and now he was standing on my left, leaning on the ramparts overlooking the city:

"But you came *to* Spain, to fight *for* Spain," David Aboulesia's hoarse voice is telling me in Yiddish. "At least have the courage of your convictions: the real Jew is no longer inside you; he remained in Liyanov. It's the Communist who came here to shed his name and his past in order to become an international soldier."

"But," I protested, "the Jew in me came to join other Jews, they are many in our ranks. Haven't you noticed them? I did not forsake the Jews by coming to Spain; this is where we met again."

"What does that prove? That many others did as you did: one hundred candles can go out as quickly as one."

I glanced at him sideways: Was this David Aboulesia or someone who resembled him? What would he be doing in Spain? Following the Messiah's trail all the way here, when it has been forbidden to tread this ground since the anathema that followed the expulsion and exodus of 1492? True, there were lives to be saved. Had he come for that? Or was it me he had come to save? Was I then in danger?

"Do you know the history of my illustrious ancestor Don Itzhak Abravanel?" he asked me in his calm, even voice, as though we were sitting peacefully in a House of Study. "He occupied the post of Minister at the court of Portugal toward the end of the fifteenth century. For this Jewish philosopher, intensely religious to boot, to be accepted by the Catholic court of Lisbon, he had to be truly great, and the country had to need his services badly. Came the time of the ordeals: forced to choose between denial of his faith and exile, he chose exile in Spain. Though a Jew, and a refugee at that, he again succeeded in attaining a high position and became Minister to King Ferdinand the Catholic. But in 1492, Don Itzhak Abravanel again confronted the same dilemma: to repudiate his faith and live in glory or leave for another strange country that would permit him to remain faithful. He chose fidelity and exile and moved to Venice where he began work on his messianic writings. Well, this man who had contributed so much to the welfare of Portugal and Spain, you will find practically no trace of him in their history books. His name shines in the history of only one people, his own and ours. This demonstrates clearly that the place a Jew occupies in universal history is determined by his place in Jewish history. In other words, if you believe you must forsake your brothers in order to save mankind, you will save nobody, you will not even save yourself."

There was something bewildering and unreal in this raucous voice invading the night to tell me of an illustrious character who may well have trod this very same ground and listened to the same nocturnal silence. I felt his hand on my arm—then I felt nothing, not even a presence.

In the distance, a sudden burst of gunfire. Then another. Two executions at dawn? Bercu? In whose memory will he survive? I pondered the question as though it mattered. Actually, nothing mattered any more.

Salud, David Aboulesia. *Salud*, Don Itzhak Abravanel.
Salud, Bercu. *Salud*, Sanchez. Paltiel is going his way. He
leaves you a poem about Cain and Abel* and their messianic aspirations.

I left Barcelona crying tears of rage.

Shall I ever forget the volunteers' shameful return to
France? Nobody came to welcome us. No flowers, no
speeches; no fanfares, no words of praise for the soldiers
of international solidarity. After the border guards, the
policemen and the customs officers, only the representa-
tives of the various offices of the Préfecture were waiting
for us, ready to plunge us back into the bureaucratic
reality of the Third Republic: papers, visas, permits, rubber stamps. We were not on their side and they treated
us accordingly.

"Since you love it so, your Spain, why didn't you just
stay there?" grumbled a gruff official.

"They'll make nothing but trouble," added his colleague. "That's how they are: they come to a country,
make trouble, then they're off to the next to make more
trouble."

The troublemakers, that was us: some fifty volunteers of
the second and third convoys. There was still isolated
fighting in free and unhappy Spain, but our Brigades were
already dismantled. On Moscow's orders? That's what our
people were saying and I believed it. Nothing was done
or undone without an order from above; and "above" was
Moscow, where a pragmatic policy of *Salud, España* was
emerging.

The French went home and the Spaniards were packed
into dilapidated and macabre internment camps. As for
me—still thanks to my precious Romanian passport—I
was free to return to Paris.

---

* This poem was never found.

On the train I was accosted by a stranger who introduced himself as Monsieur Louis. He had been directed by "certain friends" to take care of us, of me. He did not inspire confidence—he really had too much of a "clandestine" look—but I managed not to show him how I felt. After an hour or so, he became talkative:

"We see everything, we know everything. We have our people even inside the police; that fellow who examined your papers, do you think he would have let you pass like that, without difficulty, if he were not one of ours?"

The idiot. And what if I were an informer? I indicated to him that I was exhausted and wanted to sleep. I closed my eyes so as not to see anything, not to hear anything. Not to ask anything, not to refuse anything. The train was whistling, puffing, stopping, moving again; I was dozing, daydreaming. A prisoner of romantic Spain, I fled from it only to return. In love with desperate Spain, I carried it away with me like a handful of sand in my palm or ashes on my forehead.

Two years. Paris had not changed. There are cities that become estranged from themselves in one night. Not Paris. A matter of pride: at her age it becomes crucial not to change.

People were getting ready to leave on their vacations: the sea, the sun. This was the season of the newly won *paid* vacations. There was talk of war, but not too much: the wisdom of government and the strength of armies would surely prevail over the wiles of dictators.

Said the optimists: Why would Hitler declare war on France since in any case the French let him have his way? It is by not having a war that he will win it. The pessimists made similar utterances but with a slight variation: Why would Hitler rush into a war he has already won? As for the realists, who was listening?

From time to time, there was an outburst of anxiety, of malaise, but it didn't last. The theaters were sold out, there

were lines in front of the movie houses, the street vendors
hawked their junk. Elegant avenues, lively streets, inviting
store windows, successful novels, fashionable gowns. The
grumblers grumbled, the politicians made speeches, the
military paraded. The right threatened, the left countered,
the women laughed. As for the poor stateless wretches,
they were trembling, dreaming of peaceful dawns, of a
visa to some inaccessible paradise. The Spanish war had
transformed neither morals nor ideas. The Popular Front
was already history. The reactionary right barely concealed
its triumph: the future would carry it to power.

Nor had Sheina changed—except that she no longer
loved me. She had a new tenant, a painter who expressed
himself like a poet, and that made him sufficiently attractive
to give him shelter and protection and, as she put it, in-
spiration.

I wasn't angry with her, I wasn't angry with anyone. The
war and the "homecoming" had drained me of my wrath.
I observed others dispassionately, I watched myself as I
would a stranger. I belonged to nobody.

"You don't mind?" exclaimed Sheina.

"Why should I? We are adults and free. We owe each
other nothing, we promised each other nothing."

Sitting on the terrace of a café not far from her apartment, we talked of everything and nothing. I had telephoned her to tell her of my arrival; she had seemed embarrassed. I smiled to myself: She was in the middle of
making love. I knew her well enough to guess that.

"What? Who? Oh, it's you? You're here? Really?"

"I'll call you back—later," I said, hanging up.

I kept my word and called her back an hour later.

"Sorry about before," I said.

She laughed. "You're silly—but your intuitions aren't
bad. . . ."

I wasn't in the mood for banter; I went straight to the point. "Any mail for me?"

"Yes. From your father. Want to come by?"

I preferred to meet her at the café. We made an appointment for the next day. I found her a little thinner but just as ebullient. She kissed me on both cheeks, complained about the heat and the rain, the world situation and the Party, which refused to understand that she could not accommodate more than one tenant.

I reassured her: "Don't worry about me, Sheina. I have found a place to stay."

"Really?" she cried, relieved.

"Really."

It wasn't true, but she was grateful. She seized my hand and squeezed it. My other hand held my father's letters.

"Tell me," she said. "You must tell me everything."

"There's nothing to tell, Sheina."

"Nothing? You come back from Spain, you come back from the war and you have nothing to tell?"

"That's it, Sheina. I've come back from the war, I've come back from Spain and I have nothing to tell."

She found it necessary to caress my hand. "Still, my little poet, you can't be serious? You've been in battle, you've seen comrades fall, you've done things, things. You *must* tell me what it was like. Unless you've written some poems. Would you rather read those to me?"

I endured her assault calmly. "We'll talk about it another time."

"Why not now? Because . . . I live with someone? Is that it? You want to know who it is?"

"Yes," I lied again. "I do."

She began to describe the young painter: so gifted, so sweet, so wild. . . . The parting was friendly: we would stay in touch. Promise? Promise. Of course.

I saw her again on several occasions, by chance, at meetings of the Party's cultural sections. Once I thought I recognized her current lover: a friend introduced me to a painter of Romanian origin, recently escaped from a notorious fortress in the Cluj region. But it wasn't he.

I was lonely. I had lost track of all my former friends and the colleagues around Paul Hamburger. He had disappeared. I tried to find him; I followed clues, questioned mutual friends. Everywhere I was given to understand that I was treading on thin ice: new tasks had been assigned to Paul Hamburger and it was better not to ask questions. A clandestine mission into Nazi Germany? Or perhaps to the Orient? A finger indicating sealed lips, a look heavy with implications. I believed it, but not quite. I remembered my last evening with Paul; his forebodings, his advice. I also remembered my last conversation with Yasha, in Barcelona. I hoped. What else was there to do? I hoped against all hope that my friend Paul Hamburger was somewhere on a mission, therefore free, therefore alive.

I discovered the truth later, much later: Paul had been arrested as he stepped off the plane in Moscow. He had been thrown into the cellars of the Lubianka, tortured and killed. The same fate had been reserved for all his companions, all those I had tried in vain to contact in Paris.

Now that I think of it—if I had not left for Spain, if I had followed my friends, I would have undergone your interrogations earlier, Citizen Magistrate; I would have spared you sleepless nights and my wife a great deal of worry, and my son a life without future. Or perhaps one of your "services" would have liquidated me immediately?

Strange, one day as I was questioning her about Paul, Sheina almost predicted what is happening to me today.

"You knew him, Sheina. You were friends. You meet important people. Do you know something?"

We were having our usual black coffee, at the same café; Sheina was scrutinizing me, a look of concern on her face.

"I am worried about you," she said.

"Why? Because I refuse to abandon Paul? What can I do? He's my friend. He has been important in my life. If he's in trouble, I want to know. To help That's normal, isn't it? I am afraid for him. I have a premonition . . . and it is terrible."

Sheina, her mouth open, trembling, leaned toward me; her gaze was clouded. "Me too," she whispered.

I jumped. "You too? You're worried about him?"

"No," she said, barely audible. "About you."

She paused, straightened up. "Do you want me to go on?"

"Yes."

"I feel—I see—a man—you, in the dark. Alone. Prostrate."

"You're describing a prison. Or a grave. Or both?"

Fear was distorting her features. She shook herself.

"It's all nonsense, you know that. I say whatever comes into my mind—but be careful. Paul . . . went back to Russia. Don't think about him."

And yet, when I had to make my final choice—call it attraction to danger or absurd fatalism—I decided to settle in Soviet Russia. In spite of or because of what I had experienced in Spain? Because of the political situation in Europe? Was the Communist in me losing his patience? Let us say that there was nothing and nobody to keep me in Paris. Of course, I could have gone back to Liyanov—where my father, by bribing a few officials, could have "arranged" my military record as he had done earlier at the passport office—and could have lived there reunited with my family. That was what my father advised and my mother requested. The Jew in me wanted to follow their call, to kiss their hands, to rediscover his childhood. But the Communist prevailed. Moscow represented the future, Liyanov the past. Paul and Yasha, Inge and Traub urged me to seek adventure and the unknown;

my parents chained me to a structure whose foundations were too solid for my taste. And yet, had Ahuva-Tziona, my companion of a single afternoon in the Holy Land, been alive and at my side, I believe I could have rebuilt my life with her in Palestine.

Chance: what an incredible genius for organization. Is it really as blind as people claim? History surely is not, as my friend Bernard Hauptmann would have said; it knows where it is going and where it is leading us. As for me, I didn't know. I no longer knew. And yet.

Early 1939. A comrade, more lucid than the others, advises me to clear out. Munich is nothing but a farce. Hitler has fooled us all. No more doubt about that. Prague despises her French protectors, Warsaw still believes in them. Hitler swears that his thirst for conquest is quenched. People, less and less credulous, fearfully await his next blow: where and when will he strike? I watch them anxiously poring over their newspapers on buses and in the metro. In the cafés, the waiters' banter is filled with black humor, their customers' responses betray their anxiety. Place de la République, on the Grands Boulevards, in the Quartier St. Paul, in the courtyard of the Préfecture, wherever stateless emigrants and refugees congregate, I run into their questions, their uncertainties. What will tomorrow be like? Their anxiety weighs on me, their sorrow troubles me. They look at me enviously: I have a passport, I enjoy certain rights. I am not an intruder. If I feel like leaving suddenly, I can jump into the first train and that's it, I am gone. I can go wherever I wish. It makes me feel ill at ease and guilty. I don't like myself.

A depressing, sterile spell. I write nothing; I do nothing. I miss Paul. I miss Spain. I miss something. My life unfolds in slow motion. In my tiny hotel room on the Rue de Rivoli I sometimes stay for hours staring at the grimy walls, the sooty windows, motionless, without the slightest thought. I speak to nobody and nobody speaks to me; I no longer open my door to the maid; she thinks that I am ill and perhaps I am.

Ever since my return from Spain, that is how I have been; my heart is heavy with foreboding. I don't recognize myself. It's not that I feel defeated—military defeat is, after all, something I could accept—but I feel *different*. My true self is leaving me, vanishing into the distance under a bleak sky, and I remain riveted to the ground, unable to run after it, or even to shout, asking it to come back, to wait for me. I can do nothing, say nothing. I let myself sink. I sink.

I meet colleagues from the newspaper who evidently know of my troubles from Sheina. I listen to them absent-mindedly; they don't even succeed in exasperating me with their advice: One must look at things as they are, they say, overcome one's difficulties, and, once and for all, pull oneself out of this despondency that risks . . .

Pinsker has asked me to come and visit him. I do not go. He has written me a most amiable letter, insisting on my gifts as a writer, as a poet, on my duties to my readers. I do not answer. I have not opened his paper, nor that of his Zionist competitor, for weeks. What could they possibly announce that I don't already know? That the storm is near? That the Christians of Europe still have not learned to treat the Jews as equals, if not as brothers? The two editors argue with one another, insult one another as in the past. The commentators comment, the poets versify, the polemicists flounder. How futile it all is.

Finally Pinsker takes the trouble to come and see for himself.

"Why are you living as a hermit? Is that your idea of Marxism? Of a poet's role in society? My dear fellow, solitude is for the shopkeepers."

"I am tired," I tell him. "Nothing serious. Just overwork."

"Are you sure?"

"Sure."

"Come with me. Keep busy. It will do you good."

"Not now; I don't have the strength."

Then it's Sheina's turn; she appears, sits down on my bed, her breasts and mouth more inviting than ever, and asks me gently, tenderly about my writings, my "works" as she calls them. She begs me to read her a sonnet, a few verses, anything, in the name of our old friendship, in the name of . . . I refuse. I have other things on my mind, I tell her. She insists and I turn her down gently. In the end, she confesses: the Party needs me, or rather my by-line. Which explains my dear comrades' interest in my well-being.

It seems that the *Pariser Haint* has published an open letter to the Jewish poet Paltiel Kossover. Why is he silent? Is he still alive? If so, is he still free? There are disquieting rumors making the rounds about him: must he be counted among the victims of the recent purges? Or— and that is our heartfelt wish—is he among the repentants?

"The Party would like you to respond," says Sheina. "Tell those dirty bourgeois what you think of their infamous intrigues; tell them that you have not broken with the working class, that you believe in the Revolution, and in the homeland of the Revolution."

Sheina expresses herself well except when it comes to politics; then she is less than eloquent. In the old days, her exhortations would have made me laugh; now she leaves me indifferent. Let the bourgeois, the Zionists, the capitalists think what they will, let them do whatever they wish, let them write whatever appeals to them—but let them leave me in peace. Sheina, I am tired, make them understand that. I am too tired to participate in their games. Revolution and counterrevolution, Trotsky and Stalin, Bukharin and Radek, Pinsker and Schweber move about as on a screen. Their problems: I refuse to watch. I

no longer move. I no longer think. My mind wishes to
rest. Do you understand that, Sheina? Words no longer
obey me; they remain inanimate like so many anonymous
corpses. Only the Messiah can raise the dead, and I am
not the Messiah.

Carried away, her shadowy mouth half open as in the
good old days, Sheina is purring. She whispers, Oh, how
beautiful, how virile; you must write it down.

Does she suddenly want to resume an old love? I don't
ask. I don't care. If only she would go away, if only she
would clear out. If only they would all go away. And stop
bothering me. I wish to live outside life.

But that is not as simple as it seems, Citizen Magistrate.
Life catches you and does not let you go. You flee from
man and he pursues you; you run after him and he tries
to elude you.

Confined within your four walls, you believe that events
on the outside no longer concern you, yet there remains
a link between you and the world—and it is permanent—
a strange and oddly tragic link: it always depends on someone and that someone is never you. Two chiefs of state
seal a pact and it is me that a police inspector hauls out
of bed for an "identity check"; I hand him my *carte de
séjour,* my duly stamped passport and wait for him to give
them back. In a neutral, noncommittal voice he orders me
to get dressed and follow him. My documents remain in
his possession. I should be worrying, protesting, asking
questions, but I remain impassive, neutral, like him. What
can he do to me? My papers are in order, I can prove it.
Admitted legally into France, I lead a legitimate life, I
am not a burden to the economy, I cost France nothing
since I live on the monthly money orders sent by my father.

I finish dressing. We go downstairs. A black automobile
is parked near the entrance. Five minutes later I am in a
noisy waiting room packed with people and tension. I ask,

I get an answer: the police have rounded up all foreign
Communist agents. Why? Nobody wants to believe that I
don't know. What? You don't know that Russia and Germany have signed a pact—*the* pact—of the century?
Molotov and Ribbentrop. You haven't seen the papers? I
say, Impossible. Lies. Propaganda. Russia would never do
that. Never, never. They show me the headlines of *Paris-
Soir*, of *Petit Parisien*. I repeat only one word: Never.
They show me the article, in smaller print, of the Party
newspaper. They say, Read! I read. I reread. A comrade
standing near me says: Political, strategic, diplomatic
reasons, what do I know? We mustn't jump to conclusions. Now there is another word on my lips: Unbelievable, unbelievable. And I begin once again to think, to
react. Thus it has taken an event of historic impact to
wrench me from my torpor. I amble back and forth between the benches looking for familiar faces and more
information.

What will be done with the foreigners? Will they be imprisoned? Expelled? And what about the stateless, the political refugees from Germany? My case is simple. The inspector who late that afternoon makes me undergo an
intense interrogation—less intense, though, than yours,
Citizen Magistrate—comes straight to the point: I will be
expelled from French territory. And where am I expected
to go? Anywhere. To Belgium or Italy; or Germany, he
adds, laughing discreetly. Germany, I repeat, laughing.
Except, says he. Except what? Except if I agree to go home,
to Romania. In which case I would be granted an additional delay of forty-eight hours to organize my departure.
Having regained my wits somewhat, I bargain. Why not
seventy-two hours? He agrees but specifies: You better be
gone in seventy-two hours. Is that clear? It could not have
been clearer.

I leave the Préfecture and go straight to Pinsker, who
puts me in touch with someone who knows someone. I

end up meeting the comrade who takes care of cases like mine. He studies my papers in great detail, scrutinizes them, and suddenly his face lights up.

"You didn't tell me that you were born in Krasnograd!"

"Krasnograd? Don't know. I was born in Barassy."

"But that's the same thing!"

"Does it matter?"

"Does it! You were born in Soviet Russia!"

"So what? I am a Romanian citizen."

"A Romanian citizen of Russian origin. How old were you when you left Krasnograd?"

"I was a kid."

"Good. Very good. Let's go over the dossier again: You were born in Barassy, which has become Krasnograd. And Krasnograd now is part of the Soviet Union. In other words, you are a Soviet citizen. Meaning, you present yourself to your consulate, which will take care of your repatriation. Well, now, what do you think of that?"

He is getting excited, the comrade. He has found a unique solution to a problem that is not. He is proud of his ingenuity. And I am staring at him as if he were some sort of magician. He went too fast for me; he opened too many doors in too few seconds. A Soviet citizen, me? And what about my Romanian passport? And my loyalty to His Majesty the King? My nationality? And my parents? Go to the Soviet Union when my family lives in Romania? How long would it last, this separation? I must get my bearings in this collection of cities that change their names. I must think this out calmly, carefully, but the comrade doesn't give me a chance. Seventy-two hours is little. He is all excited, he cannot stand still.

"Boy, are you lucky, comrade," he says. "I am telling you, if all my cases were as beautiful as yours . . ."

He knows my past, he is informed about everything: Berlin, Spain, my cultural activities in Paris.

"Everything will go smoothly," he promises. "New pass-

port, plane or boat tickets. Don't worry about these formalities; *your* consulate will see to it."

The days go by; I am agitated, feverish, every minute
counts.

Alerted by the "appropriate department," the Soviet
consulate welcomes me as a citizen anxious to return to his
homeland. I am given a document drawn up in Russian,
some advice, instructions and a boat ticket. I am to take
the first Dutch ship leaving for Odessa. When? In two days.
I scarcely have time to embrace Sheina—*Will I see her again
one day?*—write a lengthy, confused letter to my parents,
rush over to Pinsker—who promptly announces, on the
front page, to his faithful readers, that "the poet Paltiel
Kossover, notwithstanding the calumnies of the bourgeois
press, is going home to Soviet Russia where, side by side
with our friends, he will continue the struggle for
peace. . . ." All that remains to be done is to pay my hotel,
restaurant and laundry bills, buy myself a warm suit and
underwear and . . . my time is up. Soon I am in Belgium,
then in Holland. Rotterdam. The harbor. The ship. I am
received on board, an officer checks the passenger list,
examines my Romanian passport, my Russian document,
and tells me the number of my cabin, which I am to share
with a Japanese businessman. I take a breath. Farewell,
exile.

There is a knock at the door. A sailor wants to know
whether I need anything. Something to drink? To eat?
Nothing, thank you. Sure? Sure. He leaves and I have the
odd feeling that he has not said all he came to say.

I see him again several times during the crossing. He is
watching me, spying on me. I tell myself that he probably
works for the Dutch Secret Services. But no: he belongs to
Soviet Security. He indicates that on the eve of our arrival
in Odessa. He waits until I am alone in my cabin before
he enters. He asks his usual question: Need anything? I
give my usual response and expect him to go. To my great

surprise, he remains standing there, staring at me. I invite
him to sit down but he prefers not to be too familiar. Fine,
whatever you wish. He asks me about my plans; I have
none. Where shall I live? I don't know. Acquaintances
anywhere? Yes. I know quite a few people but I have no
idea where they are—as a matter of fact, I don't even know
their real names. Paul, Yasha . . . the sailor is interested in
them, in my relationships to them. I let myself go; I tell
him about my work at Paul's side, my years in Spain, Yasha
who is important, Yasha who works for . . . I pause. I have
talked too much. How can I be sure this steward is working *for us?* And what if he were informing for the other
side? His French seems tentative; that doesn't mean anything, of course, mine is no better, and yet . . . Could he
be German? I bite my tongue; the sea has erased my underground experience all too quickly. I say no more. The
sailor—friend? enemy?—takes his leave. A piece of advice,
he says, poised on the threshold.

"Yes?"

"The less you talk, the better off you'll be."

No, he is not from the Gestapo. No, he does not wish
me harm. He urges me specifically not to speak of my
former friends, not to reminisce about my past; under
present circumstances, a past is only cumbersome. Instinctively I follow his advice.

To the questions I am asked as soon as we arrive in
Odessa, I answer that I do not know anyone in Soviet
Russia: no brothers, no friends. Why have I chosen to come
and live here? Simple: I was expelled from France and
didn't know where to go. To Romania? I am considered a
deserter there. More than any impassioned pledge of
loyalty, my frankness produces a positive effect. They
offer me their welcome. They change my francs and Dutch
crowns into rubles. And so, here I am, home, in the homeland of the homeless.

I leave the harbor and walk toward the center of town,

trailing Babel's haunting, picturesque and lovable characters: sentimental scoundrels and wretches; a human
river that flows, not seaward but toward death.

I board a streetcar that brings me into a commercial
district. I ask the conductor, Hotel? He answers in broken
sentences. There, behind the shop, small square; hotel not
expensive.

Was I right to have come? Walking down the cold street,
looking up at the buildings, I am aware that I have committed myself to a one-way street. The break with my
former life has been too abrupt. What is to become of me?
I am hungry, I am thirsty; I don't know what the future
holds for me, nor even whether I have a future. I wonder
whether my repudiated past will have a chance to renew
itself here. Also . . . I think of Liyanov and of my friends:
Ephraim, I picture him in this setting, in this land of his
dreams. I see Inge and Traub, they follow me down the
street. My whole life unfolds in my mind. As though I
were walking toward death. I cling to the past lest it
escape me. I hold fast lest I fall into the black hole that
becomes wider and wider under my very eyes and where
I feel the mute presence of my friends of long ago. I know
that one day I shall follow them, lose my footing and fall.
I can't help it; it is not my fault that I carry this suitcase;
not my fault that I chose this path over another. Chance
or fate? All the roads of my past end in Odessa. Is God
happy in Odessa?

I set my suitcase down for a moment. The hotel cannot
be far. Go on! Be brave. What could there be inside this
accursed suitcase to make it so heavy? Clothes. A few
writings. Phylacteries in a small blue bag. A few poems.
Words.

My life.

Covered up and turned in on itself, Moscow was in hiding, as if to catch its breath and conserve its heat. In icy

paralysis, its streets were empty save for pedestrians going
to work, or an occasional sled drawn by small Siberian
horses. From my first-floor window I watched the snow
falling from a low, gray sky.

I had been living in Soviet Russia for several weeks and
felt myself isolated, on the margin of my own existence.
No letters came from parents or friends. Liyanov and
Paris belonged to another world.

I hardly went out. In my room I thought of my friends,
whom I missed. I did not dare admit this to anyone:
nostalgia was not a proletarian virtue, I would have been
told. Besides, I still had no one in whom to confide.

I had been given a friendly welcome at the Jewish
Writers' Club, where I enrolled soon after my arrival in
the capital. Some of my poems published in *Dos Blättel*
were known; some had even been translated in the monthly
appearing in Piroshov. Kind things were said to me, countless questions asked about this person or that. I answered
as best I could: Yes, Pinsker was fine; Yes, Schweber was
doing good work; Yes, his praise of the Russian system
commanded attention. As for myself, I had only one question: How could I find a job?

"Wait," I was told. "The first thing you have to learn
here is how to wait. Patience."

"And I thought that in the fatherland of the Revolution people had learned to refuse to wait," I said with a
laugh.

It was pointed out that I would be wrong to make fun
of the Revolution. I took that at face value.

My visit to the club had left me with a bad taste. I had
seen from a distance the great Jewish artists and writers—
Mikhoels, Markish, Der Nister; I had shaken hands with
Kulbak, Kvitko, Hochstein. I knew and admired their
work; I even felt affection, tenderness for them: they were
my seniors, my big brothers. But I was sad. They were
muzzled and seemed anxious not to show it. They smiled,

exchanged a few words about some novel or essay, but their
hearts were not in it.

Heavy glances, lengthy silences, inexplicable head-
waggings. These Jewish novelists and poets, among the
greatest, feared clamor and the spotlight. Later I understood. Since the Hitler pact, a strange atmosphere prevailed in Moscow; of their own accord Jews lowered their
voices, tried not to be noticed. They remained in the
background, discreetly, not to embarrass Molotov. Lit-
vinov's departure from the Commissariat of Foreign Affairs
was interpreted in our club as a warning to Jews: let them
suppress their hatred of Nazism. For reasons of state the
devil was no longer an enemy but an ally. Heads downcast,
the Jews—at all levels of power—were no longer supposed
to be seen in public so as not to upset the distinguished
visitors from Berlin. They were to melt into the shadows;
they no longer counted. Their opinions, their fears, their
feelings, their lives carried little weight. Had Hitler demanded the deportation of a million Jews to Siberia, his
demand would have been studied with great seriousness,
and would not have been rejected. My seniors in Moscow
knew that better than I.

No one spoke of these matters, not even in whispers,
at the club, the Jewish theater, or in restaurants—at least,
not in my presence.

Among themselves, away from strangers, they might
have felt freer—I don't know. But I do know that politics
were never mentioned. They took refuge in a burgeoning
literature about collective farms, tilled fields, virgin forests.
I questioned one of them (I shall not reveal his name,
Citizen Magistrate, he is still alive) on this detached attitude of our famous intellectuals:

"In Paris," I said, "we fight; we denounce Nazism from
morning to night in our reviews, our speeches, and we do
so in the name of the Communist Revolution. Here you
keep silent. I don't understand."

My fellow writer, visibly frightened, whispered, "Change the subject, I beg of you!"

"But why?"

"You've just arrived, there's no way you can understand."

Another colleague was more explicit.

"You're not at the yeshiva here, young man. We're not studying the Talmud. Not everyone can speak up. Don't force us to listen to things that mustn't be heard."

A third went so far as to threaten me. "Grumbling means criticizing the Party and its glorious chief; you'll pay for this."

And they all kept repeating that I did not understand. They were right: I did not understand. I thought of Inge and her underground struggle, of Paul and his team; they had been doing their utmost to mobilize the free world against Nazism. No, I did not understand: except for the Nazified countries the Russian press was the only one not fighting the Nazi menace. It made me ill. One day, unable to contain my confusion, I mentioned it to Granek, the foremost translator of Virgil. Reserved, gentle and exceedingly shy—even more so than I—he raised his arm as if to push me away.

"You mustn't, young man, you mustn't."

"Granek—listen to me. I must speak to someone, or else I'll explode, I'll go mad."

We went out. In the street I told him of my disappointment. I told him of my years of fighting Hitler and his gang of murderers. I spoke to him of Paul, his influence, his moral impact on the intellectual milieu in France.

"It hurts me to tell you this, Granek, my friend, but I was better off in Paris. There, at least, I could cry out, warn people, fight!"

"You mustn't, you mustn't," Granek murmured, hunching his shoulders painfully, fearfully.

Granek is no longer alive. That is why I can mention that conversation. "Mustn't . . ." What mustn't I have done? Come to Moscow? Talked freely to a friend? Mobilized by the navy, he disappeared at sea in 1943. He was lucky enough to die a hero's death; had he survived . . .

"You mustn't bring up the past," Granek whispered as we walked slowly down the street where the club was situated.

And, seeing my astonishment, he went on, "Don't you know? Don't you really know what's been going on here for years? Your friends . . . are no longer."

"You mean they've left the country?"

"Oh, no, my poor friend. *They are no longer.* Hamburger and . . ."

At last I understood. Victims of the purges, they had disappeared without a trace. It was forbidden to remember them. Remembering them meant loving them, loving them meant being their accomplice.

I reeled with shock. The earth trembled, the heavens fell. I recalled my final conversation with Paul. Had he suspected what was awaiting him here? Possibly. Then why did he return? And why was I here? But it was too late for such regrets. I had to find some justification— imitate the others, sing of steel mills, the splendor of factories and the new man building them under the wise, infallible guidance of the Party—well, you see what I mean.

I got a modest job as a proofreader at the State Publishing House, French division. Lenin, Marx, Engels and, of course, Stalin: I read their works in French translation and corrected the proofs. I did my work conscientiously, as always, but without enthusiasm. After all, I am not a philosopher but a poet. There's no need to understand in order to read, and vice versa.

One day I was overcome by the desire to meet some *real* Jews. I went to the synagogue—a complete fiasco. A few frightened old men looked at me with distrust. A short hunchbacked fellow asked me bluntly, "What do you want?"

"Nothing."

"You want to pray? Where are your phylacteries?"

I left, humiliated. Yes, humiliated—what other word could describe my state of mind at the time? I began to prefer the company of writers—Russian, Tartar, Bashkir or Uzbek. Their support of a policy flattering Hitler exasperated me less than the pleas made by Jewish writers following the same orders. In fact I was seeing the Jewish writers less and less. I kept out of their sight in order not to explode, not wishing to bring disaster to the "great," whom I respected in spite of everything. For their welfare as well as mine, it was better to keep my distance.

I had rented a small room in the apartment of an old woman, who boasted of the advantages of her deafness. "In my place you'll be able to snore, stamp your feet, break your neck, I'll do nothing to stop you."

It was a three-story building on General Komarski Street. The quiet made up for the lack of comfort. The room had neither running water nor heat, but it did have dust and dirt.

Living at the other end of the apartment was a young girl, Anna, just arrived from Tiflis. She was studying at the Institute of Modern Languages. We ran into each other on the staircase or in the salon—that was what our landlady called her own bedroom—and exchanged short, polite Good mornings and Good evenings. In other circumstances I might have attempted an affair with Anna. Tall but delicate, she reminded me of the romantic princesses of ancient Russia. But I was feeling too low to see a woman's body as a source of desire. I did not feel like attaching myself to anyone.

Occasionally the landlady would shake her bony head disapprovingly; I would turn my eyes away. She would nag me: "Ah, what a generation! Incapable of grabbing hold of a woman and . . . You're young, you're healthy; she's young, she's healthy, and . . . nothing? Nothing at all? Woe to me, that my eyes should have to see such shame. Why is the good Lord punishing me like this?"

I just had no head for that. It was a grim period, for Jews especially, and also for true Communists, that is, the men and women who set the Communist ideal above political considerations and diplomatic crises. We had no friends anywhere, no allies, no support. In the street we would slink rapidly along the walls.

One day I felt the need to read something besides official speeches. I went to the club to leaf through the Communist newspapers published abroad. I expected to find some reflection in them of my anguish and confusion. I said to myself: Out there they are free to speak the truth, and no doubt they do. My disappointment was total. The Yiddish newspapers in New York and Paris, published and distributed by the Jewish sections of the Party, merely echoed our official press editorials. It was painful—yes, it really was. I read Pinsker's columns and the blood rushed to my face; the smugness of Schweber's analyses made me blush.

One day Granek, my only friend, caught me reading; I had tears in my eyes. He put his hand on mine. "You must arm yourself with patience, little brother," he said. "Think of our prophets, our sages. Is night coming? Day will come, darkness carries the promise of light."

"They're lying, Granek my friend, they're lying. We're all lying. Here and there."

Did he know the Jewish Communist editors of the non-Communist world? Yes, of course he had met them long before, as had Markish, Bergelson, Der Nister. Isn't Jewish Communist literature a closed circle? Willy-nilly, everyone knows everyone.

Der Nister and his novel, *The Mashber Family* . . . I

would have liked to become better acquainted with that austere, reserved, almost ascetic man who radiated the knowledge and fervor of Rabbi Nahman. Where is he today, Citizen Magistrate? In the next cell, perhaps? No doubt you kept him in Moscow. How I miss him! I recall his slow gait, his frail look.

Among the Jewish writers one alone infuriated me: a young poet, redheaded, arrogant, opportunistic, who signed his poems Arke Gelis. Warmly and expensively dressed for winter, he took part, uninvited, in conversations. He was not trusted: voices dropped the moment he appeared. Granek suspected him of working for the "services." I am convinced of it. During the war he wore the same uniform as you, Citizen Magistrate. He was a major, and among your people one does not become a major for nothing.

This Gelis looked happy and expansive, even on gloomy days. The more distressed we were, the more he harangued us, accusing us of timidity, passivity, hence skepticism, hence . . .

"Our policy is just and beneficial," he bellowed, his chest swelling. "Furthermore, it's moral, it defends the interests of the working class all over the world. Furthermore, it rejects the specter of war. You'd have to be an idiot or a reactionary not to see that!"

"And Hitler?" I asked him one evening, doing my best to contain my anger and disgust. "What do you make of his hatred for our people? And the cruelties suffered by Communists in his concentration camps?"

Gelis turned scarlet. "How dare you?" he cried. "You come from the decadent West to give us lessons? Hunted, dispossessed, you knock on our door, we receive you like a brother, and you thank us by sabotaging our peace policy! Is it war you want? The death of our youth? Will nothing else satisfy you?"

Embarrassed, everyone looked away. An unwholesome

silence hung over our group. I was lost, they must have
thought; I had just signed my own death warrant. Granek
seemed about to faint. There was a glint of reproach in
his eyes: "I warned you, little brother." I was seized by
remorse and terror; by exposing myself I had put him in
danger. I was about to retract, to correct myself, but
Mendelevich, the great classic comedian, spared me that
humiliation by coming to my defense.

"Comrade Gelis," he said in his majestic bass, "allow
me. Did you know Paltiel Kossover has seen the Hitlerites
at work? Did you know he helped their victims? Did you
know he fought the Fascists in Germany, in France, in
Spain? Did you know he has put his pen, his soul, his life—
I say advisedly—his life in the service of our people, the
Jewish people?"

"That's got nothing to do with it," Gelis muttered.

He shrank away. Intimidated by the authority Mendelevich exercised on all the Jewish writers and intellectuals,
the informer tried to beat a retreat. After all, Mendelevich
had important admirers—people from the Kremlin came
to see his performances.

"That's got nothing to do with it?" Mendelevich continued in a higher voice. "And you claim to be a Communist? And a Jewish poet into the bargain? We Jewish
Communists have learned to take an interest in the fate
of all who suffer, to respect everybody who joins our
struggle. A Jew who is indifferent to Jewish suffering is
like a Communist who's indifferent to the suffering of the
proletariat. Just get that through your head, young man!"

Whereupon he approached me and put his powerful
hands on my shoulders, as if physically taking me under
his protection. "Come, Kossover. Let's have a drink, and
you'll tell me what certain people do not deserve to hear."

We left the Jewish Writers' Club and went outside. It
was a fine day. A June sun—clear, silvery—was sweeping
away winter's chills and fogs. Lighthearted, lightfooted, I

danced along, celebrating Gelis's defeat. I didn't know how to thank my protector. I would have done anything to please him. He took me to his place on October Street, sat me down in his study lined with books, drawings, costume sketches, and questioned me about my life, my work, my writing. I responded without fear or hesitation. I had rarely felt so grateful to anyone.

Later Granek was to confide how frightened he had been. He had been convinced that despite Mendelevich's intervention, I would be made to pay for my audacity. Gelis had certainly reported the incident to his superiors. And since he had remained helpless in the actor's presence, he must have accused me of every political misdeed that could bring about my arrest and condemnation, if only by way of example. Frankly, I was expecting that too; I had learned the ways of the country. At night I was prepared to hear a knock at my door, and I consoled myself in advance by thinking it was still June. At least I would not freeze in prison.

But a miracle took place. Excuse me, I retract that term. War broke out, and, if it did save me from prison, it cost the lives of twenty million men, women, children, and— as we know now—it permitted the annihilation of six million of my own people. No, it was no miracle.

Still, I welcomed the outbreak of hostilities with open relief. Nor was I the only one. Listening to Molotov's speech, I felt a wild desire to shout for joy: Hurrah, at last we are going to give battle to Hitler and the Hitlerites! Hurrah, we are going to vent our wrath!

I ran to the club. Panting, overexcited, I joined my fellow writers, who were gathered around Mendelevich. At that moment I wanted to be among my own people, congratulating them, embracing them, weeping with them, laughing with them, emptying glass after glass, and aware all the while that this spontaneous celebration was the first and also the last that would unite us, the last for a

long, long time. Would there even be another? *Will I see
them again one day?* Who would live, who would die?

In the midst of the festivities, I froze. I thought of my
parents, my sisters and their children. From now on there
stretched between us a bloody, murderous front; between
us from now on there would be death with its countless
arms and eyes—death who never loses, who never retreats,
who is never sated.

Gripped by nausea, I put down my glass and shut my
eyes.

You have accused me of cowardice, Citizen Magistrate.
Jews, you have told me, are cowards: they always manage to
let others fight in their stead. Well, that is both true and
false. It is false about Jews in general; it is true about me
in particular.

During the war, Citizen Magistrate, during our great
patriotic war, I knew courageous, bold, intrepid Jews. I
knew men such as Dr. Lebedev, who, under enemy fire,
crawled on his knees to take care of the wounded, sometimes going deep into enemy territory to retrieve dying
soldiers screaming for help. Or such as Lieutenant Grossman, who singlehandedly set fire to eleven Panzers. I
knew a man—a man? no, an adolescent, almost a child—
who slipped through the barbed wire, threw grenades
under the tracks of tanks and waited there to watch them
explode. They all fought valiantly, heroically, for Russian
honor and Jewish honor, believe me. I say this not to
praise myself, but, on the contrary, to demean myself. I
was no hero. I did not fight this war as they did. I myself
fought the war with the wounded.

And the dead.

War, war, what filth. What butchery. And, above all,
what chaos.

In a single night, in the twinkling of an eye, the whole country is in turmoil. Total confusion. Nothing is where it should be. The entire machinery is out of gear. Words are replaced by shouts and orders. Yesterday's allies are today's enemies: implacable, savage, thirsting for blood. Yesterday's enemies—the capitalists-imperialists-colonialists—have become today's faithful comrades, exemplary friends. Instead of extending our frontiers, we draw them back; instead of advancing, the invincible Red Army retreats. Man? Fit only to kill, fit only to die.

At the risk of disappointing you, I shall not tell you the usual war tales animated by noble sentiments of sacrifice and valor. I claim no exploits—I won no battle, achieved no victory, saved not a single unit. Like everyone else, I answered the call for general mobilization and reported to the recruitment center; like everyone else, but no more, I wanted to enter the fray.

After the first shock, the entire country, deceived, manipulated, rushed to the defense of the invaded fatherland. With his grave, solemn "brotherly" speech, Stalin galvanized the nation. And the Jewish minority sevenfold more.

No war in history was ever greeted with so much enthusiasm. We Jews were ready to offer all, to do all, to vanquish the worst enemies of our people and of mankind. Finally we had the feeling of belonging to this country. We shared a common destiny: what was happening to others touched us viscerally. No longer the subjects or objects of some comrade or secretary-general, we were his compatriots, his brothers. Legally, politically, morally and practically, we were on the same side. We nurtured the same hatred for the soldiers of hatred. Like everyone else, we longed to sacrifice everything for victory. As for myself, I had nothing to sacrifice; I had nothing.

I can still see the scene. Kasdan, a cigarette holder between his fingers, already imagines himself at the front, leading a regiment to attack. He is trembling with excitement. Someone says, "But you've never been a soldier. You've never carried a weapon."

"So what?" he cries, infuriated at being denied a command because of such details. "Courage and patriotism, don't they count any more?"

The most astonishing thing is that at that moment we were all thinking like Kasdan. To hell with dialectics, long live faith!

Feldring, disheveled, paraphrases some Biblical passages: Hitler, like Pharaoh, will drown in blood. Feldring already sees himself making a speech on militarism in Jewish poetry and vice versa.

Morawski remains clearheaded. "Of course, we'll win, but . . ."

"But what?" someone snaps.

"I'm thinking of what it's going to cost," says Morawski.

At fifty, he's afraid of being declared unfit for service. Never mind, he'll cheat: a Jewish poet owes it to himself to lie about his age; he's always younger or older than his actual years.

The following day I learn that Kasdan and Feldring have been sent off to the air force and Morawski to the infantry. As for myself, even after a rather superficial medical examination, I have been bluntly rejected.

I lose my temper: "But I'm not sick, I've never been sick in my life!"

"No?" The doctor was astounded. "And when was your last checkup?"

"Oh—I don't remember."

"Well, comrade, I've just examined you myself and it's not so good. I might as well tell it to you straight."

"But what's wrong with me?"

"Heart."

Still, I managed. I "lost" my medical records, and in the

monstrous mess that was evident in all the services and ministries, I soon managed to change my worn suit of clothes for the no less worn uniform of the Red Army.

At last I was happy in the Soviet Union. Thus, everything can happen and did happen in a poet's life. I thought with compassion of my Paris friends under the German occupation: they did not have my good fortune.

But when all is said and done, Citizen Magistrate, do not imagine that Gershon Kossover's son, and what is more, Reb Mendel-the-Taciturn's disciple, had been abruptly transformed into a wild, brave Russian warrior or a Cossack on horseback. Despite my military garb and papers, I was no threat to the motorized enemy legions. Despite my experience in the International Brigade, I came up against insurmountable obstacles. I was full of good will, I sincerely tried, but I found it impossible to bend to the rigors of army life. The exercises—not so bad, they wouldn't kill me. The sudden reveilles, the forced marches in double time— all right too. I coughed, spit blood, suffered constant headaches and palpitations, but I never complained. Private Paltiel Gershonovich Kossover underwent combat training to the satisfaction of his superior officers.

What I couldn't bear—you'll be amused—was army speech. Too rough, too coarse, too primitive; I would blush with embarrassment, like a yeshiva student who has happened upon drunkards during a day at the fair.

In Spain it had been different. There, too, the soldiers surely were no saints; they were especially fond of women and of the curses they invented as though—God forbid— they didn't know enough of them. But in Spain I had been lucky enough not to understand them; to savor them I would have had to acquire the basics of thirty ancient and modern languages. Here I understood. And without my knowledge or desire, I began expressing myself like my barrack mates, like a true soldier of the Red Army.

We were part of the 96th Infantry Division, where all

the peoples of the Soviet Union were mixed together. Kalmuks, Uzbeks, Tartars, Georgians, Ukrainians: their eyes had seen the snows of Siberia, the sunshine of the Ukraine, the dark tides of the Volga and the Dnieper. The High Command was holding us in reserve for the Moscow offensive, scheduled for the winter. The invader was advancing, advancing, apparently invincible, irresistible, inexorable—like the God of the Apocalypse. Our cities were in ruins, our villages in flames. Why shouldn't the enemy push on to the very gates of the Kremlin? Napoleon had done it, after all. But we had thrashed that Corsican, and we would do as much or more to the lunatic from Berlin. Let him get a little closer and we'd cut off his head and drag it through the mud and snow of Moscow. We were supposed to be in training to prepare ourselves for that day. Were we? Not really. We were short of everything, even rifles. But as far as manpower was concerned, our reserves were inexhaustible.

Only, I was exhausted.

At the beginning of September I created a rather embarrassing incident during General Kolbakov's inspection. In expectation of that event there had been many rehearsals and scenes of collective madness without which no self-respecting army could function. Lieutenants were shouting, sergeants were yelling, and the poor soldiers were running, crawling, standing up, saluting, staring at an invisible point right, left, straight ahead; they presented arms, making them crackle like whiplashes, they shouldered them —another whiplash—and hop! we began all over again. So great was our fear of the general that we forgot about the front and the enemy.

When the great day arrived, the 96th Infantry Division, standing at attention, flags in the breeze, responded as one man to the commands from the colonel in charge of the base. Erect, tense, motionless, like a slab of cement, I was looking straight ahead. The general passed us in review, and, lo and behold, he decided to plant himself in front of me. He examined me from head to toe as if I were some unexpected tree dropped from the heavens and grotesquely disguised as a soldier. Petrified, I looked past the general so as not to betray my agitation. To hide it better I made use of a good old method: I let my thoughts carry me elsewhere, to Berlin with Inge, to Paris with Sheina, to Barassy with my father and mother. And my father questions me sadly: "Is that you, my son? Is that really you?" "Look and see, Father—it's me, your son." "Are you really still my son? You don't look it. You speak, you eat, you dress like an Ivan or an Alexey. Not like a Jew." "I've got my *tephilin* in my bag; would you like me to put them on?" He nods. Then I take out my bag, open it feverishly, rummage through strange objects, but cannot find them. I am drenched in hot and cold sweat: The phylacteries, where have I put my phylacteries? I am so afraid, so ashamed that I can scarcely keep my balance; I cling to my father and lie down at the general's feet, completely rigid, my arm extended according to regulations. . . .

I woke up in the hospital. An officer with a huge mustache was cursing: "A thing like you wants to hunt Germans! Stupid idiot!" He spat with disgust. "And where are your records? You've hidden them, you son of a bitch! You turn everything in the goddamned barracks upside down and you don't give a damn! You waste our time and you don't care! Do you know what we call that? Sabotage! Do you know the penalty for that? A bullet through the head."

He wanted to send me to a civilian hospital behind the front, before sending me "back home," as he said. I kept arguing, threatening to commit suicide.

"I have no home," I told him. "I don't know where to go, I'm a poet."

Absurd, stupid, ridiculous as it may seem, it was this

last argument that finally persuaded Dr. Lebedev—a Jew from Vitebsk—not to exile me. He kept me with him, but not without an explanation.

"You know the story of the fellow in love with a girl to whom he kept writing every day? She ended up marrying— the postman."

"I don't see the connection."

He was about to get angry. "You don't see the connection? Well, let me tell you . . . Damn! I told you the wrong anecdote."

He burst out laughing. "I know your type. You'd find a way to come back and poison us all. We might as well take advantage of your being here already."

That was how I became a stretcher-bearer.

"You'll carry the others until the time comes when the others carry you," said Lebedev. "That's the whole story of soldiers at war."

He was gentle, a so-called diamond in the rough. Whenever he talked about Vitebsk, a tuft of black hair fell across his wrinkled forehead and his lips twitched nervously. We got along wonderfully even though we had little in common. He drank like a fish, while I only pretended to drink. I would get angry while he would pretend to. He refused to let me smoke cigarettes, but I liked his tobacco as much as he did.

"The devil take you," he would rebuke me in a fatherly tone. "If you weren't sick, I'd make you sick; if I weren't sure of seeing you croak soon, I'd strangle you with my own hands."

"What, Comrade Doctor? You're not killing enough patients? You need more?"

I made him laugh, and he was grateful. That was my contribution to the war effort: I made people laugh. At that time, during the autumn of 1941, laughter was a precious commodity.

The newspapers never mentioned it, or only after a delay and in veiled terms, but our glorious army, caught unawares by the German offensive, was anything but glorious. I know, I was part of it. Hastily improvised, our lines of defense were hardly off the drawing board before they were broken through. Cities and fortresses opened and collapsed before enemy tanks; the defenders left their corpses there or surrendered en masse. The wounded coming in, plus the evacuation plan being studied by the staff, kept our medical personnel abreast of what was happening. After Kiev, Odessa and Kharkov, Moscow was next.

Lebedev's mood was darkening by the hour. He knew things I did not, but he rebuffed my questions brutally. I insisted; he turned his back. One evening, in his warm quarters, a bottle of vodka in front of him, and after swearing me to secrecy, he disclosed in broad outlines the fate of the Jews in the territories occupied by the invaders. The first reports from the partisans and agents operating behind enemy lines spoke of massacres.

"I don't understand, I don't understand," Lebedev kept saying, baffled.

"What don't you understand, Comrade Colonel? The Germans hate Jews, Russians and Communists. They've proclaimed that loudly and clearly enough! And now that they're putting their hands on Jews, Russians and Communists all at once, they're killing them, that's to be expected. . . ."

"Even so," Lebedev would say, while drinking, "even so."

"You don't know them; I do. They're inhuman barbarians. Capable of the worst."

"Even so," Lebedev, who was not listening, went on repeating.

He was hearing another voice, other inner voices.

"The people in Vitebsk, I know them. I grew up in

Vitebsk. I treated patients from Vitebsk, all patients regardless of nationality or religion. Why did the good people of Vitebsk permit those murderers to kill their Jewish neighbors? Couldn't they have protected and sheltered them? They didn't. Forty years of Communist education ... I don't understand, I don't understand."

There was a big difference between the two of us: I knew Berlin, he thought he knew Vitebsk. Condemned to death by Berlin, the Jews had been sacrificed by Vitebsk.

"Even so, even so," Lebedev kept saying. "I've got friends there who owe me one year, ten years of their life."

Was his family still there, in Vitebsk? I wanted to ask, but finally preferred not to know.

Days and nights flowed by as in a bottomless memory. As our armies fell back, our base became more active. In Moscow the people were digging trenches; where we were, the orderlies were preparing field hospitals. If October was marked by anguish, November was a month of disbelief. The enemy was advancing too rapidly, in too many directions at the same time; the gods of war were smiling on him. Only a miracle could stop him, but, apart from the Jews, who believed in miracles?

But a miracle did take place. It is too well known for me to dwell on it. General Winter made one leap forward, that was all. Instead of having to treat soldiers wounded in combat, our base was dealing with victims of frostbite. We were overwhelmed, but we didn't complain; on the contrary, we congratulated ourselves as though the sudden, inexplicable drop in temperature had been an exploit conceived and executed by our High Command.

It was strange: even though medically ill, and gravely so —so said my record—I showed no particular symptoms. Not only had my condition remained stable, but I felt at the top of my form.

Lebedev didn't hide his astonishment: "I saw you dying, and now you're as lively as a house painter."

"Why a house painter, Comrade Colonel?"

"I don't know. I think I saw one once at my place; he looked like a stevedore."

"Why a stevedore, Comrade Colonel?"

"I haven't the slightest idea. Because—oh, stop bothering me."

We spent the long, dull winter evenings chatting, discussing Jews, literature and philosophy. He knew I was a poet, but I avoided the subject. The front needed fighters, fighters needed stretcher-bearers, not poets. But one night, when a strange silence, a silence from the beginning of time, held sway, I could not keep from reciting for him some poems on death and dying; they weren't by me but by an obscure medieval poet, Don Pedro Barsalom of Córdoba and a friend of the Jews of Castile.

> All those dying men
> voiceless and voracious
> haunt the angel's memory
> And curse him . . .

"You read well," Lebedev remarked, stretching out on his cot. "Continue."

I began the second quatrain:

> You, death who extinguishes
> the fire that shines,
> do not extinguish the sun
> that illuminates you . . .

That night Lebedev neglected his bottle; he listened, with closed eyes. He waited for the rest of the poem, but I had forgotten it.

"Go on," said Lebedev.

I searched my memory—I appealed to my Sephardic friend, David Aboulesia, who had helped me discover the Castilian poet. In vain. Fatigue, tension, the obsession of the here and now weighed on my mind; I lived between two communiqués, between two exhortations from the political commissars.

"Well?" said Lebedev impatiently. "You're asleep?"

As a last resort, I improvised, without telling him, of course. Later, when I confessed the truth, he burst out laughing. "Which is worse? Claiming someone else's poems or passing off your own as his?"

I answered that poets give and take with an open hand: the more they take the more they give. Because poetry . . .

"You're not going to give me a lecture on writing poetry! Are you crazy?" he shot at me, sitting up on his cot.

"Excuse me. I let myself be carried away. I won't do it again."

"Look at him scowling. Did I insult you?"

I did not reply.

"Yes, I've hurt you. I'm sorry—I didn't know you were so sensitive."

"It's just that . . ."

I mumbled. I couldn't finish the sentence.

"All right, all right, let it pass," said Lebedev. "You're a funny stretcher-bearer."

"No doubt I'm also a funny poet, Comrade Colonel."

I have forgotten the childish verses I had invented for him in order to complete Don Pedro Barsalom's poem, as I have forgotten all the other poems. The winter had shrouded my voice. I watched Lebedev amputating arms and legs, I leaned over the dying, sniffing the stench of their sores, and I had nothing to say to those who would survive me. I witnessed the end of so many lives that death killed the words within me. I listened to the wind from distant steppes that rasped and bayed like a thousand beasts at the door of the slaughterhouse; it veiled my voice.

"Drink," Lebedev would say to me. "The state you're in . . ."

I was feeling bad, worse and worse. One day, overcome

by dizziness, I let myself fall down on the snow to rest. Needles were pricking my chest.

"It's nothing," I said to Lebedev. "I have some pain in my heart, it's normal. Don't you have a pain in your heart, Comrade Colonel?"

"Drink," he said. "The state you're in . . ."

Two orderlies carried me to the hospital barracks. In my delirium I saw myself divided in two—I was my own stretcher-bearer. I heard one voice, ten voices, asking me whether it hurt here or there, but what difference did it make, since I was delirious, delirious while thinking that now at last I had the right to be delirious.

As in a fairy tale, I was tended by nurses I thought beautiful, gentle and delicate. I depended on them for food, drink and everything else. Like a child, I let them care for me. I took their precise, businesslike gestures for caresses. Watching them was enough to make me want to rise up and follow them—and live. I fell in love with one and then with all of them together. I loved Natasha because she was robust, Paula because she was frail, Tina because she was red-haired and Galina because she reminded me of a gypsy girl from Liyanov. I loved them because I was weak and helpless, and needed to love. But I had numerous rivals. All the men in the ward, including the dying, breathed more rapidly when they heard them coming with a syringe or a bowl of broth. I soon forgot those radiant and enchanting nurses. Hardly had I been discharged when I stopped thinking about the hospital. What happened was that another woman had, as they say, conquered my heart. Her name was Raissa. As lieutenant in the Political Bureau of the division, she threw me into a panic every time she came to see Lebedev; she blew in like a whirlwind, charging straight toward the colonel and looking over the lists of patients. Seated on a corner of the table, she dominated officers of superior rank to her own. As for myself, a simple private, she did not even deign to accord me a regulation salute. Why was I taken with her? You'll laugh again—I liked her uniform, her stripes, her authority.

Bundled up in a heavy overcoat, and a fur hat that hid her blond hair and half her face, she would remove both with an impatient gesture. All the while she went on cursing the glacial winter that refused to release its grip, those German bastards who could not remain quietly at home, those shirkers who invented illnesses and chilblains. Today, she promised, we would see what we would see. She expressed herself like a peasant, cursed like ten and drank like twenty. And I, who still blushed at the slightest vulgarity, I liked all that. Lebedev also, as he confessed to me. Being discreet and cautious, I remained guarded; I was not about to make myself look ridiculous.

"That broad," Lebedev grumbled, "she drives men crazy, she'd turn the head of the devil himself if she met him."

I was convinced that he was sleeping with her, that all the officers slept with her—the upper ranks for periods of some duration, the lower ranks for briefer periods. And we privates were to be pitied because of our inability to commandeer anyone, not even a third-class soldier, since there was none.

Completely liberated and shameless, she subjected everyone to her whims. I imagined her in bed, in her nightdress, giving orders to her lovers: "Make love to me unless you want to wake up in prison or in Siberia." I would have gone to Siberia with her, or, at least, because of her. Instead, Siberia had moved into our midst. We shivered, we were buried in snow; our tears and our spit turned into icicles. We might as well have been in Vladivostok.

With the thaw, the division received orders to move up

toward the front. Submerged in work, I no longer languished for Raissa. Our unit followed close behind the combat soldiers. The enemy was going to launch an offensive, but we did not know on which front. Defenses and counterattacks were being prepared all around. We studied maps, scrutinized the clouds, cleaned rifles, greased machine guns; we counted the hours, the minutes. Then, one night, the sky and the ground were split. From all sides cannons started belching fire. And there were no longer dawns or dusks—war was all there was. Sallies and retreats, positions abandoned and reclaimed, villages crossed and recrossed without knowing whether we were attacking or falling back. I was plunged into a hallucinatory universe of the wounded who no longer had even the strength to groan, of mangled corpses, scattered limbs, dazed faces. In sunshine and rain, with shells flying across streams and through woods, in full attack and during lulls, I advanced with my fellow stretcher-bearers close behind the first wave, bringing back soldiers shouting for help after having shouted "For the fatherland, for Stalin." Their cries followed me into my sleep: I would wake up with a start, thinking I'd heard the cry of a wounded man whose arms were stretched toward me—toward me alone.

Surrounded by the dead, enveloped by death, I performed my duty with a feeling of inexplicable satisfaction and pride: I was no hero, yet I was exposing myself to dangers as if I had come into the world only to brave them.

Beyond the explosions of grenades and the crackling of machine guns, I heard the death rattles of my mutilated comrades; I made every effort to find them in the shell holes and beneath the smoking ruins. Little by little I learned to distinguish between the critically wounded and those not in desperate need of immediate attention: without even seeing them I could make a diagnosis. Bent over, making myself very small, I ran through the trenches among the bodies, through the puddles of blood, to seize the highest-ranking officer, then the worst-hit soldier. I ran and ran: whenever I think of the war I always see myself running and out of breath, one moment bent over a slaughtered fighter, and already on to the next one, still alive but badly wounded in the eyes, the chest, or the shoulders. In a panting but friendly voice, I would tell him the usual lies: "Don't worry, leave it to me, just hang on, comrade. Your troubles are over, two steps from here our doctors are waiting for you, they're terrific, you'll see; come, my friend, here we are; you're lucky, you're only wounded; and I know all about wounds; yours is just a scratch, you'll be fine. . . ." And the wounded man, if still conscious, clung to me with all his strength; others, half-dead, whispered broken, final incoherent words addressed to their mother, their grandmother, or the holy mother of God. And I encouraged them, I incited them all to talk, to shout, to say anything at all—as long as they were shouting they were living, and their life mattered to me as much as my own, if not more. I ran through fire and came running back to talk to the wounded and make them talk. Some of them cursed, others complained. Some whimpered and moaned like old men, their teeth chattering. Bullets whistled above us, incendiary bombs hit the sky with a barrage of yellow and red flames; men flung themselves into hand-to-hand combat yelling "Hurrah, hurrah for the fatherland!" "Hurrah for Stalin, hurrah!" And they collapsed, mowed down in the middle of their course. "Here, here—help!" Of all the words invented by God and man, only those still had some meaning. The other stretcher-bearers and I leaped toward our brothers whipped by the fire, to wrest them from the enemy and extricate them from death. Carrying them to the rear, I felt victorious; in saving one unknown comrade, I was forcing death to retreat if only to return an hour later.

I thanked God for having given me a bad heart. Had I
been in good health I would have been thrown into a
combat unit, I would have killed, I would have been
killed; I would have helped to enlarge the kingdom of
death; as stretcher-bearer I was reducing it.

Between two operations, Colonel Dr. Lebedev—morose,
exhausted, his pupils dilated—reprimanded me:

"You're going again? Do you think you're immortal?"

"As a poet, Comrade Colonel, only as a poet," I shouted,
turning my back on him.

"You're crazy. And dangerous. You think death respects
poets?"

I set down my wounded and returned to the firing line,
while Lebedev went back to his operating table. We were
both crazy. Nothing stopped us. One day, however . . .

It was near Smolensk, during a particularly brutal battle
that cost us a fourth of our combat troops. A German
soldier wounded in the throat seized me by my boots and
begged me in German to finish him off. I tried to free
myself, but he hung on. I bent over him: he was unshaven,
wild-eyed, contorted with pain. Coming closer, I saw that
he was also wounded in the stomach. His eyes unbelievably
white, his lips unbelievably swollen, he uttered phrases
interrupted by gasps: "Kill me, comrade, take pity on me,
finish me off. . . ." And I, after a moment of hesitation
and disgust, answered in my poor German, "No, not possible, not allowed, not right." He repeated the same words
sobbing, "Pity, comrade . . . finished, comrade. . . ." And,
in the midst of shellings and screams for help and the
officers' enraged orders, I tried to reassure him: "You live,
have patience; I come back get you; first I take care my
people. . . ." And, like an idiot, I kept my word. I left the
German lying in his own blood and carried behind the
lines a mustached sergeant who was rubbing his eyes and
screaming that they were scorched. He was really heavy,

that sergeant, he weighed a ton; I don't know how I managed, but I brought him back. I pushed, pulled, dragged, carried him to the emergency station, all the while telling him what he wanted to hear: his eyes were all right, he would see his wife and children and his native Kirghiz again. . . . Then I went back for the German; I dragged him and laid him out among the wounded the orderlies were bringing into the barracks, where Lebedev and his assistants, impassively, were examining, probing, cutting.

Suddenly I heard a voice that sounded familiar, though from an uncertain past: "Tell me, soldier, what do you intend doing with that one?"

I raised my eyes and met Raissa's cold, hard gaze. She did not recognize me.

"Well, soldier? Answer me!" she hissed. "What the devil is he doing here?"

"He's wounded in the neck and stomach."

"Let him croak."

"He's in pain," I said looking away.

"Our doctors are swamped and you want them to take care of these mad dogs?"

Meanwhile the wounded man had opened his eyes and was watching us; he didn't understand our words but guessed their meaning, because he started groaning again: "Kill me, finish me off!"

"Throw him out," the lieutenant ordered.

And, like an idiot, I argued. Ten steps away men were falling by the hundreds, and thousands, and here I was trying to keep an enemy alive. Luckily the German did me a favor; he had the good grace to die of his own accord a few moments later. Raissa threw me a disgusted look and left. And I wondered, Was there once a time when I found her human, when I desired her?

Lebedev, informed of this episode by the lieutenant, agreed with her. "War's war, my little Jewish poet. Emotions are good for love, and love is good for your poems; and your poems—you know what you can do with them, and if you don't, I can tell you, and you won't like that. Pity, my boy, is reserved for our brothers; care, for our fighters. As for the Germans, let them croak; let them stay in their beer halls!"

All the members of our unit thought as he did; he was the spokesman for the entire Red Army. Hatred of the invader was the order of the day, vengeance the most burning of obsessions. No mercy for the SS murderers of the young and the old, no pity for their collaborators. What else could be expected from hardened soldiers who, while repulsing the invader, came upon gallows and mass graves in every village? I too shared this thirst for reprisal on our arrival in Kharkov. Had I been able, I would have carried the ruins of the city to Germany, and all over the world. Its scorched linden trees, its broken, withered poplars—men hanging from their branches—I would have carried them into all the parks, all the streets of all the cities inhabited and embellished by men.

The outlying factory districts destroyed; the suburbs ravaged; buildings, churches, stores, warehouses, schools, homes of officials and hovels of workers: the Nazi "scorched earth" policy had left nothing but ashes. An inferno. One sergeant, a native of Kharkov, sobbing, showed me his city: "That's Sumskaya Street, whose splendor made us dream; there's Petrov Street, where my uncle, a university professor, lived; there's the square where we used to celebrate our holidays." He was hallucinating; he was seeing animated, bustling streets where we saw only death and desolation.

Our division, camped in a village a few miles outside the city, dug itself in to resist the German counteroffensive which, we knew, was coming soon. The front was moving away, but our commanding officer, General Kolbakov, received permission from the High Command to consoli-

date our positions while waiting for reinforcements. A
few days of relief, a few nights of repose, at last.

Lebedev was quartered in Kharkov itself, I with a peasant woman in the village. I had nothing to complain of; I
had better food than my superior officers. My landlady,
Olga Kalinovna, a splendid grandmother in black skirt
and kerchief, treated me like a son, her own having disappeared after the fall of the town in October 1941. Her
retarded grandson lived with her. In the evenings I asked
her to tell me about the German occupation. She would
fall asleep while speaking, but I was unable to close my
eyes until morning. Of the hundred thousand Jews who
had lived, studied, taught, worked in Kharkov, few remained. I was afraid to meet them, mutilated and tortured,
in my sleep.

I roamed around the city looking for my own people.
I questioned former officials, partisans, shirkers, military
security agents. In vain.

Then I went alone to Drobitzky Yar, where between
fifteen and twenty thousand Jews had been massacred. I
wanted to weep, but I did not. I wanted to say something,
but I said nothing. One day, I thought, I'll come back and
recite the Kaddish. Not yet. One day.

I returned there every day for an hour or two. The
place exercised a fascination over me I could not explain.
I felt I was on familiar ground, at home. These dead were
my people. What could I say to them? And yet . . . to recite
the Kaddish one must have at least ten persons; and if I
were to ask Lebedev to help me mobilize ten men . . .

"Whenever you like," he said.

One day, but when?

I went to see the black-market places. Men and women
in rags assembled to buy and sell . . . nothing at all. Empty
boxes, clothes so patched they could not be worn. A tragic
farce: someone was laughing, and I wondered who.

Our day of departure arrived. Kolbakov had ordered us
to start moving by two in the afternoon, but at eleven in
the morning the enemy launched a blistering attack. The
division fought valiantly, lost several tanks, and had to
fall back in order to avoid encirclement. Lebedev saved
his unit, but he forgot me. Wounded in the head, I lay
unconscious in a shell hole. I awoke later in a dark, humid
cellar. Blood streamed from my eyes, nose and mouth. A
piercing rhythmic pain pounded my temples. In a panic,
I tried to stand up, to get my bearings: Where was I? Since
when? And where were my comrades? I heard someone
breathing. "Who's there?" I whispered. A hoarse, muffled
sound came in response. I understood—it was my landlady's retarded grandson. I called to him to come closer;
he did not understand. But his presence did me good: I
was not alone. Then a door opened. The grandmother
entered, and, kneeling, began talking in a barely audible
voice: "God have mercy on us, they've come back; they
took the village again; our soldiers left, I brought you
into the cellar, with the help of my grandson. If they'd
found you outside they would have finished you off; if
they find you here, they'll kill all of us." I heard her as
from a distance, across other voices, other sounds, and I
resigned myself to the idea that I would not witness the
great day of victory: I was going to die like the Jews of
Drobitzky Yar—not like them, not as a Jew—but only as a
Russian prisoner. No one would know who I was, no one
would come to recite the Kaddish for me. "Promise me
you'll be careful?" the grandmother went on. "I know
them: bloody, greedy murderers, they'll ransack the
houses, let their dogs loose in the ruins—I know them. Be
careful, promise?" I did not answer. One urgent question
tormented me: "When did it happen?" "This morning,"
said the grandmother. "Before noon. They fell on us like
thunder, the whole thing started all over again." "And

Kharkov? Who's holding Kharkov, Grandmother?" "I don't
know, my dear, I know nothing. Our soldiers, I hope.
Kharkov is too big a city to let go, not like our little
Rovidok: why sacrifice our young heroes for a little village? If it's not liberated today, it'll be liberated tomorrow.
Don't you think so?" "Yes, Grandmother," I said, "I think
so." Actually I did not think so; I was not thinking about
anything except death.

She gave me a bowl of hot, sweetened water: I swallowed
a few gulps. And my blood was flowing, flowing—and my
life was flickering out. And my heart was growing heavy.

"Rovidok," said the grandmother. "I wonder if this
little village isn't more important than a lot of better-
known places? So much blood's been shed here, so many
lives lost. . . . Five times invaded and liberated, and always
at tremendous cost. Would people fight for a little place
without any importance?" "That's right, Grandma, in high
places they consider Rovidok of great strategic importance," I said to make her feel good. Rovidok, Rovidok:
I had never before heard its name.

"You'll stay here," said the grandmother, "Mitya and
I will watch over you. Be careful, my son. And we too,
we'll be careful. We'll leave you now; a neighbor might
come knocking at our door, and we better be there."

I remained in the cellar three days and two nights, delirious with fever and pain, biting my fingers and arms to
keep from groaning. From time to time Mitya came,
bringing me some warm water and a boiled potato: he
would sit down on the ground in the half-darkness and
stare at me, uttering small grunts like a beaten animal.
Was he really retarded? I didn't think so. It probably was a
ruse invented by his grandmother to keep him home. He
understood me, he understood many things, I was sure of
it. If I asked him to bring me a wet towel he pretended
not to understand. But an hour later his grandmother
would arrive with a wet rag and wash my face. "I thought

this would do you good," she would say. "Thanks,
Grandma, thanks a lot. If we win the war, and we will,
it'll be because of people like you." "You're talking nonsense. Our soldiers, our heroic warriors, are fighting the
war, not old women like myself."

During my isolation I received another visitor: a cat, a
tomcat, made his way into the cellar. At first he was afraid
of me, but little by little, he realized I was not moving; I
was not chasing or kicking him with my boot. Then he
must have said to himself: This fellow is in hiding, he's a
fugitive; I can do whatever I please. And, in fact, he did:
he became an anti-Semite, that Rovidok cat! He gnawed at
my boots, leaped onto my stomach and off again, only to
come back from another direction. How that beast kept
pestering me! I hated him more than anything else in the
world. He guessed it, and made my life even more miserable. He bit my ear, jumped on my neck, my face. It was
hard for me to hold back tears of rage and impotence.

I mentioned it to the old lady. "I'm afraid to close my
eyes; he's capable of devouring me, that vile cat." "Do
you want me to kill him?" she asked. "He's useful. You're
not my only lodger, my dear. There are lots of mice and
rats in my house." "I'll go mad, Grandma." Finally Mitya
locked the cat up in the barn. High time; I was at the
end of my rope.

When our soldiers finally reclaimed the village, and
when Lebedev saw me again at his new emergency station,
this time on the operating table, he thought I had gone
mad for good: all I spoke about was cats; I insulted them,
cursed them, called them murderers, cannibals, barbarians.
Lebedev, my friend, you who know so much about human
nature, explain to me: Why do cats hate Jews and poets?

I was evacuated to Kharkov, but I went back to Rovidok
later, much later, after the victory. With faltering heart, I
returned to Grandma Kalinovna's. Was she still alive? I
knocked at her door, listened to the approaching steps.

There she was, but aged, apathetic. I took her into my arms, presented her with a skirt I had bought in the black market, kissed her sparse white hair, her bony, bluish hands. "Cry," I told her, "it'll do you good—cry!" She shook her head: she did not want to cry. "And Mitya?" I was looking for him. He wasn't in the room, he wasn't in the kitchen. The old lady kept shaking her head: she did not want to cry. "And Mitya?" I asked again. And then the dam broke: she burst into sobs. Mitya had gone away. Carried away by the torrent of fire, her fine, mute grandson. "What happened, Grandma?" "They came back," she said, wiping her face with a corner of her kerchief. "Yes, my son, they came back again after you left." "And . . . ?" "And their last siege was the worst of all." "Tell me, Grandma. What did they do with Mitya?" "It'll upset you, I don't want to do that." "I want to know," I insisted, taking her hands in mine. But she just went on shaking her head, refusing to tell me about her grandson. "Okay," I said, "then let's talk about—the cat, yes?" She started to laugh, while tears rolled down her cheeks. It made me sick to see her crying and laughing at the same time. "If you like, Grandma, I'll stay with you awhile, I'll keep you company, I'll help you. Would you like that?" "This is no place for you," she said, struggling to regain control of herself. She was thinking of Mitya; so was I. Mitya, the victim of educated, civilized men.

My hospital stay, followed by convalescence, lasted until the fall. I took advantage of the opportunity to fall in love with Tatyana and Galina, and then with a nurse everyone called "the saint," I forget why. After that I rejoined the 96th, which was regrouping with a view to attacking the Carpathians. I reported to my company and asked to see Colonel Dr. Lebedev. A brawny, grumpy sergeant answered me: "Never heard of him." "But he's the head of . . ." "Never heard of him, I tell you."

Outside, in front of the division commander's bivouac,

I ran into an orderly I knew, one of the veterans from my old team. He embraced me. "Glad to see you, Paltiel Gershonovich!" He brought me up to date on the changes that had taken place in our unit. The news hit me like a giant fist. No need to go on, I guessed the rest. Lebedev . . I would never see him again either. I felt lost. Abandoned. Was there anyone left to turn to? I was climbing a mountain of ashes. On the other side an old man was waiting. And he was saying, "Come, my son. Come."

From then on, and until the victory, I lived in a kind of trance. I no longer sought the living; only the dead interested me, only the dead needed me. I was their companion, their savior.

The new medical chief of the division, Colonel Zaronevski, refused to accept me in his unit, and so I wound up with the gravediggers. Their commanding officer, a permanently drunk Caucasian, was recruiting whomever he could get; all you needed was two arms in good condition.

I could not understand Zaronevski's hostility. Did he resent my friendship with his predecessor? Did he think I was too weak to be a stretcher-bearer? More plausible: he detested Jews. In his eyes we were all cowards, but since our military exploits contradicted his theories, he preferred to keep us away from the front, the better to despise us.

As for myself, I went on fighting. Not for the fatherland —it had already been liberated by the Red Army—but for the corpses: I saw nothing but corpses, breathed nothing but the stench of their putrefaction. During that winter and the following spring I crawled through mud and puddles, through plains and forests, to bring them to their final assembly point.

I lived with them, for them. By dint of excavating the ground I stopped seeing the sky.

Finally, the Red Army was smashing through the enemy

defenses, liberating cities and villages set on fire by the invaders before retreating. The Germans were fleeing, and we were pursuing them, like angels of supreme punishment. Our men celebrated each victory by drinking and singing at the top of their lungs. Not I. I confess I did not associate with the Soviet heroes who joyously celebrated our triumph. I could not celebrate. I followed them, I admired them, I prayed for them, for they were inflicting the defeats the enemy deserved. But beyond that, I preferred to remain in the rear with the dead who had become my own.

The newspapers were describing page after page, the historic battles of Voronezh, Odessa, Kiev, Kharkov, Oman, Berditchev. . . . As for myself, I remember only the burnt corpses of Voronezh, the gallows of Oman, the mutilated children of Berditchev. How many corpses did I see? They were of all ages, all social and religious origins. I would invent lives and destinies for them. And attempt to unravel their final thoughts, fixed in their sightless eyes. Let no one tell me the dead all look alike; whoever says that has not seen them. Whoever says that must have looked away—I did not. I have seen thousands of unrecognizable bodies and yet I recognized them. I knew nothing about them, but I knew the thing that had been more important to them in their lifetimes than their names and trades. I once knew it, but—stupid of me—I no longer know what it was.

Those hands knotted in death—what secret did they enclose? Those arms stretched out—what justice were they demanding? A young officer weeping with rage, another with pity; their tears trickled down on me, I absorbed them all. An old man seemed to implore me, another to rebuke me. So intently did I listen to what they were not saying, I no longer heard the sounds of life.

I was going mad.

• •

The worst was the summer of 1944, when we reached the blessed, cursed city of my childhood. The Germans stubbornly refused to let go: Liyanov was theirs. They clung to it and were impossible to dislodge. Despite the ceaseless firing of our artillery and our aerial bombardments, our shock divisions were encountering too many obstacles to dislodge the enemy from his positions. Reinforcements and reserves were arriving at an accelerated pace to replace our lost men and materiel. And after each attack I would rush out to collect the shattered, trampled, abandoned human debris. And my heart would tremble. My father, my mother. My sisters, their husbands and children. Were they still alive? Would I recognize them? Sixteen years had gone by since I had abandoned them, five since their last letter. What would I tell them of my life? I could neither sleep nor eat. So near to them, and so far. Ilya, a comrade, lectured me: I was neglecting myself, I was letting myself go, I was taking refuge in death. "You can't understand, Ilya." But I was wrong: he did understand; Ilya was a Jew. At eighteen he had already seen and learned a great deal. The day we made our breakthrough and our crack troops flung themselves on Liyanov like wild beasts, he was beside me. His eyes bloodshot, he tried to calm me. No other offensive had filled me with such tension. My nerve ends were raw; I kept exasperating our commander: "Isn't it our turn yet? Are we moving?" "Not yet, the battle's still raging. Let's wait for it to quiet down." "But what are we waiting for? Comrades are dying, some are already gone, and we're twiddling our thumbs!" "Patience," Ilya said to me. "I understand what you're feeling, but be patient."

I had no choice. Our unit was supposed to follow the third wave. Ilya would not move from my side. Though younger than I, he was my protector. I needed his presence. Without him, who knows what I might have done that day at the gates of Liyanov.

The fighting was still going on in the outskirts. With Ilya at my heels I ran to my childhood home. The sun was setting, leaving a flaming sky beneath which I looked for my school, then the little market, then the House of Study. The roofs were being fired at, grenades were being thrown into the cellars, but I rushed to my house, where my parents and their children, their prayers and mine, were awaiting me. Twilight enveloped all the houses. I stopped in front of ours. Paralyzed, I could not open the door. Ilya did it for me. I was overcome by a deep, dark fear: this is not my house. I call out, "Anyone there?" No reply. I go out into the courtyard, I see the barn—yes, this is my house. I look at the apple trees, the plum trees—yes, this is mine. But the silence is not mine. And the soldier hearing it does not come from here. I retrace my steps. Here's the kitchen: "Anyone there?" Ilya opens the door to the dining room. Empty. My parents' bedroom. Empty. My fear is mounting, I am about to explode. If the house is my house, why is it empty? Where is my family? Why is nobody here to welcome me? A distant memory surfaces: the pogrom, the attic, the cellar. Might they have hidden there, as in the past? I run to see. Nothing. A mad idea shoots through me: the house is my house, but I . . . I am not I. I am really beginning to believe that when Ilya discovers a man and a woman beneath the bed in the children's room. Terrified, they get up, overturning a chair. Are they my parents? Have I forgotten what they look like? Is it possible? Anything's possible, since I am not myself. Ilya questions them in Russian. Who are they? They don't answer. In Yiddish. They don't answer. Ilya is irritated; they're in a panic. They lament in Romanian: they're innocent, they've done nothing, they never belonged to the Iron Guard. . . . I feel like hitting them, but how can you strike a couple of terrified old people? I ask them how long they've been living in this house. Forever, says the husband. Seeing the glint in my eyes, he begins again: "Oh, excuse me, excuse me. . . . You speak Romanian, Mr. Officer. . . . This house, they gave it to us." "When? Who gave it to you?" I shout. The husband stammers, "The municipality." I shout even louder: "When?" The husband tries to find words: "When . . . the Fascists . . . when the Fascists took away . . . the . . . Jews."

What did I feel? You will not understand. I felt neither anger nor hatred, neither thirst for blood nor desire for vengeance. Only sadness, heavy and all-embracing. An ancient sadness, welling up from the depths of time, tore me from the present. I was there and elsewhere, alone and not alone, more clearheaded than ever, more intoxicated than ever. My sadness was personal and collective: my memories, my gestures, the pulsing of my blood, the beating of my heart were steeped in it. Between the world and myself, between my life and myself, there was this dark mass of infinite, unspeakable, tumultuous sadness; it encompassed the first man killing the last. And I stood by, helplessly watching. Just as I stood by watching as my friend Ilya, without a word, began to slap the old man. The woman, on her knees, was wailing, clutching our trouser legs, knocking her head against the floor. Ilya went on. I watched him and was sad for him, for my vanished parents, for their son standing there. Sad for this world in its fury, sad for its Creator. Sad for the dead, sad for the survivors who would remember the dead. "Stop, Ilya," I told my friend. "Stop, what's the use?" He did not hear me. Perhaps I had said nothing. "Let's go," I said in a low voice. I took his arm and we went out into the street. Outside, Ilya stretched, took a deep breath and began cursing more and more violently, "Son-of-a-bitch bastard, son-of-a-bitch bastard. . . ."

Our company remained in the vicinity for three days. The population granted the liberators a warm welcome, spoiling us with their wines and their women. "If things go on this way," Ilya said, "I'll resign from the war and stay here in your town."

The orders from Staff Headquarters, however, forbade excesses. Romania was no longer our enemy but our ally, and the Red Army was to take that into account. We were to show ourselves understanding, helpful, good-natured. On both sides no one asked for anything better than understanding and mutual aid.

As for me, I strolled through the streets and alleys of my memory and wondered if all this was not a dream. And what if I was delirious? I am a youngster again, I am going to school, I am studying with Ephraim, I am the disciple of Rebbe Mendel-the-Taciturn, and together we are exploring the secret paths to glory; together we are hearing the sages relate our adventures while describing their own. I never left for Germany, I never lived in France, I never set foot in Spain. The Jews have not been massacred. And you, Father, you are not traveling in a sealed train, you are not traveling days and nights without air and without hope, you are not suffocating, you are not perishing from asphyxiation as you stand riveted to members of your own family and community. No, Father. You did not die that way. You did not die. And I am not living through this nightmare; humanity has not fallen into the abyss, it has not consumed its own soul.

I visited the few synagogues that were still open and insisted on hearing ten times, a hundred times, about the murderous days of 1941: the raids, the shootings, the death trains, the complicity of the inhabitants. The Fascists had worked out a program to which the whole town had become witness. It was here, on these avenues bordered by lush trees, where people strolled, met one another, exchanged greetings, wished one another a good day and a good evening and a healthy appetite. This was the road taken by housewives to go to market while discussing prices and recipes, this was where couples were formed and lovers left one another; it was here that children ran around, played ball, laughed, and their parents scolded them, while right near them, so near them, the sealed trains and their cargoes of dead and dying were rolling, rolling in circles, going from nowhere to nowhere, coming to a stop only when the last man breathed his last breath. But how was it possible? And then I stopped asking that question.

But Ilya went on muttering, "Son-of-a-bitch bastard, son-of-a-bitch bastard." Sometimes he accompanied me on my excursions and we looked like two soldiers in search of pleasure, excitement and feminine warmth.

I went to the cemetery, I wandered between the slightly tilting white and gray stones. I stopped here and there to read the names of a rabbi, a sage, a philanthropist. Here was the tomb of Rebbe Yaakov, the miracle worker who saved his community during the riots of the seventeenth century. "Why didn't you intercede on behalf of *my* community, rebbe?" I asked him in a low voice. I reproached him: "You could have shaken the Celestial Throne, Rebbe Yaakov; and if you yourself lacked the strength you could have alerted those who have it. Why didn't you enlist the aid of the Baal Shem Tov and his disciples, of Jeremiah and his ancestors, who are also ours? You were here, Reb Yaakov, and you were unable to protect your descendants. . . ." Ilya grumbled, "What are you doing talking to yourself?" "You wouldn't understand," I told him, thinking that a fellow like him, a young Communist and all the rest, a Communist from head to toe, did not, could not, believe in wonder-working rebbes. But Ilya surprised me once again: "Yes, Paltiel, I do understand." It was true. He understood. He was a Jew, Ilya.

We reached the mass grave. After a long silence Ilya wanted to launch into his litany of curses, but I held him back. He understood. He touched my arm as if to say good-bye, then went off. I was left there alone. Alone with whom? With how many victims? The grave seemed narrow to me, too narrow for so huge a number of men and women. The earth is deceptive. Alive, man needs room: offices, palaces, workshops, stores; dead, he needs but his own space: a tiny crack on the earth's surface.

Suddenly I was seized by a wild desire to open the grave, to search for my family and to bury them properly, in their own tomb. I did not. My father, on the other side of death, forbade me. He refused to be separated from his community. I thought I heard him say: Dead or alive, a Jew's place is with his people.

The sun fell, the shadows lengthened. Night was coming, announced by a dusk heavy with terror. It was time to depart. I recalled a legend that had frightened me as a child. A man fell asleep in a cemetery and spent the night there; the following day his corpse was found; the dead had claimed him. Yes, I should have left, but I could not. Impossible to tear myself away from this place; my feet refused to budge. I prepared myself to implore the dead to free me, when a voice, vaguely familiar, addressed itself to me. "And have you said the prayer for the dead?" "No," I said. "Why not?" "I can't." "You can't, or you won't?" "I cannot sanctify His name or glorify His ways—I cannot." Astonished, the voice continued: "Did you come here to blaspheme?" "I don't know," I said. "I don't know why I came. . . ."

The man I was speaking to was tall and slender; he held himself erect; he was strong, majestic. My heart took a leap: David Aboulesia! No, what was I thinking of? What an absurd idea. I put it out of my mind. I questioned him: "Who are you?" "I'm a gravedigger," he said.

"So am I," I responded. "Do you belong to a holy society? Which one?" "I'm a soldier," I said. "What are you doing here in *my* cemetery?" "My parents are buried here. . . ." The gravedigger shook his head and pronounced the ritual prayer: "The Lord has given, the Lord has taken away, blessed be the name of the Lord forever. . . ." In the deepening dusk we were two shadows uniting to confront together the mystery of the night. "The men and women I take leave of," the gravedigger said, "I make them my messengers. I tell them, 'Go and present yourselves before the Heavenly Tribunal and say that Shevach-the-Grave-digger, member of the Holy Society of the Messiah Watchers, has come to the end of his patience; say that his fatigue and also his grief are very great; say that it is difficult and inhumane to live and to die waiting, it's difficult and inhumane to carry a generation of Jews into the earth.' "

He described the bloody events that only a gravedigger could have experienced. It was he who had to receive the convoy of the dead, it was he who had to cleanse the mangled corpses. He was the last to cast a living, compassionate look on my father and mother, my sisters and their children.

Messiah Watcher. I thought of my friend Ephraim and his dreams of redemption. I remembered my father's prayers for Jerusalem. Rebbe Mendel-the-Taciturn and his keys. And—inexplicably, because he belonged to another landscape, another story—my companion David Aboulesia loomed in my mind; I heard his fantastic tales in which the adventurer leaves in quest of the Messiah the way a policeman sets out in search of a fugitive.

As he left me, Shevach-the-Gravedigger promised to take good care of my family. I thanked him. I knew he would. I also knew he would be unable to do so: I was taking my family with me; my life would become their tomb.

At the camp I met Ilya; he was not sleeping. Stretched

out on his bed, he was staring into space. He had been
drinking. I told him about my evening. "You can't understand," I said. I was wrong. He could. He understood. He
was a Jew, Ilya. He knew we are all gravediggers.

> In my dream
> my father
> asked me
> if he is still
> my father.
>
> I hold his hand
> and I ache.
> I talk to him
> and I ache.
>
> I tell him:
> call me,
> hold me back,
> try to understand.
>
> I tell him
> of my escapes
> into the future
> into the past.
>
> I tell him
> of the ashes
> and the scars
> on my forehead.
>
> I tell him
> to stay with me
> watch over me
> and never leave me.
>
> And so I see my father
> in my dream

and fail to see
myself.

Did you know
that the dead also weep?
The dead of yesterday
and before,
why do they weep?

Night loathes itself
it flees and dissolves
into dawn.

Why does night
not wish to be night?
Do you know why?

The ailing stranger
laughs and laughs;
why do I hear
him laugh so loud?

Because night
awaits him?
Because death too
awaits him?

I ask my father
to visit me
in my dreams
and give me his answers.

He listens
and makes me listen.
I know all he knew;
but,
does he know what I know?

Zusia, my Master,
Zusia, my brother,
have you changed your mind?

You said
happiness exists
and fills creation.

You said
God in His grace
prevents man
from suffering
shame
and death.

Zusia, my father,
think of your children and theirs,
your disciples and theirs,
think of them, Zusia,
and tell me then,
tell me that
suffering does not exist.

I see you, Zusia,
smiling at your brother,
the great Rabbi Elimelekh,
I hear you tell him
that everything under the sun
created by the Creator
is grace
and compassion.

Can you see the descendants
of his prophets, Zusia?
Can you see them
in the sealed cattle-cars,

in the blazing forests—
do you hear their shouts,
Zusia?

They are on fire, brother;
they are on fire, teacher,
consumed by fire
on the altar
of our people.

Please, Zusia,
be Zusia
and stop smiling—
or else do not be
Zusia.

    In my dream
    my father
    is laughing.

    Only his eyes are not.

    Why is my father
    laughing
    in my dream?

    Is it because I told him
    of my discovery?

    I have found a new Rabbi,
    I told him,
    a new sage,
    a new prophet.

    Advocating brotherhood
    and equality
    and peace among nations.

A new Rabbi preaching joy
for the poor
and the oppressed.

A prophet like Isaiah,
a dreamer like Hosea,
a consoler like the Besht.

He laughed
when I mentioned
his name.

Rabbi Karl,
our teacher Karl,
our prophet Karl Marx.

My father is laughing
and there are tears
in the silence
of my dream.

                    (Translated from Yiddish)

Your mother," says the writer, "your mother will not be coming today."

Grisha blinks. He is so busy clearing his mind of sleep that he does not grasp the meaning of what his friend is saying.

"I woke you up, forgive me."

His friend has trouble overcoming his uneasiness. He wipes his lips with the palm of his hand.

"They called me," he explains. "An urgent message from Vienna. Your mother will not be on the plane."

For an interminable and hazy moment Grisha remains paralyzed. Nothing moves him, nothing affects him. He feels nothing, weighs nothing. He is floating in a nebulous universe where the dead and the living mingle. Far from Jerusalem.

"Your mother is ill," says the writer as though to reassure him.

Grisha moves listlessly. I am stupid, he tells himself; I do not seem to be able to speak to anyone. He opens the curtains. Dawn is withdrawing before the harsh brightness that seems to spring from below, from the domes and turrets overlooking the city.

"Would you like me to make you some coffee?"

Grisha makes an effort. He is surprised by his own sorrow. That last evening with his mother, on the eve of his departure for Israel, had been less painful. And yet, at that particular moment, he had no hope of ever seeing her again. Why would she have left Krasnograd, her habits, her comfort and her friend Mozliak? And yet she did leave them. Why? That was the first question he was going to ask her. To prepare the others. Now he knows that he will not be able to ask them.

How fortunate, Grisha is thinking, how fortunate that I spent the night at home! He had almost stayed with Katya, but around two o'clock in the morning he had felt that he should go home. As though he had been waiting for an event, a message, a disaster.

He gets dressed, he feels unhappy. She is not coming, he tells himself. I shall never see her again. I shall never know the true role she played in my father's life, nor the role my father played in hers. He was too discreet, my father. Though not quite as discreet as his wife. All those adventures and affairs alluded to in the *Testament*—were they real or imagined? I shall never know that either. *Never:* that word tears him apart. Why was it so important for him to see her again? Because he no longer loved her or because he still loved her and more than ever before? Scenes from his childhood, images from his adolescence appear in his mind's eye, at first in sequence, then overlapping in time. . . . "Did you love him, tell me? My father, did you love him?" "Of course, Grisha, of course I loved him." "But then, why was his heart broken?" "Who told you that his heart was broken?" "I know it. I read his poems. His heart was broken." "But, my child, all poets have broken hearts. . . ." Another time: "Tell me how you met." "Oh, that was during the war; I don't like to talk about the war." "What was he doing?" "He was fighting, like everybody else." "And you? What were you doing?" "I was also fighting." "Your first meeting, tell me about your first meeting. . . ." She refused. He asked again; in vain. She could not foresee that one day he would know more than she did about their first encounter. She did not know there was a *Testament*. He had concealed it from her on Zupanev's advice: "I trust your mother, but as to that Dr. Mozliak, if he gets wind of our project, we're done for. Be careful, son. You are a Jewish poet's messenger, it is your duty to be careful."

That was the week of his departure. Grisha had memorized the last pages, the last verses. Just as many times before, the watchman, notebooks on his knees, was reading in a low, monotonous voice and Grisha was listening, committing every sentence, every comma to his memory, disciplining his mind, motionless, his lips half open, tensed to the breaking point. He listened, he listened gravely, intensely, barely breathing. Only his eyes mirrored life; he listened with his eyes, he listened, registering every word, every nuance, every hesitation. He owed it to himself to remember it all, to store it all, to let nothing slip by. Nobody listened the way he did; no other memory was equal to his. "What luck that you are mute," said Zupanev, scratching his bald head. "They are letting you go. They do not suspect the power of the mute. Nor did they understand my power; for them a stenographer is just barely a living object. That's how it is, my boy, the executioners lack imagination—otherwise they wouldn't be executioners."

Zupanev asked him for one last favor: "Tell me how you became mute."

Grisha made a gesture of helplessness: If I could tell, I would not be mute.

"How stupid of me," said Zupanev.

He opened a drawer, took out a pencil and a notebook and handed them to his young friend.

"Write," he said, "and . . ." He thought for a moment, then went on with a smile: "This notebook, I shall keep it together with those of your father."

And Grisha wrote. . . .

Dr. Mozliak may be working for the Security services. I have no proof. It is just an impression.

One day, coming home from school, I find him there, sitting on the sofa. My mother is standing, she seems frightened: he must be dangerous and powerful. I don't like him. In fact, I hate him.

My mother seems fond of him. She says that he is an excellent physician. That's all right with me; I am not sick. My mother is. She visits him often in his apartment above ours. As for me, even if I were down to my last breath, I would not seek his help. He frightens me.

Nevertheless, one day I was forced to ring his bell. My mother was not feeling well and she sent me to him for a prescription. I remember the white: dressed in a white coverall, Mozliak made me sit on a white chair as he himself sat down behind a white desk; it was blinding.

He wrote the prescription and said, "The pharmacy is closed at this hour. Until it opens, let's have a talk, all right?"

It is not all right. He insists. He speaks of my mother's illness. His cloying voice sticks to my skin; it makes me nauseous.

"Tell me about your father," he says.

No, never!

He is interested in my father, not in me. He puts me through a regular interrogation; I withdraw into absolute silence. He is getting angry and tries not to let it show; I am getting nervous and it does show. My father's life, my father's death, my father's poetry are not his business; in truth, I don't know much about them, but that I refuse to admit. Before my encounter with Zupanev, his place in my memory is so modest, so obscure—a photograph, a few poems—it is a personal, intimate thing. But he is obstinate. And so I stand up and go. Outside I breathe. Quickly, to the pharmacy. Thank God, it's open.

In the evening, there he is again in our home. He peers at my mother. He sits down and starts all over with his questions. My father, always my father. I run away.

He comes back the next day and the next. My mother is better but he continues to stop by evenings, to examine her and interrogate me.

At last I understand: it is me he comes to see, not Mother. His purpose? To steal my father from me. To take him away a second time; the more he comes, the more convinced I am of that.

He undoubtedly belongs to a special service in charge of brainwashing people, of draining them, of erasing their memory as one wipes a blackboard at school.

And he knows how, the bastard. He throws me a question, he repeats it ten times with different variations until I feel empty, dispossessed.

The story of the cork, for instance. I had found that cork in a drawer when I was three or four years old. There was nothing special about it but I had invented a past for it. I told myself that my father had put it into that drawer so that I might find it one day. I told myself that this cork contained a secret, a secret it was my duty to uncover. Foolishness, I know. But for me the cork was an intimate link to my father. I had mentioned it to nobody, not even my mother. Unfortunately, Mozliak saw it fall from my pocket. He guessed everything. He took it between his fingers and broke it into pieces. "You see," he said, "it's nothing but a plain cork." The bastard. He wanted to hurt me and he did. The cork he broke was *me*; I was no longer a living being, a schoolboy, but a broken cork. And it hurt, the way it does when one has a tooth pulled. It always hurts when you lose a secret.

Or the story of the sun. That, too, is a secret—only a real one. Do you remember my father's poem on the sun of ashes? Well, since I have read it, I see a sun nobody else can see: my very own sun is neither red nor silvery, nor is it a disk of gold or copper; it is a ball of ashes. Whenever I see ashes in the hearth, I discover in it a sun, a sun that shines only for me, even in the middle of the night. Mozliak guessed it, I don't know how. Yes, yes, I do know: as I answered his questions I avoided all words with any connection to the sun or to ashes; I had stricken them from my vocabulary. I said anything at all so as not to venture out on the treacherous subject of the sunny ashes. I expressed myself incoherently, I answered beside the point. And he just stared at me coldly, impassively, and bombarded me with seemingly unconnected words to gauge my reaction; I ended up betraying myself. Since then, I have lived in a world without sun.

Cautious, always on the alert, I watched over the rest of my treasures. But I was not smart enough to elude him. He was a specialist. He extracted words from me, sentences, shreds of silence; I became more and more impoverished. The more I spoke, the less I existed; he robbed me of what I cherished most. I no longer recognized myself; my curiosity was waning, I fell into a stupor. My movements and intentions were uncoordinated. I was losing my way in a dark tunnel; I felt stifled. I gave up hope, I gave up on myself. One more month and I would have forgotten everything. Then, the miracle occurred. Was it a miracle? Or perhaps an accident? Chance or conscious act? How is one to know? All I know is that, at one particular moment when I felt more cornered than ever, I clenched my teeth hard, I locked my jaws violently, opening them only to breathe and run the tip of my tongue over my parched lips. Suddenly, overcome by rage, an uncontrollable spasm made me close my jaws over my tongue.

And I cut it in two. I lost consciousness and from then on I have been incapable of pronouncing a word.

My poor mother, proud as always, confided her sorrow only to Dr. Mozliak. She could not accept that her only son would remain mute the rest of his life. "Grisha's problem is more serious," answered Mozliak. "It is mental." As far as he was concerned, I was mad. I wasn't. The proof: I was devising plans for vengeance and justice. Did that prove I was sane? Perhaps just the opposite, but then, what's the difference?

Still, my watchman friend, there is one last thing: if I were not mute, our paths would not have crossed. And, without you, how would I have built my kingdom? Without you, I would have known nothing but silence and ashes.

Y OUR MOTHER IS ILL," says his writer friend.

Grisha would like to ask, Is it serious? He doesn't know how to say it with gestures. He takes a sheet of paper and writes the question. The answer is that he is not certain; the doctors have not pronounced themselves. She has had a heart attack; she will undergo an operation.

"Unfortunately you will not be able to go to her bedside. Today is Yom Kippur, the Day of Atonement, and there will be no flight to Vienna until Sunday."

Wait, one must wait. And pray—why not? Yes, tonight he and his friend will go to the Wall, they will participate in the solemn Kol Nidre service. Tonight, up there, the verdicts will be sealed: recovery or death; forgiveness for some, reproof for others. And I? Grisha wonders. To forgive means to judge. And I don't know how to judge. I would like to know.

The city emerges from darkness. A few islands of activity. The sound of the Shofar mingles with the shrill noises from the Arab market inside the ramparts, the whimpers of small children and their mothers' shouts. Two men exchange greetings: May the year about to end take its curses along and may the one about to begin be generous with its blessings!

I shall never see her again, Grisha tells himself. Why this sadness? Since he began waiting for her, he had made so many plans. He was going to resolve all the enigmas of his past: his father's melancholy and his mother's silence. She too had secrets she had undoubtedly decided to reveal to him; that is why she had finally broken with Krasnograd—with Dr. Mozliak. That one, what exactly had his role been in all this? And Zupanev, had she seen Zupanev before leaving? Had he entrusted her with a message? Was he still alive?

Strange, Grisha thinks: I know my father better than I know my mother.

A scene flashes through his mind. On a winter evening he comes home from school and finds Raissa, graceful and regal, sitting on a chair, her hands on the table, her eyes staring into space. He drops his schoolbag and runs to console her. He takes her head into his small hands and wants to tell her so many things, sweet and gentle things, but he is moved, too moved to say a word.

She never knew—she will never know—what drove him toward her: a feeling whose name eluded him and still eludes him, a feeling both troubling and reassuring that had made his heart beat faster.

As it does now.

THE TESTAMENT OF PALTIEL KOSSOVER IX

SHE WAS SMILING AT ME, and that confused me. She had never smiled at me, not even ironically. Was it because of the victory? The entire Red Army was celebrating. The exultation was general: officers and aides were partying, getting drunk. Where we were, at the field hospital, even the patients seemed happy. I did not share their happiness.

Wounded once more, I had been hospitalized in Lublin where the 96th Division was resting at last. It had paid dearly for its glory; now it had to recover its health, and that takes time. The officers were complaining; their dream was to be the first to step on German soil, the first to hoist our flag over the ruins of Berlin. The soldiers, too, were impatient but they obeyed orders. It didn't matter where—what mattered was to fight. And our boys had fought.

And so my war had come to an end in Lublin. I was carrying a young soldier toward the rear. He was beautiful, and light as a child. I spoke to him as I always did, repeating what I always said to my dead: Don't worry, my little one, we are almost there. And he seemed to contradict me: No, we shall not get there. He advised caution: Watch out for the snipers, for the stray bullets; watch out for the mines. Watch out, watch out, easier said than done—as though the front were a street crossing. My guardian angel on my shoulders, I moved forward, tripping. Then I was lifted off the ground. Violent red pain. I opened my eyes: the impact had thrown me into a trench. Torn to bits, the young soldier was no longer young or a soldier, he was nothing but a decapitated, legless corpse. He had saved my life: I was only wounded. Surgery, sleepless nights, difficult awakenings; my eyelids weighed tons.

The front was moving away and my body clung to Lublin and I to my body. I was transferred from one hospital to another for a specific reason or for no reason. Old and young surgeons leaned over me, shaking their heads, looking worried. They had forgotten my heart, so busy were they with my shattered bones. Their turn to reassure me: Don't worry soldier, we are getting there.

As through a moist veil, I saw the doctors and nurses come and go, I heard their whispers. Was I still alive? If yes, why? If not, why was my father not at my side? What I did not know for certain was that gravediggers also die. That thought never left me. Sometimes, to distract myself, I wondered where it would happen: right here in Lublin? My head was filled with the magical and revered names of the Seer and of Rabbi Zadok of Lublin. The Yeshiva of the Sages of Lublin: my father had ardently wished me to be part of it. I called out to Borka, the Jewish medic from Odessa, who was the epitome of resourcefulness, and asked him a favor. Sure, he said, rubbing his hands. What is it: Would you like to be shipped to Moscow? Something else? A good meal? A girlfriend perhaps? He burst out laughing, slapping his thighs. "Listen," I whispered. "If I should die . . ." "Are you nuts or what? You won't die, you're almost recovered." "If I die, Borka, promise me that you will have them bury me in a Jewish cemetery." "You are nuts, completely nuts," he answered, his face falling. "Promise me, Borka." "I promise to let you have one of those beatings if you don't stop." "Borka, I beg you! For me, nothing is more important than . . ." "Nothing doing, my little idiot. You will not die, not in Lublin. Too many Jews have died in Lublin."

The hospital was moved to a primary school. There I underwent further surgery, which finally did the job. After three weeks I was transferred to a center for convalescents. There, despite my weakened condition, I was able to take part in the life of the ward. The discussions ranged from the lightning-like advance of our armies to Koniev's tactics and Zhukov's strategy. Bets were taken: Which of the two would be the first to enter Berlin? The war was coming to an end soon, that was the consensus. Some of the wounded asked to be sent home. What good was it to expose oneself now, what would be the use of dying a hero's death just before victory?

Raissa visited the hospital frequently. She had been promoted to captain and was on the lookout for the men hoping to leave. She had an eye for singling them out and the tongue to lash out at them; she called them wet rags, cowards, traitors, and they were afraid of her.

While making her rounds, she nonchalantly stopped here and there, ostensibly for a chat but in reality gauging the morale of *her* troops.

Did she recognize me? She pointed to the cast encircling my torso and asked, "When will you finally get rid of that, huh?" She was looking at my cast, not me. I answered, "Can't be soon enough for me, Comrade Captain." "Well said, soldier, well said. But make it snappy, you hear?"

The man in the bed next to mine was scolded: "Aren't you ashamed to hang around here like that, dreaming and letting yourself be served like an old retired hag, while your gallant companions beat the devil out of the enemy on his own territory?" Thus she would bring us news from the front: "Cracow has been taken, Katowitz liberated, Sosnowitz swept away; we are marching on Berlin and you

are napping? . . ." As though it were our fault. Was that
her way of being funny? Of cheering us up? Or of expressing her displeasure? She fumed at not being able to
take part in these historical but distant battles. From now
on, Lublin belonged to the past. The press was already
reporting other war news; other cities, more exotic, more
picturesque, were the focus of attention—and she, a captain, a political commissar, was reduced to taking care of a
bunch of invalids and loafers. . . . She came close to
holding us responsible. Without us and our stupid wounds,
without these cursed hospitals, she might, at this very moment, be with Marshal Koniev or Marshal Zhukov, and
the Party would be proud of her and render her the honors
due her! That is why she was so mean: she resented us.
And every day a little more. Every battle, every triumph
added to her bitterness.

My cast came off in April. But I remained bedridden
as I waited to be sent home. Nothing seemed to be happening. Came the month of May and the day the Germans
capitulated. Our division was in charge of the local parade.
It was a magnificent show, worthy of Moscow. All right,
I am exaggerating, but I am just trying to describe to you
what we felt when the division marched past the official
stand where Kolbakov and his Chief of Staff stood motionless, saluting our flags.

Even the saddest and most melancholy ones among us
opened themselves to joy. We drank, we sang, we applauded, we shouted *Long live Stalin!* and *Long live the
Soviet Union!* and we repeated in chorus, *Hurrah, three
times hurrah!* We danced in the parks, in the squares, in
the streets; we embraced, strangers offered one another
gifts and trophies. We lived this most beautiful day of
our lives to the fullest, savoring every second, every
memory; we were alive and we had won; the future was
ours, happiness was ours. We were proud, for we had
destroyed the beast; generations to come would be grateful.

That night nobody slept.

A day or two later, we were advised that we would be part of the next homebound convoy in early June. Before that, we would have to be checked out by the competent authorities and commissions.

One beautiful morning, Raissa appears in our ward carrying a bunch of files under her arm; her cold smile worries us. As usual, she walks between the rows of beds, stopping next to a noncom here, a soldier there, teasing them. Unexpectedly, she lets her blue gaze rest on me and her smile widens into a truly feminine smile. "So?" she says. "Happy to be going home, soldier?" "And how, Comrade Captain!" "You miss home, huh?" "Absolutely, Comrade Captain." "Where are you from?" "I don't know, Comrade Captain." "You don't know? Surely you have a family, a home of your own?" "I don't, Comrade Captain. . . ."

And then she does something, Raissa, that she has never done before. She sits down on the edge of my bed! Interested? Intrigued? Suspicious? She questions me about my military career, my personal life. She seems to have forgotten our earlier encounter; it was all so long ago. But no, it is not that she has forgotten; she simply has not recognized me. Refresh her memory? I remain silent. Never mind. She smiles. If I say something, she'll stop smiling. As for the business of the German prisoner . . . Even if the man I placed on the operating table had been my friend Lebedev, he would have died. There or elsewhere, in the great North. Anyway, it is better to forget. The war is over, Germany is vanquished and, most importantly, Raissa is smiling at *me*. She is not thinking of the dead prisoners, so why should I? She is captain, I am soldier. At your service, Comrade Captain!

She wants to know what I do in civilian life. I'm a proofreader, I tell her. She removes her cap; her blond hair spills down the nape of her neck, down to her vest; I want to touch it, only touch it, not even caress it; it's silly, I know, but that's her fault. I once hated her, found her repulsive. Now we have changed, we both have; now I want to feel her hair in my hand. My buddies are watching us, they don't understand: never before has Raissa fraternized with one of her subordinates. They try to listen but we are speaking in low voices as though exchanging confidences about my return home. "Proofreader? What's that?" she wants to know. I explain it to her, then I add, blushing, "I also do something else." She opens her eyes wide: "Something else?" "I am a poet," I tell her almost inaudibly. She becomes excited: "Is that true? You're a poet? Like Karovensky?" "No, Karovensky is famous; his poems are read even in the trenches. Mine . . ." "Well, what about yours?" "Mine, nobody has read but me; I don't think they're very good." "You'll recite them for me, promise?" She leans toward me: "Promise?" I nod: Yes, I promise. "Tomorrow," she says, "I'll come and fetch you; we'll go for a walk in the garden."

Now she is talking to Dmitri, to Lev, to Alexey, without any transition, while I am still all excited, flushed, torn between the desire to please her and the fear of appearing ridiculous. I should not have mentioned my poems to her. What does she know about poetry? The whispered songs, the fragments of yearnings and remorse, the prayers of the nonbelievers, how could she appreciate them? Particularly since the words are in Yiddish. I reason with myself: Why worry so much? She will not come, we shall not go for a walk, I shall not have to play the clown reciting my verses, thank God. First I loved Raissa, then I hated her, then I loved her, then . . . To hell with it. I no longer love her, I no longer hate her. I have other problems to solve. What will I do in Soviet Russia? Where will I live? Work? And what if I went to visit Lebedev's family in Vitebsk?

How stupid I am. There are no more Jews in Vitebsk. Fine, I'll go elsewhere, to Mitya and his grandmother, anywhere. I should be able, sooner or later, to find a place where a Jewish poet does not disturb people too much.

I was wrong, of course. Raissa did come back as promised. She wanted to hear my poems.

And here I am, a victim of my poetry.

Lublin suffered less than many other large cities. There was little debris in the streets. Life was almost normal. The churches were filled, the restaurants crowded. Polish and Russian soldiers fraternized. Under the trees, boys and girls rediscovered love.

Still weak, I walk with difficulty. I lean on Raissa, my right arm on her shoulder. Whenever I make an abrupt movement, I inadvertently touch her breast, and the blood rushes to my head. I often stop to rest. "Let's stop at this bench," I say. She helps me sit down. "Well?" she says. "What about your poems?" "You really want to hear them?" "Read them. I'll tell you after." "But you won't understand." "Don't be insolent, soldier." "I meant—you won't understand them because I don't write in Russian but in Yiddish." "So what?" she says without blinking. "I understand Yiddish." Oh, yes, she had learned it in her childhood; her grandparents had spoken Yiddish to her. "Where are they?" I ask. Her eyes darken. "They were killed." "When?" "I don't know." "Where?" "In Vitebsk." And suddenly I no longer see the whiteness of the sky, nor the foliage of the trees, nor the human torrent flowing toward the center of Lublin. I take a few sheets out of my pocket and begin reading aloud. She interrupts me impatiently: "How depressing, that's enough, haven't you anything more cheerful?" I shake my head. I am annoyed with myself for having given in to her. She is too cold, too indifferent to understand my poetry. I fold my poems and put them back into my pocket. "Poets are supposed to sing of love or the fatherland, or both," Raissa says spitefully. "Why can't you do that?" Of all things, *she* is the one who's offended, cheated! Her cold eyes seem hateful to me. She gets up abruptly. "Let's go back." "I was going to suggest that. The walk's exhausted me." I don't want to feel the warmth and strength emanating from her body, so I try to walk by myself. She leaves me at the door and goes off without a word. I drag myself to my bed; I collapse with a single thought in my mind before falling asleep: As a poet, I have no luck; and as for women, I'm not doing so well either.

Raissa shows up again that same afternoon. She shakes me: "Wake up!" I rub my eyes; she seems even angrier than in the morning. She hisses at me through tight lips and I think: A blond serpent. I say: "I'm tired, I walked too much." "Come on." I get up and follow her, I climb into her car. We drive along for ten minutes or so, not more, and Majdanek, surrounded by barbed wire and elevated searchlights, rises up before us in all its serenity and icy horror. "Since you're fascinated by the morbid," says Raissa, "go ahead: take a look, fill your eyes." I get out of the car, sure she will follow me, but she surprises me once more. She issues a terse command and her driver takes off. A moment later, the car is far away, leaving behind a cloud of white and gray dust resembling human ashes.

I made my way into Majdanek—and I shall not tell you, Citizen Magistrate, what I felt; that would be almost indecent. Let me say only this: I forgot my fatigue, my ailments, my disappointments, my illusions, I forgot everything; I walked and walked for hours and hours, until nightfall. I went into all the barracks, all the cells; I touched and caressed the stones, embraced the doors behind which an entire people, my own, had disappeared in a cloud of fire. No, I shall not tell the story of Majdanek; others have done it before me; let the words of the survivors live and resound; I have no wish to cover them with mine. But let me say one more thing· I felt the desire to rest there. Forever. I felt the desire to remain with the invisible dead and beat my head, as they had done, against the walls, the ceiling, to gulp the air that was escaping, to bury myself in madness, whispering and crying, cursing and praying, and repeating to myself: None of this is true, they are not dead and I am not alive. . . . Never have I wanted so much to enter into madness and death as I did that evening at Majdanek.

Huddled in a barracks off to one side, I let the shadows envelop me. I listened to the moaning, the screams of terror carried by the night fog; I saw the children pressed against their mothers, I caught their silences touched by eternity, by a dead, sullied eternity. And I vowed never to leave them.

I was alone—never have I been more alone. And yet, there was a voice comforting me: "Don't stay here, go back to the living." And, a moment later: "Raissa is right, you're attracted to the macabre." Then, after another silence: "Raissa is young and beautiful, you like her, what more do you want? Go after her, love her." "Don't ask for the impossible," I said. "This is not the time or the place." "You're wrong, it is here and now that you can and must overcome the call of the abyss, for the abyss is deeper and blacker here than elsewhere."

I recognized the voice. I wanted to submit, to accept it, but I couldn't. I had just glimpsed the truth of truths, I had just perceived man in his final convulsions; it was impossible for me to look away; I had to follow him beyond the camp and the present, into the heavens, all the way to the Celestial Throne, and there the taciturn gravedigger was addressing God in a whisper: "As a child I was a

believer, because I was told that it was impossible to give
You a name and equally impossible to deny You or defame
You in words. Only now I know! You are a gravedigger,
God of my ancestors. You carry Your chosen people into the
ground, just as I carried the soldiers fallen on the battle-
fields. Your people no longer exist. You have buried them;
others killed them, but it is You who have put them into
their invisible, unknown tomb. Tell me, did You at least
recite the Kaddish? Did You weep for their death?"

My words met a stony silence. God chose not to respond.
But the hoarse voice of a former companion echoed within
me: "You exaggerate, my friend; you go too far. God is
resurrection, not gravedigger; God keeps alive the bond
that links Him and you to your people; is that not enough
for you? I am alive, you are alive; is that not enough for
you?" "No, that is not enough for me!" "What do you
want? Tell me what you want." "Redemption," I said.
And I hastened to add, "In this place I have the right to
demand and receive everything; and what I demand is
redemption." "So do I," said my companion sadly. "So do
I. And so does He."

Feverish, delirious, carried by angels in the service of
death, I returned to the hospital. I took out my notebook.
And in a dream I wrote to my father what I had seen.

Repatriated, demobilized, I went back to my job as
proofreader at the foreign section in the State Publishing
House. The days were gray and sad, the nights long and
lonely. Nothing interested me, my life disgusted me even
though it may have seemed enviable to others. As a
wounded war veteran decorated with the Medal of the
Red Flag, I enjoyed a variety of useful privileges: no standing in line for the streetcar, free entry to cinemas and the
zoo, priority for certain foods. I had returned to the same
small room in the home of my former landlady. A volume

of my verse was about to appear in Moscow: Markish and
Der Nister had read and warmly recommended it. Visits
to the Jewish Writers' Club improved my morale, and I
managed to multiply them. I attended meetings and lectures organized by the Anti-Fascist Committee in honor
of Jewish intellectuals—Communists or sympathizers—
from Europe or the United States. I heard novelists and
poets who had been invited to present their work in progress. I liked going to see Mikhoels and his theater company perform *The Revolt of Bar Kochba*. In short, I was
doing my best to return to normal by convincing myself
that the killer had not won the game, that the gravedigger
in me could leave the cemetery, that the Jewish people
was still living, even if my own family was gone. But to
recover my balance, if not my enthusiasm, I needed something or someone—I needed Raissa's presence. That was
precisely what I needed.

One September morning, on my way to the office, I
stopped in front of a shop window near the National
Hotel. I planned to buy myself a winter overcoat. I hesitated. I am the perfect customer: sales clerks can sell me
anything, I never protest, I never bargain, I take it and
pay for it, knowing all the while I shall never wear it.

I had just decided not to go in when I saw, inside, a
woman ordering salesgirls around. Amazed, I pushed open
the door. "Yes, comrade?" asked a plump young woman.
I took off my army cap and went over to Raissa. "What,
it's you?" she cried, and shook my hand warmly. "What's
happening to you, my macabre poet?" Ignoring employees
and customers who looked at us askance, we went into a
back office to be able to talk more freely. Raissa had
changed. Without her uniform she seemed even more
feminine, more sensual. Her blond hair done up in a
bun, her eyes hard and glittering, she had that "special
something," as they say. She stood out in a crowd, no ques-

tion about that. We made an appointment to meet after
the store closed. Dinner at the Writers' Club, and then
to the theater to see Mikhoels as King Lear. "If it's sad,
we'll leave," I promised her.

Warmed-over loves and soups are generally not recommended. No doubt rightly so. Only I catch fire quickly.
That's how I am, I can't do anything about it. It's enough
for a woman to lean toward me to start my blood racing.
When a stranger smiles at me, I blush like a schoolboy
and instantly endow her with every virtue. So aware am I
of my shortcomings that I am grateful to the woman who
is not discouraged by them; to thank her I would offer her
the moon. Oh, I know it is just one complex among others
I have been carrying around since Liyanov and Krasnograd: I am just a Talmudic student who refuses to liberate
himself. As for Raissa, after our third meeting I was ready
to propose marriage. And I did. She did not seem surprised. "Are you sure you love me?" "I'm sure, Raissa: a
poet is sure of at least one thing—of his loves. And you?
Do you love me a little?" Her answer was bizarre: "If only
my poor parents could see me . . ." "Your parents?" Her
eyes were veiled. She looked at me without seeing me:
"Paltiel Kossover, Jewish poet," she said. "When you don't
depress me you amuse me." To prove that she was not
indifferent to me, she went with me three times in a row
to the Jewish theater, where that particular week they
were performing a verbose but patriotic abomination. She
begged me to read and reread my poems to her and offered
intelligent comments on them while mocking my morose-
ness. She predicted a greater future for me as poet than as
husband. Flattered, euphoric, I lived only for Raissa. As
for her, though she had never said she loved me, she had
accepted my proposal. We filled out a mass of forms and
went to the marriage bureau with Mendelevich and his
wife as witnesses. An official puffed out his chest and pro-

nounced us man and wife. The ceremony had not lasted five minutes. "If my poor parents could see me," Raissa murmured. I was thinking of my own parents, but said nothing.

Mendelevich invited us to a restaurant. Raissa was smiling, though there was mockery in her smile. I found it difficult to overcome my melancholy. I thought of those who were absent: my father, my mother, my sisters, my uncles, my teachers, my friends. I thought of Liyanov; had the wedding taken place there . . . I imagined the ceremony, the blue-and-purple satin canopy, the candles, the rabbi, the fiddlers, the speech I would have made. Here, the celebration consisted of a meal at a restaurant frequented mostly by artists; the dinner was copious, washed down with vodka and—for the special occasion—Crimean champagne. Mendelevich entertained us with his theater stories; Raissa applauded.

I was silently remembering our old traditions: an orphaned groom is supposed to go to the cemetery to invite his deceased parents to the wedding. How could I have done that? Liyanov was far away, and, in any case, Raissa would not have understood. She would have said, "Why do you need a cemetery? Your heart is one; say your little prayer and let's get it over with." "Why are you sad?" Mendelevich's wife asked me. "That's the tradition," her husband answered for me. "Couples are supposed to be sad on their wedding day: they break a glass and put ashes on their foreheads to recall the destruction of the Temple. It's theatrical, of course, but so moving." "What?" asked his wife. "Paltiel is sad because of the past?" "Of course not," Raissa chimed in. "He's sad because of the future . . . except that he doesn't know it yet." And suddenly I felt in an obscure way that we were not going to be happy.

Writing these lines today, in this place, where things seem clear and luminous, I realize that Raissa knew it too, and even before me. Then why did she marry me? Attractive, educated, with a Communist past like hers, she did not lack suitors and certainly could have found a better husband. I learned later that she had, in fact, used me to exorcise her own demons.

She had been engaged before the war. But her father had opposed the marriage: Anatoly was not Jewish. The mother wept, Raissa became angry: "He's not a Jew, he's not a Jew, so what? I am, and I don't give a damn!" "Raissa, remember," her father implored. "Remember whom? What? Leave me alone with your memories, I want to live my life, not yours." In the end she broke with her parents and moved in with Anatoly. The war separated them. Anatoly fell in Minsk, and Raissa's pain turned into rage. She began hating her parents, then all Jews; without them she would have married her Anatoly; they would have had children; they would have lived happily. . . . In the army she could not tolerate being near Jews, and when she had to be with them, she bullied them to punish her parents. She changed when she learned of the massacres in Vitebsk: all the members of her family had been buried alive. From that time on, a new feeling—guilt?—drew her to Jews— and me. Was she thinking of appeasing her dead parents in this way? Did she know that by punishing herself she made me suffer? But—excuse me, Citizen Magistrate, let's change the subject. My private life is my business.

Our wedding day passed quickly. In the evening we went to the theater to see Mendelevich in a play by Sholem Aleichem. Our friend and protector managed to insert into his text a line meant specially for us: "*Mazel tov,* good luck, best wishes for the young couple." It had nothing to do with the play, but it gave us pleasure and the audience didn't know the difference.

After the show we went to see Mendelevich in his dressing room. We thanked him. He laughed. "Did you see?

They didn't notice a thing. I could say whatever I please. Luckily Sholem Aleichem is dead."

We went home to Raissa's apartment. And there, in her bed, in her habitat, among her objects, I failed on my wedding night. Absentminded, Raissa did not seem offended. She fell asleep, but I lay there with open eyes, making plans, dreaming incoherently of a thousand futures. I had to make decisions. Galperin, the rustic poet with the childlike voice, had suggested that I translate his war cantata into French, on condition that I officially join the Party. I had discussed this with Raissa, who strongly advised me to do so. In fact, why not? The USSR had beaten Hitler and paid the price. The Red Army had liberated Majdanek and Auschwitz. Why not show my gratitude? In addition, my oldest friendships came to mind: Inge, Traub, Ephraim. . . . Of course, there were also Yasha, Paul Hamburger, the purges and the disappearances; but history is made up of many chapters.

I decided to join the Party.

My collected poems came out at the end of 1946. The reception was qualified. Certain critics praised it, others demolished it, not having understood it at all. I must say I did everything to confuse them. The volume was called *I Saw My Father in a Dream,* and not a single poem mentioned my father. At the last minute I had decided to eliminate a sort of lyrical, mystical vision in which I described a funeral procession led by my father. I ask him where he is going, and he does not answer; I ask him whence he comes, he does not answer; I wait for the procession to pass and I follow it at a distance—we walk, we walk in silence, but I hear someone talking to me and I do not know who, he speaks to me and I know I am forbidden to know who it is; I look before me and see no one, then I lower my eyes and see a little boy growing, growing; he motions to me, I recognize him; he questions me without saying a word—and I understand that it was his silence that had spoken to me earlier—he questions me without looking at me: "What have you made of me?" And behind him my father appears and he too motions to me and asks, "What have you made of me?" And my collection of poems is my answer.

Why did I withdraw this first poem? I was afraid of upsetting and shocking the Communist reader.

By and large I had no complaints. Markish generously arranged a party in my honor. A critic from *Izvestia*, invited by Mendelevich, wrote a short but laudatory column about me. It was even rumored that an account of the book and of the evening would appear in the *Literaturnaya Gazeta*. I therefore had every reason in the world to be happy, and I was, so far as possible. Our economic situation was improving. The foreign section of the State Publishing House commissioned me to do a French translation of Feffer and a Yiddish one of Zola. A second printing of my volume of poetry was in the works and I was asked to do another collection. An article of mine in *Pravda* on the poetic application of Lenin's ideas aroused considerable interest. In short, I was becoming a celebrity.

And I rather liked the fame. Not only because of the material advantages it gave me—a more spacious apartment, readings to mass audiences, lectures on collective farms, invitations to official and private dinners for distinguished visitors—but also for the power it gave me; suddenly my judgment and my actions carried weight.

Promoted to chief reader of the foreign section of the State Publishing House, I wrote reports for the mighty Ideological Commission. Manuscripts, projects, proofs, lecture notes, professional opinions—I swam in paperwork. My superiors congratulated me on my literary taste and my political instinct, and they accepted my recommendations: in a word, I was doing what they wanted.

Outside my immediate circle I was less highly regarded. People flattered me, lied to me, complimented me, but did not like me; they were jealous. Arke Gelis was carrying on an underhanded campaign against me, delving into my religious childhood. For my part I opposed the publication of his frankly worthless novel on the civil war. He managed to get people more influential than I to intercede in his behalf and the Commission disregarded my opinion; his novel was published with great fanfare.

On the other hand, I was able to intercede in favor of old Avrohom Zalmen. He had been arrested for having recited, while drunk, a sort of litany dedicated to the memory of King Saul, the greatest and most charitable of all kings because he had had the courage not to have his enemies put to death. Denounced by Arke Gelis for his appropriately insulting remarks about our immortal Joseph Vissarionovich, Zalmen was in great danger. I rushed over to see Major Koriazin in person and told him, "Avrohom Zalmen may be a mediocre Communist but he's a great poet." It seems that the matter was brought to the attention of our beloved Chief, who, it was said, ever since his days as a seminarian, felt a special sympathy for the unfortunate King Saul. If the rumor is to be believed, it was he himself who gave the order to release my crazy old Biblical poet. Gelis's defeat heightened my joy. "You see?" Raissa said to me. "The Party card brings more than material benefits."

Mostly it entailed diverse activities and obligations: ideological sessions, political meetings, lectures and signing of petitions; listening, applauding, voting. It was easy —there was the line, and I conformed to it without difficulty: the Party was right always. For me, for so many others, it had become a sort of religious order. I had only to recall my youth and substitute the Party for the Law or for God. In that way I could accept everything without reservation or hesitation. Hidden, omniscient and transcendent, the Party held the truth and the keys to the future: it knew where the most tortuous paths ended, it knew all the components of happiness. I studied its texts just as long ago I used to probe a passage of the Tractate on the Sanhedrin, that is, with the absolute conviction of finding there every question and every answer. I would even say that my religious education helped me orient myself in my new faith: more than the pure Marxists, I excelled in exegesis as well as in obedience.

Though a Communist himself, Mendelevich thought my neophyte fervor too contrived. "Don't forget," he once said, "that you're a poet first, a Jewish poet." He did not add that the Communist connection was secondary, but that was what he thought. As for me, I was too busy to think about it.

Der Nister had some reservations about me, I think: he considered me something of an opportunist. I was hurt and sought a way of explaining my attitude to him, but the opportunity never arose. I regret that. I respected the man and revered his work; his opinion of me was important to me. As a matter of fact, I often think about it: if we had had a private talk, what would I have said to him? Perhaps something like this:

"Having lost my family in cattle cars, having broken with the religion of my fathers and understood what Nazism was capable of, having escaped a thousand enemies and seen what I saw in the frozen eyes of corpses, I found in the Communist Revolution an ideal that suited me. I was doing useful work, and I was doing it as a Jew. I was fulfilling myself as a man and as a Jew. If, as in the beginning of the thirties in Germany, the Party had told me that in order to be a Communist I had to stop being a Jew I would have been conflicted: but in 1947, in Soviet Russia, that was not the case. The Party had created an Anti-Fascist Committee, organized Jewish writers and artists' clubs, sent Jewish poets to America. Mikhoels was among the most honored artists of the USSR, Feffer had received the highest decorations, Markish was adulated by the intelligentsia, and my own writings appeared in the prestigious reviews of the Writers' Union. Clearly one could be a Jew and a Communist at the same time. In foreign affairs, too, the signals were favorable. Moscow defended the claims of the Palestinian Jews and spoke in their behalf at the United Nations. Gromyko's speeches were more Zionist than those of the Zionists. It was even said that we were sending arms to the underground Jewish army. Why then should I live on the periphery, uninvolved and ineffective?"

That is what I should have tried to say to the writer I admired. But we never met alone. I had the impression he was avoiding me. This saddened me, but I was too busy to do anything about it. In charge of a division, and victim of my own fame, I was working like a horse. I was writing, and commissioning others to write. I was preparing my second volume: an epic, the story of a Jewish revolutionary turned partisan during the occupation. I slept little and poorly. I was at my work table at dawn.

Raissa teased me: "What are you trying to prove? That you're a better Communist than I?" She did not understand; she failed to see I was blossoming. My book went off to the printer's. The publication date was to be the spring of 1949. Galperin, as enthusiastic as ever, was already talking about an official party to be attended by the lions of Jewish letters. Mikhoels was going to put his theater at our disposal; Ziskind would surely agree. I protested: "That's a little premature, isn't it? The book hasn't been printed yet; it's the dead of winter; let's wait. . . ."

Once again, I had a premonition: something was going to go wrong. And—that is what happened. Mikhoels died in a mysterious automobile accident in Minsk. Strange:

when I heard the news, in my office, a passage from the Talmud came back to me: *The death of one Just signifies that mankind is ripe for great punishment.* I ran to the Jewish theater; crowds of friends, acquaintances and strangers were already gathering there, some of them sobbing openly.

There could be no doubt: certain things were about to take place. After the funeral service—solemn, impressive, unforgettable—the mechanism, once released, accelerated its rhythm. Events quickly came to a head. First, the Anti-Fascist Committee was dissolved, the Jewish theater shut down, certain by-lines in the press disappeared. Then came the campaign against Zionists and cosmopolitans. My friends avoided public places. Invitations stopped coming. I spent my free time at home with Raissa. When I tried to analyze the situation with her, she was evasive. "What do you think of all this?" I asked. "Be quiet. You have your work, I have mine. Forget everything else." She had resumed her captain's voice.

One day, on my way to the printer's, I saw Galperin in the street; his slow, stooped walk saddened me. When I arrived in front of the printer's, the workers, in a panic, signaled to me not to go inside. "But what is happening?" Old Melekh Geller, who was not really very old, pointed to the composing room. I opened the door: a dozen or so agents and militiamen, silent and surly, were methodically opening drawers, seizing manuscripts and books, using hammers to smash pages of set type, including those of my own book. Their new-style pogrom completed, they went off without a word, carrying full sets of printing plates.

At first I felt merely stunned and helpless, then I felt ill. A needling pain in my chest reminded me of my heart condition. I swallowed my pills without water. The pain subsided, but I felt so weak I thought I would faint. I sat down, facing the workers, who were expecting an

explanation from *me*. Since all these projects had passed
the ideological censorship of the authorities, how did the
militiamen dare sabotage them? When my pain had eased,
I ran to my office and telephoned the person responsible
for cultural affairs of the Party: he was not there, neither
was his assistant, his secretary was busy; a friend, an editor
at *Izvestia*, was away; Major Koriazin could not be reached,
his aide knew nothing.

It was enough to make you lose your mind. I could not
accept that the Party could condemn an entire culture,
annihilate an entire literature. And what about the books
translated from Russian? The third volume of Lenin's
complete works? And the essay in praise of Joseph Vissarionovich by young Grabodkin? Why was it necessary
to make them disappear? Nobody knew. Fighting evil
men, subversive ideas, deviationist publications—well,
such is the nature of political strife. But a *language?* Why
attack a language? Why would anyone wish to exterminate
Yiddish? Mystery of mysteries.

Of course, I tried to rationalize: perhaps the Party was
not informed. If it was, its logic escaped me, which did not
mean that it was not just or necessary. The Party must be
accepted; calling it into question means to detach oneself
from it, thus to judge it, thus to reject it. Faith, one must
always have faith; doubt is forbidden. As I repeated these
arguments to myself I thought: I have just witnessed my
second pogrom.

I came home earlier than usual. So did Raissa. My heart
was heavy, and so was hers. We had finally come to an
understanding. I told her about my day.

"It's worse than you think," she said, after a moment's
silence.

"Explain."

"I can't. Just take it from me, it's serious. Remember, I
entered the Party long before you. And I've performed

more important functions than you. My sources are trust-
worthy. . . ."

She looked despondent, downcast; I had never before
seen her in such a state.

"What do you suggest?" I asked.

"Let's leave," she said resolutely.

"Are you serious? You want me to leave my work, you
to leave yours, like that, on an impulse?"

"Listen," she said. "No discussion. Let me handle it.
Things are going to happen. It's best to be as removed as
possible. In the thirties it was the people who lived far
from Moscow and the other big cities that managed best."

Beyond the nausea, the fear and the pain, there was my
love for Raissa: oh, yes, I loved her. Her calm strength,
her decisive spirit, her courage brought me as near to her
as we had been before, at the beginning of our relationship. Was it the danger? We were one.

"Listen," she said. "You're sick, go see your doctor. Ask
for sick leave. Your wife will go with you."

"But where shall we go?"

She thought, opening her eyes wide, as she often did:
"We'll go to Krasnograd: it's in the mountains, far away;
it's a small place, just what we need."

I no longer remember why, but I took her in my arms; I
no longer remember why, but she responded to my embrace.

The events of the day had exhausted me; I could not
grasp them clearly. The militia raid, the telephone calls
into the void, Raissa's warnings: what did it all mean? Had
we fought the war—and what a war!—to end up with
this? Anguish? Flight?

We got into bed without eating, as though taking refuge
there. And Raissa surprised me once more. Instead of
waiting for me to make the first move, she snuggled close
to me, and was affectionate, tender, full of initiative. Did

she foresee our separation? She held me close, and I experienced a pleasure so intense it hurt.

The return to Krasnograd was uneventful. With a medical certificate in my pocket, I obtained the needed authorizations; our bureaucracy, luckily, is less efficient than is believed. The question of lodgings was easily settled. After the mass arrests there was no shortage of empty apartments.

To relate my renewed contacts with my native town would be to evoke my childhood; I have already done that. Yet I felt like a stranger there. The streets, the buildings and the parks, had they changed? I did not recognize them. My father's house, for instance, was no longer mine, had never been mine. I preferred not to see it again. Gone, my father's house. Gone, the city of my childhood. Barassy is far away; Krasnograd has nothing to do with my exiled childhood.

Officially an invalid, I could not seek a position, but Raissa could. Her salary allowed us to subsist for several months—several months only, because Raissa was about to become a mother.

Frankly, I tried to persuade her to have an abortion. "Bring a child into the world—*now?* How do you know where I'll be tomorrow? And what if both of us are arrested? And even if we are spared, do you really think the world deserves one more Jew?"

She was stubborn. She was bent on having her child, my arguments had no effect on her. I realized that I scarcely knew her: I knew about her only those things relating to our life together. My repeated questions about her youth in Vitebsk, her parents, her past loves wearied her; her silences made me suffer.

The waiting and anxiety continued: when would they come knocking at our door? Just as during the Spanish war and later at our own front, I was waiting for my own per-

sonal bullet. But there it had been different: I had known
I was in danger, but innocent. And here? Here I knew I
was in danger and just as innocent—but there no one had
accused me, no one had set a trap for me, while here . . .
here, knowing I had been decreed guilty, I behaved as
though I were guilty. I paced up and down my room, my
hands behind my back, like a condemned man.

At night, I lay awake listening for noises from the street
and the stairs; I held my breath. Should I wake Raissa?
The footsteps moved away . . . I breathed. Until the next
suspicious noise.

Raissa stopped working a month before giving birth.
The landlady watched her going up and down the stairs
and murmured, "Poor thing, poor thing!" Later, when
she saw us with the baby, she murmured: "Poor things,
poor things!"

In the room I contemplated my child—a boy bearing my
father's name, Gershon—and my heart melted. I was
responsible for his future, a future I imagined full of
clouds and sadness. Would I be there to teach him to walk,
as my father had done for me? Who would teach him his
first words, his first songs, the names of the birds and
flowers? Who would shield him from the evil eye? I caressed
his little bald head, kissed his moist forehead, and whispered, "May God be with you, son; may God remain with
you, Father."

I unearthed—I will not say where or how—a *mohel,* who
circumcised my son. Reciting the prayer of the covenant, I
had tears in my eyes. My son, in my arms, looked at me in
silence; and I, in silence, wished him to know joy. When
the *mohel* pronounced the name of my father, I burst
into tears.

I had not consulted Raissa; I feared an explosion of
anger. And here again, she surprised me. The coldness
vanished from her blue eyes. "He will suffer," she said,

gently shaking her head, "he'll suffer, it's inevitable, but he'll know why."

Meanwhile the noose was tightening. Disturbing news came from Moscow; Markish and Bergelson, Der Nister and Kvitko had been arrested. An embolism had laid Mendelevich low. I took the train and went to pay him a last tribute; not one of our mutual friends was there. Old Avrohom Zalmen had been put in a mental hospital; in a restaurant, he had suddenly begun shouting that he was King David's cousin: "Saul—kill me, kill me. . . ."

My turn would come, I sensed it. Prison, madness, death. Separation. I looked at my son, who seemed to be smiling at me. I looked at my son and smiled at him.

I could not understand why I was still at liberty. I knew I was under surveillance, but why was I being allowed to go on living my life as father and husband—and as voluntary exile—instead of being made to share the fate of my colleagues?

By dint of waiting for the calamity I was ready to provoke it. What if I reported to the police? I would show them my poems and tell them, "Here is the evidence of my guilt, arrest me."

I no longer knew what to do. The fear of prison seemed worse to me than prison itself. Alone with Grisha—we had given him this nickname the day after his birth—I told him stories in Yiddish, I sang him the lullabies my mother used to sing to me. Raissa returned to work and I took care of the child. When she opened the door in the evening and saw me, she sighed: I was still there. We had thought of all the contingencies: if I was arrested during the day, the landlady was to take care of Grisha until Raissa's return.

She seemed less anxious than I. She forced herself to behave normally, calmly; but I sensed her depression. She knew more than I about the dangers in wait for us. She never smiled except when playing with Grisha. She would glance at me and her gaze was too painful to bear. Trapped, I hid in the eyes of my son as I had once taken refuge in those of my father.

To pass the time, while keeping vigil over Grisha's slumber, I reread and recopied notes, poems, aphorisms. I arranged my books and clothes. I found my phylacteries one day at the bottom of a drawer, and touching them I trembled. If they could only speak, I thought. The next second, without knowing what I was doing or why, I took them out of their bag, kissed them and put them on my left arm and forehead, as I used to do in the House of Study in Liyanov. All the rituals had come back to me.

It was absurd, but I felt better. Before taking them off, I leaned over the cradle. My son was sleeping and yet I was sure he saw me through his closed eyelids.

At dinner I described the scene to Raissa and made fun of myself. "You see, I'm lapsing back into religion, I'm getting old." "You know," she said, fixing her big eyes on me, "people who have faith are the strongest, they are best able to resist pressure." I looked at her amazed: had I heard her correctly? She was encouraging me to become observant once again. . . . "Do you know the story of Rebbe Shneur-Zalmen of Ladi?" "You're joking, rebbes are your domain." "In prison he was visited by the prosecutor, some say by the Tsar himself, and he inspired them with such respect, such reverential awe, that they decided to set him free. And the Hasidic tradition says specifically that when he received his august visitors he was wearing his phylacteries." "Very good," Raissa replied, forcing herself to look amused, "if that helps you, it's all right with me."

The next day I put on the phylacteries again. This time I waited until Grisha woke up. He pulled at the straps, and that filled me with great joy.

That evening we went to bed as usual after having rocked our son to sleep. I had sung him some ancient melodies to lull him to sleep: he kept insisting on more. I spent an agitated night. In a dream I was running, breathless, to save a small blond girl who was drowning and at the same time was about to fall off a tall tower. I awoke with palpitations; it was before dawn, before the small discreet knocks on the door.

I thought of my father and of my son *at the same time*. The same thought enveloped them both, the same desire to protect them. I was overwhelmed by remorse: I had lived without being able to help them. And I was afraid: judged by either one of them, what could I say in my defense?

In prison I yielded to panic only once. Under torture? Oh, no. The beatings hurt me, but I stood up surprisingly well. My body experienced the pain, but that was not I, I was not in my body. The tears flowed from my eyes and they were not mine. I saw the olive trees and the almond trees, and not the torturers; I listened to my masters and not to yours, Citizen Magistrate. David Aboulesia was reporting the results of his messianic endeavors, Ephraim was distracting me with his underground adventures. Inge was slipping through the streets of Berlin, and I was following in order to snatch her from our enemies. Ahuva was offering me the exotic attraction of her Oriental beauty. All of them were giving me strong support; they were helping me to resist more than one temptation, and, above all, resignation.

The torturers were tearing away at my body but my imagination remained free. I screamed, but revealed nothing. The moral tortures were harder. People kept repeating that I was the enemy of everything that was pure and just, that my gods were in the service of devils, that my love of Jews masked a detestable hatred of man, that my idealism was false and hypocritical, good was bad, bad was good, and I had devoted my life to a single cause: treason. I was made to read depositions and forced to confront their authors—wretched, unhappy witnesses who denounced themselves while denouncing me, and vice versa. Oh, all those suspicions, all those allusions to my "criminal" relations with Paul Hamburger, Yasha and their friends —excuse me, their accomplices. So—I never knew anyone but traitors, informers, two-faced friends. I never would have belonged to the Party except to destroy it from within, to corrupt it in league with the agents of imperialism. I would not have gone to Berlin except to deliver Communists to the Gestapo, or to Spain except to help the Trotskyites. I was offered a chance to go free if I were to bring Bergelson and Der Nister into it. . . . Whenever I weakened and felt I was about to yield, my father appeared in a dream and saved me. As for my son . . .

I was taken home for a so-called search. Going up the stairs in handcuffs, I prepared myself for the ordeal. Breathlessly I prayed for death. Like a romantic schoolboy I asked my ailing heart to break. Before the door, I shivered with fear. I was pushed into the room, where the light, dim as it was, blinded me.

Terrified—or shattered?—Raissa, uncharacteristically, moved back to let me pass. Grisha, on the floor, looked startled: he did not recognize the bearded, stooped man who was clenching his jaw, swallowing his saliva, grinding his teeth like a senile old man. Luckily I heard a voice I alone could hear. It whispered in my ear to look up, and I did; to smile, and I did; to look carefree, and I tried that too—though I know I did not succeed. Thanks to that voice, I was able to control my muscles, my tics. "The images you take away are those you'll leave behind," the same voice told me. I paid attention to every movement of my eyelids and mouth. "Hey there, my poet friend," said

David Aboulesia, "be strong." "I'm trying," I said. Grisha
was watching me, as were Raissa and my guards, and there
I was chatting with David Aboulesia about our encounters
all over the world!

Returned to my cell, I collapse. Finally alone, I become
the child I never was, the orphan I shall cease to be. I
weep for my father and I weep for my son, I weep for my
life and for my death. Who will be my gravedigger? It
is my destiny to end in failure. Oh, it is not death that
frightens me, but the impossibility of imparting some
meaning to my past. Besides, I am not going to die, not
yet: when the Angel of Death approaches, I shall feel his
breath, I'll capture the black light from his countless eyes.
I am forty-two years old, with so many things to discover,
without and within. The weight of dust, the burden of
light. Until this confession is completed I have nothing to
fear; that I know. I still have to describe the interrogations
and to explain my choices past and present. What time is
it? It is late. I should stop writing and talking to myself,
especially since I am not alone. Someone is watching me
with a smile. Sitting in the opposite corner, under the sky-
light, his hands folded under his knees, David Aboulesia—
or is it my father?—is gazing at me dreamily. How did he
manage to enter? Nothing surprises me. I find his presence
natural and accept it. And what if the guard opens the
peephole and punishes us? I repress that fear: the guard
will open the peephole and will see nothing. That too I
find quite natural, as I find natural my need to talk. Usually
so reticent, so withdrawn, I feel like pouring out my heart.
And that seems normal to me. And what if this is really an
enemy, an informer, with familiar features and disguised
as a protector? I trust him, and perhaps I am wrong. I
should not understand, and yet I understand everything. I
understand that David Aboulesia—or my father?—has
come from far away—is it far, the other world?—to keep

me company. I also understand that his presence signifies something essential, unique, something that ought to alarm me; but I feel no fear. I feel only profound sadness, a fundamental but soothing sadness, that of Creation accepting its Creator.

I am not going to die, not yet, but I shall no longer live. I shall no longer see the passing clouds, I shall no longer breathe in the freshness of the wind, no longer smile at my son. And yet I feel no bitterness, no regret; I bear no grudges. I experience a strange sensation of compassion, as if I were sick, dying. I love all the persons I see in the distance, moving in joy and melancholy; I feel sorry for them. They are all mortal and behave as if they were not. I should like to comfort them, help them, save them. I should like to tell them the story of my life.

My cellmate stands up and leans against the damp, dirty wall. I remain huddled on the floor. I go on talking to him and I know it is useless; he knows in advance what I am going to say. I speak to him anyhow because later I shall not be able to speak. If I keep silent now, no one will understand what I have seen and heard, no one will know my final poems, my final prayers; no one will read what I have written at this very moment.

Strange: I am not thinking of death, but I see the Angel covered with eyes; he closes his countless eyelids and darkness invades the cell. Tomorrow I shall try to understand all this.

Tomorrow I shall go on writing the *Testament of Paltiel Kossover,* filling it with details, turning it into a document of the times—in which the experiences of the past will serve as signs for the future.

I shall tell Grisha what I have never yet revealed to anyone; I shall tell him that . . .

■

I remember, says Zupanov, scratching his head, I remember that night more clearly than all the others spent spying on him and transcribing his every word. Fact is I had become fond of your big child of a father. I was going to miss him. His voice, the way he had of frowning, his short staccato sighs, his pages covered with barely legible writing: how was I going to detach myself from him? He was a part of my life, that fool; he was a part of me. I had read his tales for so long that I had created a place for myself in them. I waited impatiently to read the continuation of certain chapters in order to learn of my own future. And now . . . Oh, well.

Your father did not know that he was living his last night. He could not have guessed. Not even the magistrate had any inkling. Like the rest of us, the magistrate was surprised by the telephone call from Moscow. With one brief sentence, Abakumov transmitted a clear and irrevocable order: The Jewish poet Paltiel Gershonovich Kossover was to be executed before dawn. In my presence, the magistrate tried to argue: "But the file is not ready, Comrade Minister; the accused is writing his confession. He has already admitted certain crimes, opened several breaches; I could widen those and incriminate other suspects. Could we not wait a week or two?" "No," replied Abakumov drily. "But there has not even been a trial, not even on the administrative level . . ." "Before dawn," repeated Abakumov and hung up.

We did not know it, but the same order had been transmitted that same night to all the magistrates who, in Moscow, Kharkov, Kiev and Leningrad, were in charge of extorting confessions from Bergelson, Kvitko, Markish,

Feffer and all the other Jewish writers, poets and artists of the Soviet Union.

The order came from Stalin. In a fit of madness—was he afraid that he might die before them?—he had decided to have them all liquidated that very night at the same hour and in the same way.

Let me tell you about that night, Grisha. And your turn will come to tell it. You are mute? Never mind! We shall give a meaning to your silence. Since they cannot make you talk, you shall be the ideal messenger, just as I was. Nobody will suspect you, just as nobody suspected me. One does not suspect a fountain pen, a table, a lamp; one does not worry about a stenographer. The judges and the investigators have all been eliminated by their successors, but we stenographers were overlooked. Nobody thought that we had a life of our own, an independent memory, attachments, remorse, projects of our own. And nobody will see in you the trustee and the witness of a life that enriched mine, ours.

And so you will read and reread this document and try to remember it all. And later, far from this land, you will write it down and you in turn will assume your role: you will speak on behalf of your dead father.

That is a decision I made before I met you, my boy. I made it one summer night in 1952 when you were scarcely three years old; you were asleep in your mother's room, unaware that you had become an orphan.

That night I was so disturbed that I did something I rarely do: I went out for a walk. Krasnograd at night is not so inviting. The streets are deserted, the lights are dead. Like a prison, only bigger, with invisible jailers behind the dismal facades. Every window is a peephole, every noise a moan, a cry of horror. The inmates hold their breath just as on the morning of an execution.

I stroll through the park in the direction of the river

which divides the main street in two. I come to a halt. Motionless, I listen. The river is noisy tonight. I turn my head in all directions and end up making myself look suspicious. A militiaman accosts me: "This is no place for vagabonds and loafers like you. Go home! Go on, scram, or I'll put you in jail!" He gets excited, annoyed; I do nothing to appease him. "Have you lost your tongue? Go on, you wretched drunk, get out of here!" The fellow is furious. And that is when, very quietly, without any hurry, savoring every second that increases his rage, I pull out my card and show it to him. No need to draw him a picture. The fellow has understood. He stiffens, stands at attention and starts sputtering apologies and servile formulas, enough to make you sick: "At your service, I didn't know who, how could I have guessed that . . ." I leave him without bothering to interrupt him. Even as I reach the main square, near the movie theater, I can still hear him make his apologies. Ridiculous. That's what they all are: ludicrous wretches—but I am not laughing; I cannot. That terrible awareness brings me back to your father: poor devil, nothing funny about his life! I wonder whether he ever had the opportunity to have a good time, to laugh with all his heart. Strange: I know his life yet I do not know the essential fact: Did he or did he not learn the art of laughter? I am tempted to go to him, just like that, a surprise visit, and tell him: "Listen, my dear poet, you shall be executed tomorrow morning. I am telling it to you so that you may be ready. Ivan, the 'gentleman of the fourth cellar,' already has his instructions. Say, do you mind if I ask you a question that has been gnawing me for quite some time? It concerns you: have you ever laughed, I mean, really laughed? Body and soul? What I mean is, with your whole being? For you see, in your confessions you do not speak of it and that could mean two things: either you don't speak of it because you have never laughed, or because you have laughed so much that it does not occur to you to mention it. And so, you see, I'd like to . . ."

That would be outrageous, right? I return to my solitary wanderings. Because. You understand.

The breeze rustling through the trees is mild, but I am shivering. First of all, I am sensitive to cold. And then, the idea of seeing your father again and for the last time is not one that pleases me. Does he realize that I was present at the interrogations? That I have read his Testament? That I know all about his loves, his struggles, his doubts? Does he know that I exist?

Another militiaman comes up to me; he is called to order by the first, who no doubt is following me in order to spare me unpleasant encounters. I would do better to go home and go to bed but I shall not be able to close my eyes; I know myself. I am afraid, I am afraid of, you know what I mean. I let myself fall onto a bench; I contemplate Krasnograd and I see it through your father's eyes and then through the eyes of the Angel of Death, whom your father describes so well. A man will die, tomorrow.

Today, soon. My heart beats faster. My heart is heavy, for—did you know this, men and women of Krasnograd?— stenographers do have a heart and mine is flowing over. Your father, my boy, will cost me nights of sleeplessness, I feel it. For yes, I do love him, my boy, and because of him I love you too. I decided to change your life because he changed mine. And the incredible thing is: he was never to know it.

Yes, my boy, that is one night I remember. Dawn, as always during the month of August, lights up the sky and glides over the roofs and treetops. On the other side, the mountain is clinging to night. I feel like pleading, Let night go, god of the mountain, send it back to us and keep the sun, keep it as a hostage and give us back the darkness, *let it cover the city with its shadows once more, let there be another day, another life. Under the reign of night the "gentleman of the fourth cellar" will not make the acquaintance of a Jewish poet who . . . oh, well, it's all foolishness, it's all useless, I know.*

The prison is quiet, silent. But awake. Already? The inmates are beings of a different kind; they know. Ivan has not as yet received his orders and the prisoners already guess what they are. This morning they rose before it was time. In honor of your father? Do they know it is your father's turn? They have smelled death, they feel it close at hand and that is what has pulled them out of sleep. Death and not Ivan. Ivan has not arrived yet, neither has my chief. Too early. A crazy hope takes shape in my mind: They will not come, they will not come. Ever. Killed in an accident perhaps? I am impatient. I find myself cumbersome; I would like to be rid of myself. To die before witnessing death? Here I am, delirious, rambling, casting myself in the role of martyr. Not my style. Besides, the chief has arrived. He looks drawn, sullen. Troubled. Could an examining magistrate be sentimental too? Impossible. He is annoyed, that's all. He would have liked to bring this trial to its conclusion and is being frustrated. He considered his idea of allowing a writer to express himself, of encouraging a poet to remember, a stroke of genius, and suddenly it had all gone to hell. That's neither just nor professional, if you want his opinion. Of course, he could not guess all the ramifications of the affair; he did not know that Kossover was only one among many and that the others, elsewhere, were going to be shot too. Had he known the order was coming from that high up, he would not have dared question it, not even in his thoughts. And surely he would not have displayed ill humor. He picks up a file, leafs through it, signs some papers; the final formalities in other words! Oh, well, he does not agree but the matter is closed. As far as he is concerned, the Jewish poet Paltiel Gershonovich Kossover has ceased to live. One day, another examining magistrate would be sitting in his place, signing the same forms relating to his predecessor. While writing, without looking up, he asks me: "Do you really want to accompany Ivan?" "Yes, Citizen Magistrate." "Whatever for?" "Oh, I don't know, but . . ." "But what?" "Nothing. Except that I have never seen the 'gentleman of the fourth cellar' at work and I was wondering . . ." "You wouldn't be something of a pervert, my dear Zupanev?" "Just curious, Citizen Magistrate . . ." And so my chief shrugs his shoulders and goes on with his work without speaking to me again. As for me, I cannot stay put. I must force myself to remain seated on my usual stool from which I saw your father fight a battle that was already lost. Surreptitiously I glance toward my secret drawer: my favorite poet's writings are still in it, well protected. I promise you, my little poet. But I really should let him know this, reassure him with a wink, a gesture—but how? No, that's a bad idea. A cruel one. What is the use of warning him that he is about to die? If I make him understand that I am taking care of his Testament, *he will guess immediately; he is not stupid. He'll guess that if I am prepared to take such a risk, Ivan must not be far away. . . . And there he is, Ivan. He has come in without knocking. He shakes the chief's hand and throws me an absentminded good day. Elegant, dressed in a well-tailored uniform, he is a handsome man, only I find him ugly, repugnant. I pretend that I am working but I am too nervous to transcribe the routine nonsense. I watch Ivan as he pulls out his* nagan *and checks it. He is a professional, Ivan, a meticulous fellow. Having satisfied himself, he stuffs his* nagan *back into the regulation holster attached to the belt under his vest. My chief looks up, opens his mouth, closes it, opens it again. Dutifully, Ivan* asks, "Shall we go?" "Let's go," says my chief. I stand up when he does. Ivan turns to me: "What do you want? You know the regulation. . . ."

"He is curious," my chief tells him. "He has followed so many cases, he wishes to be present at the ending, to get an idea." "To each his own," mutters Ivan, displeased. "All right, let's go."

Automatically, I check the clock, which has stopped—and my watch. I like to situate important events in time. I remember looking at my watch, but what was the time? Strange, this lapse of memory. For I remember everything else: the morning light was blue; my chief was continually moistening his lips; and I had awful stomach cramps.

Silently, single file, we walk behind Ivan. Here we are in the subterranean labyrinth of the "isolators." Green bulbs on the ceilings, empty hallways. Ivan stops in front of a cell and motions to us not to make any noise. Such is the procedure; one opens the door gently, oh so gently, and surprises the condemned man in his sleep. One tells him that he must undergo another interrogation, and suddenly the problem is no longer a problem. The secret of success lies in surprise and speed. Except that your father, my boy, receives us standing as though he has been waiting for us. I am impressed by his calm. His face is scarred, his clothes are in tatters, but he looks noble to me. Foolish, don't you think? Briefly, he dominates us, intimidates us. He is the one to speak: "I worked all night, Citizen Magistrate." "Excellent," says the examining magistrate. "I am sure that it is excellent. I shall read it this very day." A silence. My chief is undecided. Ordinarily, the condemned man is led to the fourth basement where the "gentleman" shoots a bullet in his neck and leaves without any further ado. For your father, the program is different. The execution is to take place in the cell. "I have come to review with you the description of what you

call the pogrom at the printer's shop," my chief is saying.
He spreads some papers on the cot and your father bends
down to reread them. For a moment his eyes meet mine:
he has just seen me for the first time! I am overcome by
fear—he will mistake me for Ivan. To prevent a misunder-
standing, I introduce myself: "Zupanev—I am the stenographer." Your father is reassured: if the stenographer is
here, it really does mean only an additional inquiry to
elaborate on some detail. Suddenly, he sees Ivan behind me;
he would like to know his name as well but he restrains
his curiosity. As for Ivan he returns his gaze and says
nothing. "Very well," says your father. "Let's see that
passage." He begins to read and my chief pretends to
listen. And, God knows why, I suddenly remember my
maternal grandfather. I was three years old, or four, when
he took me with him to the synagogue; it was a holiday;
the men, lost in meditation, seemed to be listening to a
distant voice. What voice were we four listening to now?
I watch in horror as Ivan pulls out his nagan and pulls
my sleeve to take my place behind the condemned man.
I feel like howling to warn your father. Paltiel Kossover
is entitled to leave this stinking world like a man, facing
death, spitting in its face if he so chooses. But I remain
silent. Following your father's example, I tell my mind to
go away, and the whore obeys me: my thoughts fly to the
desk, to the notebooks neatly lined up in the secret drawer;
others will be added. And one day, one day, my dear
Jewish poet not yet assassinated, one day your sparks will
start a fire. And on that day I shall laugh! Do you hear me,
Paltiel Gershonovich Kossover? One day you and I will
surprise mankind with our laughter!

And those fools of magistrates and executioners who
see nothing! They think that they are finished with this
Jewish poet—one more—and his work. They think they
can control time as they dominate man: "To be preserved

for eternity," reads the rubber stamp that seals their files. But eternity couldn't care less about them—and neither could I. I'll show them what their stamp is worth! And what I do with their secrets. I'll show them, yes I will.

Now Ivan is behind his victim: I watch him as he raises his arm slowly, slowly. The barrel almost touches the nape of your father's neck. My eyes become blurred, there are knots in my throat: the Angel of Death is not a monster covered with eyes, but a well-dressed man armed with a nagan. Abruptly your father shatters the silence. He is speaking softly: "You must understand, the language of a people is its memory, and its memory is . . ." A muffled explosion tears through me. The poet collapses, slides slowly, gracefully to the ground, his head slightly to one side as though dreaming. Ivan motions to us: it's all over. The magistrate and the executioner exchange procedural remarks: burn the corpse; also his personal effects; also his wretched ritual objects; burn it all, erase his name from history by striking it from all the records. While they talk I contemplate the poet's face and promise to avenge him. That bastard Ivan will not have the last word; he means to obliterate your death just as my chief took away your life—but I am here. Those fools forgot me. The perfect witness, that's me. Though invisible, I was present as they transacted their filthy business. I heard it all, understood it all and filed it all away! Imagine their faces, those fools, on the day your father's song will come to haunt them from all corners of the globe. On that day I shall laugh, I shall laugh at last, for all the years I tried so hard to laugh and did not succeed. Thank you, poet. Thank you, brother. I leave you but you're not leaving me.

Back at the office, I hear the chief make his report—brief, neutral, concise: "Your order has been carried out this morning at 5:34 A.M." He gives the necessary instructions. He calls for tea, for buttered bread. As for me, I *experience a strange sensation: my heart is broken but I know that I shall laugh. And suddenly it happens: I am laughing, I am laughing at last. And if the Chief doesn't notice, it's only because he is a blockhead, like all the rest.*

It's idiotic, even unjust, but it is the dead, the dead poets who will force men like me and all the others to laugh.

I tell your father and I repeat it to him. Even though he is no longer living and no gravedigger will ever lower him into the ground because the ground is cursed and so is heaven. Never mind. I shall carry him, your big child of a father, I shall carry him a day, a year, ten years, for I must hear him laugh as well. That is why I implant in you his memory and mine, I must, my boy, you understand, I must. Otherwise . . .

ABOUT THE AUTHOR

Elie Wiesel received the Nobel Peace Prize in Oslo, Norway, on December 10, 1986. His Nobel citation reads: "Elie Wiesel is a messenger to mankind. His message is one of peace and atonement and human dignity. The message is in the form of a testimony, repeated and deepened through the works of a great author." Wiesel is Andrew Mellon Professor in the Humanities and University Professor at Boston University and is the author of more than forty books. He lives in New York City with his family.

THE FORGOTTEN

A distinguished psychotherapist and Holocaust survivor is losing his memory to an incurable disease. Never having spoken of the war years before, he resolves to tell his son about his past—the heroic parts as well as the parts that fill him with shame—before it is too late.

0-8052-1019-9

FROM THE KINGDOM OF MEMORY

The essays and speeches collected here include reminiscences of Wiesel's life before the Holocaust and his struggle to find meaning afterward, his impassioned testimony at the Klaus Barbie trial, his plea to President Reagan not to visit a German S.S. cemetery, and his speech in acceptance of the Nobel Peace Prize.

0-8052-1020-2

THE GATES OF THE FOREST

A young Jew hiding from the Nazis in the forests and small towns of Eastern Europe allows another refugee to sacrifice himself in his stead. As he struggles with his guilt, one question recurs: How to live in a world that God has abadoned?

0-8052-1044-X

THE TESTAMENT

On August 12, 1952, Russia's greatest Jewish writers were secretly executed by Stalin. In this novel, poet Paltiel Kossover meets the same fate but, unlike his historical counterparts, he is permitted to leave behind a written testament. Two decades later, Paltiel's son reads this precious record and finds that it illuminates the shadowed planes of his own life.

0-8052-1115-2

THE TOWN BEYOND THE WALL

Based on Wiesel's own life, this is the story of a young
Holocaust survivor who returns to his hometown after the
liberation, seeking to understand the mystery of what he
calls "the face in the window"—the symbol of all those who
just stood by and watched as innocent men, women,
and children were led to the slaughter.
0-8052-1045-8

THE TRIAL OF GOD

When three itinerant actors arrive in a small Eastern
European village to perform a Purim play for the Jewish community, they are horrified to discover that all but two of the
Jewish residents have been murdered in a recent pogrom.
The actors decide to stage a mock trial of God, indicting Him
for allowing such things to happen to His children.
0-8052-1053-9

TWILIGHT

The story of a man whose search for a friend who saved him
during the Holocaust leads him to question the very
meaning of survival, this novel of memory, loss, and madness
resonates with the dramatic upheavals of our century.
0-8052-1058-X

Available from Vintage

A JEW TODAY

In this powerful collection of essays, letters, and diary entries,
Wiesel probes such central moral and political issues as
Zionism and the Middle East conflict, anti-Semitism in the
former U.S.S.R., the obligations of American Jews toward
Israel, and the media's treatment of the Holocaust.
0-394-74057-2